ANNE WOODWARD ... ago, or maybe Yorkshire ad... teaching English to enraptu... to the classroom and said hello to her writing cabin. When not writing, she enjoys baking while singing loudly, and walking in the countryside, keeping quiet.

Follow Anne Bluesky @annehosmwriter.bsky.social Threads annewoodward.author

For Mark!
Happy reading!

ANNE WOODWARD

THE ART OF

MURDER

Anne

NORTHODOX
PRESS

Northodox Press Ltd
Maiden Greve, Malton,
North Yorkshire, YO17 7BE

This edition 2025

1
First published in Great Britain by
Northodox Press Ltd 2025

ISBN: 978-1-915179-61-6

This book is set in Caslon Pro Std

Cover and text design by T J Keane

Printed and bound by CPI Group (UK) Ltd,
Croydon, CR0 4YY

For Patricia

CHAPTER ONE

NOVEMBER - THE DAY AFTER THE FIRE

I stare into the smouldering abyss of what was once Dad's studio. Horror at what's happened clenches my heart and I can't erase from my imagination the silent film replaying the young woman's death. The stench of burnt oil paints, canvasses, and turps saturates the air. It catches the back of my throat; my eyes water. Another, unfamiliar, smell undercuts the scene. Dread of what it might be crawls over my skin. The film starts again, so I screw up my eyes and shake my head. Vision be gone.

The front door is destroyed, consumed by flames. It's a screaming mouth, a gaping hole in the charred wall. Through the gap, the sky lowers over the rest of the building. At the edges of the grey ashy expanse, low remnants of wall show where the building used to be. It's smaller than I remember.

* * *

I'd expected to find police officers swarming everywhere but found only a lone security guard's vehicle blocking the entrance to the shed. As I climbed from the car, a middle-aged, pudgy bloke waddled towards me, his head tilted in curiosity. He reminded me of a chubby starling chick that'd fallen from its nest. He halted by the front bumper, the pebbles grinding beneath his shiny boots.

'Can I help you, miss? This is private property; have you made a mistake?'

'Don't think so. Where are the police?'

'Cutbacks. They were here until…' He checked his watch. 'Noonish? Said they'd be back tomorrow.'

'Right. Oh, I'm Sia l'Ussier. This is, used to be, my dad's studio.'

The guard squinted at me. 'You're a l'Ussier?'

'Yes. Dad's agent said she rescued some paintings? Thought I'd take a look; I'm curating an exhibition of Dad's work, at my gallery in Deerdale.'

'They're in the hut.' He shuffled towards the shed, dredging a key from his pocket.

'You have a key?'

'Police give it me.'

He hauled himself into the vehicle and reversed it enough to make space in front of the shed. His dismount from the vehicle was a sight I hoped never to behold again. Relief eased my discomfort when he unlocked the padlock and pulled open the shed door. Stacked against the back wall were several paintings. I almost pushed him aside in my haste to get to them, dropped my handbag on the floor and pulled the front painting from the stack. It was barely recognisable under the scorching and was it my imagination, or was it still warm? I cast it aside and took the second, the third, the fourth.

'How safe is it?'

The security guard blinked, startled by my question.

'The building is dodgy; there's so much supporting structure gone. See for yourself.'

'Why aren't forensics still here?'

'Said they needed to be elsewhere. Not a public service anymore, y'see. Privatised and made worse, if you ask me, because they have to answer to their shareholders or suchlike. Is a disgrace.'

He shook his head, tutting.

'But they're coming back, you say?'

'Mm. Tomorrow. I shan't be on duty then. I'm only here till seven.'

'Do you mind if I wander round the back?'

'You shouldn't, not really.' He gave me a sympathetic smile. 'But I don't suppose a quick shufty will do any harm. You've got ten minutes.' He made a drama of consulting his watch.

'Thanks.'

He dawdled to his van, opened the rear door and took out a flask. The sound of liquid pouring into a metal cup accompanied me as I walked from the front to the corner of the building.

* * *

So, I find myself here, my emotions in such a mess I've no idea how to continue. It's disconcerting: forensics have abandoned their work, the place still warm. I should complain. The frosty grass crackles as I walk the length of the studio. Inside, a surprising amount of debris is recognisable; I supposed everything would be destroyed. It's easy to see where easels stood, and cupboards, at least one of which is still intact. Can I reach it, see what's inside? Why do I want to do that? Madness. No crazier than believing a figure has been removed from Dad's painting.

Pallid footprints, a gruesome aura around the perimeter, imply plenty of activity. The garden, untouched, sits gloomy, drained of colour, its life sucked out by the fire. Now you really are being fanciful, Sia. It's winter; course there's no colour.

I stroll to the back fence, close the gate, and lean on the fence to survey the studio. The side wall opposite where I walked is only half destroyed. Nearer the front, the corners meet, and there are remnants of glass in the open window. Open? I scan the ruins, but find no other windows, open or otherwise. Have

I been ten minutes? Disquiet niggles as I search again. To clear my head, I face the soothing browns and greens of the woods, allow my mind to drift. Undergrowth partly submerges the path. Patches of crushed greenery hint at the passage of animals - a fox or pheasant. I remember its route from when I was a girl and played here while Dad painted, so its winding to the boundary fence is easy to trace. What carefree days they were, when I was safe in Dad's love, shielded from Mother's constant fault-finding. I stand still but as hard as I listen, no screech of pheasant disturbs the quiet.

'Miss?'

The guard's call interrupts my reminiscing; I wave and stroll towards him with a pretend air of calm.

'Have I had my ten minutes?'

'More like fifteen. Sorry to insist, but I'd hate us to get into trouble.'

'Yes, thank you for your understanding. I'd hate it, too.'

We return to the shed, and my abandoned handbag, which I'd forgotten. Let's hope he hasn't had a rummage through it while I've been snooping. I crouch by the paintings, feeling Dad close as I rove my eyes over his work.

'I'll take the paintings, if that's okay with you?' I say over my shoulder.

'Aye, they said someone from the gallery would collect them. Shall I help you load?'

'Thank you, that'd be good.'

'Miss, I'm curious. Are they valuable, them paintings?' He nods at the ones I've spread against the wall side by side. They're all smoke damaged, to some extent.

'Not in terms of money, except perhaps for their novelty, but they're priceless to me.' I stand and stretch my back. The paintings' character changes when I see them at this angle. Just like those in the gallery. 'These are ones Dad rejected, abandoned or decided to come back to…' The lump in my throat takes me by surprise. A treacherous tear buds in the corner of my eye and slides down my cheek before I can halt it.

'Must be hard for you. Losing your dad, and then this.' He eyes the paintings. 'His others must be brilliant if these are the also-rans. What a talent.'

'They are.' I speak through trembling lips, my effort to keep them under control failing. 'You should visit our gallery in the city.'

We gaze at the paintings together in silence. When I hang them for the exhibition, I shall leave the damage. It adds something to them, gives them a sense of poignancy Dad would love.

We take twenty minutes to pack the car. While he positions the last one, I pick up my handbag. He arrives at my side as I sling the strap over my shoulder.

'Thanks again for your help. I appreciate it.'

'You're welcome. Good luck with the exhibition; hope there's no mishaps.'

The guard's words send zigzags of uneasy electricity along the hairline behind my ear, just like the ones I had in the gallery when I first spotted something weird going on with the painting. If I were superstitious, no doubt I'd be scrambling for my Ouija board or consulting the runes for an explanation. The crunch of the gravel under my shoes adds an undertone of edginess which jiggers up my calves. I get into my car, turn the key in the ignition, the engine coughs into life and I reverse towards the road. At the gate, after a clumsy three-point turn, I glance into the rear-view mirror at the studio and, as though superimposed upon my vision, an image of the altered painting at the gallery flashes and is gone.

CHAPTER TWO

Rather than drive straight back to the gallery with the paintings, I wend through the leafy lanes towards Ashgrove Bog. It's my favourite place, where I come whenever I need to sit, alone in the quiet, and contemplate. Only one car here when I swing into the car park. Moments later, I'm striding out towards "my" bench with my blanket under my arm, my breath pluming, and my fingers crossed that the people from the other car haven't decided to rest there, too. Much to my relief, it's unoccupied. I love the view from here - the lake with its shaggy fringes under which often hide various water birds with their youngsters. Not in winter, obviously. I plonk myself on the bench and let my eyes rest on the mirrored surface of the water. The air nips at my skin and I fold in on myself, the blanket wrapped around me like a cuddle. Not even a sparrow chirrups; no squirrels scamper along the branches of the ancient oaks skirting the lake. I absorb the silence, grateful for it.

But the silence lacks the power to overwhelm the jagged edginess I've felt since my discovery two days ago. I wish I could organise the mess in my head, unravel the knots, separate the strands. Just they refuse to be unravelled, and Dad's thread is entangled with them all. Vic thinks I'm barmy, deranged by grief. In all the years he's been my boss, he's never closed the gallery. Now, though, he wants me out and keeping busy running errands to distract me. And to see a therapist. When Vic's wife died, I never realised he'd had therapy; I need to pay more attention. Perhaps he's right. Since Dad's accident, it's been imperative to stay in control, not to allow myself to fall apart. Could the altered painting be my mind playing tricks on me, my innermost self, fighting to be acknowledged? Huh. Innermost self. Yet, it makes more sense than the alternatives. Who could've gained access to the gallery, altered the painting so expertly Vic questioned the woman's existence? No-one. That leaves Dad. He came back and erased the woman from his painting. Don't talk rot, Sia. Dad's gone. That's the crux of the matter. I expect when I return to the gallery, the missing woman will have returned. Or I'll discover her in a different painting, like Vic hinted. I wish it had been Dad, even as I know it's impossible. And besides, what would provoke him to take such action?

Movement under the foliage across the lake, and ripples span out, breaking the reflecting surface into rings that spread and disappear. I squint, focusing on the far bank. A small, brown creature shakes water from its back and scampers out of sight. Dad said there were water voles here; I wonder if that was one? Tendrils of bitter air creep under the edges of my blanket and I hug it tighter.

'Lovely creatures, water voles.'

I swing round. Beside me sits a woman wrapped in a huge, padded coat with a fur edged hood that obscures much of her face. It doesn't hide her smile. How did I not notice her arrive? I gape at her.

'Sorry, did I make you jump?'

'I wondered if it was a vole. You did, a bit.'

She pulls her collar up to her chin, the fur tickling her bottom lip. 'I'm drawn to the lake's serenity, and the voles. Gives me space to think.'

'Me, too.'

We gaze at the lake, its stillness restored. Usually, I'd resent when another person dared to share my space, but it doesn't seem invaded by this woman. Perhaps it's because she sits as motionless as me and doesn't push to continue the conversation. Time feels suspended. I glance at my mobile; to my astonishment, nearly an hour has passed since I arrived. I shouldn't linger; Vic needs me at the gallery, no matter what he thinks, and I need to do something useful. Check the painting.

'Have you found any answers to your problems while sitting here? When not disturbed by a vole?' She asks without looking at me, her face toward the lake.

'Not really.'

'Want to say the words aloud? See if it helps? Stop you telling yourself you're barmy because you're not talking to yourself? I'm a good listener. Tell me your story.'

Weird, she uses the same word as me, when I sat alone. I rest my gaze at the lake, my nerves jangling. I suppose I could; what harm in talking to a stranger I doubt I'll meet again? And so, I tell her about Dad, his accident, the exhibition and the fire. I even tell her about Mother and, finally, haltingly, about the altered painting…

'It sounds mad, but sometimes I get the sensation the paintings watch me as I stroll the gallery after the visitors have left, prisoners keeping their gaoler in sight, ever hopeful of snatching the keys and making good their escape.' I give an unsteady laugh. 'Crazy nonsense. They're just paintings, but Dad's so talented. He's given them dual personalities; qualities only visible to those who live with them, who love them enough to explore beyond the obvious.'

I glance at the woman; she's closed her eyes. I don't think she's asleep, bored to death by my setting the scene. I should stop waffling; get to the point.

'Well, that evening, I scanned the pictures for the exhibition of his work we're putting on, including the painting we'd hung earlier called The Boardroom Bosses. The air shivered. I buttoned up my jacket, but the hairs on my arms quivered even as I rubbed my hands up and down my sleeves. Behind my ears, along my hairline, a subtle twitch.' I sound unhinged, even to me, but my need to off-load makes me press on.

'I couldn't work out what was wrong with it. Lord, we'd spent hours getting it right. Poor old Vic, my boss. His back was killing him, but it was perfectly set up by the time we'd finished.'

I take another surreptitious glance. She nods for me to continue. Glance not so subtle. I go on. 'Imagine the painting, if you can; the businessmen at the front grin back at you, smug in their success. Those sitting behind try to suppress their glee at being part of such notable company. The back row ignores you; they're too busy making deals. Seated in the middle, men shovel papers from table to table. Dad had captured their self-satisfaction brilliantly.

A bolt of realisation almost knocked me off my feet. Where was she? The woman peering over the be-suited man's shoulder, dead centre? The space between me and the picture rippled. She wasn't there. I know she was the sole woman. I'd made sarcastic comments to Vic. He said it was probably someone's secretary getting in on the action. And laughed when I got cross with him. A conversation he seems to have forgotten.

I checked the information plaque, but it was useless. Why hadn't I insisted on naming everyone in the portrait? Too many. I remember saying no-one would care. If only Dad hadn't been so obstinate about photos. But no. "People who genuinely appreciate my paintings should visit the gallery regularly or, better yet, buy one." And I'd been stupid enough to abide by his wishes. I could have double checked. I searched the painting again, thinking maybe I'd misremembered where she was, but knowing I hadn't. It was a thorough portrayal of masculine power on the board.

I didn't ring Vic like I meant to, got side-tracked by a call from my boyfriend. But that's a whole different story. Anyway, after our chat, I looked back at the painting. The woman was still missing. Like I expected her to magically reappear when I turned my back. The painting conveyed masculine completeness. In the half-light, the men's eyes followed me, challenging me, daring me. They knew what had become of her.'

My companion listens in silence, only the occasional nod confirming she's paying attention. 'Little wonder you needed the solace of the reserve,' she says after a long enough pause to make certain I've finished. From under her hood, she stares at me through the fur. 'I can't advise you, but to be frank, I wouldn't dismiss what's happened to the painting.' She stands, and a faint scent of musky roses washes over me.

'Thanks… I think.' When I stand to face her, she's a little shorter than me, so all I see is that smile beneath the fur-lined hood. 'I should be getting back.' I step away from the bench, bundling my blanket into a rough parcel, and head towards the car.

'You'll get to the bottom of it,' she calls. 'Good luck with the exhibition; I'm sure it'll make your father very proud; see ya.'

Did she call my name? I spin round to ask, but she's gone. The path along the lake is empty; she must've taken the route through the trees. I squint into the dappled gloom, but nothing disturbs the quiet. No footsteps crunch the leafy carpet, no twigs snap underfoot. She's disappeared as quickly and silently as she appeared. I shrug, trying to dislodge my unease, dump the blanket in the boot and get into the car. Time to return to the gallery and Dad's exhibition. And to check that painting.

CHAPTER THREE

Vic sits with Detta, Dad's agent for many years, on the bench in the part of the gallery where Dad's paintings hang. She has her back to me, her customary straight shoulders bent, as though she holds her head in her hands. Just what Vic needs; another woman in an emotional state. Vic smiles, his eyes sad. I hold up a bag of doughnuts and shake them, raising my eyebrows in question. He gives me the thumbs up, so I gesture making coffee. His second smile is more reassuring.

I take three coffees on a tray, and the bag of doughnuts clasped between my teeth, to where they sit. Detta straightens herself as I approach and plasters a fake smile on her face.

'How are you, Sia?' she says, taking a mug. She is grey with tiredness. Her complexion, the envy of every woman I know, is dull and smoky, as though she wears her experience of the fire.

'Better now I've collected the paintings you salvaged from Dad's studio,' I say through gritted teeth, hoping I won't drop the bag. 'You saved loads; how did you manage it?' I offer the doughnut bag, but she waves it away, so I place it on the tray between the remaining mugs.

'I'll tell you everything one day. It's a bit soon just now…'

'Oh. Course. Sorry. Vic?'

He pulls out a doughnut and helps himself to a mug. 'We've been discussing the exhibition, Sia.'

Something in his voice twangs my senses like an adrenalin shot. 'What about it?'

'We were wondering if it wouldn't be prudent to postpone it – given that Tina lost her life in the fire.'

I stand there, the tray and doughnut bag in my hands, like a simpleton unable to understand his words.

'But I've been working on it for ages. And we agreed, after Dad's accident, we *had* to go ahead.'

He doesn't look at me, his coffee suddenly deeply fascinating. 'Vic?'

'It might appear disrespectful,' he says at last. 'To Tina's family.'

'We could pay tribute to Tina.' I wave towards the front door, as if they can see what I'm waving at. 'I've got the paintings in the car. Thought I'd show them as they are, scorch marks and everything.'

Vic tilts his head, thinking. 'It's an idea…'

Detta shakes her head. 'I'm not sure about this, Sia.' Her voice, usually so mellifluous, has a sharp edge.

'We could invite her significant other to the opening. Ask them to unveil a plaque in Tina's memory.' I sound desperate, even to myself, but if we don't hold the exhibition, what am I supposed to do?

'Wife. Tina's wife.' Detta sighs. 'It's a bit soon to be thinking like this. Discussing it seems wrong.' Her eyes cloud, but she holds me in her gaze. 'Let's not be hasty.'

Within me, an unruly, furious adolescent wants to scream how unfair it'd be to postpone. Rage fills every part of me, and my head feels like it's exploding. It takes a mammoth effort not to stamp my foot. Control, Sia. You're thirty-five, not fifteen. 'No, of course. Vic and I must discuss it, though.' I try to catch his eye, but he's even now focused on his damn coffee. 'The exhibition's almost ready.'

Detta finishes her coffee and stands; she puts the mug back on the tray I'm still holding, my own coffee untouched. 'I know your dad's exhibition is important, but bear with me, eh?'

Her soft tone undoes me, and I look at her properly. 'How are you? It must have been hideous.'

She smiles, a genuine smile, and squeezes my arm. 'Relieved. Horrified. Sad. Aching…'The smile disappears. 'I didn't start the fire, I promise you.'

'What? Why would you..?'

'To stop the paintings being exhibited. The police have been asking questions.'

I frown. 'But how would they know you didn't want them on display? That was a conversation between you and me.' As soon as I utter the words, I know I'm lying; I told Mother when I asked for her to give Detta permission to visit the studio. For reasons I cannot understand, I say nothing, but my duplicity appals me.

Detta shrugs. 'Don't look so shocked. They're just doing their job. Now, has anyone told your brother?'

'Sandro? I haven't.' I turn to Vic. 'Have you?'

'No, I doubt anyone has. And he'll be holed up working on that new David. It'd be best coming from you; you're closest to him. You go. Take advantage of the gallery's closure.'

'People might think you're trying to get rid of me,' I say, only half joking.

'Dear girl, as if.' He pulls me into an embrace so unexpected, Detta and I exchange startled looks. He coughs, like he's just remembered himself, and pulls away. 'Go now. Get it over and done with.'

'Right. Mind if I drink this first?' I slide the tray onto the bench Detta vacated and take my mug. The coffee's almost cold, but I swig it back, anyway. I grab a doughnut. My mouth full, I say, 'We could check Mother; make sure she's okay.'The familiar leaden dread creeps over me. At least with Sandro by my side, Mother should be more manageable.

Vic and Detta laugh. I put on my most innocent of faces, a

challenge as I've stuffed my mouth with doughnut. 'What?'

'You've hardly changed since you were a child,' says Vic, giving me his indulgent "Oh, that Sia" smile.

'A real sweet tooth,' says Detta. She kisses me on my doughnut-filled cheek; I'm like a hamster. 'Take care. I'll see you soon.' She blows Vic a kiss and departs, leaving a faint smoggy perfume in her wake.

'Before you go, Sia. Don't forget your appointment with Kim Brown, will you?'

'Kim Br..? Oh, the shrink. I won't. But I'm not imagining things, Vic.'

He glances at The Boardroom Bosses, and I follow his gaze. The air ripples as before, like heat haze, but Vic doesn't notice. 'I'm sure you're certain about the missing woman and you may be right, but I struggle to fathom how.'

I step closer to the painting, and the men peer out at us, pleased with themselves, complacent. 'They're so horribly self-satisfied.' I jab a finger towards the man in the blue jacket. 'Especially Mr Smug here. Looks like he's got away with murder. Bet he knows where she is and could take us to the body.'

'Sia!'

'Sorry. Recent events have dislodged my filter.'

'Go and tell Sandro.' He takes me by the shoulders and guides me to the main door. 'Give him my love.'

* * *

Sandro declines when I ask him to come with me to see Mother. His reaction to the destruction of Dad's studio was predictable; said everything would work out. Wish I had his sunny disposition.

Rather than give her more ammunition with which to attack me for being an uncaring daughter, I give myself a stern talking-to in the car and head for home. If that's what you'd call it these days.

CHAPTER FOUR

It's a short but tedious drive to Mother's from Sandro's workshop across Deerdale. Headlights glare and tail lights flash in the dusk. This is my least favourite time to be in the city, when its ancient grandeur is masked in hazy light and the traffic fills the streets with noise. Dad's studio would've made the perfect place for an art gallery, and I could reach it from my flat without entering the city centre. Vic's been nagging me to spread my wings. Could we rebuild? Maybe I should put it to Mother. If she's not in a mood. Or drunk.

The windows are ablaze when I pull up in front of Mother's house, like she's afraid of the dark. She, who when I was a child never appeared frightened, stands peering from the bay window, as if expecting me. Perhaps Sandro called to tell her I was on my way; God, I hope not. My heart heavy with dread, I kill the engine and step into the bitter night air.

'Do you need all these lights on?' I squint as I enter the hall. The walls jump out at me, brilliant white and heartless. Gold-framed mirrors reflect the stark chandeliers that hang in the hall. I switch off the main light and the entrance becomes a place of welcome once more, illuminated only by the soft lamp on the telephone table next to a vase filled with pink and purple winter flowers.

'In here, Artemisia.' The voice smoothed by alcohol retains its edge. 'Don't go round turning off the lights.'

'Mother.' She allows me to come close, air kiss. The scent of her, her softness, her beautifully draped dress send shivers through me. 'You've started early.'

'Don't get sergeant majorly with me. I'm the mother here. And my glass is empty.' She sighs. 'Just like my heart.' She holds the glass out for me to take, her blood-red nails so fierce and out of place with her impossibly tender hands. A corpuscle of wine nestles at the bottom of the glass.

I stroll through to the kitchen. The surfaces gleam. A lone bottle stands watch over the abandoned room. I dim the lights, take the handset and press a button. The kitchen is diffused in lavender from under the wall units. My heart loses some of its heaviness. When we first had these coloured lights fitted, Sandro and I drove Mother and Dad wild, constantly switching them to disco mode. I smile briefly at the memory and pour the wine.

I find her sitting by the unmade fire, staring into the darkness of the grate. 'Let me get a fire going. It's cold enough.'

She shrugs, accepts the glass, and takes a deep drink. I feel her eyes on me as I set the fire going. The daily help, whoever it is this week, has banked it up. I just need to light it. Within moments, a trickle of warmth comes from the fire. I switch off the overhead light. Mother says nothing. The room relaxes into comfort, and I slouch into the other settee.

Mother eyes me with unsuppressed disappointment. Her favourite emotion, to misquote Joni Mitchell. I sip the wine, a Merlot - we share a weakness for it - and stare right back at her. It takes all my willpower not to look away. 'About the studio...'

'What remains of it. That unfortunate young woman.' She shudders, much like I do whenever I think of Tina Shaw. 'You can't possibly want to discuss the studio's future now?'

'Not discuss, just put an idea to you for consideration.'

She arches a perfectly shaped eyebrow and tilts her head, her bright green eyes challenging. I am ten years old again, speared in her icy beam. 'Go on.'

'Vic's been telling me I should spread my wings, become more independent-'

'Can't disagree with that. Your little exhibition may be an important event in Deerdale, but it's not going to make your name known further afield, is it? Even with the prestige of your father's paintings.'

This was an error of judgement. I should've waited. It's too soon. I can't tell her Vic's had second thoughts since the fire. My empty stomach growls nervously. 'Shall I make us some supper? Don't know about you, but I'm hungry.' It's not quite the truth; I'm too nauseous to be hungry but eating might help. It has before.

She follows me through to the kitchen and sits at the table while I rummage about in the cupboards, searching for anything I can use to create something vaguely appetising. The subject of the studio is dropped as we struggle to make small talk while I throw together an assortment of tinned veg, noodles and a chicken breast from the fridge. I slosh in some garlic purée and soy sauce. Despite my edginess, the aromas from the wok stimulate my taste buds and hunger returns. I serve the meal on to two plates and join Mother at the table.

We eat in silence until she says, 'Pity Detta's housekeeping was wasted.'

'Pardon?'

'When we talked about her visit to the studio, I suggested she arm herself with a dustpan and brush - give the place a spring clean.'

I splutter on my noodles. 'Pardon?'

She smiles, glacial innocence in her eyes. 'You know how fastidious she is. I thought the dust might offend her.'

I snort into my glass, despite myself. 'Mother...'

'What?'

I shake my head. 'Nothing.'

We spend the rest of the evening watching reruns of Cagney and Lacey until Mother's eyes begin to droop and her wine glass hangs precariously in her elegant hand. I slip it from her and place it on the small table.

'Mother.'

She stirs. 'What's the time?'

'Time we were in bed. I must be at the gallery early tomorrow.' Another untruth, but that's how I manage my visits to Mother. Keep them brief, avoid warfare and my being left bleeding.

She holds out her hand for me to take, and I ease her to her feet. She looks into my eyes. 'I hate night times. They're the worst.'

'I know.' And I do. It's the same for me. Even Theo's arms wrapped round me as he sleeps don't bring the comfort I crave but, at least I have that. Sometimes. My throat constricts. 'I know.'

'Well, don't just stand there, maudlin. Help me upstairs.'

In bed, I stare through the shadowy dark at the ceiling. In the dim light from the ornamental lamppost in the garden, the lack of me hits, as it always does, like she's erased me. My mobile, on the bedside cabinet, springs into life. Theo, wishing me sweet dreams. I tap a reply, turn it face down on the cabinet and hunker under the duvet.

In the morning, I let myself out of the house before Mother awakes. The air hacks into me, its freezing fingers lancing my lungs. Defrosting the windscreen takes ages, even aided by the blowers on max, but the chill inside is blunted by the time I drive away.

I journey at a speed that wouldn't make a snail break into a sweat and eventually tumble into the slightly-less-cold-than-outside gallery. 'Sorry. Everyone's on a go-slow today.'

'Coffee's on. Shouldn't be long.'

I unwind my Doctor Who scarf and loop it over the hook in the office, hang up my coat, rub my hands together. 'I should get a new car. Half an hour without discernible heat. Was like driving an igloo.'

'How was she? Did Sandro go with you?' Vic rakes his long salt and pepper fringe from his face; it falls to its original place at once.

'Drunk. Sad. No, I went alone.'

'Did you discuss Detta?'

'Detta? No, why?'

He stares along the gallery towards the door. 'She was so adamant those paintings your dad did of her weren't to be exhibited…'

Oh, Christ. I talked to Vic about it, too. I'd forgotten. Still, Detta has too, now. 'So?' What does it matter if we cancel the exhibition? I bite back my words.

'She has a motive.'

'Vic, don't be ridiculous. Detta wouldn't commit arson.'

He rubs his chin. 'Did she and Heather ever actually admit Detta got there first?'

'What a way to put it. Mother's aware, course she is. What caused her acidity when I asked about Detta viewing the paintings, heartburn? She couldn't understand Detta's determination for them to remain out of the public eye. Dad wasn't going through a Van Gogh phase, was he?'

'Now you're asking. No idea. They'd split before I met Frank. In fact, I'm sure he and your mother were married by then.'

'Whatever, it's history. They're gone, so Detta needn't worry about anyone seeing them but her. Unless…'

'Unless?'

'She photographed them. Vic, d'you think she would've?'

'No. She'd respect Frank's wishes.'

'I would've, wouldn't you?'

Vic laughs. 'My dear girl, no-one has ever wanted to paint me in the raw.' He laughs again, and chuckles as he walks to the office, leaving me alone with Dad's paintings.

His spirit leaps from the paintings, from every face, every limb, every gesture. I love the way he captures the essence of those he's painted. There's Betty, with the girlish smile. Harold stands over her, his hand on her shoulder so protective and just a little sinister. A shudder passes through me. I'm glad Theo isn't like Harold. I couldn't function with anyone overbearing. Theo. Will he badger me again? I wish he'd let it drop. 'He doesn't understand me,' I whisper, shaking my head at Betty. 'You do, though, eh?' She smiles at me, a twinkle in her eye. She knows what I mean. See that brood round her feet? It's a wonder she's got the energy to smile.

The other paintings watch me standing here talking to my favourite. It's daft, but my mood improves after our daily chats. Is it a sign of madness? Like mother, like daughter? Perhaps.

I scan the room, taking in the animation of Dad's paintings, and can almost hear them chattering amongst themselves. Oh, Dad. How unfair it is. Your exhibition *will* go ahead and astonish everyone. But you won't see it.

CHAPTER FIVE

TWO DAYS LATER

Kim Brown invites me in with a sweep of her hand. Taller than me, she doesn't appear close to retirement. Her long grey hair glows with health as it tumbles over her shoulders. Her hazel eyes twinkle. My blood stops racing and calm flows through my veins.

'Please, sit.' Even her voice has a smile.

As I step in, I'm enfolded in a warm hug. A hint of lavender and peppermint hangs in the air. On the walls, ethnic pictures throw comforting colours into the room. The carpet's like one of those rag rugs from the past, a patchwork of reds, pinks, purples and cream. I wiggle my toes, imagining its texture on my bare feet.

I position myself on the pale blue couch. It gives just the right amount under my weight, the multi-coloured cushions supporting my back.

Kim sits on a matching chair.

'Before we begin, I must make it clear - Vic Wells has paid for six sessions. Are you happy to continue? Or would you rather I refund him the money?'

'That's typical Vic. No, don't refund the money; he'd be so hurt. I'll thank him when I get back to the gallery.'

Kim nods and smiles.

'Sia. That's a pretty and unusual name. I bet it has a story.'

She folds her hands on her lap, long fingers tapering to nails the colour of latte, and tilts her head in question.

'It's short for Artemisia. After the painter Artemisia Gentileschi.'

'I can see why you shorten it, although the full name has beauty, doesn't it? Does anyone call you by it?'

I laugh. 'Only Mother, particularly when she's angry.'

'Is she angry often?'

The russet eyes search my face, lock on to mine. I don't know what to say. Always.

'Sometimes.'

'Tell me about her.'

'She's a painter, like my dad.' I stall, the calm of the room suddenly oppressive.

Kim watches me, expressionless, her eyes depths of wisdom. Like she knows all about Mother.

'She likes to dress up.'

'Does she? What as?'

'I mean, change what she wears. It depends on her mood. One day she'll be in designer dungarees and loafers, the next a Dior gown.'

'Even when she's painting?'

'She hasn't painted since Dad…' I can't say the word; I'm ridiculous. 'Since he…' I screw my eyes tight.

'Died?'

I nod, horrified by the tear burgeoning under my closed eyelid.

'What does she do instead?'

Alarm shrieks through my thoughts, my head a scramble of panic. Tell the truth, my inner voice urges. Don't, whispers the fear, wheedling and unctuous. I take a deep breath, my eyes still clamped shut.

'She drinks.'

My words dissolve into the air, absorbed by the stillness of the room. When I open my eyes, I half expect to be sitting alone, so still does Kim sit by me. But there she is, silent and watchful.

'She drinks a lot. Mother was always partial to a glass of wine, but nowadays it's a bottle.' My betrayal begins. The fear sits, lodged in my ribs, shaking its head and oozing regret. I haven't the energy to push it away.

'How much do *you* drink?'

The question takes me by surprise, and I pull back until I am pressed hard against the cushions. 'I enjoy a glass of wine.' A picture of the Merlot I sank a couple of nights ago takes shape behind my eyes. 'Sometimes, I overdo it. Don't we all?' My laughter is shaky and insincere. It has guilt laced through it.

'How worried about your mother's drinking are you? Have you tackled her on the issue?'

I'm a sullen schoolgirl, caught out not telling her parents about a detention. '… I haven't really said much. Made the odd comment. Nothing specific.'

'Why not?'

'Not the kind of subject one discusses with Mother.' Were they my words? Did I say that? Not the kind of subject *one* discusses? Dear God, what will she think? 'What I mean is-'

'Yes?'

'It's difficult.'

'Since your father died?'

I wish she could read my thoughts. That I didn't have to express them out loud. She looks as though she could, gazing at me with understanding and empathy. Yes, I'm sure she could. I will her to hear them. She sits, unnaturally still. Waiting. For me to speak.

'No.'

'How do you feel, since your father died?'

A complete curve-ball. Somehow, I curb my impulse to whack her across the face for springing such a question. Heat crawls up my neck, a creeping tide of fury. 'How do you think?' If words had edges, these would be chef-knife sharp.

'You tell me. Everyone reacts differently. Your mother drinks. What do you do?'

'I work.' The admission emerges as a sigh from the deepest part of me. 'I work.'

'And when you're not working?'

I look her in the eye. 'I exist.' The truth of it smacks me. All this time, I have been fighting to keep my feelings restrained, hidden. Even from myself. 'I haven't cried, apart from an occasional tear.'

'Not everyone does. It doesn't mean you don't love him.'

'Oh, God.' My mouth tightens. My skin over my cheekbones spasms, and tiny daggers fling themselves along my lash line. The terrifying spectre of losing control looms over me. I push down the sob in my throat. I will not succumb now.

Kim leans over, pulls a tissue from the box on the low table. She offers it to me. 'You're allowed to cry.'

'I can't.' The words hiss through my clenched teeth. My jaw throbs with the effort.

'Take it.' She gives the order in a tone as soft as a caress. 'It'll come upon you when you least expect. Best be prepared.'

A moment passes.

'We've not talked of your father. Are you up to it?'

'I'm not sure. What do you want to know?'

'Tell me about the exhibition.'

'It's celebrating his forty years as an artist. We thought it'd be brilliant to dig out paintings from each decade and display them collectively, to show his journey from rookie painter to the master he is now.'

She nods. 'How come you were working on it together?'

'Vic Wells? Owns the gallery where I work; he liked the idea. He's a real fan and has known Dad for years. We, Vic and I, consider the place Dad's. There's so many of his paintings hanging there.'

'How was it, working with your father?'

I can't stop myself grinning. 'It's brilliant. He's such good company. We laugh a lot. On the same wavelength, according to Mother.'

Kim half smiles. 'And is the exhibition still going ahead?'

The medicine ball question thuds into my solar plexus. I cannot speak, any words I might utter lying battered under its weight.

She waits as I summon the strength to answer.

It takes all my power to mumble, 'Yes,' in a voice unrecognisable as mine. I want to explain the greater significance of Dad's exhibition, the importance of its success. But I can't. Vic hasn't agreed yet, but talking to Kim has strengthened my resolve. If nothing else comes from this meeting, that's a step forward.

'Perhaps you can tell me more next time? Shall we synchronise our diaries?'

I nod and she picks up a large book I only notice now from the table. I scrabble in my handbag for my mobile.

'Same time next week; is that all right for you?'

'Yes.'

As I scroll through my calendar, she writes my name in her diary. I make a note of my appointment, drop my phone into my bag, and take out my purse.

She dismisses it with a subtle wave of her hand. 'Remember? It's taken…'

'Vic.'

She nods.

'Thank you.'

We stand. She steps back to let me pass.

Outside, the November sun makes a feeble attempt to shine through the thin cloud. The cool air teases my cheeks. Something tangled inside me has unfurled, just a little. In the car, I switch on the ignition and Joni sings.

CHAPTER SIX

THE NEXT DAY

Vic takes the package I offer, his brows deep over his eyes. 'What's this?'

'A thank you. For Kim. I'm sure she'll help.'

'Ah. Knew it.' He pulls open the package and gasps. 'Darling girl. There was no need but thank you.' He offers me the box. 'Care to share, with coffee?'

'Hoped you'd say that. Yes, please. Shall I pour?'

We sit at reception, the aroma of coffee in a heady mix with the sweetness of double chocolate cookies. I lick crumbs from my fingers.

'This won't do. There's an exhibition to organise.'

'Sia, are you sure-?'

'Yes, Vic. I am. I called Detta last night and asked her to contact Tina's wife. She's going to invite her to open the exhibition – the whole thing.'

'I'm astonished you've persuaded her. Did you give her the Heather treatment?' He frowns. 'And if Tina's wife says no?'

I ignore his reference to Mother. 'Worry about that if she does. For now, we soldier on.' Detta was surprisingly willing when I asked her, despite her reservations the other day. Survivor guilt coming into play, perhaps?

He grunts into his coffee and wanders towards the office. I don't understand why he's still so hesitant. Especially when the salvaged paintings are such beauts. The small gallery will look wonderful with them against its moss green walls. Perhaps Detta can help me choose suitable frames, although the unframed ones in the big gallery have impact.

My head full of musings, I amble to Dad's pictures. 'Now then, Betty. Can't chat right now. Got work to do.' Next to Betty and Harold, The Boardroom Bosses still smirk. What have you done with her? Their faces reveal nothing but masculine confidence. If I could step into the boardroom with them, it'd be no different. They're so completely in control. Possibly, she was never there. That's what Vic thinks, I'm sure.

From the stack ready to be hung next, I withdraw the family portrait Dad did when I was a kid. I prop it against the wall beside the Bosses and walk across the room to study it. I'll never tire of looking at it. How happy we are. I love the way Dad and Sandro smile at each other over my head, sharing a private joke. Even Mother looks pleased about something. He painted it during her short-hair phase. She could be mistaken for my older sister. And Boy. The sweetest creature. Should I get another dog? Sorry, Boy, if you're listening. Don't mean it.

Vic strolls to join me, and he stands eyeing the picture. 'You're going to put it next to the Bosses?'

'Considering. I appreciate the contrasts – the colour and warmth of the family compared to the grey cynicism of the corporation.'

He nods, pensive. 'Yes, yes. That might work. Frame?'

'No. Don't want to contain its joie de vivre.'

'See what you mean. Hm.' He walks away, still nodding, like an ancient oil well head.

I slouch back against the wall. Thank goodness this one wasn't at the old studio. Tina Shaw. Should I go with Detta to see her wife? No. Not sure I'd handle it right. Detta's approach will be discreet, empathetic.

The phone rings but Vic answers, so I rummage through the other paintings in the stack. I am hauling one such from the pile when Vic calls me from the office door.

'Sia, it's the police.' He waves the phone at me. 'They want to talk to you.'

'Me?' I mouth at him. With a strange griping in my gut, I take the phone from him.

'Miss l'Ussier?'

'Yes.'

'We want to talk to you concerning the fire at the old studio. Would it be convenient if one of our officers dropped by the gallery this afternoon? Just for an informal chat.'

'I suppose so.'

'Rightio.' The line goes dead.

'They want to question me about the fire.'

'I expect they're talking to everyone involved with Frank.'

'Why? No-one ever goes there anymore. I went out of curiosity, nostalgia? And I wanted to rummage through the paintings in the guard's shed.'

'It surprised me they gave you access. Isn't it part of the investigation?'

'Not the shed, no. The guard had no objections once I'd explained. Helped me load the paintings into the car. I told you that.'

He looks thoughtful. 'You did. And it bothered me at the time.'

'Anyway, someone's coming here this afternoon.'

* * *

I sit behind the desk, mentally kicking myself for not tidying it before they arrived. The police officer and his sidekick frown at me across the carnage, and I strain to hold my features under control. I'm reminded of those old cop shows of my childhood and half expect the sidekick to lick a pencil before taking notes. If he does, there'll be no accounting for my behaviour.

'I had to find out if I could use the paintings Detta – Ms Jackson – had saved, in my exhibition. I told the bloke at the gate.'

'When were you last at the studio? Before that?'

'Can't remember. Years ago. Dad didn't use it much anymore, except for storage.'

'Apart from Ms Jackson, had anyone else been there? To your knowledge?'

'Mother, I think. The same day as Detta. Yes, I'm sure she did.'

'Any idea why?'

'Knowing Mother, to have a sneaky peek at the paintings before Detta. So, she'd know if any paintings were missing later.'

The police officers exchange glances.

'Is that a concern?'

I realise my mistake. 'No. Not at all. Mother likes to play games. Keep people on tenterhooks. She'd assume Tina'd tell Detta she'd been; put Detta on edge. That's how Mother operates.'

'So, you have no concerns à propos Ms Jackson's visit to the studio?'

'None.' I am a little too strident, my answer too immediate. 'In fact, I asked her to search for paintings to use in Dad's exhibition.' I try to modulate my voice, to sound calm and unflustered. My conversation with Mother about the nudes needles through my brain.

'I see.'

The sidekick coughs. 'Explain why Ms Jackson went to the studio?'

Doesn't he listen? He delves his hand into his pocket and pulls out a tube of mints. He prises one out and offers the tube to me.

I shake my head. Hate mints. It's all I can do to clean my teeth every day. Why doesn't someone invent a toothpaste that isn't minty? I remember having a lovely strawberry one when I was a kid.

'Miss l'Ussier?'

'What? Detta. Yes. I said. To find suitable paintings for the exhibition.'

I have no idea why I don't mention the nudes, and, as though he read my mind, the inspector says, 'Was Ms Jackson looking for specific paintings?'

'No.' I'm hell-bound, for sure. Why shouldn't I tell them about the nudes? None survived the fire. 'Haven't you asked Detta this?'

'Yes. She corroborates your story.'

My relief is short-lived.

'But your mother doesn't.'

'Eh?'

'Do you believe Ms Jackson wanted any of the paintings at the studio destroyed?'

They suspect Detta started the fire. She had a motive, and she'd been swift to assure me she hadn't started it. Was that guilt? Why did she say that? So soon after getting here? It's not Detta. Course it isn't.

'No.' I don't sound convincing at all, my 'no' whispered into my chest.

They watch me, their faces professionally blank.

'She can't have started the fire. She's just not like that. I trust her completely.'

'Do you? That's good.'

I'm under suspicion, too; they consider me an accomplice. My face burns with guilt.

The inspector stands, and his sidekick follows suit. 'That'll do for now, Miss l'Ussier. We may need to speak to you again. Remember anything significant, call.' He flicks a card on to the desk. 'My direct number is on there. Leave a message if I'm not available.'

'Right. Will do.' I follow them out of the office to the main door. They nod at Vic as they pass. 'Bye.'

The door sighs closed, and I stand watching as it cuts off the outside world. When I spin on my heels, Vic stands by reception, his eyebrow arched in question.

'Right, next painting. We'll never be ready at this rate.' I make a show of being calm and walk determinedly towards Dad's corridor.

Vic's footsteps creak behind me. I stop and face him. 'What's the matter?'

He raises his eyebrows. I shouldn't exclude him.

'They… wanted to know if Detta had any reasons for wanting the pictures destroyed. I reckon she might be a suspect. In cahoots with me.'

Vic explodes into laughter. 'Sia, why on earth should they think any such nonsense?'

'Because, I'm guessing, Mother told them she wanted to find the nudes.'

His laughter dies. 'Oh.'

'Quite. They told me my story agreed with Detta's but not with Mother's. It's obvious she's told them Detta didn't want the paintings publicly displayed. It's exactly the thing she would do. For devilment.'

'Shouldn't you speak to her?'

'Mother or Detta?'

'Your mother. This could be nasty for Detta.'

'It won't make any difference.'

'Why didn't you or Detta mention the nudes? Could they have another reason for their suspicion?'

'Vic, listen to yourself. Of course there's no other reason. What other reason could there be?'

She loved him, romantically, once. Perhaps she never stopped and has been jealous of Mother all along. *I'd* certainly want to rub Mother's face in it if I were in that situation.

'… that's all.' He looks at me with expectation, wanting me to react to his words when I haven't listened.

'I can't explain why I didn't tell them. It didn't feel right.'

'That'll convince the jury.'

'Excuse me? What do you mean?'

'It's arson, Sia. They will charge someone. There'll be a trial. You may well end up in the dock.'

Nausea hits me in the knees. Which is an odd sensation. I lick my lips. It doesn't help. So, I meander away to Dad's paintings. 'That won't happen.' Do I sound confident? I doubt it. 'You going to help me with this or are you busy doing *important* gallery stuff?'

'No. I'll help.'

In the pause before he follows me, the air sighs with resignation.

* * *

My mobile buzzes. Theo. No-one else calls me at work. 'Hello you.'

'Doll, how's it going? Just on a prep period, so thought I'd call you.'

He's ebullient, his voice musical with happiness.

'It's all good. Vic 'n' me have hung more paintings and I've written the blurb and got it printed. And the police have interviewed me. All in a day's work. You?'

He doesn't speak. His breathing rasps into my ear, like audible thoughts. 'The police?'

'Yeah. Routine, apparently.' I hear suspicion everywhere. 'Nothing to worry about, although they warned me they may need to speak to me again.'

'That's pretty much routine, yes. The studio belonged to your dad.'

'Listen to you, mister expert.'

'Don't forget my brother's with the force.'

I giggle, hold back the urge to wish the force be with him. 'I haven't forgotten. Will he have any insider goss on our case?'

'Wouldn't say, even if he did.'

'Pity.'

'Why?'

His question is a pinprick to my conscience. 'No reason. Just being daft.'

'Arson is serious, Sia. You shouldn't joke about it.'

'Rowan Atkinson reckons you can make a joke about anything.'

'You know my thoughts on him. Got to go. See you soon. Be good.'

And he's gone. 'I love you, too.' My mobile stares back at me, devoid of expression. Of course. Foolish woman. It's inanimate.

'Arranging another tryst with the handsome school teacher?' Vic smiles and hands me a mug of coffee.

'Chance'd be a fine thing.' The mug sits warm and comforting in my clasped hands. 'He's too busy trying to impress the boss. Wants the top job so he works all hours. Haven't seen him for, well, since the weekend.'

'Poor you. But how much sweeter your next assignation will be.'

'If he's not too tired.'

'Susan tried teaching. Trained and everything. Lasted two years. Said it was the hardest work she'd ever done.' He gets a faraway look in his eyes.

'That's what Theo says - no-one understands how exhausting the job is. The only time he's human is in the holidays.'

'Which reminds me.' He snaps out of it like he's made a decision. 'When's your next appointment with Kim?'

'Thursday. It's in the diary.'

'Good, good. Lovely woman. I'm glad you took to her.'

'I did. Thanks for the tip.' I've said it before, but it does no harm to repeat myself. 'The next session might be harder, though. Got the impression she was breaking me in gently last time.'

'Sounds right. It can feel like a hammer blow, the things she asks. Still, you'll feel better in the long run.'

Curlicues of apprehension coil and uncoil in my gut. Since my first session with Kim, my doubt has increased. I have to keep telling myself it's for my own good. I struggle to rekindle the optimism. It's like someone else experienced the spark of hope, not me.

'I can do without any hammer blows, thank you very much.'

'You'll manage.' He waves his mug at the walls. 'It's taking shape. You were right about the placings, by the way. The family portrait is perfect next to the Bosses, for many reasons. You're getting the hang of this curating business.'

'Is that supposed to be funny?'

'What? No. Can't you take a compliment, young lady?'

I drain my mug and clonk it on to the floor. 'Yes. Thank you. I'm glad you approve of what I've done so far. It matters.'

He ruffles my hair, like I'm six. 'You have an artistic streak in there. Just different from your mum and dad.'

'Will Mother agree?' I know the answer, and it's unfair to Vic, but the words are out before I can stop them.

'How can she not? You're doing a fine job. Your dad's paintings never looked so imposing.'

'That's good to hear. But I'm not expecting her to say anything positive.'

'Some people struggle to express their feelings…'

'Vic, stop. It's sweet of you, but we both know Mother is not such a person.'

He sighs. 'Don't take it to heart, whatever she says or doesn't say. Your dad would've been very proud.'

I press my lips together and blink at him. The muscles in my neck go rigid; my torso takes up the signal and every part of me hurts; cramp wrenches each fibre into spasm. It will pass, but a moment of panic seizes me, and I'll be tender for hours.

Vic looks away, pretends to scan the room. He strolls to the few paintings still to be hung. 'What're your plans for this lot?'

I take a deep breath. 'They're the ones Detta salvaged.' I join him by the pictures. 'I thought I'd hang them along there.' And I point to the wall adjacent to the entrance where I imagine the paintings to hang. 'They'll be the first ones people encounter when they enter.'

He tilts his head. 'You want them to see those? The fire-damaged ones, before the rest?'

'Yes. It shows the circular nature of life. These are among Dad's earliest paintings – so visitors should see them first. But they are also, in some ways, the last because they survived.'

He nods. 'Yes. But what about Tina Shaw's wife? Won't seeing them first seem rather heartless?'

'Not if she's warned. She's aware the paintings will be here, and I'll tell her where they are. If we hold the opening ceremony in here,' I wave my arms, my palms open, 'she'll have passed them before she has to say anything – and they won't be in her direct line of vision, either.' I'm thinking on the hoof here as I haven't given Tina's wife much thought and Vic's questions throw me off guard. I don't want the poor woman to break down; it's a possibility.

'Let's see how they look first. Decide then.'

He's not convinced. But I reckon I'll win him over when he sees them in place.

The rest of the day, we spend hanging the paintings and writing the blurb. Vic re-opens the rest of the gallery. The winter sunshine has brought people into town, and a steady trickle of visitors ambles through, curious about what's hiding behind the cordon. I phone John, the printer, who offers a decent price for posters and asks for photos of the paintings to include.

'There won't be any. Couldn't we just have one of the gallery?'

'Photos of the paintings, especially the more obscure works, would have more impact. Even a picture taken with your phone would do, if you're concerned about the quality?'

'I'd like to keep it under wraps until the opening. How about that? I'll photograph the paintings covered with dust sheets?'

John tuts. 'It's most unusual not to have photos of the paintings – at least one – when trying to promote an exhibition.'

'Yes.' I count to three. 'But my father never allowed photos of his works. You know that, too.'

I can almost hear him shaking his head and looking heavenwards. 'Send me something. Make sure it's not too ghastly.'

'Okay. Thanks, John.'

I'll photograph the fire-damaged ones, just a corner here and there exposed—a hint of what's underneath. It'll be tantalising if I get it right. John's talking tosh. And if Mother's got any of Dad painting, that'd be brilliant. No. I'll go on the internet. Bound to be one of him I can use.

CHAPTER SEVEN

A WEEK LATER

Jenny takes ages to answer the phone. I check the time. It's possible she's still in session, although unlikely. She's been my closest friend since sixth form, like a separate me. I hate the half-empty vibe in our flat when she's in Brussels working. True, I encouraged her to develop her career, but her success has come at a cost.

'Hello you.'

'Bonjour mademoiselle. Ca va?' My French accent is appalling.

'Yeah. Over worked and underpaid. As ever. What's new?' Each word exudes tiredness.

'They've arrested Detta on suspicion of arson.'

'I beg your pardon?'

Jenny's disbelief echoes my own.

'When are you coming home? I'm desperate for a cuddle, litres of wine and shed loads of monosodium glutamate.'

'Aren't you getting them from Theo?'

'It's not the same. I need you. Anyway, Theo's not keen on Chinese food.' Or my drinking; his barbed hint about it plays through my mind; I press my inner mute button.

'There're a couple of lengthy sessions this week. Then back for a few days. Although there's talk of my being needed in the House for a while.'

I groan. 'That's worse, somehow. Knowing you're in the country but not here, with me.'

'I'll be home for weekends. Nothing happens in the House at weekends. Not like this place. But tell me about Detta. They can't be serious?'

I well up, my throat suddenly dry and tight. Deep breath. 'Mother told the police about the Detta nudes. That gave them the motive. Detta was there when the fire started – apparently arsonists often hang around to see the impact of their handiwork.'

'But it nearly killed her!'

'They're not convinced by Detta's story. She says they think she didn't mean to kill Tina, but that's the other thing hanging over her. They could escalate it – to manslaughter.'

'Oh, my God.' Jenny's voice is a whisper of incredulity. 'Poor Detta.'

We're quiet for an age. I imagine Jenny in her modern, stark apartment and guilt steals over me. 'Sorry. I shouldn't have called, but I needed to talk to you. Now you'll worry and feel impotent because you're over there and I'm here. Sorry. I'm sure I'll manage. Vic's being brilliant, as always-'

'Stop gabbling, Sia. It's fine. I shan't fret. Obviously, I wish things were different, especially coming so soon after your dad, but I have faith. You'll manage. Have you been to that counsellor you told me about? What's her name again?'

'Kim. Yes. She's helping.'

'Good. Can't you discuss with her your need for cuddles and wine and stuff?'

'Yes, but it's not the same as doing it, is it? I can't stay up till the early hours with *Kim* and get sozzled, can I? And drinking alone isn't fun.'

'You haven't been, have you?'

'Not much. Can't risk facing Vic with a hangover.'

'Don't do it at all, Sia. That way ruin lies.'

'I know, don't nag.'

'Not nagging. Just reminding.' There's a pause and I picture

Jenny glancing at the clock. 'How is Theo?' Her tone stiffens as she mentions his name, and I hesitate. How strange, after all our years as friends, I should be awkward about Theo. Jenny's always adored him.

'Busy,' I say at last. My thudding heart tells me I'm lying by omission. 'He's adamant about this promotion; he does nothing but work.'

Jenny, even in a different country, is not fooled. 'Has he been badgering you again?'

'He's not had time.' My laugh sounds hollow even to me. 'I wish you were home so we could talk properly.'

'Just tell him straight, Sia.'

'Must go. Meeting him for supper at the school. It's dining in night.'

'That'll be nice. Give him my love.'

'Will do. Love you.'

'See you soon. Love you, too.' And, with a noisy smooch into my ear, she's gone.

I hate this moment, the one immediately after a chat to Jenny when she's in Brussels. The emptiness of the flat crowds me, and my thoughts echo in the vacant rooms. I need Joni. I put my code into my iPad, and she serenades me with *Chelsea Morning*. There's not much sunshine through my windows on this grim November evening. Heavy clouds scud, desolate, over the town and half naked trees bend in the wind, trying to hold on to the few leaves that cling without hope to their branches. Only when the Christmas lights are switched on, will the city regain its vibrancy. Then, there'll be a storm and half of them will stop working so that swags across the high street will dangle, patchily illuminated and sorry for themselves.

I try to shrug off my blues, but *Down to You* swims into my thoughts, the plaintive solo piano before she sings. In my wardrobe mirror, my refection stares at me, lost. It's gone: what

I took for granted, assumed was solid. I pull my favourite warm dress from its hanger. The deep golden-russet wool glimmers. I run my hands over its softness: if a Jenny hug is unobtainable, the dress must make an acceptable substitute. Theo will approve – all he sees is how it clings to my body.

Moments later, the woman in the mirror doesn't look so abandoned. Isn't it astonishing how clothes can affect you? Joni knows a thing or two. The lustre of the dress reflects my hair, which falls on to my shoulders in loose, auburn curls. My crowning glory, Dad always says. I pull on a pair of orange flats and the outfit is complete. I swipe my bag from the sofa, my coat from the hook, and brace myself for the bitter chill outside. At least dinner is guaranteed to be delicious, warming and filling. And there will be wine.

CHAPTER EIGHT

AFTER THE DINNER AT SCHOOL

Theo pushes open the door and steps aside to let me pass into the hall ahead of him. He pulls the key from the lock and tosses it in his hand, as he always does. A fizz of anticipation zings through me. He'd taken me by surprise when he'd said he'd come home with me, smiling his sexy smile and making my knees turn to jelly.

I chuck my bag on to the chair and roll my shoulders. He's behind me in a moment, his firm hands massaging the knots in the muscles at the bottom of my neck. I tip my head forward and let him edge his thumbs along my spine. Each movement unlocks more tension until he reaches the small of my back. I don't want him to stop.

'Have you got any scotch?'

His question shatters my luxuriating; the muscles knot again in arthritic spasms. 'Somewhere. Wouldn't you rather go to bed?'

Wine has made me bold. My face flushes, but I don't care; I want to wrap myself round Theo under the duvet. I'm hoping for sex, but I'd settle for a body hug.

He takes my hand and drags me to the sofa to sit by him. 'Forget it. We need to talk.'

I am trapped. Disappointment aches in my core, radiating heaviness into my limbs. And resignation courses through my knowing veins. 'Do we?'

He ignores my question. 'Sia, doll, I came back with you

tonight to talk to you, to ask you something.'

Here we go. I guess I couldn't keep it at bay forever.

'The head has asked me to apply for the job. He spoke to me this afternoon. Said it was a formality, but the school must follow procedure.' He stares at me, his grey eyes earnest yet seductive. 'The interview will be next week. I could be deputy head by the end of term.'

Silence sits thick upon me. We both know what comes next. A deputy needs a wife who will throw herself into the life of the school, encourage the boys in extra-curricular activities, and live in one of the tied cottages. And take pleasure in doing so. The whole scenario fills me with horror.

'Well done.' My words are not totally insincere. I am proud of him, appreciate how hard he's worked. 'I never doubted you.' And I mean it. His ambition has driven him since the day he started at that God-forsaken place.

'Then you know what I want to ask you..?" His intelligent eyes hold me in their grip. We met when he brought a busload of kids from school to the gallery two years ago and his eyes were the first thing I fell for. They never fail to reduce me to trembles. I'm unable to look away, even as I prepare to shatter his dreams.

'Theo, I can't.'

He takes my hand in his. 'Sia, will you marry me?'

'Haven't you listened? I can't marry you. I said so before you asked me.'

'Why not? We're good together, aren't we? Neither of us ever looks at anyone else. And we're not getting any younger.'

And now for the body blow.

'I want to be a father. Of your child. You know this.'

Gently, I pull my hand from his. 'I do… as much as you know how much I don't want marriage, children, the whole domestic thing. It just isn't for me.'

He studies his hands; the hands I long to caress my skin, tousle my hair, explore my most intimate places.

'I thought you were just putting it off because it scared you.'

'Scared me? How?'

'Commitment, childbirth. I dunno.'

Can I tell him? Let him have the truth behind my determination never to marry? Never to have children? He sits, a man thwarted by the woman he loves. Although I can't remember the last time he said so.

'Is it me and my children you crave? Or is it convenience? Ready-made family?'

'How can you ask me that? You know how much I love you.'

'Do I?'

Although we sit together, the space between us is gradually widening, as if the sofa is pulling us apart. He watches me across the divide.

'Yes, you do. I should tell you more often-'

I laugh. 'You're right there.' I try to be kind. 'Theo, your feelings aren't the issue here. It's mine, and your utter disregard for them. When have I given you reason to suppose I want any of it? I love you. I'm happy with the way our lives are – well, I'd like us to be together more but-'

'We would be together more! We'd be living in the same house and wake up together every morning.'

'Couldn't we do that without getting married?'

'I'm not sure.'

'Do we have to live at school?'

'I do. It's part of my job. And the deputy's house is terrific. You'd love it.'

We aren't getting anywhere. The hope in his face shreds my heart. 'I don't want to live at the school, Theo.' Tiredness overtakes me; my limbs leaden, my head aching. I stand. 'Are you staying? I need to go to bed.'

For an age he stares at the floor, doesn't move. He pulls himself from the sofa and takes me in his arms. He's all-encompassing, reassuring and strong. But it's an illusion, just a physical thing. I let myself lean into him anyway, and I could stay in his caress all night, ignore the longing in my weary body for sleep, and surrender to him.

'Let's turn in. It's been a long day.'

In bed we lie, our legs entwined, enfolded in each other's arms. His heartbeat flutters against mine. Within minutes, he is asleep. I slide my arm from under him, my legs from his, and curl up into my usual sleeping position, my back towards him. His breath tickles my skin, but I don't move. I may never feel it upon me again and I want to make it last as long as possible. In the darkness, far away across the city, the Minster clock chimes, and I resign myself to a sleepless night.

'Tea?' His voice brings me to consciousness. I have slept after all.

He stands there, a naked silhouette, a mug in each hand. I can't stop myself grinning. I sit up, plump my pillow, lean back and reach for the mug. 'Thanks.' It's hot and threatens to burn my mouth. Perfect. I have trained him well. I'd have this every morning if I moved in with him at the school. Would it be so bad?

He slips back into bed, and we sit in companionable quiet drinking tea, the light from the hallway cutting through the shadows of the bedroom. I flick on the bedside light and wince, even though it's only a soft beam from under a cream lampshade.

'What's on the cards for you today?'

He lowers his mug. 'The application letter. And three sixth form lessons. You?'

'Your favourite day. Can't the letter wait until tomorrow? Or are you on duty this weekend?' His calendar is pinned on my kitchen noticeboard and I have a momentary prick of guilt. Should I be aware of when he's on weekends? Probably.

'Just in the morning. I could write it in the afternoon, but I'd rather get it started, at least.'

'Do you need references?'

He shrugs. 'No idea. No-one's said.'

'I'll be your referee. I'd make sure it'd be glowing – tell 'em how masterful you are in bed and-'

'Don't. Don't make fun of me. It's important.'

'Not making fun. Just trying to be amusing. I know it's important. Sorry.'

We say nothing while we finish our tea. He clatters his mug onto my dressing table on his way to the bathroom. The shower radio bursts into life, a man's voice droning through the sound of cascading water. I amble to the kitchen and, while listening to his movements in the bathroom, prepare our breakfast. It comforts me when he's here. Could we carry on as normal if he gets this promotion? What if my refusal to join him at the school stops him being appointed? The horror of the idea tears through me. How selfish I must seem. But then, why should I alter my life for him to progress in his career? Isn't my career important? Things are never straight forward, are they?

He appears at the door, handsome and smelling delicious: the perfect boyfriend action figure. I'll never stop finding him desirable. I hand him a fresh mug of tea. 'Will you get the job, if you don't have a wife – or fiancée – in tow?'

'They appoint bachelors – I'm a prime example. But the accommodation isn't as good. They prefer married men. Family values and such. None of the senior staff is unmarried.'

'Oh.'

'But that's not the main reason I want to marry you. You do believe me, don't you?'

'Honestly?'

He nods.

'Not sure.'

We've reached an impasse. Again. I see no happy way out. Each solution brings problems I fear we won't be able to manage.

'Breakfast. Is hard to think straight on an empty stomach.'

But muesli, fruit, yogurt and nuts have little effect on my thinking, which stubbornly refuses to become clear. It continues to race in circles, never reaching a satisfactory conclusion.

Theo bolts his food and springs to his feet. 'Gotta go.' He plants a kiss on the top of my head. 'Please, consider it? I'll call you.'

His departure is like someone has plugged in a giant vacuum cleaner, which sucks away everything not pinned down. The flat is at once empty. But it's me who isn't pinned down, not Theo. I stack the dishes in the dishwasher and slam it closed. It shudders, as if it's considering its bonds of restraint. Which is how I would feel ensconced in a school cottage.

My mobile buzzes. Theo. I wish he wouldn't text while driving. *Bringing Mark with me to the exhibition. He's a fan.*

I reply with a thumbs up emoji and two kisses. Mark Hubbard. What did Mother say about him? 'Cannot imagine how Oxford accepted that man. He's clearly…' Oh, what was the word? I can't remember. She wasn't impressed, although most people look second best next to Theo.

At the gallery, an hour or so later, Vic tells me the police have called again. 'You're to go to the station. ASAP.'

'What? Now?'

'I'd say so, yes.'

I don't even begin to unravel my scarf, but spin on my heel towards the door. 'See you later.'

In the traffic, my mind fills with agitated questions. Will they ask me why I didn't mention the nudes? Charge me for withholding information? Should I call Mother before I go in, make sure I know what she told them? My stomach roils and the muesli churns in rebelliousness. Wouldn't that be dandy, throwing up on the police station floor? I laugh, despite myself. How could I indicate my guilt with more certainty?

I edge into the police station car park. It's rammed with vehicles. Great. I must park on the road and risk getting a parking ticket. How much worse can things get? Just as I manoeuvre between two lines of parked cars, a young man waves at me across the car park and points. I think he's telling me he's leaving, so I pull round and sure enough, he gets into his van and pulls away. I wave a thank you and drive into the space. It's still nippy, the air coming from the heater no warmer than outside, but I dig out my mobile and call Mother.

She answers almost at once. 'Artemisia? Have you seen the time?'

'Yes. We civilised folk are washed, breakfasted and dressed by now. Aren't you?'

'Me, civilised? Never. That would stifle my creativity.'

'Mother, what did you tell the police about Detta's nudes?'

There's a pause before she speaks. 'Tell them? Why, the truth, of course. Why?'

'Because they've arrested her?'

'Oh, that.'

'Yes, that. What, exactly, did you tell them?'

'Exactly,' she says, mimicking my tone, 'what I assume you told them.'

My turn to pause while I gather myself to stop the torrent of fury and frustration just itching to pour forth. 'Please tell me. I'm at the station for more questioning. I'd appreciate it if you told me.'

'Now I understand why you call at this ungodly hour. I told them Detta requested entrée to the studio because she wanted to find the nudes.'

'But that's not-'

'I told them you wanted her to check the old paintings, but I had to mention her strong conviction the nudes should remain hidden.'

'Oh, Mother. You had to, did you?'

'They seemed to consider it important.'

'Aren't you even a smidgen bothered that Detta has been arrested? That she might go to prison?'

'Not if she's guilty, no.'

'She isn't guilty. I am certain she isn't.'

'Artemisia, I fail to see how you can be so sure. She had a motive, she had access to the paintings.'

'So, why didn't she just steal them? We'd not have known any better.'

'Desperate people don't think logically. And anyway, Tina…' Mother shivers audibly down the phone. 'Poor girl, would have seen her remove them.'

'Maybe. I still think she's innocent.'

'Let the police do their work. Then we'll get the truth, won't we?'

The phone dies in my hand. Goodbye, Mother. Thanks for your help.

The man at the desk picks up the phone and tells someone I'm here. He tells me to take a seat. I sit hugging my bag in the cool of the waiting room. Posters warning of Cyber-crime and instructing how to be safe at night when out alone adorn the walls. Aren't the police supposed to make you feel safe? These posters amplify the dangerous nature of the world. Laughter echoes from behind a set of double doors and footsteps approach.

'Miss l'Ussier?'

I stand.

'This way, please.'

It's the officer who came to the gallery. He strides along the corridor with purpose, and I trot behind him. His suit jacket is crumpled from too much sitting and there's a thread hanging from his shiny elbow.

'In here.'

He opens the door into a small windowless room with a table and four plastic chairs. On the table is an old-fashioned tape recorder and a couple of empty paper cups.

'Coffee? Tea?'

'No thanks.'

He invites me to sit. Just as I scrape the chair from beneath the table, the door opens and a uniformed woman officer, who is ridiculously pretty with gleaming fair hair tightly wound into a chignon, and dimples like Doris Day, enters. She should be a kissagram. She closes the door behind her and sits with the officer at the table, facing me. My guts rumble, and the situation becomes serious.

He fiddles with the tape machine and turns to me. 'My name is Detective Inspector Smith and with me is PC Broden. It's… 9:45am on Friday, November 22nd. We are interviewing Miss Sia l'Ussier.'

My mouth is dry. I wish I'd asked for a cup of water. I'd not be surprised if, when they ask me something, all that comes out is a squeak.

'May I call you Sia? It's a bit of a mouthful, your surname.'

'Of course,' I cheep.

'We want to discuss events of 11th November, if we may?'

I nod. And PC Broden jots something in her notebook. So that's why she's here. Tape recording not enough.

'When we last spoke to you, you told us Miss Jackson had gone to the old studio on your orders.'

'No. I said I'd asked her to look for paintings to use in the exhibition. I didn't order her to go.'

'Was her visit your suggestion?'

I sense a trap. PC Kissagram looks up from her notepad. She has the unerring gaze of a gorgon. I study my fingernails.

'We decided together.'

Their disbelief is tangible, rolling over me like a sea fret. They say nothing, waiting for me to continue, listening for the snap as I ensnare myself.

'None of the family catalogued what was there, paintings-wise. So, we decided Detta should go and check. We hoped there'd be something for Dad's exhibition.'

'And what did she find?'

Heat blooms on my skin, my ears blaze. It crawls from my

collarbone to my neck; the blotchy, florid evidence will condemn me.

'Half a dozen canvases. We were both delighted.'

'What else did she find?'

'Excuse me?'

'Other than the canvases? The ones I assume you're using in the exhibition?'

Snap.

A flicker of understanding passes between them.

'She found other paintings, ones not suitable for the exhibition.'

DI Smith raises his eyebrows. 'Why unsuitable?'

'They were nudes. Not typical of Dad's work, nor in keeping with the other exhibits.'

'Isn't there a nude painting of your mother in the exhibition?' His voice is as smooth as oil. It slips and slides into my ears. I hunch my shoulders, trying to rid myself of its unctuousness.

'May I have a cup of water now?' How I get the words out is a mystery. My mouth is doing a passable impression of a Saharan valley, my tongue sticking to my teeth, gritty and rough.

He nods at the PC. She slithers from her chair, and in no time, returns bearing a cup. She places it on the table. The DI tells the tape machine of her actions.

The water is warm and metallic. They are determined to deny me comfort. But then, they think I am Detta's accomplice. What do I expect?

'Why aren't the nudes Miss Jackson discovered worthy of your exhibition, yet the one of your mother is?'

I cannot disparage my dad's paintings. I have never seen one that doesn't deserve to be hung where everyone can see it. They are masterpieces, without exception.

'They were intimate, private.' I reach over and deposit the cup on the table. They watch my every movement. 'Unlike Mother, the model for the paintings did not want the world and his wife gawking at nude paintings of her.'

'Who is the model?'

My hesitation only makes matters worse, yet I do not want to say her name. I gather my strength, look him in the eyes and say: 'Detta.'

And the world thunders betrayal in my skull.

'Why didn't you inform us of this initially, Miss l'Ussier?'

Suddenly, my name is no longer unpronounceable. Any trace of geniality has disappeared. The gorgon has a playmate.

'She's not an arsonist.'

'But she had reason to dispose of the paintings, didn't she? Hadn't you mentioned to her you were considering using them in the exhibition?'

I gape at him. How..?'

Like a mind-reader, he says, 'We talk to anyone involved. Someone overheard you having just this conversation with Miss Jackson.'

Vic.

I have made a huge mistake; should've told them the truth from the beginning. Now, they'll be convinced we're both guilty. God, I could even end up in prison, too.

'Yes, we spoke about it. Detta didn't want the paintings displayed. She never said why, but I guessed it was because she and Dad… were a couple at the time he painted them.'

'Did she say she wanted to dispose of the paintings? Or did she just want them to remain unseen?'

'Will my mother get to hear what I say?'

'Only if it comes out in court.'

'Detta asked me about buying the paintings. But she never so much as hinted at getting rid of them.'

'Why are you worried about your mother finding out?'

'Because Mother views Detta as a sort of rival. She knows they were together before she met Dad. If she thought Detta wanted the paintings, she'd play games with her. Nasty games.'

It's peculiar how relief soaks through me as I tell them the truth. The dryness in my mouth has gone, the heat recedes along my neck, below my collar.

'I'm sorry I didn't say this at the start. I was trying to help Detta. She isn't an arsonist. And she's devastated by Tina's death.'

'Could you drink a coffee now? Or tea? We could probably scrounge a biscuit from somewhere, if you fancy it.'

The change in his demeanour unnerves me. Is he trying to trick me into another betrayal? My mouth dries again. I swallow hard.

'Yes, please. Tea.'

He nods at PC Kissagram, aka the gorgon, who scowls, her dainty face a study in disagreeability. But she leaves, pulling the door to behind her with a fierce clank. Like a prison door.

DI Smith tells the machine she's gone. He turns to me, one side of his mouth in a half-hearted smile, his teeth glinting behind the full lips. What do they say? Like a shark grinning at its dinner?

'When did your mother visit the studio?'

'I told you before. I don't know the exact time, but it was before Detta.'

'How long did she stay there?'

'I've no idea – wait, no. Detta said Tina told her Mother was in the studio for half an hour or so.'

He consults his manila folder, riffles through the pages, stops and reads for a moment. Perhaps he's testing me, testing the truth of my answers. I bet Detta has told him what Tina said. He shuts the folder.

'Yes, that tallies. Why did your mother visit the gallery, if Ms Jackson was seeking out other paintings for the exhibition?'

'To unnerve Detta, no other reason. I told you last time, she enjoys manipulating people.' As you're trying to manipulate me and unnerve me. We've been through this, so why ask me again? The guard. I bet he's told them I was snooping around.

PC Gorgon, I can't think of anyone so glowering as a kissagram anymore, heaves through the door carrying a tray. Three plastic cups in brown holders totter alongside a couple of cling-filmed packs of biscuits. She dumps the tray on the table, slopping murky brown liquid on to the tray. It leaches under the biscuits. 'Tea and biscuits, sir,' she says, the 'sir' heavy with impudence.

'I hope you don't take sugar. PC Broden has over-looked it.'

'It's fine.'

I help myself to a cup. The tea, though tasteless, is hot. It percolates through me. The plastic wrapped biscuits drip on to my trousers when I take them from the tray. Inside, knock-down Hob Nobs lurk. They have as little flavour as the tea: the perfect accompaniment. When I get back to the gallery, I shall so enjoy a cup of proper coffee, and who knows, there might be a cookie left. It feels as if I have been here for hours. I search for a clock and recoil; they've only questioned me for an hour. My sessions - an hour each - with Kim pass in a flash. Time is a most disconcerting thing.

'Let me go over what we've discussed today,' the DI says, with his mouth full of biscuit.

Don't they teach manners at police school? Hark at me, sounding just like Mother. Anyway, it'd be parents, not-

'You confirmed Miss Jackson wanted to prevent the nude paintings of her being placed on display.'

His words are an accusation. He goes through everything we've discussed, scanning the PC's notes. I want to listen carefully, so I don't miss any mistakes, but he speaks too quickly. I forget what he's said as soon as the words are gone.

'If you would just stay here for a few minutes, we'll get the notes written up and you can sign them as an accurate record of our conversation. Is that all right? More tea?' He switches off the tape machine and ejects the cassette, which he slips into his pocket.

'That's fine. And, no thank you to the tea.'

His smile this time is warmer, more genuine. 'Don't blame you. It's crap, isn't it?'

He and the PC rise from their chairs in unison, like synchronised swimmers doing a dry run. As soon as they leave, I stand, too. My backside is numb from sitting on the plastic chair. It's a relief to stretch my legs. There's nothing to look at; the walls are bare. And it's cold; I hadn't realised how chilly till now. Adrenaline keeping me warm, I expect. Isn't that how it works? I rub my hands together and blow on them. It makes no difference, so I tuck them into the folds of my scarf. I'd appreciate Doctor Who's assistance. We'd travel back in time – witness how the fire started.

DI Smith returns, wielding a sheet of headed paper.

'Read through this, and if everything's okay, sign and date the bottom. You'll need to print your name as well.'

He places the paper and a ball-point pen on the table and stands over me as I read.

'How necessary is this, when you've recorded the whole interview?'

'It's easier to access the information on paper. The tape's for back-up, proof we didn't put any undue pressure on the witness.'

'I see.'

I sign and date the statement, print my name at the bottom.

'Can I go now?'

'You're not under arrest. You were free to leave at any time. Thank you for your help.'

He extends his hand, and we shake. It's the most bizarre thing to do, like we've just settled a deal. Perhaps we have, of sorts.

He walks with me to the main door. 'When is the exhibition opening?'

'Couple of weeks. It could open now; we're virtually there.'

'I may pop in.'

'I'll watch out for you. May even provide you with a decent cuppa.'

'I'll definitely come, then. Goodbye.'

During my return journey to the gallery, the interview replays in my mind; my answers to their questions jostle in a tumble of worry. I'll call Detta once I've spoken to Vic. I hope she'll understand the betrayal wasn't done willingly.

CHAPTER NINE

DECEMBER 2ND, THE DAY OF THE EXHIBITION

The gallery shimmers in unexpected December sunshine. Dad's paintings gleam with life and humour. Leaving them frameless was a good idea - the movement from one to the next is seamless. Even Vic commented on it.

Detta walks towards me, smiling. I try to return her cheer, but my nerves about the opening, and the sliver of doubt which nestles in the back of my mind, make it tricky. She was understanding about my police statements, but since the interview, I've sensed a change in our relationship. Although it could just be my imagination. I force my face into a bigger smile. Let's hope it seems genuine; I want it to be.

'Sia, you are a magician. Deerdale will laud your exhibition. I wouldn't be surprised if it's taken up by national media.' She takes my hand and gives it a squeeze.

My blush is a sincere enough response. Who doesn't like to be praised?

'Thank you. I am chuffed with the way it's turned out. Just have to see what my fiercest critic says.' The thought of Mother, who should arrive any minute, sends my stomach into hyper-driven somersaults. I pull my hand from Detta's and rub my tummy.

'Silly girl. She'll be proud of you, overwhelmed by your talent and success.'

'That'll be a first.' I cannot keep the cynicism from my voice.

'I'm looking forward to Sandro's reaction, though. He's always said I can do it. Even when I was working with Dad, he said I should work independently.'

'He's right. You're a natural. Vic says you'll be in demand after this.'

'Really?' The frisson of delight Vic's confidence in me creates momentarily banishes the nerves about Mother. 'Wow. That's exciting, and a bit scary... work in other galleries, you mean?'

'That's the implication, yes.'

'Never thought about it.'

Detta looks at me as though I'm bonkers.

'Honestly. I kind of assumed I'd always be here, as a guardian of Dad's work.'

'Branch out, use your education and training to the maximum. You've so much knowledge about other artists, it'd be a shame not to reap the benefit of your expertise.'

Is she making fun of me? I can't tell. It wouldn't be the first time. But she has got me thinking. 'You could be r-'

'Artemisia, come and show me round your little exhibition.'

Detta shrugs and pats my arm. 'Indulge her vanity for a little while. She'll be purring over everything before you can say Prosecco.' She winks, and love for her floods through me.

'Mother. I'm glad you've come.'

I arrange my face in a welcoming smile, which I know doesn't reach my eyes, and stride towards where she stands with Sandro at reception. Sandro steps towards me, intercepting Mother.

'Sia.' He takes me in his arm. 'Mum's edgy,' he whispers in my ear. He steers me round to face Mother. 'Here she is, Mum.'

We air kiss. Mother pushes me away to arm's length and scrutinises me. She's judging my clothes and finding them wanting. I try not to sigh. My tweed culottes and matching waistcoat keep me warm, and I adore how the greens bring out the auburn in my hair. Mother doesn't care for polo necked jumpers, either, even if they are merino, but in a gallery that's often chilly, it makes sense to wear something to keep out the cold.

'At least you're not wearing jeans,' she says, slipping her hand into the crook of my elbow. Her grasp is tight, her narrow fingers digging into my arm. I'm sure I'm not imagining her tremor. 'Come on then. Don't keep me standing at the threshold like a paying customer.'

I guide her towards the first paintings. Before them stands an easel displaying an enlarged version of our promotional picture. The brief notes explain how the first paintings were salvaged from the fire and pays tribute to Tina. Opposite the easel, on a low table, Tina smiles at us from a gilt frame. She looks unbearably young. In a second gleaming frame, sitting beside a dainty vase of flowers, is an outline of her life. It includes her fascination with art and her heroic saving of Detta from the fire. On the wall adjacent to the table hang three of Tina's embroideries: scenes from graphic novels, full of vitality and colour and wit. Mother ignores them.

'Why have you not cleaned the paintings?' Her voice quivers, anger only just beneath the surface.

'Visitors need to see how close they came to destruction. How these beautiful works were almost lost to us.' I sound like the brochure. Hardly surprising, since I wrote most of it.

'Don't give me that. You just couldn't be bothered.'

Behind her, Sandro shakes his head, resignation in his eyes. 'Mum, that's not fair. Sia's worked incredibly hard. Give her some credit.'

She waves away his comment without turning to face him. Instead, she moves on to the next paintings, not bothering to look at these early ones individually. Her face is a mask of indifference. I was a fool to hope she'd be impressed. When I try to move away from her, hurt zinging through me, she grabs my arm more tightly.

We stand in front of the family portrait, and I silently dare her to say anything disparaging. Betty looks on, I swear with a sympathetic expression, the sparkle in her eye muted. Mother relinquishes my arm. She steps closer to the painting, peers at herself and then back at me.

'I can see you in me here. Cut your hair and you're very like I was. Not as slender, obviously, but the likeness is quite something.'

'Who'd have thought it?'

I say the words before my usual filter kicks in, but she smiles. 'Indeed.'

A commotion at reception rescues me. Vic gestures at me across the gallery.

'I'll have to see what he wants.' I glance at the clock. 'It might be Claire.'

'Who's she?'

'Tina's wife. She's opening the exhibition, remember?'

I walk away before Mother can speak. I don't need to hear her resentful complaining, especially as she absolved herself from the organisation of the exhibition. Ahead, Vic talks to Claire, takes her coat and offers her a glass of wine. He's at his solicitous best and Claire, laughing, takes a glass.

'Only one, though, Vic. I don't want to be drunk when I give my speech.'

'Hello, Claire. Nervous?'

'Sia, hello. Mm, just a bit.' She takes a sip of wine. 'Done nothing like this before.'

'Would you like to see Tina's table? Might be best.'

She nods, understanding what I'm getting at. She must possess courage to agree to this. Not sure I could. I said nothing at Dad's funeral, unable to utter a sound. Didn't sing any of the hymns, couldn't join in with the responses. Stop castigating yourself, Sia; this isn't a funeral.

Together, we approach Tina's table. Claire catches her breath as she gazes at the pictures on the wall. They are framed, but

Tina gave the pictures a 3D quality. In one, a superhero thrusts his fist over the frame like he's punching the onlooker. Claire touches his hand with her fingertips.

'I remember her sewing this.' Her fingers trace the outline of the fist. 'It's one of her first, which is why I chose it for the exhibition.'

I don't know about Vic, who stands close, but I hold my breath. Will Claire keep it together?

Claire sups her wine and reads the words in the frame. She's read them already. I wanted her approval before going ahead, but it's like she sees them for the first time.

'Yes. Yes, this is nice.' She turns to me, her eyes misting. 'Thank you.'

'Did you want to see Dad's paintings again? Remind you of how they're displayed?'

'No, if you don't mind. I'd rather sit in the office and go over my speech.'

Vic takes her arm. He murmurs to her, and she leans into him, her grief obvious. I watch them go into the office, my heart full.

Mother stands by the family portrait. Hasn't she moved since I left her with Sandro? She clasps her handbag - a huge designer thing with gold chain handles - like a shield. I cannot imagine what she carries in it and for a moment, I have a vision of a tiny dog peeping its head from between its folds. More likely, a hip flask of gin.

'You might have put my portrait somewhere we could see it more. Why have you stuck it in a far corner?'

Sandro looks at me, like he's curious, too. He probably reckons I've made a blunder, but I haven't. Whatever Mother's injured pride may say.

'It's in the best light of the gallery, Mother. No other painting is lit in the same way - it illuminates you.'

She stares hard at me, tiny black dots in the centre of her green eyes. Eyes like weapons. 'Of course I noticed that. But…' She gives up.

Over her shoulder, Sandro grins at me, and I swear the Hallelujah Chorus has broken out, showering my mind with sparklers. I can't stop myself grinning back at him.

'You've done a brilliant job, sis. Well done. D'you fancy a drink, Mum? Before the rush?'

'Yes, dear. Fetch me one, would you?'

'Are you going to stay here? There're chairs in reception.'

'Don't fuss, Artemisia. I shall stay. It gives me a good view of everything.'

'If you'll excuse me, I have to make sure Claire's okay.'

I march away before she can protest, my little victory still singing in my ears. It's nearly time to open. From outside, the voices of people waiting on the pavement creep under the doors. I half expect to see smoke-like vapour arise from the gap.

In our office, Claire leans on the desk, her notes in one hand, her wine in the other. She gives me a nervous smile and holds out her notes to show her trembling.

'You'll be fine. Focus on an individual, mid-crowd, and address your speech to the bridge of their nose. You'll fool the audience into thinking you're making eye contact. Works for me.'

'You get nervous?'

'You bet. Never sure how they'll react.'

Vic pops his head round the door. 'The press has arrived and that chap from Look North is waiting in reception. Talk to them, Sia?'

'Now? Haven't you given them my press statement?'

'Of course, but they want to speak to you. Go on; tremendous free publicity?'

'Time to take my own advice. Be back in a jiffy.'

I run my hands through my hair and check my face on my mobile. Not perfect, but remember you are Heather I'Ussier's beautiful daughter. Ha ha. Warning murmurs, telling me not to mess up, silence the singing in my head. Shoulders back. Slap on a smile. And I'm out of the office, heading towards the Look North bloke whose name escapes me, which is embarrassing, especially as I watch his programme almost daily.

'Hello there. Didn't expect to see you here today. Thanks for coming.'

He's much smaller in real life than he looks on the screen, and he smells fabulous, like a forest after rain. His camera woman decides, after a recce, the perfect place for my interview is beside the family portrait. My heart shrivels. Mother stands there, peering along the gallery at us, the hope in her eyes unmistakable. She'll want to muscle in. She's adept at stealing thunder.

But I cave. As we stroll towards her, the Look North man asks questions about the exhibition. He tells me he'll ask some of the same ones again on camera. By the portrait, his face lights up when he sees Mother. She is radiating glamour: her make-up is flawless, her gorgeously understated suit in olive green and the blouse that matches her eyes gives her the aura of a film star.

'Could you stand next to your mother, perhaps between her and the portrait?'

I shuffle to where he wants me to stand. The camera woman pins a microphone to my waistcoat and asks me to step a little closer to Mother. I try to keep my eyes from wondering in her direction. Her triumphant gaze takes in everything, like the beam from a lighthouse through the darkest night. Where are the rocks upon which I might founder?

'Ready? Shall we begin?'

I nod. The camera woman smiles, and he launches into his spiel.

He turns to me. 'So, why this exhibition here, and now?'

I give him the patter, tell him about how Dad and I were working on it together. But as I draw breath, Mother puts her hand solicitously on my arm and looks into the camera.

'Artemisia has produced a wonderful little exhibition in her father's memory. It's a miracle how she has taken up the challenge, in the tragic circumstances.'

Look North man tilts his head in question. 'It must make you feel gratified that your mother is so supportive.'

The camera woman pulls the camera back to me. I feel myself held in its lens, a frightened mute. I catch Mother's smile in the corner of my eye. 'Yes. I suppose it must.' The words come from somewhere.

The interview lasts a few more minutes. I answer his questions without thinking, forgetting what I've said as soon as I've uttered the words. Next thing, he's shaking my hand and telling me to watch the programme tonight. I follow him and the camera woman back to reception where Vic and Claire wait with Theo and Mark. They must have watched the whole sorry thing, seen Mother's thievery. Theo puts his arm round my shoulder and draws me close.

'You did brilliantly. Love your answer to the question about your mother's portrait. Bravo.'

I have no idea what he's getting at, but I take comfort in his embrace, burying myself in his arms and pretending the world has disappeared, pretending Mother did not hijack my interview. The shame of my performance ebbs. It's possible I'm over-reacting.

Vic taps me on the shoulder. 'It's time. Shall we?'

* * *

Applause echoes through the gallery and Claire sighs, her relief obvious. The crowd disperses, wandering off to view the paintings. A small group gathers round Claire, who shakes her head. I bet someone's asked to buy one of Tina's creations. Can't see Claire parting with them.

The gallery fills with people who discuss the paintings and the air hums with their voices. I fetch myself a glass of wine from reception. Mother sits - someone has brought her the high stool from the back room - in regal splendour, allowing her attention to fall upon anyone she deems worthy. Notably, worshippers eager to offer a compliment or two. She laughs at a joke, holds out her glass and Mark Hubbard snatches it too keenly from her and bowls through the crowd towards me.

'What are you up to? Fawning all over Mother?'

He pours the Prosecco too quickly, and it erupts over the top of the glass.

'Blast.' He takes a handkerchief from his jacket pocket and mops up the spillage. 'Your mother is utterly gorgeous. Could "fawn" all day, if she'd let me.'

'She would.' If it was anyone but you. Poor Mark. I've no idea how he's avoided Mother's wrath. 'Shall I take that? Haven't spoken to Mother for a bit.'

'No, no. I'll do it. We're getting on famously.'

He takes up Mother's glass like it's a trophy and minces through the people towards her. She gives him a smile to deaden the soul but accepts the wine. It's good he's keeping her occupied, I suppose. Saves me from having to be the subject of her scientific appraisal. Counterfeit. That was the word she used. Good word, Mother. But is he? Really? God, how we laughed the night we lit the Chinese lanterns after Dad unveiled his latest painting. None of the buggers took off, except Mark's. 'I've got it up,' he says. 'Well, that's a first,' says the poker-faced little cow with him. Makes me smile even now, after all this time. And Mark, hand on hip, camp as you like, 'You weren't complaining when I serviced you this morning.'

'Excuse me, Sia?'

A cultured voice, with a hint of an accent I can't place, springs me from my memories.

'Yes?'

I squint at him. About Dad's age, his eyes sparkle like nature designed them that way. How can I know this man?

'Daniel Rose - we've spoken on the phone.'

'Have we? Sorry, I don't remember.' I drink some more wine,

taken over by the absurd notion I must impress him, and feeling stupid. Good start.

'It was before Frank passed away. He and I were going to collaborate on a piece for my magazine.'

Perhaps Daniel came to Dad's funeral. Yes, that explains how, weirdly, I remember him and don't, simultaneously. The mess I was in then. I offer my hand.

'We meet in person, finally, then.'

He laughs and takes my hand in a firm but reassuring grasp. 'Indeed.'

He holds on to my hand a little longer than necessary. It doesn't feel creepy at all. Nor does the way he looks at me with those twinkly eyes.

'I came because I wondered if, if I could interview you? For the article? Naturally, I'm interested in you, but must confess I've pages to fill in the February issue.'

My turn to laugh. The audacity of it. 'Would you like a drink?'

'No, thanks. Never touch the stuff.' He puffs out his chest like he's proud of himself.

'Okay. Don't mind if I refill, do you?'

'Not at all. Be my guest.'

'Is that another invitation, Mr Rose?'

'Yes. Please, dear Miss l'Ussier, would you do me the honour of granting me an interview?'

How preposterous he is. And charming. He regards me with an air of mischief. Doing an interview with him would be a whole lot of fun, I'm certain.

'Did you know my father well?' The question pops out from me without my having given it conscious thought, but now I've asked, I want the answer.

Daniel becomes serious, the playfulness gone. 'I did, yes. We've known each other since before you were born. I wrote the article about his first exhibition, in The Guardian, that sealed his breakthrough.' He shakes his head. 'We had the mother of hangovers the following day.'

'That's how I know you!'

He frowns.

'Couldn't place you when you spoke to me, but of course, I've read everything about Dad. I've read your article. You were a bit, a bit, edgy in your praise, I remember.'

He blushes, just a hint, his smile returning and shadows fading from his umber eyes.

'Guilty as charged.' He lays his hand upon his chest, slender fingers tapering to well-manicured nails. 'You spotted my jealousy, I'm afraid.'

'Why? Why jealous?' But before he speaks, I know what he's going to say.

'Frank was so much more talented than I. As I admired everything he created, envy ate away at me knowing my own meagre abilities would never match his.'

Bingo. It's like hearing my own thoughts echoed back at me.

'I get that. It's the same for me. Not a creative genius, like him. Or my mother. Or my brother.'

'But you are. Look around you. What you've done here is bursting with creativity - the way you've hung the paintings, made optimum use of the light and the gallery's features. It's a work of art in itself.'

I refill my glass, unable to meet his eye or graciously accept his praise. It sits uncomfortably upon me.

'Frank was modest, too.' He whispers, like he's telling me a secret.

A sip of wine, and I can face him.

'You've already been round it, then? I assumed you'd just arrived.'

'No, I've been here since that poor young woman opened it. She's a plucky girl. Not sure I'd have such composure so soon after losing a loved one.'

'Same here. She's amazing.' It's easier to talk about Claire. 'I told her she would get offers for Tina's embroideries but-'

'Far too precious to part with.'

'Mm.'

'So, is that a yes? To the interview?'

'Yes.'

'We'll need to do it soon. Deadlines and all that. And I want to focus on your exhibition, so it's current.'

'Right.'

He takes his mobile from his pocket. 'Would you be able to talk to me next week? Say, Monday or Tuesday? I'll come to the gallery, if that's easier for you.'

'Can I call you, once today is over? I should return to the other guests.'

'Of course.' He replaces the phone and withdraws a card. 'There's my personal number.'

I slip it into my pocket. 'Nice to meet you, Daniel. I'll call. Promise.'

He nods, turns from me and heads towards the door. I make my way back into the gallery where Mother is holding court still. Within the group of adoring admirers, Mark stands dangerously close to her, his gaze fixed upon her. Another sip of wine, and I am ready.

'Still here, Mother?'

'I've not had a chance to escape - too many people desperate for a genuine connection with your father's paintings. I do hope I haven't overshadowed your little exhibition.'

Curls of irritation wiggle up my spine, but I smile. 'Nothing could do that.' Daniel's words whisper in my head. She can say what she wants. A genuine art critic has said it's bursting with creativity. My heart sings.

'My dear.' She slithers from the stool and clutches my arm. I try not to wince. 'I want to see my portrait again now the light has changed. See if you're right.'

The crowd parts for her to pass, like a female Moses through the Red Sea. I mumble thanks to them, and guide Mother towards her painting.

Across the gallery, Theo waves his empty glass at me. I shrug. If he wants another drink, he can get it himself. Mother holds on tight, her nails pearlescent blue, like dainty bruises.

In the late afternoon sunshine, Mother's portrait is breathtaking, a modern Mona Lisa with a smug, enigmatic expression. The light from the tall windows shimmers across it and its complexion glows. She fixes it with jade scrutiny, one eyebrow gracefully raised. No wonder Dad loved her so much; her extraordinary beauty is captivating. As she regards her younger self, her expression softens. Has she ever gazed upon me that way? Not that I can remember.

I wait for her to speak. No way am I going to ask her opinion. She'll assume I'm craving approval and deny me. It's easier to say nothing. Visitors jostle us as we stand. Some tell me how wonderful the exhibition is, how much they've enjoyed seeing Dad's timeline in paintings. One or two remark on Mother's portrait, but most seem to understand that she's having a private moment and leave us alone.

Without dragging herself from admiring her own features, Mother says, 'I want to kill him.'

'Who, this time?' I can't keep the weariness from my voice. Let's hope she thinks it's from all the work I've put into the exhibition.

'That Mark Hubbard.' She hisses his name, like it's something disgusting she's spitting out. 'He has hardly left my side since he arrived. Odious man.'

'He's all right.'

'He tried to inveigle his way into your father's circle, and now he's trying it on with me. I won't have it.'

'Mother, what are you talking about? Mark hardly knew Dad.'

She pulls herself away from worship and pins me with an icy

stare. 'Mark Hubbard nearly ruined him. Who accompanied him to the casino? Who encouraged his gambling?' She spins on her heel and looks along the gallery to where Mark stands, in conversation with Theo. 'Mark bloody Hubbard.'

'What?' I splutter my wine. Mark has a gambling problem? That's news to me. He's lazy and unambitious, but gambling? 'Are you sure it was him?'

'Of course I'm sure. You won't believe what I could tell you.' She takes a deep breath. 'So that's all I shall.' Her eyes freeze; I'll get nothing else from her about Mark, Dad and gambling today. If ever.

And does she deign to mention how her portrait glisters in the light, like it's the brightest star in the darkest sky? No. I repeat Daniel's words silently, telling myself the exhibition is a triumph. She'll never say such a thing. Aching tiredness comes over me. I long to sit, to heave my weary legs on to my coffee table and sink back on to my sofa.

'Seen enough?'

She sighs. 'I have. Ask Theo to take me home.'

Please. 'All right. Meet you at reception.'

I push through the gathering, coming to a halt in front of Betty and Harold.

'It's so unfair,' says a woman's voice.

'Typical patriarchal attitude. Men!' replies another.

Two middle-aged women stand reading the blurb next to the painting, their faces grim with disapproval.

'That's why Betty's one of my favourites.'

They blink at me, probably astonished to be interrupted by a stranger.

'I'm Sia l'Ussier - I created the exhibition of my father's works.'

They gasp in unison, their grimness taking flight as smiles light up their faces.

'How do you know about Betty's piano playing talent?'

'It's incredible, but her family was aware of her talents and chose to discourage them. Harold was a bit of a bully sometimes, but she loved him. Betty's sister visited her once, when Dad was in attendance, and she let slip the family secret. She told him, and he told me years later. When I researched Betty myself, I discovered she was a gifted pianist *and* a singer. The music you can hear today? That's Betty.'

'Goodness. Is Betty aware you've discovered her secret?'

'No, sadly. But her children are - there're a couple of them here today. Isn't that marvellous? It's why I've had to be, shall we say, diplomatic, in my notes about the painting.'

The woman closest to me squeezes my arm. 'I think it's wonderful, what you've done. Given that dear lady a second chance.'

'Thank you. Betty'd be pleased.'

The women gaze afresh at the painting. 'She looks different now.'

'That's the beauty of art. She looks different in the evening, too, when our visitors have left and I'm alone.'

'Artemisia, you were organising my lift home?' Mother appears at my side, furious at being upstaged by two dowdy, middle-aged women.

'Oh! You're the lady from the painting.' The first woman clasps her hands together. She looks from Mother to me. 'You must be mother and daughter. You're so alike.'

Mother stands a little taller. She almost smiles. 'Indeed. Do you like my portrait?'

'It doesn't do you justice,' simpers the second woman.

The first one shoots a glance at me. 'It could be you in the painting. You're the image of your mum.'

'Nice to meet you. Sorry, but we have to go. C'mon Mother.'

We're on dangerous ground now. I must get Mother away before these women cause her to spontaneously combust. I haul her away from them, my grip tight on her arm. She follows in my slipstream, quietly fuming, her muscles rigid in my hold.

Mark appears before us. Just what I need. His smile is lop-sided, his head tilted. He is unsteady on his feet. 'Shall I take the lovely Heather home? It's not out of my way.'

'Don't be ridiculous. You're drunk. Theo can take her.'

He looks crushed but I don't care. I just want her out of here. 'Where is he?'

'He's gone to the little boys' room.'

Mother and I shudder in unison.

'Have you seen Sandro?'

'Not for ages. That rather sweet girl, connected with those sewing thingies. He was with her.'

But the area by Tina's table is empty.

'Right.' I steer Mother toward the office. 'Stay here. I'll find Theo.'

She says nothing but glares at me like it's my fault Sandro has disappeared, and Theo answered the call of nature just when she needed him. Why she wants him to take her home, I don't know. Perhaps she arranged for Sandro to bring her but not take her home. I'll wring his neck, if that's true.

Back in the gallery, there's no sign of Theo. I can't take her; I've had too much wine. Maybe Vic will do the honours. But I can't see him either. What the hell is going on? Have they all deserted me, to cope with Mother in murderous mood alone? As those women said, Men!

'Sia.'

Theo calls from across the gallery, and he pushes his way through to me. 'Mark came into the gents. Thought something pervy was going on. Says Heather needs a taxi?'

'Please. There's no one else who's sober enough.'

'Perhaps you shouldn't have drunk so much - not on your opening day.'

Another dig? If he's joking, his timing is atrocious.

'I haven't had that much, but I don't want to risk driving.'

'I'm coming back for you then, am I?'

'Would you?'

He kisses my cheek. 'Course, though I must nip into school to do some admin. Now, where is she?'

We head over to the office. Mother stands rigid, dead centre, as if she wants to avoid touching anything. I cringe at my mess – Vic'll insist on my tidying it now the exhibition is open.

'It's not usually like this. We've had things on our minds.'

She quivers. 'I'm sure.'

'Ready, Heather?' Theo puts his smile on full beam and offers his arm. 'Let me take my favourite starlet away from all this.'

Starlet? All this? All this? He takes humouring her too far.

She takes his arm, and does that Princess Diana thing, looking up at him from below her lashes. I want to smack her. I want to smack both of them.

'See you later. I might be a couple of hours. Is that okay?'

'There's always stuff to do.'

Theo guides Mother to the door, holds it open and allows her to pass in front of him, in a waft of some expensive perfume she's sprayed on while I was out of the room.

'Bye, Mother.'

She doesn't turn but waves her bruisey fingers at me. I suppose that will have to do.

CHAPTER TEN

I close my eyes and let the quiet cocoon me. Vic left a while ago, so I wait for Theo alone. But I'm not alone, am I? Not with these friends surrounding me. Betty's stopped singing and playing the piano. She stands there, happier than she's been – ever. Even Harold has a satisfied, proud expression, his grip on her shoulder affectionate rather than domineering. I bet he'd have loved her to have become a famous pianist. Singer, not so much, but a pianist. They have kudos, don't they?

'Well done, Bets. You wowed them today. Might get a recording contract. I'll have to pay to talk to you.'

I pull myself up from the bench. Theo should be back soon. No doubt he and Mother are discussing how to persuade me to marry him and move into one of those cottages. I wish she wouldn't encourage him; it's not her life.

I amble towards reception, past Dad's rescued paintings, and turning my back on the Bosses. If she's still missing, I'm not sure how I'll react. And if she is back, I'll have heart failure, so I don't look.

The dark outside buffers against the windows, like cold cellophane. The gallery walls hunker down, bringing the paintings closer. After the activity and fuss of the day, it shrugs its shoulders to unknot the tension, and the radiators clunk as they lose heat.

The hairs on my arms tremble, my skin prickling with the chill. Behind my ears, my hairline twitches. The strain of today must be taking its toll. I hug myself, rubbing my hands the length of my arms. It makes no difference. The tips of my fingers whiten as if bloodless. I come to a halt in front of The Winning Hand, my senses piqued. The other paintings blur out of my peripheral vision; I home in on this one. And the truth screams at me. The eighth poker player. He's gone. As the words *it can't be happening* form in my mind, my brain tells them to shush. He should be there, leaning his elbow on his linen-trousered knee, grinning at his friends as the old man deals. They share a joke, all smiles. But here, none of them notice he's disappeared.

I read the blurb. Stupid. I know what it says. I wrote the words. But I didn't write there were eight men. Why didn't I include that fact? Because everyone can see that, and I needed to keep the blurb brief. Idiot! Was he there when the exhibition opened? Did visitors see eight or seven men? I glower at the notices warning people against taking photographs. This is your fault, Dad. Acid ferments in my gut. You and your precious no photos rule.

In a few strides, I am standing facing The Bosses. She's still not there. I am not imagining this. People are disappearing from the paintings. Vic found no sign of tampering. Did he look close enough? I career to the office, rummage through the desk drawer in search of a magnifying glass. My fingers curl round the metal handle and I hoick it from its hiding place under catalogues and a stapler. I run back to The Winning Hand.

I drag a chair from reception because this one's hung higher and totter on it, peering at the place where he should be. I lean close, any closer and I'll be climbing into the painting, and I study it through the lens. The surface is perfect, the brush strokes as they should be. The background continues, the shading seamless, with no hint of anything having been painted over. But I know these paintings, their every detail, every nuance. And he should be there.

I clamber from the chair, scurry to the opposite wall and view the painting from a distance. The absence is striking; Dad's painting unbalanced with a vast swathe of nothing he would never have countenanced.

The door creaks and Theo arrives. Is he startled to see me,

hard against the wall, staring at a painting with a random chair dumped in front of it? The magnifying glass sits heavy in my hand, inferring my guilt. He stands by the entrance and frowns. Don't ask. Please, don't ask.

'Are you ready?'

'Yes.' My answer emerges, fast, punchy, like I'm hiding something. I slip the magnifying glass into my pocket. 'Just having a last recce.'

'You'll see them in the morning. Hurry. I want to go home.'

'Right. I'll get my bag. It's in the office.' He knows that. It's where I always put it. Why explain? So I can smuggle the magnifying glass into the office, although why I must be underhand mystifies me. The chair fights back when I haul it back to reception and drop it with a thud.

My hands shake when I stuff the glass under the catalogues, and slam shut the drawer. I pull my scarf from the hook, wind it round my neck and slip into my coat. Grab my bag, and I'm at his side.

'Let's go.' I jangle the keys; it hides my trembling.

On the way home, I shut my eyes and pretend to sleep. I can't talk to Theo. Not while I process what has happened today. If it was today. But it must have been. Wouldn't I have noticed before the exhibition started?

'Noticed what?'

'Eh?' I stop slouching. 'What did you say?'

'You said you'd have noticed. Noticed what?'

'Think I must have been dreaming. No idea.' I gaze out of the window to avoid looking at him. My cheeks burn. We crawl through the evening traffic. It's Monday; why so busy?

'Is something on your mind?'

We stop as the lights go red. They're always against me when I'm in a hurry.

'No.'

We pull up outside my flat. He doesn't turn off the engine and relief overtakes me. Since our talk the other night about marriage, my nerves quiver whenever we're alone together.

'I won't come in. Expect you're tired after today. What are you doing Wednesday?'

What an odd question. 'Work, as usual. Why?'

'Let's have supper together. At the Indian.'

My favourite place to eat in Deerdale. And midweek, it should be easy enough to book a table. My stomach rumbles in anticipation. He can't press me with awkward questions in a public place, either.

'Yes, that'd be lovely. What time?'

'I'll book and message you.'

He leans forward and kisses me on the mouth. The touch of his lips on mine sends zingy delight straight to my arousal button. I wish he'd stay the night, despite the quivering. But the engine idles.

'Wednesday, then. Don't forget to text me. Shall I meet you there?'

'No, I'll come and collect you.'

He pulls back, presses the seat belt catch with his thumb, and it slackens. My signal to leave. I unsheathe myself, grab my bag from the footwell, and open the door. In the dull light of the interior lamp, he is pale, dark circles under his lovely eyes.

'You look tired, too. Have an early night.'

He nods, but his expression tells me he'll do no such thing.

I stand on the path, watching him wave as he drives away. I wave back, uncertain he'll see me. The night air trickles over my skin, like iced water, a shock after the warmth of Theo's car, and I scurry to the door, keen to be inside.

The following day passes in a blur. By closing time, I can barely lift one foot in front of the other. I slouch at reception trying to count our takings. It's impossible.

'Vic, I'll do this tomorrow. Too tired to think straight. Need my bed.' I scoop the cash into the box, tip closed the lid and heave myself to my feet. 'I'll put the box in the drawer.'

'Don't. Leave it there. I'll take it home. You go. You look exhausted. I'll lock up.'

'Thanks, Vic.'

My limbs drag as though made of osmium and my arms complain as I pull on my coat. The five-minute walk to the car stops time. I climb in, slumping into the seat with the grace of an exhausted toddler.

I shouldn't drive this tired. Those signs on motorways tell you tiredness can kill. What I could kill is a mug of hot chocolate while soaking in a steaming bath. For once, I'm glad the traffic is slow. Easier to navigate when everything's moving at a snail's pace.

It's dark under a starless sky by the time I trudge to my front door, push the key in the lock and turn. The door edges open and I halt at the threshold.

The kitchen light glows at the end of the hall, and a smell redolent of spaghetti Bolognese wafts to greet me. I drop my bag and hurry towards the kitchen, my weariness forgotten. By the cooker, Jenny turns, smiles and puts the spoon she's holding on the counter.

'Saw you arrive. Bath's running. You have a soak and I'll pour you a glass.'

'Sod that. Give us a cuddle.'

We hug like we've been apart for years rather than weeks. As I take in her familiar scent, tears fill my eyes. I snuffle into her shoulder. She untangles herself and holds me at arm's length, studying my face.

'Hey, what's the matter? Don't tell me the opening wasn't a tremendous success. I've spoken to Detta, and she says it's been fabtastic.'

I laugh through the tears, hiccoughy and overcome, at her using our favourite word from school. 'Fabtastic. Yes. It was.'

'But?'

I unfurl my scarf and dump it on the table. She tuts and scoops it up. 'Put it somewhere else, not on my table. We're about to eat.'

She bundles it into my arms. 'Scoot. Bath and PJs. Then come and tell all.' She pushes me towards my room. 'Go on, go.'

In the heat of the bath, the day's events tumble through my head. Jenny brings me a glass of red and I take a huge draught, grateful for its velvet smoothness and richness on my tongue. The Winning Hand. I drink more. Inside my head slides forwards as I lean back on the bath pillow and balance the glass on the edge. I close my eyes; the painting swims before me, in soft focus but with enough definition to register its missing player. Have I drunk too much too quickly? Am I over tired? I can't decide. I curl the chain round my big toe and yank the plug from the plughole.

In my PJs, I slouch back into the kitchen, refill my glass and sit at the table. Jenny strains the spaghetti, spoons a dollop of green pesto into the pan and mixes them together. Basil and garlic mingle in the steam. Despite my fatigue, hunger churns in my gut.

'You said you couldn't get away.' My voice is reproachful, annoyingly. It wants to divulge my feelings even if I don't. 'Can you come to the gallery tomorrow?'

'Mm. That's the plan.' She speaks with a mouth full of spaghetti. 'Got here this afternoon.'

She plops spaghetti on to two plates, sloshes the Bolognese sauce on top and sprinkles fresh parmesan to finish. She hands me a plate.

'Buon appetito.'

'Saluti.'

We eat in contented silence, savouring the flavours, before launching into conversation. Something we began as gauche teenagers we never let slide.

'Go on, then. Tell me the but.'

Her bright eyes hold me in their beam. I can never hide my concerns from Jenny. I explain the second disappearance.

'What does Vic say? Or Sandro?'

I shrug. 'I only saw it when everyone had gone, and I was waiting for Theo to come and bring me home.'

'What did he say, then?'

'Didn't tell him.'

She takes a sip of wine, holds the glass at rest on her mouth. 'Why not?' The words swirl round the glass like she's trying them out.

'I couldn't.'

'Because?'

'He's asked me to marry him, and I've said no.'

The clonk of her glass on the table is an exclamation. 'You did it?'

A spiral of pleasure twists within me. I smile at her from behind my glass. 'I did it.' Now I've said it aloud, it feels real and right. The hours I've wasted during the long dark nights seem just that – a waste of time. I needed someone to tell. Kim's face flits through my mind. I could have told her, and maybe I will now Jenny knows. 'You can't imagine my relief.'

'I never thought you'd do it. Fancy you still having the ability to surprise me. Good for you. How did he take it?'

'Not sure. We're still seeing each other. He still applied for the job. Just waiting for the interview – but it's academic; the job's his.'

'Is the sex just as good?'

I snort wine into my glass, wipe my face with my hand. 'Yes. But not so frequent.' That's not true. Our sex life had dwindled before the proposal. He's always too busy or too tired. 'I miss it.'

'Are you going to ditch him? Find someone more available? I guess it'll just get worse once he's deputy.'

I can't say I haven't considered it, but breaking with Theo doesn't sit well with me yet. 'Sex isn't everything.'

'You're not going through an early menopause, are you?'

We fall into laughter. I wish she could stay, not return to Brussels and her high-flying career.

'I have been moody and temperamental. That's what Vic says. He reckons it's why I'm seeing the missing people. It was him suggested I see Kim.'

'You said. But you don't agree.'

'Not entirely. Seeing Kim is helping me cope with losing Dad, but I don't think grief is making me see things.'

'How would you explain it, then?'

The hilarity disappears in an instant. 'You'll think I'm raving.'

'Try me.' She rests her fork on her plate and stares at me, no trace of mischief in her face.

The words are in my head, but they're in a scramble and I can't unscramble them so I'll make sense. As I try to decide, everything the words imply sounds ridiculous. I squirm at the nonsensical ideas muddling through me.

Jenny says nothing. She takes another sip of wine, her eyes on mine while I tussle with my thoughts.

'I think-'

Hammering on the door cuts me off. We leap to our feet but stand gaping at one another.

'What?' I can't be sure if it's Jenny who's spoken or me.

Jenny sprints down the hall to the door and she wrenches it open. Sandro and Theo barge into the flat. 'Where's Sia?' Sandro's voice, edgy, sharp, cuts through the air. My heart thuds out of time. Dread seeps over me like cold slime.

'Sia.' Sandro rushes to me and takes me in a rough embrace. Mother. Has something happened to her? Why'd he be so distraught otherwise? Behind him, Theo stands rigid. He is white-faced, his eyes troubled.

'Has something happened to Mother?' I pull away from him, stumble to my chair and fall upon it.

'No.' Theo steps forward. 'It's Mark.'

None of this makes sense. They're over-wrought about Mark? Neither of them respects him. What is going on?

Jenny sits opposite me. Theo and Sandro join us at the table.

'Sia, I can't tell you any other way.'

I have never seen Sandro this serious. My light-hearted, easy-going brother is like a strange clone of himself.

He takes my hand in his. 'Mark is dead.'

The painting materialises, with cinematic clarity, in my mind's eye. The missing man is Mark. My certainty overwhelms me. But I cannot speak of it. Not yet.

'How?' Jenny asks, but we both want the answer.

Sandro and Theo exchange a bewildered glance. Theo nods, and stares at me like he's waiting to gauge my reaction.

'Someone has shot him.'

'Don't be ridiculous.' And I laugh. To my shame, I laugh.

'He's not.' Theo talks as though he's speaking through water, in ripples rather than words. 'I heard it, Sia.' He doesn't take his eyes from me as he whispers, 'I heard it.'

My supper gurgles up my throat, wine and Bolognese in a nauseating mix. I swallow hard.

'I assumed it was a car back-firing, so I didn't act.' His eyes glitter with tears. 'I just cursed and went back to my marking.' He rakes his hand through his hair. 'I might've saved him…'

'Mate, nothing could've.' Sandro looks at me. 'It was point blank range. He didn't have a hope.'

Jenny coughs. Is she battling regurgitation, too? In her pale face, her blue eyes brim with anxiety. 'Why'd anyone want to kill Mark? We aren't living in America; who owns a gun in this country?'

Sandro shrugs. 'Got any wine left?'

I fetch two glasses from the kitchen and a bottle from the wine rack. It slips in my shaking hands as I battle to withdraw the cork. It makes a hideous pop when it's released. My nerves shriek.

Sandro takes the bottle from me when I try to pour. I shake so much I slop wine on to the table. He hands a glass to Theo and orders him to drink.

In the heavy quiet, Theo takes a huge slug of wine. And he speaks. 'The police figure the murderer was someone familiar to Mark, someone he trusted. Forensics reckon no signs of a break in, nor a struggle…'

'Christ,' Jenny whistles under her breath. 'Does that mean it's someone you know, too?'

'It's possible. I must go back. The school is in lock-down. Head argued with the police as he understood my insistence we tell you in person.' He stands, sways a little, and takes another draught of wine. 'Police expect me back.' He stumbles towards the door.

'Theo, Mark isn't a particular friend of mine, so why did you say I should be informed?'

He grabs the door handle, his knuckles pale, and turns his gaze to Sandro. 'You coming?'

'Course. I'll drive.'

'Theo.' His name cuts through the room on my ragged call. Now he turns. 'Why come to tell me?'

'He was at the gallery. I don't know. I had to get away. Couldn't think of another reason for them to let me leave. Said I'd be an hour, tops. Got to go.'

He darts away, shock rendering me incapable of rising from my chair. Sandro flies after him, yells a quick goodbye, and is gone. Jenny and I sit in stunned silence. I can't unscramble my brain. Jenny pours more wine, and we drink, both staring into nothingness, our spaghetti congealing on the plates.

'You're connecting it with the painting, aren't you?' Her eyes stay focused on something in the distance, or not focused at all, like she's processing her own thoughts as I try to mine.

She's right. It takes her saying it for me to admit it. First Tina and now Mark. A woman, then a man. It can't be a coincidence, can it? But that means I am raving as I feared. Jenny will call the madhouse and get me admitted. I drink more, to put off having to speak.

'Sia?'

'Yes.' As soon as I say the word, it ceases to be outrageous. My past cynicism, which had erupted in my even daring to consider it, quietens to a subtle roar. 'I don't believe in coincidences.'

She takes up the plates from the table and carries them into the kitchen. She clatters them on to the draining board; a fork crashes to the floor, its echo drives through me, jarring. I wince. And drink more.

Back at the table, she tops up our glasses. 'Was Mark jealous of Theo?'

'What? No. Why?'

She sits opposite me again. 'Just wondered.'

'You're not suggesting Theo did it? That's just stupid.' But her words don't hurt me as perhaps they should if I believed Theo incapable of murder. 'Why would Mark's jealousy turn Theo into a killer?'

'If he tried to scupper Theo's promotion?'

'But that's a done deal. You're seriously wrong there, my friend.'

Jenny laughs into her wine. I can't help myself. I try to control the grin tugging at the corners of my mouth but fail. We hold each other's stares while we snicker into our glasses.

'Stop. Stop.' My chest aches from the effort of trying to behave appropriately. Poor Mark is dead. Shot. In the grounds of the school. I snort again. I am a despicable human being.

'Who then?'

I don't understand why she's pressing on with this. We can't solve it. That's why the police exist. 'I've no idea. But I bet the police will interview me again. Two dead people, in suspicious circumstances. It's inevitable.' And I remember that DI Smith never turned up at the opening of the exhibition, despite his promise.

Our laughter dissipates, and we sit once again in silence. Even outside, no sounds interrupt our contemplation. No car tyres whoosh along the tarmac, no sirens pierce the night air. It's like living in a vacuum.

I heave myself from my chair and go to the window. I pull back the curtain and search the view for any sign of life. Nothing. No-one walks along the path, the traffic lights at the end of the road blink for nobody. In the inky sky, edged with fluorescence from streetlights, no aircraft trails cut across the stars emerging from the clouds.

In the school's direction, I stare hard to see if I can spot police blue lights, but there's no sign. No doubt I'm too late. Poor Mark. What happened tonight? Who saw him last? What did they say to each other? Was he scared? I would've been.

'Sia?'

'Mm?' I turn from the window; the curtain falls with a whisper.

'How close were you and Mark? You weren't… dabbling?'

'No, I wasn't. Hardly knew him. Only saw him with Theo. Don't think I've ever seen him without. Are you turning into Madam Poirot?'

She smiles. 'Just eliminating you from my enquiries.'

I wander back to the table, sit, and drink again. 'It's odd that another person has died so soon after a figure goes AWOL from one of Dad's paintings.'

'It's almost like he knows.' Unmistakable sarcasm drips from her words. 'Shall we have a séance?'

Her face is expressionless. She's aching to laugh but struggles to contain and hide it.

'Cow.'

And we erupt once again. My muscles relax, tension recedes. How I wish it could be permanent, but tomorrow, real life will thrust itself into my face again. And Mark will still be dead.

'Did I tell you; I'm doing an article for a magazine?' Why Daniel Rose should pop into my mind, I've no idea, but there he is. 'Dad was in the middle of arranging it with this journalist. He came to the opening and asked if I'd do it instead.'

'Your Dad?' She drains her glass and pours herself more. 'He is being busy.'

'I wish it had been him.' My sigh comes from somewhere profound. 'No. Guy called Daniel Rose. He's a specialist art journalist. Known Dad for years, apparently. Dad never spoke of him, but that's what he says.'

'Is he genuine?'

'He didn't show me his press credentials, if that's what you mean.'

'Now you're being saucy. What magazine does he work for?'

'Own. It's his own mag. Called, oh what did he say? Hold on. I've got his card.'

I scramble to the couch, where I dumped my bag and rummage through it. Of course, the card is wedged in under my sunglasses, hairbrush, and purse. I remove it with a flourish. 'Here.' I read the card as I return to the table. 'No magazine title, just his name and number. And a very modest tag-line – *An award-winning writer with style and insight.* D'you think he made that up himself?' I sling the card across the table and Jenny picks it up.

'I bet that's a quote from someone; maybe when he won his award. And the winner of the most self-satisfied writer award is…' She drums her fingers on the table and consults the card. 'Daniel Rose.'

'He didn't give me that impression. He was funny, charming. I liked him.'

'You're gagging for sex.'

'He's the same age as my dad. Don't be revolting.'

'Is he married?'

'No idea. And it doesn't matter. Just stop. I'm not even thinking about him in that way.'

'Bet you are.'

'He's very attractive, and if he were thirty years younger, I'd consider it. But, no. Just no.'

She lets the card drop on to the table. 'Stranger things have happened. You wouldn't have admitted that a few weeks ago.'

'Things have changed. Theo's been avoiding coming home with me, says there's too much work to do. Imagine living at the place. Yes, we'd breakfast together, but after that, it'd be who knows what time I'd see him again. And they'll expect me to play wifey and get stuck into school life. Yuk.'

She leans across the table and squeezes my hand. Tears spring from nowhere. I gulp and take a swig of wine.

'You've had a time of it, haven't you?' She squeezes again. 'But you're coping. Your exhibition is a triumph, you're seeing the counsellor, and you've taken a stand with Theo even though it's been hard. Good for you, Sia. You're taking control of your life.'

'I hadn't cried since Dad went – until I'd seen Kim. Now, I cry at the slightest provocation.' I wipe my face with my hands. 'And at such random moments.'

'I've heard it gets you like that – grief.'

'You heard right.' I take a tissue from my pocket and dab my watery eyes, catch the drips from my nose. 'Any eligible bloke'll see my snotty face and my puffy eyes and skedaddle in the opposite direction. If I split up with Theo, I'll be alone till the end of time.'

'I'll buy you a Rabbit for Christmas.'

A laugh fizzes up my throat. 'Thanks.'

'Talking of Christmas, you haven't forgotten I'll be home for a week, have you?'

'Haven't thought about it at all. Too busy with the exhibition. Now it's up and running, I can start organising.' My words take a moment to filter through my mind. 'It'll be the first without Dad.' I hide my face in my hands, and tears course over my fingers unchecked.

Jenny says nothing but lets me cry. In the hush, strains of 'Waterloo' emerge from my bag. Jenny jumps up and retrieves my mobile. She hands it to me. I don't recognise the number, although it registers somewhere in the back of my mind. I swipe the front and press speaker.

'Miss l'Ussier? You'll know why I'm calling. Could you call into the station tomorrow? To assist with our enquiries into the murder of Mark Hubbard?'

I'm instantly sober. No more tears. 'Why do you need my help?'

'We're talking to everyone in contact with Mr Hubbard in the days leading up to his death. It's standard procedure. If you could? Tomorrow? Morning, if possible.'

'Yes, all right.'

The phone clicks and PC Gorgon has ended the call.

'She sounds a lot of fun.'

'She's a cross between Doris Day and Miss Trunchbull. Actually, quite frightening.'

'No doubt she'll go far in the force.'

'Shall we go to bed? I've had it for today, and if I've got to be interrogated by PC Broden, I'd best be wide awake and with it.'

'Yeah. Let's leave all this.' She waves her hand across the detritus on the table. 'I'll clear it up in the morning before coming to the gallery. Will you go straight to the station?'

'I'll text Vic. Tell him I'll be late.'

We hug and make our way to our bedrooms. She goes into the bathroom first while I cleanse my face. In the dim light of the bedroom, I stare at my reflection in the mirror. I look ancient; dark circles cup the bags under my eyes and my skin is pasty under the slap. Thank heavens for foundation and blusher. I'll need as much help as I can get tomorrow.

CHAPTER ELEVEN

THE NEXT DAY

I sit in the office, drumming my fingers on the desk. The computer screen is still frozen. We should get a new one. This heap of junk was no doubt installed as part of the original building, circa 1800. Perfect after a late start.

Christmas shopping has started in Deerdale. In the lead-up to the opening, I didn't notice the Winter Fair being set up, nor the lights being strung across the wide streets where pedestrians throng. Once PC Gorgon had finished with me, my trudge through the city allowed me the opportunity to wonder at its transformation. The tree in the central square towers over everything, nearly as high as the surrounding buildings. Shop windows with their red, gold and snowy sparkly displays entice shoppers to over-spend. Even in my tired frame of mind, I appreciate how radiant the city looks, dressed up for the festive season.

But the thrill is absent. Instead, a hollowness inhabits me. How will we endure Christmas without Dad? A vague recollection of a conversation at the wake runs through my mind. Didn't Mother say Christmas as usual, at her house? Dread fills the hollow. Mother, Sandro, and me. Could it be any worse?

The screen flashes and the cursor dives diagonally across it. Life is restored. I open the gallery email account and grin at the screen: Look North has emailed. They want a follow-up interview at the tv studio. Vic should do it; he's the senior curator. I reread the email. No such luck. They've asked for me.

I scroll the unreads. Nothing from Daniel Rose. He asked me to contact him, but if he's keen to interview me, wouldn't he call? He said he wanted to do it early this week, but it's Wednesday. A feeling I associate with Theo ferments in my gut: disappointment. I dig out Daniel's card from my bag and play with it, turning it over in my fingers. Should I call him? I'll have a coffee, see what Vic thinks.

'Yes, call him. I expect he's very busy, and if he asked you to call, he'll wait. He won't call you.'

Vic's right, of course. I carry my coffee into the office and pick up Daniel's card. Each of the giant buttons on the office phone clunks with a distinct note. I pretend I'm playing a strange percussion instrument and I always try to make a tune from the numbers I press. Daniel's tune doesn't jar. Sometimes, it's just a cacophony. I lodge the handset between my shoulder and ear, go online and search the news media for mentions of the exhibition. A couple appear. I've just pressed print when he answers.

'Daniel, it's Sia.' I'm shy talking to him, which is absurd. The heat surges up my neck. Thank the Lord he can't see it.

'Hello. Enjoyed your slot on the television. Well done, you kept your cool.'

'Thanks. It wasn't easy.'

'I bet. Heather can be a handful, can't she? Has she seen it?'

'Undoubtedly a hundred times. Not sure she realises the telly adds half a stone. She'll be a tad miffed, to begin with, but she'll soon get over it, when her friends call to tell her how fabulous she was.'

Daniel chuckles, his laugh vibrating in my ear. 'She won't be too upset, having to defer to you?'

'She won't see it that way. It was her interview, not mine.'

'That's not true. You were marvellous.'

How pleased I am to hear his words is idiotic, but they make me sit straighter and smile at the phone.

'When shall we do your interview? Can you come to the gallery tomorrow?' I flick the page of my diary. Only my appointment with Kim. He could choose his date, but I want him here as soon as possible.

'That'd be great, yes. I've a meeting at half eight. How does elevenish sound?'

'I'm writing it in my diary – in ink, so it's fixed.'

He takes a sharp breath and I swear I hear him smile. 'So shall I, the instant we finish our conversation.'

'Excellent. I'll see you tomorrow. Oh. Do you prefer tea or coffee? Or hot chocolate?'

'Hot chocolate. You can spoil me.'

'Got it. Bye.'

I replace the receiver, the fiery skin on my neck a dead give-away. I shall have to stay here till it subsides, or Vic will get the wrong impression. The first article has printed, so I lift it from the tray and read.

Smug doesn't begin to cover it; how my heart sings as I read. The review of the exhibition is glowing. Apparently, I have "artfully" displayed Dad's paintings, making "striking" use of the gallery's architectural features and light. Vic has to see this.

Visitors roam the gallery. Vic stands talking to a pair of Chinese women, whose heads nod with everything he says. He gestures to "The Winning Hand". The women step closer and peer at it. I hold my breath. Has Vic noticed? He's still talking to them when I approach.

'…and although Frank l'Ussier liked a dabble, this painting doesn't glorify gambling in any way. A few critics said it did, when he unveiled it, but Frank always maintained he showed the natural pleasure one gets from winning.'

The women smile, thank him, and move on to a different painting. Vic remains where he is, deep in contemplation. He does that, sometimes.

I touch his elbow. 'Vic, read this.'

He takes the sheet from me, pulls his glasses from the top of his head, and reads. As he does, a smile breaks across his face. 'I say, dear girl, how wonderful. Promise me you won't let these rave reviews go to your head?'

'I might. Daniel Rose is coming to interview me tomorrow, and Look North has requested a follow-up at the studio.'

'My dear, you'll be a media sensation. It's time they recognised your talent in the wider world.'

'Thanks, Vic.'

I hug him, and he squirms out of my embrace.

'Yes, well. Things to do.'

He hands me the sheet and blusters towards a group of students who discuss Betty and Harold. They part to allow him to join them, and in moments, they are attentive to everything he has to say.

"The Winning Hand" is still minus one. Of course. I can't get over how wrong it looks, nor that Vic hasn't noticed. The whole imbalance is so alien to Dad, he must have clocked something amiss. It's possible he doesn't know Dad's work as well as he thinks.

I wander back to the office and spend the rest of the morning slogging through admin. The gallery has a constant stream of visitors; the traffic manifested in eddies of light, shadows and sunbeams falling across my desk like a giant is playing with a switch.

At lunchtime, I pull myself from my chair. My back is stiff, and my foot has gone dead because I've been sitting too long. My mobile lights up. It's a text from Sandro. I rub my ankle and wriggle my toes as I open the message. It doesn't concern Mark; a pleasant surprise. Bill Sharp, our family's accountant, has called a family meeting. Maybe he's sorted out Dad's finances at last. The meeting is at Mother's tomorrow evening, supper included. Supper. Great. Making small talk while trying to eat. Still, I expect Mother will hold court and I'll be able to eat at my leisure. Which reminds me. I'm hungry. I drop my mobile on to the desk, rummage in my bag for my purse, pull on my coat and scarf, and go out into the gallery. Vic is still ensconced in the group of students, so I don't interrupt him. I'll buy his usual festive season lunch and hope he's not had an unexpected change of heart since last Christmas.

The Winter Fair animates the city, gives it a joie de vivre unique to the season. I jostle through hordes of shoppers towards the row of food stalls that line up under the trees. Although it's still daylight, the trees cast shadows over the stalls and the tiny white bulbs suspended from their branches glitter through the murk. My latent Christmas spirit stirs. There are so many foods to buy, from German sausages to paella, which makes me smile. Never knew paella was a Christmas delicacy. From the size of the crowd at the stall, it certainly is. I push my way to my favourite. Overhanging the front, fake snow glistens from the wooden arch. The woman serving at the counter wears an elf costume complete with red and green apron, and a hat with knitted plaits. She must be sixty if she's a day, and she dispenses her tasty offerings fast, so I'm soon at the front of the queue.

'Yes, love. What can I get you?'

'A Yorkshire roast wrap and a spicy cheese toastie, please.'

The air cuts into me. I stamp my feet while she cooks our meals. At the next stall, they sell mulled wine and I'm tempted. The perfume of cinnamon and herbs wafts over me as I wait. Once I have our lunches in my hands, I hustle to the stall and order two cups. The guy balances the cups on a cardboard tray with holes so I can carry them without spilling them as I battle through to the edge of the crowd. In the fresh air, being surrounded by people, my spirits lift, and I saunter back to the gallery happier than I've been for ages.

Back at the gallery, students still surround Vic. I dump the food on the desk in the office, hang up my coat, but keep the scarf wrapped round my neck. He's in full flow when I reach him. I cough. The students gape at me, their pens hovering over their notebooks.

'Sorry to interrupt. You're needed on the phone.'

Vic makes his apologies. The students chorus "Thank you" and we head back to the office.

He spies the goodies on the desk. 'You dear thing. Thank you. It was getting intense out there. My bones complain if I stand around too long; I'm getting old.'

'Nonsense. But they have had their money's worth.'

It's a standing joke, given how little we make. People donate, rather than pay an entrance fee. Art is for people, Dad said, but sometimes people don't pay.

Vic sits on the chair, and I lean against the edge of the desk as we tuck into our lunches. The cheese from my toastie strings on to my chin; I scoop it up on my finger and push it over my lip. The contrast between the crisp bread and the soft cheese is a huge part of the pleasure I get from eating these cholesterol-filled sandwiches. I've no idea what spices they use, but I've never been able to replicate them at home. And I have tried so many times.

'We've got a family meeting tomorrow night.' I take a sip of mulled wine. It's instant festivity. In my head, Dean Martin tells me it's beginning to look a lot like Christmas.

'About the will?'

'Not sure. Sandro didn't say. Bill's invited.'

'It'll be the will. I'm astonished how long it takes solicitors to manage estates.'

'Wouldn't know. This is my first experience. Haven't given it much thought, what with everything else that's happened since Dad went.'

Vic nods and takes another bite of his wrap. Still chewing, he says, 'Understandable. You coping better? Kim's helped?'

'Yes.' I lean over him and turn the pages of the diary. My next appointment is in a couple of days.

'Any more news of that poor chap, Mark? I can't believe someone shot him. In Deerdale, at St. Bede's, too.' He shakes his head and takes up his mulled wine. 'What is happening to the world?'

'They've closed the school early, so the boys are happy.'

'And how is Theo? It must be a terrible strain on him.'

I shrug. 'Yes. They weren't close, but they were colleagues. Theo feels responsible.'

'Poor Theo. Not his fault, though, is it?'

'No. The head brought forward his promotion. He's liaising with the police, contacting parents, dealing with the media. The head's left everything to Theo. Bloody man.'

'Sia, that's not like you.'

'Well, what's he doing? Not much, if you ask me. Theo had an awful experience with one tabloid reporter. Didn't say which one, but they well-nigh accused him of pulling the trigger.'

'Have you seen him?'

'No. We communicate by text.' The festive feeling recedes. 'The head wants him to stay while the police are on site. He doesn't know when he'll get away.'

'That will mean you won't see him much over Christmas?'

'Don't expect to till afterwards. He'll go to his parents for what's left of the holiday.'

Vic studies me, regarding me with a similar expression to Kim when she's about to spear me with a troublesome issue to discuss.

'Dare I ask, is it over between you two?'

'Been over a while, Vic. But neither of us has been courageous enough to admit it.'

'I am sorry. Always considered you the perfect couple.'

'So did I, once. Then, Theo asked me to marry him, and everything changed.'

'Did he? Don't you want to marry him? He's a good catch,

surely? Frank regarded him highly.'

'Mother will be heart broken, too. It's not for me, though, marriage. I could've stayed just the way we were forever.'

Vic finishes his mulled wine and throws the cup into the bin. 'Well, that's a shame. That you and Theo think differently, I mean. But you must do what's in your best interests. You'd only end up resenting him if you married him unwillingly.'

My heart swells with love for Vic. No-one could replace Dad, but Vic is a brilliant reserve, the perfect uncle. 'Thanks. That's my opinion, too.' I gulp the rest of my wine and chuck my cup into the bin, where it lands with a sigh. 'Time to get back to work.' I head out to the gallery.

A handful of our regular lunchtime visitors chat, drawing strangers into their conversations. They do an excellent, unpaid, service to us.

An elderly woman I've not encountered before leaves the group and seats herself stiffly on the bench. She rummages in her shopping bag and withdraws a sausage roll. Crumbs spill to the floor as she takes her first bite. Hasn't she seen the no eating signs?

'Excuse me.' I try to keep my voice friendly, although people ignoring our instructions re food annoy me.

She jerks her head towards me, tale-tale crumbs on her lips. The startled expression in her eyes convinces me she knows.

'I realise it's tempting, with it being warmer in here, but I'd appreciate your not eating in the gallery in future.'

The woman folds over a greasy paper bag lodged in her basket and tucks it in; an attempt to hide the offending article. She licks her lips, sucks a recalcitrant crumb from a fingertip.

'Sorry. I rarely break rules.'

'I'm aware I sound petty, but the paintings tempt people to touch them, even though they shouldn't. Fingers are bad enough. Dirty fingers can cause all sorts of damage. And we borrow exhibits, so we must take care of them.'

'Yes, I understand. And consider myself chastised. Rightly so.' She smiles, the creases in her face deepening, so I reckon she's unfazed by my reprimand.

'Do you have a favourite? In the exhibition?'

She scans the paintings, her eyes alighting on "The Winning Hand". 'Something about it intrigues me.'

A Catherine wheel spins in my gut. 'Oh?'

'In the other paintings, the people fill the canvass, make them alive. This one seems unfinished, somehow. Is it?'

The Catherine wheel whizzes. My stomach rumbles. 'In what way unfinished?' I hold my breath, willing her - and yet dreading her - to say something's missing.

She tilts her head, concentrates on the painting. I sit beside her and stare with her. The space vacated by the smiling poker player screams to be noticed.

'What's your level of expertise with poker?'

'Non-existent, why?' What is she getting at? 'Is it important?'

'Possibly. When my husband was alive, we played in a syndicate. Perchance it was peculiar to ours, but we always insisted on an even number of players.'

The Catherine wheel sputters and comes to a halt. It sits, burned out and smoking, heavy. 'Perhaps it was just yours.' My words are hollow. Even in my ignorance, I know it's not a peculiarity of her syndicate. Others are bound to share the same approach. Somewhere deep in my memory whispers the notion that poker players are often paired.

'Perhaps. We liked to play in pairs, but it's not everyone's cup of tea. But this picture,' she points to the top left-hand corner – his place – 'shows a paired game, I'd swear to it. And if I'm correct, where's the eighth man? Popped out to attend to the call of nature?' She laughs. 'Not very artistic, is it?'

My laughter is shaky. 'Are you questioning my father's artistry?' I try to make my voice light, but I hear the hurt.

'No dear. Not the picture; I'm intrigued by the notion a player has left the game. The picture is charming. Makes you wonder, though, eh? Who is he? Where's he gone? Everyone loves a mystery, don't they?'

The gallery becomes hushed, like everyone is pondering her questions. I cannot look away from the painting. I picture Mark sitting in the empty place, smiling at the other players. Is one of them my dad? No, it's one of his earlier paintings. He didn't know Mark then, did he? What am I thinking? The missing man isn't Mark.

'Interesting theory, but I'm sure this is how it's supposed to be.'

I can't explain why I lie to her. Her face crumples and the excitement she may have stumbled on to a secret fades from her eyes. Visitors start talking again. She takes the stick leaning on the end of the bench and uses it to pull herself up to stand.

'Been nice talking. I'll come again. Maybe we can find a mystery in another of your father's pictures.'

Her shoulders are hunched as she shuffles towards the main door. Regret blossoms. I should've humoured her longer. I can't dwell on it because at the entrance, Jenny stands aside to let the woman pass. She waves and saunters over, takes me in a hug and kisses my cheek.

'Sorry I didn't come earlier. I overslept, felt wretched, so crawled back to bed armed with water and paracetamol. How's your head?'

'Fine. No hangover whatsoever.'

'You heavy drinkers can take it.'

'I'm not a heavy drinker, thank you very much.'

She links arms with me. 'Show me round then.'

I guide her to Tina's embroidery pictures, and she gasps. I've yet to meet someone they haven't impressed, apart from Mother, and I wish Claire would consider selling one or two. Jenny runs her finger over the out-stretched fist, just as Claire did at the opening. The sameness of their gestures is profoundly touching.

I tug at her arm.

Dad's early paintings shimmer in the cool afternoon sunshine, their colours enriched by its pale-yellow light. I say nothing as Jenny reads my blurb at each one. She comes to a halt in front of "The Winning Hand".

'This is the one, yeah?' She whispers into my ear. The little hairs spring to attention and a shiver ripples from my neck to my toes.

'Yes. I'm not the only one who's convinced someone's missing. That old lady you held the door open for? She thought so, too.'

'Does she know your dad?'

'She didn't say. Said she played poker and to her, the game looked out of kilter – it requires an even number of players.'

Jenny stares at the painting. 'Top left, yes?'

'Yes! Not just me, is it?'

'Well, we agree it looks odd, all that space where your dad might have painted someone…'

'But?'

'Doesn't prove he existed, does it?'

'No.'

'Show me the other one.'

We walk through the gallery, Jenny giving cursory glances at the paintings we pass. We stop before The Bosses. 'This one.'

'Tell me again who's missing.'

She nods as I explain, peers at the spot where the woman should be.

'This one's not so obvious. You're sure she was in the painting?'

'Certain.'

We sit on the bench facing the painting, where a man shuffles along to the end to give us space.

'You've no photos, have you?'

'None. I may be forced to disobey Dad's wishes.'

'Gosh, you are taking this seriously. You've always baulked at the idea.'

'Make life easier. And we'd be able to commission posters of Dad's most well-known pieces. Vic's been saying so for years, but Dad refused. Could be an excellent source of income.'

'You need to talk it over with Heather and Sandro. And Bill. He might have a document from your dad that forbids photography.'

'True. Funnily enough, Mother's called a family meeting with Bill tomorrow. If there's time, I'll ask him.'

'Don't forget to tell Vic.'

'Tell Vic what? Hello Jenny. Lovely to see you. How's Brussels?' Vic leans across the bench and kisses the top of Jenny's head. She jumps up and throws her arms round him.

'Hello Vic. Good to see you, too. Brussels is busy, as always. She's thinking of photographing the paintings.'

His surprise is comical, his eyebrows shooting up his forehead, so his glasses appear in danger of being dislodged.

'Just thinking. Nothing definite. Our brochure would've had more impact had we splashed a photo of Betty across the cover.'

'Cannot disagree with you on that one. What's prompted the change of heart? Oh, the disappearance?'

'Disappearances.'

I've spoken the word before I can stop myself. He frowns.

'There's been another one?'

'Come on. I'll show you.' Jenny grabs his arm and hauls him away. I sit, unable to rouse myself. The arguments rage in my mind. Dad hated photography, just as those tribes who believed photos stole your soul. It wasn't a whim. But should I continue to abide by his wishes now he's gone? The gallery would benefit. We might even sell more paintings. And posters, postcards, proper brochures. More revenue opportunities. The real issue, however, is if I had photos, I'd have proof. Because something tells me, it will happen again.

CHAPTER TWELVE

DECEMBER 5TH

Why on earth I should have butterflies is beyond me. It's only Daniel I'm expecting, not the King. Truth is, though, I have been on tenterhooks since we arranged this meeting yesterday. I hardly slept and now I have bags under my eyes like suitcases. It shouldn't matter, but it does.

Overnight, from my sleeplessness emerged the decision, and this morning, I began photographing the paintings. The shock on Vic's face, so comical, helped distract me from the guilt. He followed me round the gallery for a while, shaking his head. We did laugh. I can always delete the photos before doing anything with them. That's what I told Vic, anyway, and I might just do that. I could feel Dad's reproachful and disappointed eyes on me as I moved from painting to painting as if he were trailing me, too, subtly trying to slip the camera from my grasp. I swear the blithering thing grew heavier with each picture I took. Have I dared to view them yet? No. What if the missing people show up? Lordy, I really am losing my marbles.

Daniel arrives on time. Casually dressed in light blue chinos and a navy jacket, he looks much younger than his years, despite the silver at his temples. Jenny's teasing rings in my ears and I tell my brain to stop listening.

'Sia, hello again.' He stretches out his hand and I take it. His grip is firm without being overpowering, his hand warm and dry.

'Come into the office.' I turn on my heel, my face flushed. He must not see how he affects me. 'We have tidied up in your honour.'

'I'm flattered.'

'You should be. We didn't make the effort for Mother.'

We chuckle, our quiet laughter like two-part harmony. Like when Dad and I used to share a joke, or a whimsical moment. Warmth and yearning percolate through me.

'Please.' I gesture to Vic's battered old chair. 'Sit.'

'If it's okay with you, I'd rather conduct the interview in the gallery, by the paintings. I find conversations more stimulating that way.'

'Right.'

He pulls a tiny notebook from inside his jacket, flips it open, and rummages in his pocket. He withdraws a stylish golden retracting pencil.

'That's beautiful. May I ..?'

He passes me the pencil, and I gasp. 'It's a Pat Kanoe.' The pencil looks smooth, but its barrel is striped, three stripes every so often all round so that it has purchase when I grip. 'Have you got the matching pen?' The pencil sits comfortably between my fingers, the perfect writing instrument slightly weighted towards the top.

Daniel smiles and retrieves a matching pen from the same pocket. 'Don't know why I carry it - refills aren't obtainable and it's long since given up the ghost-'

'But it feels wrong to carry one without the other.'

'Yes.'

I hand him back the pencil. What an intriguing man he is. I hold back from telling him I have a similar set at home. Don't want him to think I'm getting all deep and meaningful at our first interview. Dad gave me my set for my twenty-first birthday, and I have always treasured it.

'Where did you get it?'

His face clouds. I've asked the wrong question.

'From a dear friend, as a gift, years ago.' He tucks the pen away. 'Shall we?'

In the gallery, we leave the awkwardness behind, much to my relief. Daniel stops by the early paintings. We stand before them in silence for a while. 'Haven't seen these in years. It's like a school reunion. Was Frank aware these were included?'

'No. We rescued all those along this wall from the fire. This one,' I point to the painting nearest reception, 'nearly got overlooked, being so much smaller than the rest. But by the scrawls on the back, we've deduced it's probably the oldest one here. Although we can't be certain. Mother never put us right, so I guess we're correct.'

The painting shows three soldiers sitting in sunshine, on an unruly haystack, smoking. It makes me smile each time I look at it.

'I love their carelessness; it's a blistering day, and they lounge on a haystack, smoking. Utter madness, but there they are, sticking two fingers up at authority and danger. See how weary they are. I reckon they're on a break from fighting in the First World War. Behind the front line, enjoying a fragment of peace before their imminent return to the hell of the trenches.'

'Why World War One?'

I point to the horizon. 'Smoke plumes in the distance; that's a battle raging. Besides, their uniforms give it away. And the muted colours, like an ancient photograph. I'm particularly fond of the soldier here.' I gesture towards the painting once more. 'Unlike his mates, his smile is uncertain, as though the photographer's just said, "Say cheese," but he's too anxious. His face is filled with pathos.'

Daniel scribbles in his notebook. 'But Frank painted real people, people he'd met. How do you account for that here?'

'In the early days, he did quite a lot using old photographs for inspiration, despite his aversion to having his own work photographed. That's my guess with this one. I'd love to find the original photo. Could hang it beside the painting. That would be something, wouldn't it?

Especially if the photo had some sort of provenance.'

'Haven't you tried to discover one?'

'Of course. Drawn a complete blank. It's possible it's a family photo, but Mother claims to know nothing and none of Dad's relatives are alive to help.'

Daniel hums thoughtfully while he writes. I go on to tiptoes to read what he's put, but everything's in shorthand.

'Don't worry, I'll let you read the article before it goes to print. Before Frank's accident, what was your role in the exhibition's organisation?'

We amble through the gallery as I talk. The bench in front of Betty and Harold is empty. When I tilt my head to suggest we sit, Daniel nods and we take up our positions. Betty twinkles at me and Harold glowers. He clearly disapproves of my consorting with Daniel. I clamp my mouth shut to prevent the guffaw that rumbles up my throat from bursting forth and embarrassing me. Behind my amusement sits something not so comfortable; the notion that Dad is also watching and not whole-heartedly approving. I cannot shake the conviction he would rather I didn't participate in the interview.

Daniel stops writing. 'Sia?'

'Where were we?'

He half closes his eyes to peer at me, like he's focusing a pair of binoculars, homing in on me.

'You said it was only natural for the exhibition to go ahead, as planned. Why did it seem natural to you, when others might have disagreed?'

Just the kind of question Kim might ask, and I struggle to answer. The reasons are simple in my heart but so hard to explain in words. How do I describe to Daniel, someone I've only just met, my profound need to hold on? To admit aloud, here in a public place, my most intimate dread?

'It just did.' How pathetic I sound. 'Call it instinct, if you like.

Others questioned my motives but, once I'd told Vic, we agreed to hold a celebration of Dad's work, not just a retrospective.'

'Is there a difference?'

His gentle tone masks the cutting nature of the question. Is he implying we went ahead just as a money-spinner, taking advantage of circumstances to raise funds for the gallery?

'Yes. A retrospective lacks the, the warmth of a celebration.' The fire of indignation burns in my belly. 'We've displayed the paintings in deliberate order, not strictly chronological, but determined by how they enrich one another. It brings out the subtleties of the brush strokes, demonstrates how his techniques developed or his use of colour. So, we set one or two apart; stops them bedazzling the others.'

'Like the portrait of your mother?'

'Yes. While our family portrait enhances those close by due the wonderful way Dad imbued it with sunshine and light. It spreads to the others, giving them so much more depth.'

I don't want to dwell on Mother's portrait, but Daniel stares down the gallery towards her. He closes his notebook and strides away in her direction. Must I lose everything to Mother?

He comes to a standstill in front of her. She smiles knowingly at him. I can barely bring myself to look at her. To me, she is wanton and needy; careless, yet demanding. It's all there in her vivid green eyes. I half expect her to say something patronising.

'She was perfection in beauty.'

The wistfulness in his voice gets under my skin more than I expect. I say nothing, not wanting to betray my feelings. Jealousy, I hear her say, is a very destructive emotion.

He turns to me. 'You're so like her.'

'Yeah, so I've been told. She doesn't agree, though.' But her comments during the opening whisper in my ear. She does. I can't think why I deny it.

'Your eyes are a different colour, but the resemblance is striking.'

'I have looked in a mirror.'

His face closes, and he looks at his notepad. He strides back towards The Bosses. My heart lurches. I've upset him, and now he's going to want to discuss The Bosses. Does he know Dad's work well enough to spot the disappearance? I scramble to catch up.

'This one is interesting, the subject being so different from what Dad usually picked.'

'I thought so when he agreed to the commission. The speculation in the press - critics claiming he'd sold out, gone commercial - nearly ruined him.'

'Yes, I read it during my research for the exhibition, and discussed it with Dad. He reckoned it was a lot of fuss and bother about nothing.'

'Did he do it for the money?'

'Not really. He saw the painting as another challenge, trying to make the suits seem human. I reckon he succeeded.'

I cannot stop staring at the space vacated by the missing woman, but I must avoid catching Daniel's eye. He'll realise, I suspect, if our eyes meet.

'Odd subject to find interesting; is there another, unusual, aspect of the painting that fascinates you?'

A lump the size of a planet forms in my throat. My brain turns to mush. 'No.' It's all I can do to squeeze out the word. I focus on the painting.

'Because, for me, it's the style he's adopted, the technique. His brushwork is utterly unique here.' Daniel fans his hand over the painting, coming to a halt with his fingers pointing exactly at the spot. He frowns.

My rib cage tightens, my breath coming in sharp rhythm.

The silence is full of sounds. If my head were a film score, jagged violins and a ragged drumbeat would play. I haven't taken my eyes off the painting, the precise place in the painting, since we stopped in front of it. Like I am guiding him, showing him where to look.

'Here, this chap leans on the table, the papers in disarray. The brushwork is more obvious. Frank makes the curl of the papers' corners urge you to slip your fingers under them and tidy them up.'

I exhale with a sigh. 'Yes, I see what you mean.'

'And I love that he's wearing a red handkerchief in his breast pocket - an almost feminine touch.'

My glance strays to Betty, and I swear she's grinning at me beneath her winsome smile. Her eyes are full of devilment.

'Would be a pretty colourless affair, otherwise, wouldn't it?' My courage thrills me, encouraging Daniel to consider the painting further. 'But I suppose it looks okay in the boardroom, which is, no doubt, all rich wooden panels and leather chairs.'

'The artist must consider where the painting will hang when it's a commission. As you know. I must say, though, it's a stroke of genius to hang it beside the Parmenters. The contrasts are fabulous.' He jots something in his notebook.

'Betty's one of my favourites.' I take a step nearer to her and she twinkles at me. I'm on much safer ground here. Betty wouldn't ever up and leave. Of that, I am certain.

'Tell me why.'

He gets the whole spiel, jotting languidly as I chatter. My misgivings evaporate while I talk to him about Betty's history.

Daniel whistles through his teeth. 'It's incredible such attitudes still existed during our lifetime.'

'Well, in yours anyway.'

He grins. 'Yes, quite.' He flips the notebook shut. 'I'm done here. Can I take you for an early lunch?'

My gut spasms. Hadn't been expecting that. My appetite disappears in the instant.

'Thank you, no. I've stuff to do here, and it would be unfair to abandon Vic without warning.'

Vic wouldn't have minded, and I keep my fingers crossed

Daniel won't ask him if it's okay. I'm confident I can keep my composure in the public arena of the gallery, but across a table for two in a cosy restaurant? No. Far too dangerous. I'm not attracted to him, of course I'm not, but I sense a connection which I find disturbing.

Daniel shrugs. 'All right. I'll get this written and send you a copy as soon as.' He pauses, and I fear he is gearing himself up to say something he finds awkward. 'About photographs.'

Did he hear Vic and me talking about them? I can't remember if we spoke before or after Daniel arrived.

'What photographs?'

'That's my point. Mine is an art magazine. I can't carry an article about an artist sans photographs.'

He's right, of course. Yet, I'm cornered. My decision, so recently made, sits fidgeting in my heart. I may, even now, erase the pictures.

'When did you say you were hoping to use the article?'

'As early as February, if I can swing it with the editors.'

'You aren't the editor?'

'I own the magazine, contribute, influence what goes in, but I leave the final choices to my editors.'

'I see. Give me a day or two? It's an enormous step. I assumed you were aware of Dad's phobia?'

He nods curtly, his eyes full of disappointment.

'I've actually taken some photos. They're not up to much. I'll send you a couple when I've seen them on the big screen. They're still in my camera.'

He grins, his eyes shining like a toddler's when receiving an unexpected Christmas present. 'Can I see them on the camera? I've got a good eye - I'll be able to tell if they're suitable or not.'

'Just a minute. Can you wait here?'

How do I handle this? I scurry to reception, where Vic sits chatting to a man I recognise as one of our regulars. I gesticulate at Vic as I approach, praying the man won't turn round.

'If you'll excuse me, my curator needs to discuss something with me. Lovely to see you again. I'm so pleased you like the exhibition.'

He worms his way off the chair and slithers into the office. I smile apologetically at the man and follow Vic.

'He wants photos.' My voice sounds like it's been taken from the soundtrack of a 1940s spy film. 'He wants to look at the ones on my camera.'

'Course he does. He'll want stunning photos to help sell the magazine. He'll probably want to use one for the cover.'

'What?' This news shakes me to the bone. It is totally contrary to Dad's wishes. 'But, but that's going too far.'

'Is it? What are photos for, then? You've photographed your dad's paintings, so use your imagination and do something spectacular with them. The front cover of a prestigious art magazine would be a brilliant start.'

His words knock the panic from me. What he says makes sense, and it would bolster the gallery, as well as send the magazine circulation through the roof.

'Got it. Right.'

I make for the door.

'Thanks, Vic.'

Daniel is studying "The Winning Hand" when I go back to him. I stop before I reach him and watch. He approaches paintings in the same way as me. I recognise that posture, having been teased about it for as long as I remember. He's taking in as much detail as possible, finding something challenging and intoxicating about the painting. There isn't a painting in the universe that doesn't affect me, even those I detest – Oh, God. Is this when he notices? It's impossible for anyone with a trained eye to miss the emptiness, not to notice the incongruity. I walk quietly towards him and stand by his side.

'You're familiar with this one?'

He swings round, his face a study in bafflement. 'I thought I was.'

Sirens wail. Are they in my head or outside the gallery? I can't work it out.

'What do you mean?'

'It wasn't like Frank to leave so much… nothingness in his paintings.' He points. 'Between these two players, don't you feel an absence?'

'Yes. I toyed with commenting about it in my blurb but decided against it.'

'Why?'

Mother always says one lie begets another and now I need to think fast. Not my strongest ability.

'I wanted nothing negative. It's a celebration of Dad's work, not a critique.'

Will he see through me? My reason isn't completely fabricated, and it soothes me to think I'm not being totally dishonest.

'Yes, I see.' He shrugs. 'Are you going to show me your photos, then?'

I am so relieved, I'd probably agree to anything.

'Yes, yes. Come into the office. And I'll make you that chocolate I promised.'

While Daniel scrolls through the photos - I hadn't realised how many I'd taken – I fuss about making hot chocolate. Anything to avoid hanging around while he examines each one for an eternity. Vic leans against the door frame, an infuriating "I told you so" smile on his face. I thrust a mug into his hands.

'I'm going into the gallery. We can't both abandon it.'

My mug wobbles as I stride away from him. I can feel his amused gaze on my back. I stand straighter, and search for some poor, unsuspecting visitor to corner and lecture. The gallery is almost empty, only our regulars dotted about. I can't bother them; they've heard it all before. I need Kim, right now, sitting on a bench ready to listen to me. But I shall have to wait.

I stay out of the office long enough to finish my chocolate. When I return, Daniel and Vic huddle close, staring at the camera.

'Yes, definitely that one for the cover.' Daniel looks up. 'Sia, these are wonderful. You should consider turning professional. I wish the photographers at the magazine were this good.'

His good opinion of my photos fills me with unreasonable happiness, as if his judgement is important. No matter how I try, the smile won't disappear. I can't justify my reaction. He'll withdraw from my life once the article is in print. The happiness is quelled, a little. Now we've met, I must admit I'd enjoy getting to know Daniel. Not like that, I assure the tiny squirmings in my gut. He's intriguing.

'Which one did you choose for the cover?'

Vic holds the camera out for me to see the tiny screen. It's my close-up of Betty, her sunlit complexion even more dewy, like an advert for an expensive moisturiser. Her lips are full, sensual and the colour of Pink Lady apples. Her eyes flash with mischief. She would adore being a cover girl. I hand back the camera.

'Good choice. She'll become a pin-up.'

'Could you give me a memory stick with the photos? You'll retain copyright and will be paid accordingly.' Daniel is suddenly business like.

'Okay.'

'Good. I'll be off, then. Get the thing written. With your photos, this article will be an exclusive publications *internationally* will envy in perpetuity. Frank's antipathy towards photography will be the making of us. And it's not going to harm the gallery, either.'

He kisses me on the cheek as he pushes past. I watch his silhouette through the patterned window separating the office from reception. He leaves a faint trail of something expensive and masculine in his wake.

'Have I done the right thing?'

Vic puts his arm round my shoulder. 'Your dad would be very

proud of you. I'm sure he'd say you've made the right decision.'

His words sound reassuring, but I cannot shake off the doubt which niggles at the back of my mind. Having not viewed the photos myself, I've no idea what they'll reveal about the disappearances.

'Pass me the camera, please. I should have a look at them before sending them to Daniel.'

'Don't delete any.'

'What about the duff ones?'

'There aren't any. Promise you'll not delete a single one.'

He holds my gaze, looking sterner and more determined than ever before.

'I promise.' But in my pocket, as he passes the camera, I keep my fingers crossed.

CHAPTER THIRTEEN

LATER THAT DAY

Arranged around the grand table in Mother's formal dining room, we look a sorry bunch, the room's stately furnishings doing nothing to create a relaxed atmosphere. Without Auntie Marian to watch over him, Uncle Isaac drinks steadily. She will be furious when he gets home, blotchily flushed and not quite coherent. Detta has barely spoken a word throughout the meal, and her plate still has plenty of food on it while the rest of us have finished. It must be hard for her; Mother has made no secret of her conviction that Detta is the arsonist. Sandro tries to keep Mother entertained most of the time with his tales of tragedy. His latest piece is not behaving itself, the wood grain not going where he wants and so ruining the line of the sculpture. She pretends, convincingly, to be enraptured by his animated descriptions, which are worthy of their own show at the Edinburgh Fringe. Bill attempts to chat to Detta, but he's failing. He looks over at me now and then, tries to include me, but my contributions don't make his task any easier.

Opposite Mother, someone set Dad's place for dinner as though he's been delayed at the studio and will join us later. Much as I try to avoid looking at the unused cutlery, the empty glass, I can't because where Bill sits across the acres of white linen makes it impossible. The gleaming cut glasses and glinting silverware only underscore his not being here.

Mother taps her glass with a spoon. The talking dies and everyone looks at her. She coughs, takes a sip of wine. 'Now we've eaten, it's appropriate for Bill to take us through the issues surrounding our finances.'

Detta places her knife and fork carefully on her plate. She clasps her hands on her lap, her eyes lowered. Sandro pulls his napkin from his knee, crumples it into an untidy ball, and drops it on the table. Bill tops up his glass. Uncle Isaac pulls his fork from his mouth and clatters his cutlery on to his plate. He looks around the table belligerently. When Bill offers me the decanter, I cover my glass with my hand and shake my head. I may be staying the night, but I don't want to get drunk.

'Bill?' Mother's imperious tone comes as a warning; best not keep her waiting.

From beneath the table, Bill produces a leather document case, withdraws a sheaf of papers and sets them on the table next to his plate. He takes up the top sheet and regards us over his half-rimmed spectacles. He reminds me of Badger from that ancient Wind in the Willows series on television I loved so much as a child.

'The arrangements are complicated, so, with your permission, I'll not bore you with details but provide you with an outline of how matters stand.'

'Trying to fob us off again.' Uncle Isaac mutters into his glass, but we all hear him, and studiously look away, giving Bill our attention.

Bill ignores him. 'Frank made a variety of investments during his career, many of which were abroad. Nothing illegal, although people might question their morality – especially in today's climate, where tax evasion is frowned upon.' He scans our faces; all of us, even Uncle Isaac, fix our gaze upon him. 'Inherited foreign investments may incur a tax, either in the country of origin or here in the UK. Where taxes are paid in another country, it's possible to get tax relief here.'

My eyes glaze over as he speaks. I blink, and glance round

the table. It's not just me Bill's leaving behind. With regret at refusing a top up, I drain my glass. Can I reach the decanter without interrupting Bill?

'So, while Frank's will is clear, the tax situation is not. Therefore, I can only distribute funds from the monies wholly in this country. I have spoken at length with our lawyers. They advise me to make interim payments to certain recipients while I sort out the matter of the foreign investments. You'll understand, we must retain sufficient funds to cover tax demands.'

'So, we're no nearer to getting to the cash?'

We all gasp and stare at Uncle Isaac. He pours himself another glass of wine, and takes a mammoth glug of it, slurping as he does. While there's a break in Bill's talking, I reach over and slide the decanter across the table and fill my glass. From the corner of my eye, I see Mother's disapproving glare.

'I'm afraid so, in your case, Isaac. And you, Detta. However, I can give an allowance to Heather, Sia and Sandro.'

'That's ridiculous!' Uncle Isaac erupts from his chair, bloated and florid with anger. 'I'm more of a blood relative than them. I should get something.'

His chair topples backwards and crashes to the floor. Detta shrinks away from him, caught in the full force of his shouting.

'Sit down, Isaac. Don't make an ass of yourself. In the eyes of the law, we are more family than you are.' Mother's icy tone is underscored by the sub-zero flash of her green eyes; a Medusa, she holds him in her unwavering scowl.

Sandro springs up and rights Uncle Isaac's chair; he guides him to sit.

'The law is an ass.'

His bloodshot eyes scan us, one by one. It's hard to believe he's the same man who is such an entertaining uncle when he's sober. Whose idea was it to set him up in the drinks business? I try to keep his better side in mind, but it's difficult when he's drunk, and it happens more and more.

'Then you're in good company.' Mother glares at him. 'Now, let Bill finish.'

Bill takes another sip of wine. 'I believe there will be considerable sums due, once we have resolved the foreign matters, but when you deal with the government, it's very much their pace, not ours, that determines when things will be settled. And it doesn't help us to aggravate officials overloaded with paperwork.' He takes up a second sheet. 'Then, we must address the problem of Frank's studio.'

I can't look at Detta, but I know she's blushing and no doubt wishing she could be anywhere but here. Mother stares at her, though, like she is trying to turn Detta into stone.

'Until the fire, the future of the studio was straightforward. Now it's part of a police investigation, it cannot be handed over until they have finished. There's no guarantee the building is salvageable, so selling the land may be your only profitable option. I have investigated its insurance policies, and they cover it for arson, but how much the insurance company will hand out is uncertain. We may have a fight on our hands.'

The room is heavy with unspoken reactions to Bill's words. He regards us, his concern obvious in his kind, dark eyes. His gaze comes to rest on Detta, who still keeps her head bowed.

'Detta, I am sorry this is awkward for you, but your presence here is necessary, as Frank's agent and his closest confidante. He'd have wanted it this way. No-one here believes you are guilty...' He spears Mother with a challenging expression. '... and we'll support you to the hilt. We want you to rest assured.'

Mother raises an eyebrow but says nothing to contradict him.

'Thank you.' Detta's whisper is almost to herself.

'So, as far as interim payments are concerned, I shall make these from the estate account next week. Each of you, Heather, Sia and Sandro, will receive £10,000.'

'Why can't you split the money five ways, and give each person less?' Isaac bangs his fist on the table. 'This is a bloody nonsense. Just a way to stop me and the arsonist getting what's due.'

Detta is on her feet and flees before we can stop her.

'I'll go. Uncle Isaac, that was cruel.' I bite back further words of castigation in my hurry to reach Detta before she leaves the house. She's in no fit state to drive and I want to apologise for Uncle Isaac's spitefulness.

I find her in the unlit front sitting room. She doesn't move or make a sound when I enter, so I sit on the floor at her feet and take her hand in mine. Unsure what to say, to bring her comfort, I wait for her to speak. She squeezes my hand, and that's enough for me.

We sit in silence for ages. From the dining room, discordant voices clash like battle scenes from a Benjamin Britten opera. I strain to make out what they are saying, but they jumble and merge, so it's impossible.

'It *wasn't* me who started the fire.'

'I believe you.' Does she remember my reaction when she first told me of the fire? My suspicions must have been obvious to her.

'You didn't to begin with, did you?'

My discomfort at her words stops me from replying. The horror, the aching disappointment, of seeing her closest friends suddenly wondering if she's an arsonist must be crucifying. My shame has me blushing, even in the darkness.

'It's all right. You believed me when it mattered. The Inspector let it slip, your defence of me when they interviewed you.'

'Detta, I'm sorry.' She's not to know the struggle with doubt that preceded my declaration.

'You're still grieving. It messes with your mind. Suppose they will use that argument about me when it comes to court. Deranged former lover becomes arsonist through grief.'

I pull myself on to my knees and throw my arms around her, bury my face into her. She strokes my hair.

'It gets better, honestly it does.'

She comforts me while she's in distress. I am enveloped in emotions: love for her, respect, and disbelief at her strength. I'm not sure I could be so calm and brave.

As we sit in our embrace, the voices from the dining room continue to rage. A shaft of light, severed by a man's shadow, splices the sitting room.

'Sia? Detta?'

'In here, Sandro.'

He switches on the lights, dimming them to avoid the glare, and closes the door behind him.

'Uncle Isaac's still being obnoxious. Mother has called for a taxi to take him home. She's accused him of embezzlement, says Auntie Marian should divorce him and run the pub herself. He's apoplectic.'

'Is she right?'

Sandro slumps into an armchair. 'No idea. Wouldn't be surprised. He's always flirted with the shadier element.'

I pull myself away from Detta and sit facing Sandro. 'He and Dad always have lots of meetings. I thought they were close.'

Detta runs her hands through her hair. 'Not that close. The meetings were business. Your dad has a stake in the pub.'

'Does he?' What a revelation. Did Bill allude to it at the reading of Dad's will? I rack my memory, but what I can recall about the day is cloudy, mired in misery. I don't think I listened, or at least, nothing went into my brain. 'Did he leave it to Uncle Isaac?'

'No. I expect that's why Isaac's so furious. It wasn't specifically mentioned, so it goes to your mother.'

Sandro and I take a deep breath in unison.

'That explains a lot. Poor old Uncle Isaac.' Sandro shakes his head. 'As far as I'm aware, he and Mother have never agreed.'

'He's another one she says takes Dad away from her. Always complaining about his visits to the pub. D'you think she'll take any interest? Or will she sell her shares or whatever to Uncle Isaac?' I can't imagine Mother actively involved with the pub, or Uncle Isaac.

'Don't be surprised if she hangs on to her share, just for devilment.'

The ringing of the doorbell interrupts our conversation. I'm on my feet in an instant.

'That'll be the taxi. I'll get it.'

As I reach the front door, Bill propels Uncle Isaac from the dining room. Mother walks behind them, a brandy goblet in her hand and serenity on her face. She's won this battle. Bill ushers Uncle Isaac into the taxi, pays the driver, and stands with Mother on the steps until the tail lights disappear. They turn together and re-enter the house.

'Thank you, Bill. I can see he's going to be a problem. But I expect there'll be a way of getting rid of him.'

'You can always give him your stake in the pub.'

Bill's suggestion, so mildly made, stokes Mother's fury in an instant. She swings to face him, her eyes ablaze.

'Give him? Give him? If you think Isaac will get more than the minimum due, you are mistaken. I'll see him in hell first.'

Bill shrugs. 'It was just a thought. Consider it erased.'

Mother puts her glass to her lips. 'As he should be,' she mutters into her brandy.

We gather in the sitting room. Detta appears composed; she nurses a brandy, too. Sandro points at the decanter, in question. To hell with it, I'll have one. I'm not driving, after all. He pours a large measure, passes it to me and gestures to Bill, who declines.

'I'll be on my way. Thank you for a delicious supper, Heather.' He bends in a slight bow and leaves us.

My main worry now is Mother. Will she behave herself, now that Detta is alone with us? I need to distract her. How can I..?' Got it.

'I had an interview with a bloke called Daniel Rose today.

He'll publish it in his magazine.'

'Daniel Rose? When did you meet him?' Mother's pupils are like pins – the sharp end.

'At our opening - said he and Dad had negotiated an interview and suggested I do it instead.'

'I knew nothing of this. Are you sure? He's not to be trusted. He could have strung you a line, just to get inside information.'

'Mother, he seems perfectly pleasant-'

'So do sharks, from a distance. You should keep yours. Cancel it.'

'For heaven's sake. It's just an interview for an arts magazine – which he owns. He said he'd known Dad for years. And you.'

Is Mother's blush embarrassment or fury? 'What? And you believed him?'

'Haven't you known him for years? He was very gushing about your portrait. Said you were "perfection in beauty".'

Embarrassment or fury, or whatever, evaporates. She preens, sits up straighter, and looks at me from under her lashes. It makes me want to heave.

'Really? He said that?'

'Reckon he's got a thing for you.' Sandro's voice is full of amusement.

Mother turns to him. 'He always did.'

I have to rein in my urge to shout, 'Gotcha!' Mother seems to have forgotten the nastiness with Uncle Isaac.

'Very well, then. Yes, we moved in the same circles. Many years ago. Before you were born, Sia. He was jealous of your father – of his talent, his success…'

This confirms what Daniel said, so for once, I take Mother at her word.

'But he and your father fell out, and we stopped moving in the same circles. Your father never spoke of him again.'

'Why did they fall out?' How catastrophic a disagreement could cause such a schism?

'Your father never said. I felt it best not to question him.'

That's at odds with the Mother I've grown up with. Maybe she was a very different person in her younger days. The mystery of it irritates me, though. I want to know everything. Perhaps I shall ask Daniel when we meet again. I have the photographs to sort out for him. My gut does a back flip. The photographs. Should I tell Mother now? It might be the alcohol making me reckless, but on I plough.

'I must see him again. I've got photographs to go with the article.'

She flies from her armchair and slaps me hard across the cheek. My face blazes under my hand, tears flow over my fingers.

Sandro and Detta are on their feet. He grasps Mother's arm and pulls her away from me.

'You know your father's wishes concerning photographs, you wretched, ungrateful girl. He put you up to it, didn't he? This is Daniel Rose's doing.'

From behind my hand, I face her. 'No, Mother. It isn't. I had already taken the photos. I thought it was time.'

'Did you? Did you? He's hardly cold in the ground and you take it upon yourself to trample over his lifelong belief. How could you?'

'Mother, sit.' She shakes herself free from Sandro but does as he suggests. She sits glowering at me, the fury palpable across the divide.

'I'm sorry. Vic and I discussed it.'

'So even Victor knows before I do? Charming. Who else? No doubt you've had cosy chats with Theo? Jenny? Detta?'

'No. Just Vic.' I'm not good at lying, but I need to calm the situation before she loses control. She's been so contained since Dad's accident, no outbursts at all. Although it's felt like a powder keg, it's been preferable to her explosive rages.

'Mum, I'm sure if Dad knew his paintings were to feature on the cover of a celebrated art magazine, he'd relent, especially as he wasn't painting so much. Think of the interest in his paintings it'll generate – Sia's bound to sell more pieces.'

Bless Sandro. I have said nothing to him, but he sees how it could work in our favour.

'And I don't expect the magazine will suffer, either. Your father has been renowned for his insistence on no photographs. This is quite a coup for Daniel Rose.'

She's right, although I hadn't couched it in such terms in my head. There might have been cynicism in Daniel's motives. My instincts tell me otherwise.

'Please don't be angry, Mother. I agree, but I'd be a fool to countenance passing up this opportunity. The gallery will benefit, too. Everyone does.'

'Except your poor father.' She shakes a lace handkerchief from her sleeve and makes a drama of dabbing her eyes.

Sandro pulls her into a gentle embrace, something I couldn't do in a million years. She'd shake me off with a barbed comment about my being over-emotional. But she submits to Sandro without a murmur. And I sit here hoping the crisis is over.

* * *

Ten days later, the promised advance on Dad's estate sits in my account. Riches don't bring happiness; I'd give it back in an instant to have Dad by my side. No doubt I should invest the money but I've no interest. Hah. Literally no interest. Would Uncle Isaac be affronted if I offered to invest in the pub? I'd ask Auntie Marian, but we're not well enough acquainted; it might embarrass her I know their financial position. Money truly is the root of all evil. But I could buy myself a new outfit or two. Jenny says I should spend a little, save a lot. That's her mum's philosophy, apparently: used to be her mantra on pocket money days. Must have been great having a mother who doled out pocket money. Not like mine, who opened a bank account when I was too young to appreciate it. She deprived me of that normal, satisfying experience of catching coins clonking into my childish palm. Will you listen to yourself, Sia, hear how ungrateful you sound?

Mother's words at the family meeting echo in my head. Again. Are Daniel's motives cynical? I'll discuss it with Kim. Cripes, is that the time? I'd best be on my way, or I'll miss my appointment. The clutter on the desk can stay till I get back. If I promise Vic I'll tidy it when I return, he won't nag me too much. Hopefully.

With my mobile slung in my bag, and my coat half on, I leave the office and go in search of him. He's easily found, despite the crowd. This time, he's surrounded by a group of women, all in rapt attention as he speaks. It's Deerdale's WI, who visits every year. Vic loves it when they come, says they're the nicest group and the most interested in the paintings. They make a hefty donation, too, which may colour his opinion just a tad. With the exhibition in full swing, he's got loads of new information to impart, so he'll be in his element.

It's impossible to interrupt him, so I make a hurried retreat to the office, scrawl a note promising to tidy things later, and prop it against the computer. I pull my coat on properly, button up and hurry to the door.

A minute past my appointment time, I knock on Kim's front door and try to calm my racing heart. The lights were on my side today, so I've driven like a thing possessed through the city, getting sworn and gesticulated at by bus drivers, blokes on bikes and one old woman who shook her walking stick at me.

'Sia, come in.' Kim stands aside and I pass through into her consulting room. The December sunshine suffuses the room with soft light and warmth. She follows me in and closes the door behind her.

'How are you today?'

'Tired. The gallery is still hectic, thanks to the success of the exhibition. I'm kept busy; we both are.'

She says nothing, waits for me to continue. I love these quiet moments, when Kim lets me gather my thoughts. To begin with, awkwardness at the silence convinced me I harboured a subconscious guilt, but not now. So, although my mind is chaotic, I take time to pull one idea from the mess.

'You remember during our last meeting I told you about when Uncle Isaac got stroppy with Bill Sharp, over the allocation of funds? Mine came through. It's an immense sum of money and it squats in my account, waiting for me to spend or invest.'

'Have you considered this before? What you'd do with your inheritance?'

'No. Never needed to.'

'And now?'

'Jenny and I chatted about it over supper the day they deposited the money in my account. She has firm ideas about what I should do but...'

'But?'

'It doesn't seem right to spend it; it's like stealing.'

My stomach knots as I speak and my throat tingles as if I'm on the verge of throwing up. In my head, the argument resumes: the one between 'The money's yours' and 'But I can't; it's wrong.'

'How would your dad react to your reacting this way?'

'Tell me not to be so daft, to spend it and enjoy it.'

'Why is it like stealing?'

My eyes fill with tears. The answer forms inside my head in letters a mile high, but I can't utter the words. They travel from my brain to my mouth but get lodged on my back teeth like acidic leftovers. I swallow as best I can with a tightening throat and try to push the words into the air.

'Because he didn't give me the money himself.' The next words tumble out more freely, now the tricky ones are uttered. 'An official, an accountant or banker, took the money from Dad's estate and gave it to me. He had no say in the matter. Because he couldn't.'

She nudges the tissue box towards me, and I grab a handful. Loss of control in front of Kim happens so often I should be accustomed to it, but I am crippled for a moment, too busy blubbing into tissues and trying to mop up its effects. At least I have stopped apologising.

I sit here with the soggy crumpled ball of tissue in my hands, the worst over, and laugh without meaning it.

'You must get sick of dealing with hung-up, weepy people. How come you don't lose your composure and tell us to pull ourselves together?'

Kim smiles. 'I'd soon lose clients with that approach, not to mention my professional reputation.'

'Hadn't thought of that. I couldn't do it.'

'How are you coping with the run-up to Christmas?'

I sniff rather unglamorously. 'Christmas? By keeping busy with stuff at the gallery. I've designed a set of cards, and another of gift tags. Next year, we might commission wrapping paper, but I don't know how, yet.'

'How do you feel about Christmas itself?'

'Dread mostly. Coupled with the desire to hide in my flat and get neezled.'

'Neezled?'

'Intoxicated. I stumbled across the word while researching something. Great, isn't it? Truthfully, I'd prefer to drink myself unconscious and awaken after the event.'

'Why such a powerful reaction?'

'Two days cooped up with Mother. Sandro'll be there, but without Dad, I'm expecting it to be grim.'

'What can you do to prevent it becoming grim?'

Is she trying to annoy me? Why should I fight the grimness? What about Mother and Sandro? Don't they have a role to play? Irritation bubbles like a caustic Prosecco. I'm glaring at Kim; I can sense my eyes narrowing and wish they wouldn't. Don't want to upset Kim. But what the hell, she's upset me.

'Why is it my responsibility?' My words emerge from my ten-year-old self, outraged by the request to exercise the dog. In the rain. 'It's always my responsibility.' Yep, definitely channelling my inner child. The horrible, bothersome one nobody likes. I can't help it, but I sit sulking at Kim like she's Mother.

'It isn't. But you're the one who reckons it'll be grim. Perhaps your mother and brother don't look at it in the same way.'

To say I'm brought up sharp by her reply isn't an exaggeration. We've covered many awkward and painful issues over the weeks, but for the first time Kim's made me feel like a spoilt child kicking against her elders and betters because she doesn't want to admit they're right and she's wrong. Damn it. I'm at a loss.

'How can you make the time at your mother's more bearable – for you? What strategies might you use to keep yourself from hating every minute and thus prevent...'

'A major falling out?'

Kim smiles and nods: her invitation for me to reflect upon her question and, eventually, offer an answer.

'Mother is facing her first Christmas without Dad, so it will be bleak for her.' The words spoken hit hard, even though they are my own. What a selfish cow I can be. 'I'll need to exercise restraint when she's difficult, try to consider her feelings and my own.'

In the silence, the horror of Mother's situation slams into me in a way I've never encountered. I've realised she's grieving, that she misses Dad but always in a kind of academic way, not a human way; I haven't appreciated how desolate she must be. She feels the same as I do.

'Difficult is Mother's modus operandi, so I've learned to mitigate the awfulness over the years. In doing so, I've blotted out recognition of her emotions, failed to acknowledge how events hurt her, words hurt her. My words.'

'Responsibility rests with everyone involved, not just you.'

'But if I'm to get through Christmas unscathed, as much as I can, it might help to remember her pain, mightn't it?'

'I would have thought so. But there's a fine line between empathy and being a doormat.'

'Right. Empathy with an edge. Got it.'

'You're all affected, each facing your first Christmas without your dad. You, your mother, and Sandro are vulnerable.'

'I wish you could talk to them, too, give them the pep talk. It'll be a battle trying on my own.'

'Only if you regard it as such. Your determination to factor in your mother's emotional fragility should go a long way to help. Tell me about your brother. You don't speak of him often.'

'Sandro? We're close, always have been.' I nod at her, as might a self-satisfied toy on the rear shelf of a car. 'We take care of each other.'

'Can you take comfort in his presence? Find elements of festive spirit in his company?'

'I'm sure I can, yes. Seeing it that way, the prospect doesn't seem so hideous. Sandro and I will see that Christmas isn't mired in sadness.'

'And we'll meet again on…' She checks her diary. '…the 9th January.'

It's time to leave already? Can't believe our session has ended; I only arrived five minutes ago.

'Right. 9th January. That's nearly three weeks.'

'We discussed the break, remember? I'm visiting my sister in New York. But you'll have my mobile should there be an emergency.'

'Yes. No, of course.' I delve into my bag, pull out a card and a small gift bag. 'Merry Christmas, Kim. And thanks for everything. You're a life saver.'

'You save yourself, in the end, I just help you find the way. Thank you.'

We stand in unison, laugh awkwardly, and I follow her to the front door.

'Merry Christmas, Sia. See you in the new year.'

'Bye, Kim. Happy travels. Hope it snows in New York.'

She grimaces. 'I don't. I won't get home.'

Throughout the drive back to the gallery, Mother's grief haunts me. How have I been so self-centred not to appreciate her sadness? Too wrapped up in my own. From now on, I shall try extra hard to be more understanding. Good luck with *that* whispers the cynical voice in my head, sounding remarkably like Mother.

CHAPTER FOURTEEN

CHRISTMAS EVE

Christmas Eve, Betty. Poor Jenny. What a time for her grandfather to succumb to cancer. Our flat, despite the tree, lacks the festive mood. I shouldn't complain. He's her favourite grandparent, so my missing her doesn't compare to her grief.

These weeks since Mark died, strange. The police haven't contacted us, nor given us a clue to how investigations into the fire are progressing. Theo told me I "require" patience. Require. His transformation into senior management rattles apace.

Business here, though, terrific. You must have noticed we're busier than we've ever known, with people complimenting Dad's exhibition. My exhibition. And Vic's. Shouldn't exclude him, although he keeps telling everyone it's all my doing. Won't be long till we switch off the tree lights and head our separate ways for the Christmas break. Although it's only two days, that familiar knot of dread tightens as closing time approaches. And it's only two nights at Mother's. Anymore and I'd need counselling. Oh. More counselling.

My mobile pings from inside my pocket. Do I want to attend to a work's email this near to closing? It's impossible to resist though, isn't it? I drag it from its resting place and see three new emails. One from Daniel. Typical man. It's doubtless to wish me a merry Christmas, as he told me he never sends cards. Wonder if he knows his staff sends them on his behalf and that a rather witty greeting sits on my mantelpiece at home?

Photos? Is there a problem with them? He never said when we last spoke. It's tricky to read on my phone, so I make my way to the office to open it on the big screen.

How could they? The back-stabbing bastards. My heart in an assault of my ribcage, I run into the gallery. I must speak to Vic. He's sitting alone, poring over a catalogue.

'Vic!' I shout as I scurry towards him.

He looks over his glasses at me. 'What's the matter?'

'Daniel bloody Rose is what's the matter.' I stand beside him, my hands on my hips, my breathing rapid and raw. 'He's bowed to pressure from Mother and changed the cover of the magazine.'

'What? You mean-'

'Mother's interfered. Again.'

'But she-'

'Has nothing to do with it. This time she has overstepped the mark. And as for him.' Hot indignation flares through me. 'I thought I could trust him. Obviously not. Can't tell you how livid I am.'

'No need, dear girl. I can see that. With every reason, too. Wretched man.'

Vic's not one for swearing, so even this language is startling. Part of me is thrilled he's so on my side. But it doesn't erase the fury eating away at me.

'I'm going to speak to him. Tell him he can't do that. Either it's Betty, as agreed – or I withdraw permission for the photos to be used.'

'Can you do that? You didn't sign a contract, did you?'

'No. Gentleman's agreement. Huh. That's a joke.'

Vic looks at his watch. 'You'll never catch him now. Most places closed at lunchtime. You'll have to wait till Friday.'

I stamp my foot and Vic smiles. He stands and puts his arm round my shoulders. 'Dear Sia. Don't let it ruin your Christmas.

You're not a woman to break a promise to. He'll be sorry he ever crossed you by the time you've finished with him.' He chuckles. 'Let him enjoy his last Christmas.'

We laugh, but the rage doesn't abate. To use one of Mother's phrases, I could kill him. 'Only because you've asked me. He's a fortunate man. Till after Christmas. Then he will wish he'd never been born.'

I stomp back to the office, take one furious glance at Daniel's email, and switch off the computer. I am still fizzing as I put on my scarf and coat. If only Jenny were home, I'd spend a glorious evening with her devising my revenge. It's tempting to go home and be alone for Christmas Eve. Our first Christmas without Dad to hold us all together and Mother pulls this stunt. It's like she wants us to fall out. I shan't give her the satisfaction. I shall be the epitome of graciousness and the dutiful daughter. Some of us know how to behave.

Vic strolls into the office, his face crumpled into that sympathetic expression. On anyone else, it'd be annoying, but on him it's reassuring. He drops the catalogue on to the shelf and takes his coat from the stand.

'I have a gift for you. Just a little something. I hope it pleases you.' He takes a small and beautifully wrapped package from his coat pocket and offers it to me. 'Merry Christmas. And thank you for making this place such a success. Couldn't have done it without you.'

The dinky present is surprisingly heavy. I place it carefully in my handbag and withdraw my gift for him from the desk drawer. My wrapping is darned good, too. Has to be. There's always the hint of competition between us on this score.

'Thanks, Vic. Here's yours. Honours even?'

He takes it, turns it over, and inspects my handiwork. 'Reckon so. Thank you.' He kisses me on the cheek. 'Merry Christmas, Artemisia.'

'Merry Christmas, Victor.' Another little ritual.

He stands back and gestures for me to leave the office ahead of him. At the front door, the icy night air cuts through me. I hunker into my scarf and rummage for my gloves in my coat pocket.

'D'you think it'll snow?'

Vic gazes at the sky. 'No. Light's the wrong colour.'

'See you Friday.'

'Indeed.'

I stride into the dark, the river's gentle lapping against its banks a whispered imperative to get home. Home. Perhaps I should go there first. Call Theo and ask his opinion of Daniel's treachery. He's got enough on his mind. Will he even be at his parents' house yet? I don't know when he was leaving; nor did he come to that.

In the end, I drive straight to Mother's, resisting the temptation to pop into a wine bar first. Christmas Eve at Mother's. What have I done to deserve it?

Sandro's car is parked in front of the house when I arrive. That's something. I shall be more able to keep my temper with him around. The risk of being stranded alone with Mother gone, my liquefied guts settle. Bloody Daniel Rose. Sparks of fury flash behind my eyes as I unload my overnight bag and my sack of presents from the boot. I slam it closed with a satisfying clunk and head for the house.

'In here.' Sandro calls from the kitchen, his voice mingling with the aroma of something savoury and delicious. I can't remember if I had any lunch and I'm starving. Hope he's cooked. It'll be something wonderful if he has.

My bags dumped at the bottom of the stairs, and my coat draped over the banister, I seek him out. He's wearing one of Mother's pinnies and looks fourteen. A tall glass in his hand sparkles with bubbles.

'Merry Christmas, sis. Here, have this.' He gives me the glass and takes up another from the counter beside him. 'Cheers.'

'Cheers.' We clink glasses and I take a gulp of the champagne.

It's good stuff. Of course. 'Where is she?'

'In her room, getting changed ready for dinner. Says Givenchy is too classy for dinner in the kitchen with the kids.'

'For once, I agree. Hope she's putting on a pair of Levi's and a Marks and Sparks blouse. What's for supper? It smells divine.'

'Salmon and cod fish pie with celeriac mash. Served with a green salad of fennel and dill.'

'Sounds perfect. A brilliant contrast to Christmas dinner, too. Can I help?'

'Set table? Has she got any fish knives?'

'Do we need them, for pie?'

He shrugs, so I don't bother searching for them; ordinary knives will do.

I could fool myself we're eating in a posh restaurant by the time I've finished. Mother has a variety of fancy napkins and place mats, so I make the effort. I don't want us to forget it's the festive season, so I choose a burgundy tablecloth, silver place mats and napkins. A couple of tea lights in low glass holders complete the ensemble.

'Isn't that sweet?'

Mother materialises behind me as I light the candles. She proffers her cheek for me to kiss. I kiss the air closely enough for her subtle perfume to hint its expense at me, and she swans away to take the glass Sandro has filled for her.

She wears a floor-length robe of startling blue that emphasises the green of her eyes. Its simplicity gives her grace and makes her as striking as I have ever seen her.

'Mother, you're gorgeous.'

She smiles, looking appraisingly at me. I wish I hadn't spoken. Even a compliment lands me in trouble.

'You came straight from work, I take it?'

'Yes.'

'Has she got time to change, Sandro?'

He winks at me over his glass. 'Yes, but there's no need. She looks terrific as she is.'

'Hm. Artemisia?'

'I doubt what I've brought with me will be good enough for you. But if my work clothes offend you so much, I'll slip into my jeans.'

Before she can respond, I'm off, swooping to pick up my bag and taking the stairs two at a time. I haven't brought my jeans with me, but it was worth it to see the dismay on her face. How old are you? Fifteen? I settle for my comfy navy culottes and a new t-shirt I bought especially. It's dark blue with a snowy night scene on the front, embellished with glitter. I love it, but Mother will hate it, thinking it tasteless. I hum to myself as I skip downstairs in my slippers. Something else to drive her mad. I am a terrible daughter.

Sandro stifles a laugh when I enter the kitchen and tops up my champagne. Mother takes a deliberate sip of hers and eyes me with disdain. Deck the halls with boughs of holly, fa la la la la, la la la la. 'Tis the season to be jolly, fa la la la la, la la la la.

'I hope you intend to wear something more formal for dinner tomorrow?'

'Mother, this is my formal.' I do a twirl beside her. 'Don't you love my festive shirt?'

'How long, Sandro?'

'Ten minutes, max. Sia, could you mix the salad?'

He keeps me busy, and Mother occupied in idle chat, until it's time to eat. And the fish pie is sublime. None of us say much while we eat, just savouring every mouthful. Sandro's cooking to the rescue. He opens a second bottle of bubbly and pours us another drink. I could swig it like lemonade. Mother watches me as she delicately forks another sliver of pie into her mouth. Even her staring is provocative, and the urge to throw my champagne in her face is only tempered by its deliciousness and the way it makes my head fizz.

She holds her glass aloft, looking from me to Sandro in

expectation. In obedience, as small children, we pick up ours and await her pronouncement.

'Let's drink a toast to your father on this first Christmas Eve without him.' She glances dramatically at the empty fourth place at the table, takes a deep breath and places her manicured hand on her heart. 'He was my world, my muse, my guiding star.'

Dear God. She's Googled how to stun your audience with a saccharine speech. My glass shakes in my hand. I want to down it in one and get on with finishing my meal. But Mother has more to say. Obviously.

'Your father should be here with us tonight, telling jokes and sharing stories, but he isn't. So, we must manage, the three of us, and try to keep the spirit of Christmas in our hearts, for him. To Frank.' She tilts her glass towards the centre of the table, and we mirror her. The glasses clink.

I want to scream. Instead, I empty my champagne glass and nod at Sandro to refill. He does so without hesitation. Mother tuts and takes a genteel sip. So much expressed without words.

We continue to eat in silence, no jokes or stories forthcoming. What did she expect? Sandro and I to turn into Gary Delaney and Sarah Millican? Tonight always promised to be the worst. I wish I'd stayed at home until morning. Christmas Eve alone seems so much more preferable than this agony. What conversation can I start when everything is likely to set her off? Daniel's duplicity cuts into me. I still can't believe he'd acquiesce to her. He went schmaltzy over her portrait. But who doesn't?

'Artemisia, are you getting drunk? I wonder if you have the same genes as Isaac.'

She smiles as she speaks, as if she's making a light-hearted jest, but her eyes, direct and hard, tell me she's doing nothing of the sort. I drain my glass with as much defiance as I know how.

'Yep, right on both counts, I expect, Mother. At least I don't resemble him. It's my good fortune to take after you, so they say.'

'Sia.' Sandro's quiet interjection is heavy with warning.

'What?' I plough on, the warning ignored. 'I do. Lots of people commented at the exhibition, and after my appearance on Look North.'

'*We* were on Look North. Have you forgotten I was by your side?'

'How could I forget? Standing there oozing glamour and gorgeousness and faux support.' I hold up my glass. 'Sandro?'

He shakes his head but fills it. 'Mother?'

She pushes her glass towards him across the table. 'There was nothing faux about my support.'

She pauses; my forthright mother, struggling to find the right words? If she claims to have been proud of me, I might choke. I wait, the room suddenly filled with anticipation. Even Sandro is unnaturally still.

'It was difficult, seeing his paintings gathered together and him not there.' She swallows a catch in her voice. 'I rarely say what I should.'

'That's true.'

She glares at me. 'But I appreciate the effort you've made at your little gallery.'

She couldn't do it, could she? Couldn't just come out and praise me or my exhibition? Champagne tingles on my tongue and in my throat; I am swallowing rage. It fizzes impotently in my gut.

'I guess that's something.'

'Sia, Mum – behave. It's Christmas Eve. Can't we be nice, for Dad's sake?'

'Of course.' She smiles. 'Have you concocted a wonderful dessert for us?'

Another opportunity is gone. Am I being immature to want her to praise my achievements? I'm not a child anymore. Her good opinion has no impact on my professional success.

I help Sandro clear the table and check the fridge. Half a dozen bottles fill the bottom shelves. I pull one out. 'More bubbly, you two?'

'No. Put that away. Top shelf. I've chilled a bottle of Chateau La Rame.'

Moments later, we're back at the table tucking into a red fruit trifle, the base undoubtedly soaked in half a bottle of the dessert wine we sup while eating. I am gloriously squiffy, as that girl from the play I studied at school said, much to her mother's irritation. It makes more sense to me now than when I was a teenager, although I remember having my suspicions, even then.

'If you don't mind, I shall retire to my room. I must meditate before bedtime.' Mother drops her napkin on to the table as she leaves. She doesn't say goodnight.

We soon clear the detritus of the meal. Sandro and I adjourn to the sitting room to lounge by the light of thousands of tiny white lights on the tree, softened by the glow from the fire. We sprawl over the settees, two adolescents again, ungainly and inelegant but relaxed now Mother's out of the way. Sandro swirls a brandy in a huge goblet, and I sip more champagne. For a while, we watch the flames in silence. The warmth and the gentle light soothe my fractiousness.

'What's eating you tonight?'

Sandro's question pierces my contentment, and Daniel's betrayal snaps into focus. He listens while I explain what Mother has done.

'Phew. No wonder you're angry. You did well to keep a lid on it, sis. What will you do?'

'Email Daniel and demand a meeting. I won't let them push me aside. It's my gallery, my exhibition and my bloody interview.'

'Good for you. And good luck. I have a feeling you're going to need it.'

'I'll drink to that.'

We chink glasses. I'm suddenly sober, and ready for bed myself. But I don't want to drag myself away from the fire and the tree. The room wraps me in Christmassy fog: warm and comforting. It reminds me of an illustration from a Dickens novel.

Only an hour later, however, we retire for the night. Sandro kisses my cheek as he wishes me sweet dreams. He slopes towards the kitchen with our glasses clinking between his fingers, his movement fluid and graceful. I have to turn away and head upstairs before I run after him to double check it's not Dad.

Christmas Day dawns grey and raw. My skull feels tight under my skin and a headache threatens. I scramble from under the duvet and search through my wash bag for paracetamol. The shower helps wash away my nascent hangover. I dress quickly - slipping on my pink silk organza dress I bought last week, especially for today. It falls like a whisper over me and the hem swings with natural grace. I spin in front of the mirror, admiring the way the fabric ebbs and flows round me, as if it were aware of my inner rhythms. Daft woman. But my confidence blooms.

The house is quiet downstairs, the curtains in the sitting room still closed. I pull them open to let in the day, which shines brighter than I expect into the dimness of the room. I press the buttons on the handset to switch on the tree lights. No cards on the mantelpiece. Mother must have received a few, surely? I wander along to the kitchen, peering into the dining room on the way. No cards in there, either. Maybe she's got them upstairs in her dressing room.

By the time Sandro appears, I have set the table for breakfast and laden the countertop with the ingredients we need. I am tying the apron round me when he joins me.

'Merry Christmas, sis.' He plonks a kiss on my cheek.

'Merry Christmas. Did you sleep well?'

'I did, thanks. Although it always feels weird sleeping here again, don't you think?'

'That's why I don't, if I can avoid it. Hard to believe we lived here.'

'Know what you mean. I wonder when Mum'll show?'

'Doubt she'll be late today. She'll make the effort, won't she? If she didn't have a nightcap after her meditations last night.'

'She wouldn't do that. Would she?'

'Do what?'

Mother stands in the door, her head tilted to one side as if she's assessing us. Sandro and I laugh in unison.

'Have a drink in your dressing room.'

'Good heavens. You must think I'm a lush. No – although your father and I used to take a brandy to bed, in the days before you were born. Thought it terribly decadent.'

'Because it was. Merry Christmas, Mum.'

Sandro is by her side in a moment and takes her into a fierce hug. She eyes me over his shoulder, with something that could be affection, a smile almost discernible.

'Merry Christmas, Mother. Breakfast will be ready soon. Coffee? Or tea?'

Breakfast passes without incident. Once the table is empty of crockery, cutlery and condiments, we start the dishwasher and take a fresh cuppa into the sitting room. It's time to open presents.

The room is too spacious and Dad's absence echoes from every corner. I hadn't noticed it in the half-light last night, but now it's inescapable. How are we going to endure it? Sandro positions himself on the floor by the tree, just where Dad always sat. We'd agreed it made sense for him to hand out the presents. Now, it's all wrong. Mother sits at the end of the settee, her usual place. I don't know where to sit. If I settle in my regular spot, I'll feel miles away. I sit in Sandro's place, opposite Mother, and sip my tea, trying to relax, but discomfort perches on my shoulder.

Under the tree, an array of stylish, matching and fabulously wrapped parcels is arranged as professionally as a department store window. I have to smile. My gifts and Sandro's wreck the perfection, but it looks cosier, more like a family's offerings.

Somehow, we endure it. Sandro amuses Mother and me with his silliness while ensuring neither is left without a gift to unwrap. We ooh and ah as we discover what treasures Mother has chosen for us, but the most genuine pleasure for me comes when I undo Sandro's gift. Inside a small box nestles a silk scarf in shades of pink. I pull it out and drape it round my neck. It's a perfect accessory for my new dress.

'Were you spying on me when I went shopping?'

'No. I've had that for ages – ask Mum. She was with me when I bought it.'

'Really? Did you help Sandro choose it? It's gorgeous.'

She doesn't confirm or deny her influence on the selection; disappointment, my constant companion, settles. How nice if she'd… oh, never mind.

'I love it. Thank you.'

The rest of the day we spend watching whatever is on the telly until it's time for the Queen's speech. This is our signal to abandon the television to prepare for dinner. As tradition demands, we adjourn to the kitchen together. The turkey is cooked; Mother's domestic cooked it earlier in the week, so it just needs carving.

Christmas dinner passes without Mother and me falling out. We even share a laugh once or twice, and I catch Sandro smiling at us. None of us mentions Dad, but I bet he's on their minds, as he is on mine. Thankfully, Mother didn't set a place for him at the table, which I'd been dreading.

In the sitting room, hours later, we lounge about, looking at our gifts and sipping coffee. If I close my eyes, I can pretend Dad is here, too, snoring on the other settee.

'Artemisia.'

Mother's voice cuts through my inner ramblings.

'Mother?'

'Has Daniel Rose contacted you concerning the photographs for the magazine?'

Millions of fireworks burst into life in my heart.

'Yes.' Careful, Sia. Behind my eyes, torrents of blood crash against my brain.

She nods. 'Good. He said he would, but as you hadn't

mentioned it, I was wondering.'

'He emailed me yesterday.' Keep it tight. It's Christmas Day. Don't get involved in this.

Sandro's expression, a scared animal caught raiding the grain supply, nearly makes me laugh.

'What did he tell you?'

I sit up straight. I cannot avoid it, despite my best efforts, so I fix Mother with unblinking eyes.

'That you had asked him to put your portrait on the cover.'

She has the audacity to smile.

'It makes so much more sense. People associate me with your father far more than Betty Parmenter.'

'It's my interview, and those are my photos. You had no right to interfere.'

'Not interfering. Helping.'

'How dare you sit there and spout such a lie? It's about you. It's always about you.'

'Sia, leave it for now.' Sandro's impression of a scared creature gets better.

'I will not leave it.' I turn back to face Mother. 'This interview is none of your business. You were wrong to speak to Daniel, and he was wrong to listen to you. And he'll know how wrong when I tell him-'

'Tell him what?'

'If he doesn't go back to our original agreement, I shall withdraw my permission to use the photos.'

She leaps to her feet. 'You wouldn't.'

I stand. Can't have her physically looking down on me. 'Watch me. It's as we agreed or not at all.'

'You wretched girl. You have always sought to anger me.'

'No, Mother. You manage that by yourself. Just by breathing.'

Her eyes widen, the jade fiery with rage. I know what's coming. So does Sandro. He jumps to her side and tries to take her in his arms, but she'll have none of it.

'You are the most ungrateful, spiteful girl. Why do you torment me? At this time, especially? When any mother would expect succour from her only daughter?'

It's a new angle on an old argument but it means the same. Next, she'll tell me my faults, and how she's had to tolerate me all my life.

'Ever since you were born, you've been a trial. An unaffectionate, wilful child without consideration for others, you've not changed a scrap. Why I've endured you for so long, I don't know.'

'Nor do I, Mother.' I collect my gifts, stuffing them into my arms in a precarious muddle. 'Tell you what. I'll do us both a favour and leave. You obviously don't want me here. You and Sandro can enjoy a cosy evening together without me spoiling things.'

I march towards the door, without looking at either of them. They can both go to hell. I don't stop until I reach my bedroom, when I kick the door shut behind me and throw the presents on to the bed. In a blur, I pull my overnight bag from under the bed and chuck my belongings into it. I struggle to close it, stuffed as it is with the gifts and my things, but I manage.

At the bottom of the stairs, Sandro waits for me, my coat over his arm. In the sitting room, Mother is ranting. I can't tell what she's saying, but I can guess. I shrug into my coat and find my car keys in the pocket.

'Should you drive? Shall I get a taxi?'

'On Christmas Day? You're joking, right?' I can't keep the snark from my voice but right now, I don't care. 'I'll be fine.'

'Sis, call me. When you get home.'

'I'll text. Not in the mood for talking. Anyway, you'll have your hands full.'

'Sandro, is she gone? Come here. I need you.'

'Merry Christmas.'

If he catches the sarcasm, he doesn't react. I haul my bag to the car through the bitter air. In moments, the engine is idling, and

I wait for the windscreen to clear enough for me to see out. He's not at the front door, which is closed, the wreath twitching in the wind like it's in its death throes. Shadows cross the window of the sitting room. She's still raging; I can tell by the fast movements. Poor Sandro. A small patch clears on the windscreen; I pull out of the drive, Joni's *River* the perfect accompaniment.

CHAPTER FIFTEEN

TWO DAYS AFTER CHRISTMAS

Daniel's sitting under one of those outdoor heater thingies, nursing a pint of lemonade when I arrive. I pretend I haven't seen him, go inside and push through the crowd to the bar. Yesterday alone, I had plenty of time to practise what I'll say, although it doesn't need that much rehearsing. Jenny shared my fury when I called her, and Theo was aghast he'd pull such a stunt. Their indignation and words of encouragement have bolstered me no end. Not that I have had a second's doubt. I order a large red wine and elbow my way back to where he's waiting, a blanket folded over his knee. I pause at the threshold. His grey temples aren't distinguished and round his eyes, laughter lines have morphed into crow's feet. He's aged decades. Troubled by conscience?

'Daniel.'

He's on his feet and scrabbling to keep the blanket from falling. I put my glass on to the table, undo the top button of my coat, grab another blanket, sit and tuck myself in, my bag between my feet. He looks at me with sorrow in those umber eyes. Good. I hope he's had a miserable Christmas, overshadowed by guilt and dread.

'Sorry the pub's so busy. Never thought. D'you want to go somewhere else, somewhere we can talk without freezing to death?'

'This is fine.' I wrestle with my facial muscles, trying to keep the smirk from escaping. Journeys in my car with its dodgy heating must have toughened me up. Under the heater, and with the blanket, it's not unbearable. And the river makes a soothing companion.

He takes a sip of his lemonade but shows no sign of enjoying it. Another ping of satisfaction. When I try my wine, I have to stop myself grimacing. It's probably not that awful, but after the stuff I've had in the last couple of days, it tastes rough.

'No doubt you want me to explain.'

'Wrong. I want… no, I demand, that you go back to our original agreement.'

'I understand. But I'd like to explain. If you'd bear with me.'

'Why should I do that?'

I take another sip of the god-awful wine. My body is rigid, like someone's rammed a fencepost up my coat. And my mouth is almost too tight to drink. My neck twitches.

'No reason I can imagine. As a favour to me. An appeal to your generosity of spirit?'

I shift my chair closer and lean over the table, the fencepost buckles. I should get his assurance and leave, but something holds me back. Curiosity, most likely. What excuses he might create.

'Go on, then. I'm listening.'

'Thanks.' He takes a breath, coughs into his palm. 'Before you were born, Heather and I were … close. We hit it off the moment we met and there was always a spark between us.'

'But she was married to my dad.'

'She was. And I was married, too. To Julia.' He takes a great swig of lemonade and clatters his glass on to the table. 'There was no affair, but we couldn't escape from the truth. In the end, Frank confronted me.'

Well done, Dad. A papa lion, seeing off the competition.

'He was decent about it, but adamant I must have no further contact with Heather. He made me promise to stay away, and to never communicate with her again.'

'Mother said you'd fallen out, when I told her I was doing the interview.'

'Did she say why?'

'No, although she said you "had a thing" for her. She was horribly proud when I told her your reaction to her portrait.'

He chuckles. 'I bet. She never lacked self-esteem. At the exhibition, I avoided her, which luckily for me, she helped by staying by that family portrait. But it was a spear to my heart, seeing her again. And knowing she was free. I'm sorry. This is insensitive, but I want to give you the truth.'

I bite my bottom lip, afraid I'll cry. And I mustn't. I have to appear strong and in control.

'How does this affect what photo you use for the cover?'

'She came to see me. I don't know how she found out where I live.'

'Wasn't your wife there?'

He looks at me, his face ashen. 'She died. Many years ago.'

'Oh.' My heart clenches as the enormity of his words hits me hard. Could they be on the brink of rekindling their relationship?

'I can guess what you're thinking. Something about her tempted me when she turned up on my doorstep. I was putty in her hands.'

'Bit clichéd, Daniel.'

He smiles as he takes another drink. His eyes regain their twinkle. Damn. Where's my indignant fury? Mother's knowing sneer forms in my mind. Thank you. There it is.

'And that doesn't excuse your betrayal. Not to mention total unprofessionalism.'

I lean back and wait for him to react. He drains his glass.

'No. You're right. I've had a wretched time since.'

'Good.'

He squints at me. 'There's a bit of her ruthlessness in you, too.'

'So you know the danger of messing with me.' I smile the sweetest smile I can, without it reaching my eyes, which I haven't taken from his face.

'It'll be your Betty on the cover, as agreed. I've been so stupid. Will you forgive me?'

'That depends.' What am I saying? I'm going seriously off script here. I push my half full glass away from me. 'Buy me a drink and I might consider it. But not this stuff. It's vile. See if you can rustle up a decent hot chocolate.'

He leaves to battle the crowd inside the pub. No-one else is braving the cold, even under the heaters, which push out enough warmth to stop it feeling like Siberia. But it sneaks in between the tables. My feet go numb in my boots.

The river nudges against the tarpaulin-covered leisure craft, which bump against the wharf. I love it here in winter, when the tourists are indoors, the riverside is deserted, and I have my city back.

Daniel and Mother. Why didn't she admit it? Too proud? Or ashamed she nearly strayed. Perhaps she did. And Dad forgave her. What if he's lying? Trying to make me sympathise with him, so he can wriggle out of his error of judgement. I don't know; I'm inclined to believe him.

He places a mug of steaming hot chocolate on the table. 'Hope you're okay with Bailey's. It's got a shot.'

'Love it. Thanks.'

'I've never understood its appeal. Must be a feminine thing.'

'Not so. Theo likes it.'

'Theo?'

Now what do I say? I lift the hot chocolate to my lips. The faint smell of Bailey's wafts into my nostrils. 'My boyfriend.' No reason I should tell Daniel of the trials we're going through. The chocolate is delicious. Perfect for outdoors.

'Was he at the exhibition?'

'Yep.'

'The tall, horribly handsome chap with the winning smile?'

'That's the one.'

'Is he an artist?'

'No. He's a deputy head teacher. At St. Bede's.' Pride at Theo's success emerges from somewhere. 'Just been promoted, in fact.'

'Christ. He's the one dealing with that murder case?'

'It's been ghastly.'

'I bet it has. Poor bugger. Theo and the murdered bloke. What was his name?'

'Mark Hubbard.'

'That's right.' He shakes his head and takes a long draught of his drink. 'You never think it will happen to anyone you know, do you? It must have shocked you.'

'Yes. Daniel, about the magazine cover.'

'It's done. Back to the original, as agreed before I had my mad moment. For which I apologise without reservation. Am I forgiven?'

I savour the Bailey's hot chocolate, eyeing him over the rim of the mug. This must be how she feels when she has someone in her power. Can see why she likes it.

'I'll hold judgement until I've seen the cover.'

'You are a tough one.'

'Not really. I don't care for being double-crossed.' An eruption of laughter threatens, and I struggle not to spray hot chocolate over the table. I must resemble a gerbil with my face full.

Daniel laughs with me. He passes me a gleaming white handkerchief, and I mop up the dribbles on my chin like a ten-year-old. He holds his palm out when I try to return the hanky to him. 'Keep it. It's a symbol of my surrender.'

'Thank you. I'll launder it and get it back to you.'

'No need. Got hundreds. I insist on decent handkerchiefs.' He shudders. 'Cannot abide paper tissues.'

'I get what you mean. I'd much prefer a proper hanky, but tissues are so much more hygienic, aren't they?' My turn to shudder. 'The thought of washing dirty hankies – no thank you.'

'It's a generation thing.'

'Possibly. Although you've never seemed old to me.' Oh, God. Listen. He'll think I'm flirting. I gabble on. 'Unless you've got a guilty conscience. You looked a hundred when I arrived.'

'Felt it. But not now.'

'Don't count your chickens until the magazine is out.'

'What will you tell Heather?'

'Me? I won't. You will.'

He nods. 'Does she have any idea?'

'We had a row on Christmas Day.'

'Oh.'

The last drop of the hot chocolate is heavily laced with Bailey's. I could drink a pint of it right now. Poor Daniel. A dreadful task awaits him, and his pallor tells me he knows just how much it's going to hurt. Special rapport or not, Mother's rage will be spectacular. Let's hope Sandro's nearby with extra meds. Daniel might need medicating, too.

'I'd best be going. I promised Vic I'd be less than an hour.'

'Right.' He stands as I do and takes the blanket, which he folds. He holds it close to his chest, like a real-life comfort blanket. 'Is everything okay between us now? Now I've seen the error of my ways? And promised to put things right?'

'We're heading in the right direction. But you've tested my trust in you. Don't cave as soon as Mother makes a fuss – which she will.'

'I won't, I promise.'

'Goodbye, Daniel. Take care.'

'Sia?'

'What?'

'Thanks. You'll never appreciate how much this means to me.'

I laugh. 'Oh, I will. When the magazine sells out and you become internationally famous. That'll give me a good idea.'

He stares at me with such intensity I have to look away.

'There's so much more to it…'

'Bye, Daniel.'

I don't want to think about what he means, whether it's me or Mother torturing his conscience. I smile to myself despite the brutal air cutting into me as I stride along the wharf and try not to imagine Daniel's forlorn figure standing where I left him.

* * *

The Minster bells toll in the new year, fireworks illuminate the sky in Technicolour and the night air fills with revellers' drunken cheering. Across the frosty rooftops, their carousing sounds like a crowd scene from a black and white film from the 30s.

Dressed in my PJs, I lean on the windowsill of the sitting room, breathing in the cold through the open window. My mobile is silent by my elbow. No-one can get through now. I tried to text Theo just before the bells started, but the message wasn't sent. No doubt everyone in the country is texting absent loved ones, but only the lucky will get connected before daybreak.

I pull the window closed, draw the curtains and take my phone to the sofa. The telly shows London ablaze with so many fireworks, white light dominates the screen. From behind it, the London Eye is visible as a spectral skeleton on a purple backcloth. My glass is empty, so I refill it from the conveniently placed bottle of Merlot next to my foot.

'Cheers.' I lift my glass and toast the crowds on the television. A young presenter I don't recognise tells me how much more excitement will follow, but I doubt whatever's coming next will enthral me much. The programmes leading up to the midnight hour were sadly lacking in festive spirit, so I don't hold any hope for the rest. I point the handset at the telly and silence falls.

When did I last spend a New Year's Eve alone? That would be never; I've celebrated with friends or family all my life. I take another slurp of wine. Its rich warmth, blackcurrant aftertaste and the hum it's placing in my head justify the price I paid. The label says 14% proof. No wonder I'm enjoying it; that's nearly sherry, that is.

Dad would love my choice of new year tipple, fond as he is of

Australian wine. The neutron star of grief blossoms in my gut: a silent explosion of blackness. I'm immobile, save for the tipping of the glass to my lips. Nothing else exists as my limbs grow leaden and I am absorbed by the blossom. Moments pass in this dark fog, my submission as natural as breathing. My unhappiness comforts me as I allow myself admittance. The truth of Vic's words becomes clearer; I must allow myself to grieve, to immerse myself in order to heal.

On the low table between the sofa and the telly, my Christmas gift from Vic gleams in the lights from the tree. I take it in my hand where it nestles, tiny and dense. It reminds me of the evenings last summer when I visited Vic to see the hedgehogs that come to his garden. I fell in love with the snuffly, surprisingly swift little critters. The one in my palm stares at me with the same intensity as the live creatures. I still get a frisson of awe remembering I had a close encounter with a hedgehog. I close my eyes and conjure the dampness of the grass as I lay still, at the same level as the hoggy while it explored Vic's shrubbery and then hustled across the lawn to where I lay waiting. We made eye contact, just for a moment, and it thrilled me to my core. Vic's presents are always thoughtful, unusual. The hoggy carving puts a smile in my heart, momentarily elbowing grief aside.

My mobile lights up; Theo's face grins from the screen. I drop the bronze hoggy on to my knees and snatch the phone.

'Happy new year, doll.'

'Happy new year, Theo. Where are you?'

'About to ask you the same thing.'

'Doesn't sound like a party. You still at your parents'?'

'Look out your window.'

I scurry to the window, hoick back the curtain and there he is, standing on the pavement, waving a bottle at me. Laughter fizzes in my head. I throw open the window.

'Are you mad? Get yourself up here; you'll have the neighbours complaining.'

I tug the window shut and scamper to the front door, where I peer through the spy hole, awaiting his appearance on the landing. About to ask me the same thing, indeed. Man's an idiot. His distorted frame arrives at the top of the stairs, so I unlock the door and fling it open. I cannot stop myself grinning like a loon.

Theo saunters to the door, pulls me into his arms, and plants a sloppy kiss on my cheek. 'C'mon, let's get this beauty opened.'

We stumble to the sitting room, entwined in each other, but Theo holding the bottle aloft, so it doesn't smash against the walls. I'm breathless as we fall on to the sofa, and too happy to argue when he presses me into its corner and kisses me. He doesn't stink of alcohol, so I assume he's sober. More than I am.

'Right, where's your corkscrew?'

He pulls himself from me and stands, a sentinel in search of a bottle opener.

'In the drawer next to the hob in the kitchen.' I point towards the kitchen, in case he's forgotten the way. 'Over there.'

'I remember where the kitchen is. Don't go away.'

He returns with two glasses and the corkscrew, the bottle tucked under his arm. He plonks himself next to me.

'Couldn't cope with another minute at the parents'. Their idea of a new year celebration is listening to Radio 3 until midnight, drinking a mug of Ovaltine and going to bed.'

He holds out the glasses for me to take while he uncorks the wine. I'll be so sozzled by bedtime, I'll be hung-over for a week. But I don't care. He's here with me and we're going to celebrate together. Okay, it's late, but who cares?

New Year's Day dawns, fanfared by clog dancing men stomping across my forehead to the Trumpet Voluntary. From the depths of the duvet, I pull my mobile into bed and am blinded by spears of light from its screen. It's only possible to tell the time by squinting and that makes arrows of pain fly across my eyelids, where an evil demon has sharpened my ingrowing lashes. It's 10:45.

Theo and I slouch in the sitting room drinking coffee and nibbling toast, neither of us in the mood to shower or dress. I hope no-one comes visiting. We'll pretend we're out. By late afternoon, he says he's feeling better, so he trundles to the shower to wash away the excesses of last night. He's being kind; I drank far more than him, having made a start on my lonesome in the hours leading up to his arrival. He's a great bloke, so discreet.

While he's in the shower, I clear the detritus from last night. Under the coffee table, evidence of our debauchery: the empty wine bottles, the glasses and several half empty packets of crisps and assorted savoury snacks. No wonder I'm dehydrated; I must have had a year's worth of salt before we fell into bed. The fact everything's under the table – rather as we were – is testament to my attempts to tidy up before retiring. I hate leaving a mess.

Theo emerges from the bedroom fresh, shiny and smelling delicious as though he's spent the night at a health spa. If it weren't for the clog men, I'd wrestle him to the floor and have my wicked way with him. Even the thought makes me woozy.

'Leave the rest to me. Have a shower; you'll feel better.' He relieves me of my rubbishy load and nods towards the bedroom. 'Go on.'

He's right. Under the heat of the powerful jets, the clog men retreat to stand ready for action later. I stand, water cascading down my body, never wanting to leave the cubicle's sanctuary. I close my eyes, let the droplets fall from my hair on to my face. It's bliss.

A loud knock on the en suite door breaks my submersion. Through the watery glass, Theo's figure wobbles, framed by soft light from the bedroom.

'Sia, I must go. Promised the parents I'd attend their New Year's Day soiree with their neighbours.'

I switch off the shower and step out. He holds out a towel and wraps it round me when I take another step towards him. I lean against him, enveloped in warmth and softness.

'Thanks for keeping me company. It was the best new year.'

'As far as you remember.'

'Quite. Are you safe to drive? Won't you still be over the limit?'

He pulls me closer and rubs my back, my shoulders, my bottom. I shall start purring soon.

'No. It'll be fine.'

He tilts my face so I can gaze into his grey eyes. Bet mine are an attractive red. He kisses the end of my nose.

'We had a good time. Glad I came.'

His lips are on mine, and we kiss as though it's our last.

I pull away, the idea too horrible to countenance.

'I'll see you soon?'

He kisses my cheek. 'Of course; no idea when, but soon. Head expects me back at the grindstone tomorrow before the boys return.'

'But you've hardly had any holiday. It's not fair to expect you back before term starts.'

'It's nothing too arduous, just admin. I'll call you.'

He ruffles my hair, grins and abandons me, standing here with shivering legs and longing in my naughty bits. Pity Jenny didn't give me the Rabbit she threatened.

CHAPTER SIXTEEN

A WEEK LATER

On the desk, my mobile stirs and Sandro's face fills the screen. I snatch it up before he rings off; it's always a challenge with him - he's so impatient.

'Sandro?'

'Have you spoken to Mum yet? It's two weeks.'

Not this again. 'No.'

'Why not? The pair of you must make amends.'

'Must we? She could phone me, visit me at the flat. She knows my number, where I live.'

'It's not like you to be so stubborn, sis.'

'I've had it with her.'

'You don't mean that.'

'Really?'

'Yes, she's furious about the magazine, but that'll pass. Once people see it and rave over her portrait again. You'll see.'

'She called me a traitor to the family. Accused me of collaborating with Daniel to deny her.'

'You said. But she doesn't mean it.'

'You heard her. Sounded like she meant it to me.'

'Please, sis. She misses you.'

'Oh, p-lease.'

'She does.'

'Sia, do you need to rush off?' Vic catches me by surprise. He hadn't said goodbye, but I thought he'd left.

'I'll have to go. Vic wants me.' I swipe the screen and Sandro is silenced. 'Not particularly, why?'

'Thought we might go through those paintings in the rack, double check they're labelled correctly. Can't have them delivered to the wrong client.'

'Okay. It'll take my mind off family matters. That was Sandro. Pleading, again.'

'He's worried.'

'There's no need. She'll just have to live with it.' I sound so confident. Wish I was. Mother's vitriol since Daniel spoke to her has been spectacular. And she blames me.

'I wish we didn't have to part with The Painting Lesson.' I change the subject, hoping Vic will take the hint, as we stroll towards where the rack of sold paintings leans against the wall. 'It's my favourite.'

'Which one? Isn't it in the exhibition?'

'It wasn't to begin with. I kept it back, thinking we could display it once it was over, so it wouldn't get sold. I wrote an extremely brief, dull blurb hoping to put people off buying it. Didn't work.'

'You devious little minx. Which is it? Show me, before it's packed off.'

'You must know it – it has the father bending over the mother's shoulder as they admire their children's handiwork. The expression on his face lights up the whole painting, he's so proud of them.'

How can Vic not know the painting I mean? He draws it from the rack, props the painting against the wall and turns to me, frowning. 'Are you sure this is the painting?'

'Why wouldn't I be? It's my favourite.'

My skin behind my ears tingles. Oh, no. Not now. Not again. The hairs on my arms jump to attention, and the sensation of icy water trickling between my shoulders skitters down my back.

He beckons me to stand next to him, says nothing, but tilts his head towards the painting. The room capsizes and re-balances.

'He was there.'

'When?'

The mother still gazes proudly out from the centre, like she's wanting the world to acknowledge her children's artistry. But the sketch the father held in his hand, that should lean on her shoulder, she holds. This disappearance is different – the painting's been altered. Nausea clutches my heart.

'Just before I racked it, ready for dispatch.'

'Did you photograph this one? Before you stowed it?'

My heart deflates. 'No, nor the rest of this batch.'

The chill doesn't cause my shakes. Deep in my consciousness, the certainty it's a bad sign spreads like frost on a window. Someone is going to die.

'Sia, this must be about your father, can't you see that? You must see Kim, as soon as possible, or this will send you crazy.'

He puts his arm round my shoulder, and I lean into his warmth and strength but today, his magic doesn't work, much as I want it to. We stand staring at the painting. I wish no-one had tampered with the painting; I wish it could be restored. Huh, I believe in wishes as much as I believe in horoscopes, God or the afterlife. And yet, something extraordinary is happening. How can people disappear from paintings? What if I've remembered them wrong? Isn't it paranoid to accept warnings about death as true? My blood zings through my veins and my heart pumps hard. I haven't made a mistake, I'm certain. That could be a psychotic idea, zapping through my brain on faulty synapses or whatever they're called. No-one admits they're mad, do they?

'You're right. I'll call her. See if she can fit me in for an emergency appointment.'

'Hold on though.' Vic's tone stops me in my tracks. 'If you're right, won't the buyers realise there's something wrong with the painting?'

'Not necessarily. They bought it as a gift for a private school down south somewhere. It's going straight there.'

'That's a pity. Should we get in touch and ask them to call in? Take a look at it?'

'On what pretext? That we've lost one of the figures?'

He rubs his chin. 'Hm. Yes, that would sound bizarre.'

'And they'd want their money back. Oh, Vic, let's do it. We can keep the painting.'

'You certain you're not pranking me?'

'I wish I were that clever. And I'd never compromise one of Dad's paintings.'

'No, no. Course not. Are they being collected tomorrow by the carriers?'

'No. Everything's going on Friday.'

'Right. You make that appointment with Kim, and I'll shut up shop.'

In the office, I call Kim, but it goes to her answer-phone. I can't think of a message, so I hang up. I'm seeing her on Thursday. Don't suppose my psychoses will kill me before then. Vic switches off the lights, edging the gallery into darkness which steps towards me. I grab my mobile and scramble out, bumping into Vic in my haste.

'Just saying night to Betty.'

He shakes his head, laughing.

In the gloom, she eyes me with concern, Harold, too. I swing my mobile light across them.

'Don't you start. I've got enough on my plate without you two ganging up on me. I'll see you in the morning. Better have your best smiles for me. Not in the mood for anything else.'

I switch off, plunging us into darkness, and wander towards Vic, standing in the dim security light by the front door.

'I've got your stuff.'

He holds up my coat and helps me into it. I wind my scarf

round my neck and unburden him of my handbag.

'Did you speak to Kim?'

'No. Answer-phone. Got an appointment on Thursday. I'll be fine till then.'

We part on the street. Vic strides away, plumes of air billowing above him as he walks. I shove my hands in my pockets and head towards the car. My footsteps chime in the empty night. At the corner, a cigarette flares orange and fierce in the shadows; a man loitering in a doorway blows smoke rings into the dark. I speed up, rummaging in my bag for my keys and holding them tight. At the entrance to the car park, I glance over my shoulder. He's stepped into the muted lamplight, and he faces me. I duck under the archway and run to my car.

On the way home, listening to *Little Green*, something in the song works its way into me and I turn towards Mother's house. It's possible Sandro is right; I'm not helping matters with my intransigence. Good word, Sia. Dad would hate to think we were estranged. If you were here, Dad, this wouldn't be happening.

CHAPTER SEVENTEEN

A WEEK AFTER THE THIRD DISAPPEARANCE

Mother doesn't respond when I call from the front door. I close it behind me and step into the hall. She isn't in the front sitting room, nor the kitchen. The place feels like a show home; even the scent of the flowers on the telephone table underscores its emptiness. No cooking smells, no trace of Mother's perfume. Where the hell is she?

At the bottom of the stairs, I stand motionless and listen. Could it be possible? After so much time? I sprint through the kitchen towards the utility room. On the back step, I scan the darkness of the garden, hugging myself against the evening chill. Yes. There's light at the far end – she's in her studio, at last. Now what? Do I go and knock, risk disturbing her? Or should I leave her to it? She's not expecting me, so if she's in the middle of something, she'd not be best pleased. Guess my bridge building will have to wait.

I close the door and retrace my steps. It's after seven, and my stomach complains. Better to go home and eat. I can drop in tomorrow. It was careless of her to leave the front door unlocked. I lock it as I leave, comforted because no marauding strangers will get in and steal stuff while she's painting. A little thrill passes through me. I'd convinced myself she'd never paint again. Who knows, this could be the start of her recovery; make my task easier.

Halfway through my supper, Theo calls. I imagine him sitting surrounded by exercise books in his grand new office, slouching in the enormous leather chair the head gave him when he was appointed. Wouldn't get that in your bog-standard. Don't start, Sia.

'We've decided not to use his cottage anymore. I can't see anyone wanting to live there, can you? We're contemplating getting it demolished and making a garden there instead.'

'Don't blame you. Have the police finished their enquiries, then? As far as they concern the school?'

'I think so. Sia, Mark's parents came. Jesus, it was tough. Poor old things. His mother was in a terrible state. He was their only child. Can you imagine?'

'No, it's hideous. For everyone concerned. Will there be a funeral now?'

'They want us to hold a ceremony here, in the school chapel. The head's agreed. After that, they'll take him home to bury him in their own churchyard. They're both devout. No idea where Mark got his atheism from – uni, I imagine.'

'You sound dreadful. Theo, why don't you spend the night with me; let me smother you in TLC?'

He chuckles, but without warmth: it sounds like a marble in a bottle.

'Thanks, doll, but I've got stacks to do here. Maybe at the weekend?'

He says nothing of my going there. They frown upon unmarried cohabiting. The head told him in no uncertain terms the school's trustees won't tolerate such an arrangement, especially from a senior member of staff. It touched me he asked, but I was unsurprised by the response.

'Rightio. Talk soon. Love you.'

'Night, Sia.'

My supper has coagulated while we talked. It might be midweek, but my soul needs a glass of wine. Theo has stopped telling me he loves me, and it hurts. Our relationship is dying, but it's taking an eternity to breathe its last. I fetch myself a glass, fill it to the brim, and settle again at the table. Would it be cruel to finish with him while he's grieving? As if I'm not. It muddles my head and my heart. Best to wrap it in tinfoil and hide it at the back of the fridge of my emotions. Blimey, Sia. Where did that come from?

The wine improves my supper no end. Despite everything, I'm not too miserable when I dump my empty plate and cutlery in the sink and fill it up with hot water. I'll leave them to soak. Wash them up in the morning. I close the kitchen door, hiding the mess, and make myself comfortable on the sofa. How about watching something diverting on telly for an hour? Before I go to bed, alone.

Channel hopping is frustrating, but nothing grabs my fancy. No political quizzes, no nature programmes. Everything's cooking or sport. So, I flick to the news section, find a channel I trust and click, hoping to catch up on the day's madness. I might get lucky and there'll be something funny on the local news.

It's no good, though. It's so interminably boring, I drift off, the newscaster's voice a distant hum far away from my fuddled brain. Until something familiar pierces my consciousness. She says Daniel Rose, and I am at once awake and sitting upright. Why is Daniel in the news? She moves on to another story, saying they will bring more information as they receive it. What information? I grab the handset and scroll through the channels until I reach another news channel, but after two minutes, it's clear they have nothing on Daniel.

My iPad is on the sideboard. I snatch it up and press in my four-digit password. As soon as they appear, I touch the news icon. Identical headlines as the television news shout at me, so I scroll, my fingertip clumsy on the screen. Daniel's face appears and I cannot take in the headline. It can't be right. Someone's made a horrible mistake. My hands shake so much I can hardly hold the iPad steady enough to reread the words: Art critic found dead: misadventure suspected.

I fall on to the sofa, numb, staring at the screen. There is a brief sentence under the photograph, but it makes no sense. How can this have happened? What does misadventure even mean? Who can I ask? I don't know, I don't know.

I sit, cradling the iPad as if it might offer me answers or comfort, but it gives neither. We spoke only the other day. His remorse felt so genuine. I sensed friendship growing, despite the betrayal. And now he's gone. My chest tightens, the same way it does when I'm at Kim's discussing Dad. Poor Daniel. He won't see his article in print or be able to revel in the plaudits from jealous rivals over his scoop on Dad's paintings. Just like Dad and the exhibition.

'Waterloo' trills from my handbag. When I pull my mobile from its depths, Theo's face lights up the screen.

'Theo…'

'Sia, I've just seen the news. What the hell?'

'I've only just seen it myself.' The sob chugs up my throat. 'Oh, God, Theo.'

'Shall I come? Do you want company?'

'Yes, yes, please.' I cry, my chest lurching with every intake of breath.

'I'm leaving now.'

Theo's face disappears, so I drop the mobile beside me. I grab the iPad, tap in my password once more and, fumbling, get it wrong. Twice. Third time, icons appear. I tap the news and scroll the page. Daniel twinkles from the screen; the headline jars, at variance with his smile. He's dead. I liked him, really liked him. We had a connection, am sure he felt it, too, despite the hoo-hah about the magazine cover. He showed interest in my career, spoke positively when we discussed my professional development - unlike Mother, but so like Dad.

I fall on to the cushion, bury my face in it and plunge into weeping. My face is hot and wet, my body aches with it, but I can't stop. Every part of me hurts, my grief for Dad sharpened by Daniel's passing. Mark and Tina swirl in the mix of my thoughts in a topsy-turvy maelstrom. Their faces come and go like I'm watching a film noir I don't understand. Wasn't I paying attention when life became so painful and messy?

Theo's key in the lock startles me. I sit up and wipe my sleeve across my face. There's no hiding my anguish, but he needn't see me all snotty. He's by my side in an instant, his strong arms cradling me. And I weep again. He murmurs, but I can't make out what he says, don't care. Just glad he's here, holding me, so I am not alone.

'Sia, let's go to bed.'

He lifts me gently from the sofa and leads me to the bedroom. He wipes my face with a tissue, sits me on the bed, and helps me undress. His gentleness is sensuous, arousing. We kiss, our mouths barely connecting, but an electric rush sparks through me. In bed, he holds me close. His scent fills my senses. Our love-making is tender, slow and exquisite. He brings me to a whole-body climax. It prickles my skin, warms the spaces between my toes, makes my chest, shoulders, neck, scalp flush with waves of comforting heat. I subside into his arms, replete. My eyes heavy, I nestle into him, and he holds me in the shelter of his embrace.

* * *

Theo rolls over, grumbles in his sleep, and settles. Streetlights glimmer under the curtains, casting shadows across the room. The bedside clock announces it's three minutes to four. I should go back to sleep, but something niggles at me, stops me from turning my back on the red numbers piercing the gloom. I sit upright, the niggle sharpened. Daniel Rose.

I crawl from the bed, slip into my dressing gown, and pad into the lounge. The faint aroma of stale last night's supper lingers, and I regret not doing the dishes. The television handset sits on the coffee table, the tiny light in the corner of the telly tells me I didn't switch off. I don't care. The telly flashes into life at the press of buttons. Problems in America, another Beast from the East barrels its way towards us and negotiations for a trade deal stall. I press the red button and a choice of news stories presents itself. Nothing on Daniel. I didn't imagine it, did I? No, the residue of last night's love-making reminds me. Theo came round to be with me because he'd seen it, too. So, why has it disappeared from the news, when they reported initially?

My hands deep in hot, sudsy water, I wash up while the kettle boils and the news channel updates. When I've done the dishes, and brewed a cup of Earl Grey, if they haven't updated, I'll call someone. Right. Who? I could call that policeman; his card is in my purse. Don't suppose he'd appreciate a call at this time of day, though. I sigh. Will have to wait.

By half past four, I'm sitting with said cup of tea in front of the television, still waiting for an update. I have a twinge of shame I've let world issues - ninety-nine per cent bad - pass me by all these months. Must revive the habit of reading the paper. And doing the crossword. No wonder my brain is turning to mush. I've let things slide.

'And now, more on the death of art critic Daniel Rose, whose body was found by his cleaner yesterday.'

I sit still, not even taking a sip of tea.

'According to his wife, from whom he was estranged, the circumstances of Mr Rose's death are suspicious. What those circumstances are have yet to be disclosed, but early reports show Mr Rose died in his bath, alone, at home.'

Wife? He never mentioned a wife, not a living one. The newsreader moves on to another story, so I flick the remote and the screen goes black. I sip my tea. Why might Mrs Daniel be suspicious that he died in the bath? He could have had it too hot and died of a heart attack or fallen asleep. Can that happen? Poor man. Dying alone. Why were they separated?

Theo grasps my shoulder, nearly knocks my tea out of my hand as he kisses my cheek.

'Any more news?'

I tell him what I've heard.

'I bet he'd had a couple of drinks. That'd explain it.'

'He didn't drink. He told me so the first time we met.'

I make Theo a cup of coffee, and myself another Earl Grey. We sit on the sofa, like an old married couple. I love sitting here, ruminating over things. If only Theo lived here. but then, where'd Jenny live? She could still live here, stupid. She has her own room. If only.

He drains his mug. 'Better get sorted. No-one knows I'm out.'

'You made an escape bid from prison?'

He frowns at me. 'No. They'll worry. We always sign out, and I forgot.'

I shrug. Still sounds like a prison. 'You shower first, then. I'll get breakfast ready.'

'Just toast for me. I'll have a proper breakfast at school.'

He swans off to the bathroom and I head for the kitchen. Our routine is familiar, despite it being ridiculous o'clock in the morning. But it irritates that he'll get a "proper" breakfast at school. I could have given him that here. And we'd have spent longer together. I don't suppose it matters, not if we're going to separate. The thought brings an unexpected lump to my throat, and I wish it wasn't so. Who will comfort me if not Theo? That makes me sound horrible. Am I using him? No idea. I can't help myself smiling despite the hurt. Until he has someone else, I guess I'm free to carry on with him. Am I fooling myself, trying to convince myself I don't care? Artemisia, you are a dreadful woman with no heart. But the words don't convince. When I imagine Theo with someone else, desolation overwhelms me even as I accept our relationship is doomed.

Table set, toaster loaded, kettle filled. He comes into the

kitchen just as the toast pops up, half burned, half under-cooked. I tweeze the slices from the slots with my wooden tongs and plonk them on his plate.

'There you go. Finest toast this side of Deerdale.'

He reacts with only a smile. At the table, we munch through toast laden with jam – Theo – and peanut butter – me. I drink more tea. He'll not want to kiss me before he sets off if my breath stinks. The meal, if that's what you can call it, is soon over and he's standing, taking the last dregs of coffee and clunking his mug on the table.

'Will you be okay? Shall I call later?'

'Can't tell. Should be okay at work.'

'Call you tonight, then.'

He kisses my cheek, pulls away before I can encircle him with my arms and tempt him to stay longer. And goes. I stand at the table where he left me for a moment. This won't do. It may be early, but I need to shower, dress and get to work. That'll stop me wallowing. And I know the best way to kick start my day.

I rummage in the sideboard until I find the USB stick. I switch on the sound-system – well, the portable music thingy Theo gave me for Christmas – and plug in the stick. Volume up loud and hope the neighbours appreciate the cheerful collection.

Joni sings "Dancing Clown" and I caterwaul with her. I swing the machine as I sashay to the bathroom. She serenades me while I shower; the fiery water needles on my skin. I close my eyes and jig, lathering myself with something sweet smelling

As I towel myself dry, we harmonise to "Big Yellow Taxi", her last version with the lilting accordion, which reminds me of holidays in sunshine.

In under an hour, I'm in the car, pulling away into the traffic. It'll be a nice surprise for Vic to find I've arrived ahead of him, more so if I've got the coffee brewing and the heating warming the place. I shiver. The morning is bitter, frost gleaming on rooftops and windscreens scraped; the gallery will be freezing.

A woman on the radio informs me it'll be a slow commute today because it's the coldest morning of the winter so far, with the possibility of snow later. I turn my heating to maximum, more in blind optimism than genuine hope. The steering wheel is painful to hold, and I wish I'd put on my gloves. I picture them on top of the sideboard and curse.

As the traffic is light, I make steady progress. I don't have time to let thoughts of Daniel dominate me, but he's there, lurking just beneath the surface. I pull into the car park round the corner from the gallery and park in my usual place, surrounded by vacant spaces, for a change. From the car park to the gallery front door, it's only a few minutes' walk and today, I'm glad. The icy air bites into my skin. I sink my chin into my collar and march ahead.

I hear the shouting before I turn the corner: men's voices in an urgent chorus. Why are they yelling? At the junction, I hesitate. A crowd pushes against the half-open gallery door. Through the gap, Vic gestures and speaks, but I can't make out his words. What's happening? I quicken my step.

A man on the edge of the crowd turns, sensing my approach, and he yells. The man runs towards me, the others follow his lead. I back myself to the wall as they surround me, shouting and asking questions.

Anger erupts from nowhere. I fling out my arms, catching the arm of one man, who lets out a stream of invective. It gives me enough time to slip through them and hurtle towards the gallery. Vic hauls me inside, shuts the door, and locks it. Running footsteps echo along the pavement. We stand in reception, gaping at one another.

'What the..?'

'The press. They want to talk to us, well, you, about Daniel. I got here early because someone rang me at stupid o'clock asking questions. Thought we might have a problem. I tried to call you, warn you, but it went straight to answerphone.'

I pull my mobile from my bag. Three missed calls. 'Sorry, Vic. I must've flicked it on silent by mistake.'

'No matter. You're safe for the time being. I'll call the police. See if they can disperse the mob.'

For the time being? What does he mean? I've no chance to ask him as he disappears into the office and his urgent tones as he talks tempt me to follow him. I unwind my scarf, hang up my coat, and collect our mugs from the cupboard.

Vic hangs up the phone. 'They're on their way.' He shakes his head. 'This is a nasty business.'

'Is it? Why?'

'Just a feeling in my bones.'

'Vic, I have a feeling in my bones, too.'

'Oh?'

'I think.' I stop. Can I say this aloud? 'I think there's a connection between the disappearances and the deaths.'

'You think there's a connection?' Vic looks at me as if I've just said I'm planning to drown a kitten. 'Sia, I assumed Kim's sessions were helping?' He slumps on to the chair, a sigh from somewhere deep passes his lips. Behind him, the coffee machine bubbles and hisses. What time did he get here?

'They are. I haven't cried so much since adolescence.' I sound sarcastic, but I'm being genuine.

'That's not what I mean.'

'It doesn't alter the fact – people are going missing from the paintings. I can't explain it, but they are.'

He shakes his head. 'Sia, even for you, this sounds deranged.'

'Don't you think I've had that concern? Course I have. Frightens me to death.'

'But?'

'I'm not imagining things. And before you say it, I'm aware a psychotic would declare the same.'

The phone rings. Vic snatches it from its cradle, ums and ah-has, and replaces it. He stands. 'They're outside, the police.'

I follow him to the door, my stomach in knots, and my eyes watery with indignation and grief.

Behind the police, the gaggle of reporters has shrunk. They run towards the gallery as the police cross the threshold, but Vic is quick. He slams shut the door and engages the bolt before they reach the step.

DI Smith and PC Gorgon – my favourite police officers – stroll towards reception. She eyes the coffee machine.

'Like a drink?' Pavlov would be pleased. 'It's fresh.'

'Thank you, yes. Your exhibition and the promised decent coffee at last.'

'Indeed.' I turn to the gorgon. 'How do you want yours?'

'Black. No sugar.' Her manners haven't improved. It'd not kill her to be civil.

'Sorry I didn't make it sooner.' The Inspector shrugs. 'It's been a busy time, more than usual for the festive season.'

I pour four mugs of coffee, grab a handful of milk pots from the cupboard under the machine, and remove the tops. They remind me of toilets with the lids up. Used to make me giggle when I was a kid. I pass DI Smith his, take my time over the gorgon's. Then remember she wants hers black.

We drink without speaking for a minute or two. What will they want from us? How will they protect us from the reporters? How will we open the gallery with a posse of journalists loitering outside?

DI Smith lowers his mug, holds it between his hands like something precious. 'The interest in Daniel Rose is a surprise. He's not that well known, outside the art world.'

'Art critics aren't, unless they're on television.' Vic sips his coffee. 'Daniel was on the brink of becoming famous. His scoop with Frank's paintings will have a profound impact on the art world. People will clamour for more.'

The gorgon deposits her mug on the counter, takes out her notebook and scribbles something in it. 'What's his scoop?'

Vic rubs his chin. 'Photographs. His article is interesting because of the photographs that will accompany it. Frank l'Ussier had never, in his lifetime, allowed anyone to photograph his works. It will set the art world ablaze.'

She writes it all down in her book; a dim-witted pupil who doesn't understand what she is writing. Her face, contorted in concentration, exposes her ignorance.

DI Smith nods, his mouth turned down at the corners. He's mulling over what to ask next, any fool can see that.

But the gorgon doesn't hesitate. 'Why would it make such a difference? How can you guarantee no-one has sneaked a photograph during his exhibitions? Sounds unlikely anyone could prevent it.'

Her querulous tone is so patronising, I want to chuck the dregs of my coffee at her. 'Dad's always made his wishes regarding photos abundantly clear. Maybe someone has a grainy, out-of-focus snap somewhere, but no-one has decent photos of his paintings.'

She turns her icy blue eyes towards me, the lifeless eyes of a beautiful doll. 'You can't be sure, can you?'

'It changes nothing. The article will set the art world alight; the magazine will become a best-seller and interest in Dad will be stratospheric. You cannot deny its importance. The photographs' importance.'

The bravo in Vic's expression urges me to continue.

'That rat-pack of reporters can sniff a sensational story. If there's something suspicious in the way Daniel died, they know it will sell their papers. It's gossip and scandal they're after.'

DI Smith smiles at the gorgon. 'That's you told, PC Broden.'

'Won't do the gallery any harm, either.'

'Now.' He frowns at her and addresses Vic and me. 'We can

disperse the reporters, set a cordon round the gallery. But that'd also stop your visitors from gaining admittance and persuade the journos there's an important story to unearth. Or, we can allow a representative in here to talk to you, send the others packing and hope you can continue your day in peace. A peace of sorts. I doubt they'll leave you alone until they've got what they want.'

On cue, the phone bursts into life.

'Don't answer it. If it's important, they'll call back. You both have personal mobiles?'

We nod.

'Do not give your numbers to anyone. Use only the mobiles for personal calls. The mob will discover them, but if you're lucky, the furore will abate before they start pestering you.'

It sounds very serious; are Vic and I in the middle of the investigation? Our only connection with Daniel is through the interview.

'I don't understand how the reporters found out about the article?'

DI Smith shrugs. 'I can't answer that yet. You clearly had a significant relationship with Mr Rose. And we need to investigate that, too. To get an idea of his movements, his contacts in the days leading up to his death.' He pauses, considering whether to say more? 'We suspect his death might not have been straightforward.'

Peanut buttery saliva gurgles at the back of my throat, and my brain evaporates through my skull. My knees tingle. 'What do you mean?'

'I expect you've seen the headlines – why else be here so early? His cleaning lady discovered Mr Rose last evening. She had returned to his flat to collect her shopping bag, which she had inadvertently left there earlier in the day.'

The gorgon coughs. 'Sir.'

He brushes her intervention aside with a cursory waft of his hand in her direction.

'From initial findings, it looks as though Mr Rose had been drinking.'

'But he didn't drink – he told me that the day the exhibition opened.'

The gorgon scribbles.

'There were traces of alcohol in his mouth. Forensics will investigate, search for evidence of any drugs that might explain Mr Rose's collapse in his bath.'

None of this makes sense. He definitely said he didn't drink. 'Will there be a post-mortem?'

'It'll take place today.' He glances at his wristwatch. 'In two hours.'

'So soon?' Their speed astonishes me.

'It's always done as soon as possible after death. Before cells begin to deteriorate.'

'I see.'

'Anyway, Miss l'Ussier, we're not here to fill the gaps in your knowledge of police procedure.'

The gorgon smiles that frigid smile. Imagine kissing her. Like kissing an ice sculpture, one in no danger of melting. I shudder.

'I'll organise someone to clear the mob. Meanwhile, we need to clarify your dealings with Mr Rose. You may not think you have much useful to tell us, but we can use everything you say to fill in holes in our information. Helps us to join the dots.'

'I'll refresh the coffee pot.' Vic collects our mugs and makes towards the bathroom, no doubt to give them a quick sloosh round before making the next lot. DI Smith turns his back on us and pulls a mobile from his coat pocket. He talks hurriedly and so quietly it amazes me the person at the other end can hear him.

'Shall we go into your office? Get things started?' The gorgon gives the instruction in a honeyed tone which could be mistaken for an invitation for a girly chat, but she doesn't fool me. The sharp eyes spear me like one of those infra-red pens teachers in the bog standards complain about. Listen to me. Theo has so much to answer for; that's not my thinking at all.

'Miss l'Ussier?'

She gestures towards to office in a manner that brooks no argument, and I scuttle through the door. I make a show of going to sit behind the desk and inviting her to sit opposite me. Now she's a naughty schoolgirl who's been summonsed, not me. My inner crowing is short-lived.

'How well did you know Mr Rose?' She sits on the edge of the chair, her long legs crossed and the note-pad on her knee. She tilts her head.

'Not well. I met him for the first time the day the exhibition opened.'

She scribbles. Bet her short-hand is perfect. Can imagine her perched on the boss's knee. Stop it, Sia.

'Why did he attend?'

Can she truly be this dense, or is she playing with me? 'He's an art critic.'

She blinks in slow motion. No, it's me who's the idiot.

'And?'

'He was in the middle of organising an interview with my father. After Dad's accident, Daniel wanted to do the interview with me, instead.'

'Daniel.' She says his name under her breath and scribbles in her wretched notebook. 'What arrangements did you make with Mr Rose?'

If inflection could underline speech, hers would be in bold black ink. Mr Rose. The skin in front of my ears prickles. That line from Macbeth whispers in my ear, even though my thumbs aren't itching, yet.

'We arranged my interview the following week, here at the gallery.'

'Is that all?'

'Pardon?' What's she getting at? Is she an undercover reporter from some red top, trying to trick me into saying something indiscreet? Bloody woman.

'What else did you and Mr Rose discuss?'

'Nothing. We made the appointment. That's it. Oh. I asked him if he'd prefer tea, coffee or hot chocolate. He said hot chocolate.' Not going to divulge the playfulness of our chat. None of her business.

'This conversation occurred at the gallery, the day the exhibition opened?'

'No. He gave me his card, and I called him the following week.'

'There are no witnesses to this conversation? On the phone?'

'No.' I'd hate to be guilty of a crime and have her question me. Shame crawls over me, despite my innocence – I only half believe in it, myself.

Vic blusters in backwards, turns and places two mugs of coffee on the desk. He stands there, looking like a puppy after praise.

'Thanks, Vic. You're a lifesaver.' I grab the mug with the milky coffee and take a gulp. 'PC G… Broden, help yourself.'

Behind Vic, DI Smith hoves into view. 'Excuse me, Mr Wells.'

Vic stands aside to allow the policeman into the room. His presence crowds the office and claustrophobia threatens.

'I will speak to this reporter chappie. It's the one who covered the exhibition, Sia. You know, the one who wrote that positive article after the opening? He'd be the best bet.'

'Good idea. Thanks, Vic.'

The gorgon takes no notice of Vic. Throughout the brief exchange, she jots stuff in her notebook and stares at me. It's unnerving. Is she human? More likely, a new species of robot officer. She gives me the creeps. DI Smith stands behind her, his hands resting on the back of the chair. He reads her notes.

'What was your impression of Mr Rose?' He's cordial, unlike her.

I look up from my coffee. 'I thought he was nice, liked him. Wouldn't have agreed to the interview otherwise. He seemed genuine.'

She scribbles. The scratching of her pen across the page is rhythmic and regular. And annoying. 'Was it his idea to take photographs?'

'No. I'd started photographing them a couple of days beforehand. It was a coincidence, a good one for him.' I stop myself saying his name. The gorgon reacted as though my calling him Daniel was important, so I won't repeat that mistake.

'Did you only meet him the once?' She widens her periwinkle eyes. Guess it works on some people. 'For the interview?'

'No, we had a second meeting. I'd sent him the photos on a stick, and he'd gone through them with his editors.'

'Where did this second meeting take place?' She holds her pen, ready to write everything I say.

I look at DI Smith. 'We met at the Green Dragon.' My heart is racing; this sounds like a date. Heat, betraying and unwelcome, edges up my neck.

'Were you alone with Mr Rose?'

'Yes, but the pub was heaving, so we sat outside. It was a short meeting.'

'What did you discuss?' Still that gentle tone, an invitation to speak, not an order, but her softness doesn't mask her determination, her steeliness.

'I told you, we discussed the photos to go in the magazine.'

'Couldn't you have done that on the phone?'

'No. Well, yes, but it was important to speak to him in person. He'd changed his mind which photos he wanted to use, and I wanted him to explain – to persuade him to go with our original plan.'

'It was such a big deal?'

Here we go again. Mother muscling in, interfering. 'My mother had called Daniel.' Bugger. 'She wanted final say on what photographs he used. He changed his mind in deference to her wishes.'

'But it was your interview? Your photos?' The gorgon doesn't miss a trick. That stupid schoolgirl look was pretence.

'Yes. But Mother.'

They focus their stares on me, a sniper's cross-wire holding me in their grip.

'Mother had ideas of her own.'

'How did you react to that?' She looks at her note-pad, the shadow of a smile on her beautiful, sneering mouth.

'Is this relevant?'

'Just helping us get the full picture of events leading up to Mr Rose's death. Please answer the PC's question.'

'I was livid. I had chosen a terrific close-up for the front cover and Mother persuaded him to use another.'

'Do you know where Mr Rose lived?'

What the..?' The change of subject throws me.

'No.'

They think I fancied him. Not content with trying to pin being an arsonist's accomplice on me, now they're trying to get me to admit being involved in another death.

'Why should I?' I sound belligerent but I don't care.

The gorgon stops scribbling. She scowls. 'Just covering all angles.'

'I've told you everything I can.' I stand, holding the edge of the desk to mask my trembling. 'We are done here.'

They exchange resigned smiles; the gorgon slips her pen and notebook into her pocket and DI Smith opens the door for her to pass through ahead of him. He pauses.

'We'll keep in touch. No doubt you'll be keen to know how the case is progressing. And we may need to speak to you again.' With a curt nod, he leaves me.

I sink on to the chair, wrung out. I have no reason to fear the police, yet it ferments in my gut. Vic's voice rings out goodbyes, the gallery door creaks as it opens, thuds as it closes. He continues talking in subdued tones. The reporter, of course. It brings me no comfort, his presence. I'll stay in here. With luck, he'll finish his interview with Vic and go away.

Vic appears in the doorway. 'You managing?'

His gentle enquiry has me reaching for the tissues as tears well. 'I'm fine.'

He comes in, shuts the door and sits in the chair vacated by the gorgon.

'We'll stay closed today. I'll stick a notice outside, on the door. Stock-taking or some such. He wants to talk to you. Are you up to it?'

'Why? What can I tell him you haven't? I don't want…'

'Leave it to me. I'll get rid of him and pour us another coffee. Or are you sated with caffeine?'

'I'd appreciate gin, to hell with coffee.'

He consults his fob watch. 'A bit early for that, my dear. Why don't you press on with admin while I finish with our friend from the newspaper?' He pulls himself from the chair, with accompanying grunts only older people make. He winks at me. 'Won't be long.'

In quiet solitude, I fire up the computer and lean back, waiting for it to come alive. It hums and whirs, but the screen stays dark. I close my tired eyes. Tina, Mark and now Daniel. What do they have in common, apart from me? DI Smith never mentioned Tina, nor Mark. They must still be investigating, surely?

From my handbag, 'Waterloo' pipes into the office. I grab hold of it and on the screen is an unknown number. Have they found me? I leave it to play out the rest of the song, holding it in my palm, and wait for the message icon to appear. Moments later, sure enough, a red dot forms at the base of the phone icon. I press it and listen. The caller, with a cheerful London accent, tells me they want to talk to me concerning Daniel. He mentions a sum of money which makes me choke and gives me a number to call. Why are people so interested in him? And why do they assume I have the answers to their questions? I need to talk to Kim. I flick the pages of my diary; my appointment's on Friday. Could she fit me in today if I called and said it was urgent? Bet she would. I call her.

THE ART OF MURDER

* * *

I sit in the car outside Kim's house, early. Vic looked relieved when I said she'd squeezed me in to her busy schedule. It wasn't until I'd finished talking to her, I realised how early it still is. By the sounds of things, she was in her kitchen, having breakfast. I shall have to apologise. It's still a freezing morning, but at least I didn't have to scrape the windscreen. Hark at me, grateful for small mercies. I check the time on my mobile. The post-mortem will have started. What if they find drugs and alcohol in Daniel's body? What will that prove? Accidental death? Suicide? Or that misadventure thing? Whatever they find, it's too sad to bear.

I ring her doorbell and she's there in moments. She ushers me inside and the warmth of her house envelops me. We head towards the consulting room. In the thin winter morning light, the colours of the furnishings glimmer. I love this room.

'What's the problem?'

Her directness takes me by surprise. Is she cross I called, because she doesn't look angry? No, the kindness in her eyes gives me confidence.

'Have you seen the news headlines today?'

'No. Why?'

'Daniel Rose, the man who interviewed me for the magazine? Someone found him dead at his home yesterday.'

'Oh.'

I tell her everything, seeing the headlines, the reporters' siege and the police at the gallery. She listens without comment, but jots notes in her book. I take a deep breath.

'And, before this, another person disappeared from one of Dad's paintings.'

'How does Mr Rose's death affect you?'

'I'm shocked. We'd fallen out over the magazine cover, but he'd made amends, and we'd sorted it. So…' My lips tremble and I clench my teeth, gathering my control to speak again. 'I hoped we'd become friends. I liked him.'

She says nothing, waits for me to continue but conflict and nonsense fill my head. I want her to believe me but when I tell her what's going on, it sounds ludicrous. Daniel wasn't a lifelong friend so why do I feel cut adrift by his death? And repulsed by Jenny's joke about fancying him? The gorgon's inference of the same. Then, there's the article. Will they publish it now he's dead? Has my argument with Mother been for nought? No. She's messed with me for the last time. I'm certain the last disappearance isn't a fluke, either. But where's the link? Where is it?

I open my eyes, surprised I'd closed them. Kim sits opposite. The hush of the day settles like fine dust upon us. I'd like to sit motionless and let it stay undisturbed, so restful is its presence, and different from the turmoil in my head. I'm not here for silence though.

'Tina and Mark's deaths were tragic, but it's a greater loss with Daniel.'

The words bounce around my brain, but I struggle. I take another deep breath.

'It's silly; I'd known him a few weeks, but it's as though I've lost a loved one, not a near stranger. Like losing Dad all over again.'

'Why do you think that?'

'Daniel and I connected; I'm sure I didn't imagine it. Despite the fall-out, there was something between us that felt profound.'

I can't stop the tears spilling on to my cheeks. Kim pushes the tissue box towards me, and I grab a handful. Crying is supposed to be a release, isn't it? Not for me; my nerves are pulled tight, their pizzicato vibrations discordant. And I continue weeping, the dust of silence dispersed into the air.

'Sorry. Bet you love having an unexpected client who sobs through what should have been a quiet morning.'

'You needed to come. It's fine.'

I wipe the damp from my face and chuck the tissues into the waste basket. Sitting facing her, I search for something to discuss. Perhaps all I needed was her company, her calming presence. Her stillness is unlike anything I experience with anyone else.

'I can't shake the feeling Dad's warning me, when he erases a person from a painting - and I'm sure he's behind the disappearances. But he's dead, so how can that be possible? And how come I'm even considering it?'

'Sounds like you're processing what's happened and trying to make sense of it.'

'But that's the thing. It doesn't make sense. I suppose Daniel being Dad's generation, I might react to his death more, especially as he knew my parents years ago. Maybe their friendship has created a bond and I'm intuitively tapping into it.'

Kim makes no comment and I'm not surprised. I'm talking like some kind of new age hippy, spouting baloney. But I can't ignore the yelling of my intuition; God knows I've tried. Should I confide in Kim how noisy my head has become? Or is that my route to the funny farm?

In the quiet, someone's piano playing in a nearby house comes, muffled, through the walls. Far away a church bell tolls; it could be the Minster. Life outside continues as normal while my own becomes stranger.

I stand and gather my bag in my arms, holding it close like a shield.

'Sorry. I'm wasting your time. Thought I had something to discuss, but it turns out I haven't. I just needed a cry, and I could have done that at home. Sorry.'

'No apologies required. You're sure there's nothing else?'

She remains seated, regarding me with compassion, or what I take for compassion, and waits for my reply.

I want you to tell me I'm not going crazy, that there's an explanation for what's happening. I want you to make everything normal again.

'There's nothing else.'

In my head, the door to enlightenment and relief closes, leaving a thin rectangle of light piercing the darkness. Why I need to lie to her, is a mystery, but I do it anyway.

'Thanks for listening. It helped.'

She follows me to the front door. 'I'll see you Friday? As planned?'

'Yes. Thanks again for seeing me at short notice. I feel a bit of a fraud now. Sorry.'

And I do. It was foolish of me to hope she could help. Maybe I need a priest rather than a shrink. Huh. That certainly sounds like madness.

'Bye, Kim.'

'Bye, Sia.'

In the car, waiting for the lights to change, a familiar voice whispers in my head, its message at odds with its softness. There will be another disappearance. Someone else will die unless I can prevent it.

I'm in determined mood by the time I knock on the gallery door and Vic lets me in. 'Vic, I have to complete the photographic record of the paintings. Today.'

'Hello Vic. It went well with Kim, thank you. Yes, I'd love to hear how you've dealt with the press while I've been out.'

'Sorry. It did go well.' I link arms with him. Let's hope he can't tell I'm lying because I can't explain to him how weird the session with Kim was. We stroll towards reception. 'Tell me everything.'

Next to the coffee machine are two white paper bags, each grease stained. I gasp, hunger suddenly rampant. 'Vic! You bought lunch. You absolute angel.'

'It's early, more like elevenses but Kim's sessions often made me hungry – especially the middle of the day ones.'

As I chomp through my cheese toastie, Vic brings me up to

date. Tomorrow's local paper will carry a lengthy article about Daniel, including the interview with Vic.

'It'll be sympathetic, I'm sure, but don't be shocked if you're described as distraught.'

'Eh?' I splutter on my mouthful of toastie.

'You didn't want to speak to him, remember? I had to make an excuse.'

'Right.'

'And I let him have a couple of photos. Hope you don't mind.'

'Which ones?' I do mind. I mind a great deal, but how can I admit it without sounding petulant?

He fidgets in his chair, holds my gaze with troubled eyes.

'Which ones, Vic?' But I know what he'll say.

'The early one of the soldiers, and, and your mother's portrait. That's the one he wanted most – he had a wander and liked it.'

I sigh; how I hate being right sometimes. 'Will it detract from the magazine's article? It's Daniel's scoop, after all.'

'I don't think so. Hope it'll enhance it – give the readers a hint of what's coming.'

'Let's hope you're right.' I chomp into the toastie, tear a lump from it and ram it into my mouth.

* * *

Towards five o'clock, when the shadows cast by the streetlights cause the paintings to adopt their alter-egos, I have most in digital form. We view them together, Vic whistling periodically at my genius with the camera. Have to admit the results please me, in particular the close-ups.

'You know, Sia, we could make a collage of the close-ups and use it for the cover of our next brochure. Wouldn't that be tantalising? Prick the visitors' curiosity. What do you think?'

'Great idea. We could theme it – if I took photos of eyes, say.

Have them staring at the visitor from the cover. I like that idea.'

'So do I.' He stretches his back as he stands straight. 'But you can't take them now, the light's wrong.'

'I'll do it in the morning. I assume we're opening tomorrow?'

'If there's no welcoming committee.'

'I meant to tell you and events overtook me. I think Mother's painting again.'

'Oh?'

'Mm. I drove over to patch things up with her; she was in her studio.'

'What's she painting?'

'No idea. I didn't go in; just saw the light under the door. Thought better of disturbing her. More than my life's worth.'

'Well, that's good news. I wonder if she'd relent and let us hang a painting or two here?'

'Let's not get presumptuous. We'll see what she's done, first. Besides, I bet she'd say no.'

'I expect you're right. Shall we finish for the day?'

We switch off the computer, drain the coffee machine and recharge it ready for the morning. I wander to Betty to say goodnight. Everything sorted, Vic and I let ourselves out into the bitter night air.

'Any plans for this evening?' Vic pulls on his leather gloves, locks the door and slips the key into his overcoat pocket.

'No. Might call Jenny. She's in London. It's worse, her being in this country.'

'Does she come home for the weekends?'

'That's the plan. Although she didn't last week. They've given her a swanky apartment for the duration so she might not want to come home.' The truth of my words startles me. Haven't said them aloud to anyone else. 'I'll see what she says.'

'See you tomorrow.' He salutes and marches away into the frosty night, his breath pluming above him.

I push my hands into my pockets and trudge to the car park, my footsteps a muted echo in the empty street. I hitch my bag strap across me and grip it to my chest like I might a shield. As evening falls, no-one else walks hereabouts except occasional drivers, like me, heading towards the car park. It mystifies me where the people are, who abandon their vehicles here. They must make the long walk into the city centre. It's not a shoppers' car park, and I watch for one or two regular cars, but I've never seen their drivers. The place is deserted, peculiar shadows thrown across the yellowed stripes of the parking bays. Dull neons illuminate the low ceiling, which barely help, so it's fortunate I always park in the same place, more or less. I press my key fob and the lights of my car flash. In their temporary beam, something moves. I stop. I squint into the darkness. Nothing. It was probably a pigeon or a cat.

'Miss l'Ussier?'

A man steps out of the shadows. My heart stammers, the muscles in my chest contract.

'Can I talk to you about Daniel Rose?'

I cannot make out if it's the reporter Vic spoke to or someone else. I squint into the murk; how close is he to my car? What might happen if I make a dash for it?

'Who are you?'

I hope my fear isn't obvious, but my voice sounds brittle and staccato.

'I'm came this morning. Police turned us away.'

He must be a reporter, one of the unlucky ones. They don't give up easily, do they?

'You could be anyone. What's your name?'

He laughs into his collar. The hairs up the back of my neck bristle, the skin on my face pulls taut.

'Is it true you were the last person to see Daniel Rose alive?'

Am I furious or afraid? My heart thumps in my ribs and my

stomach knots. I rummage in my bag, grab my mobile and hold my thumb on the home button. I hold it in the air, my hand shaking.

'Come out of the shadow. I can't talk to you if I can't see you.'

He emerges from behind a pillar, and I flex my thumb. A flash of silver light crashes against the walls and vehicles. The man curses, and footsteps recede into the darkness. I run to the car, haul myself in and slam closed the door. I press the lock, its satisfying clunk the best sound ever. Without taking my bag from where it's slung across me, I ram the key in the ignition and turn on the engine. The lights blaze against the wall. I thrust into reverse, edge out and swing the car to face the exit. In the headlight beam, nothing stirs. Whoever he was has got away. I take it steady to the road, looking to all sides. Nothing. At the exit, I fumble slotting the card into the machine. The barrier rises, I press my foot on the pedal, and the car lurches forward. In my rear-view mirror as I drive away, a figure steps out of a doorway.

My nerves zing throughout the journey home, but my heart rate calms the further from the car park I drive. In silence. Joni: even she can't work her magic tonight. I was the last person to see Daniel alive; was that his assertion? His question implies I'm the killer. What am I thinking? No-one has mentioned murder, not in public. But Vic has, and Kim. So have I, in private: someone murdered Daniel. How can this certainty be so strong?

I loiter in the car when I arrive home scanning the area for anything odd or suspicious. One of my neighbours comes out of the block. He's a paramedic, going on duty, I expect. I open the door.

'Dave, how's things?' I release the seat belt, grab my bag, pull the key from the ignition and climb out of the car. 'You on nights this week?'

He saunters over, loping like an athlete, and grins. 'Yep. They're getting their own back for my having holidays over Christmas and New Year.'

'Oh dear. I couldn't work nights. Don't know how you do it.'

'It's not too bad, once you're used to it, and if you don't mind dealing with drunks.'

I shudder. 'No, I couldn't do that, either. Just a wuss, me.'

As we chat, I get out my flat keys. I jangle them in my palm. 'Hope you have a quiet night.'

'That'd be a first. Good night.' He lollops away, hands in pockets. I dash to the front door.

I pad round the flat, look in every room by mobile torch light. Satisfied I am alone, I pull closed the sitting room curtains and switch on the sideboard lamp. Everything is as it should be. My nerves are still strung like a Stradivarius. In the kitchen, I am thankful I tidied up this morning, an eternity ago. The microwave clock says it's almost six. No wonder. I've been up for fourteen hours.

Once I've divested myself of my coat and scarf, I prepare supper. It's a throwback to my student days, and my go-to comfort food. Tinned chopped toms, oodles of spices and a bag of rice. It's boil-in-the-bag stuff these days, so I don't have so long to wait. And, unlike those days, tonight, I chop cooked chicken into the mix. The rice ready, I spill it into the pan with the other ingredients and stir until mixed. Tom'n'rice must be eaten from a bowl, using a spoon; Mother would faint at my lack of niceties like a knife and fork. I grin at my rebelliousness. Pathetic at my age.

It's a juggling act, carrying the warming bowl to the sofa and switching on the telly. I go to the apps and select an episode of my favourite general knowledge quiz. It isn't long till I'm chuckling at the random nature of the stuff I learn, and the antics of the team members. By the time I've finished my supper and watched the credits roll, my eyes lids are heavy and my body aches, like I've done a marathon session at the gym. Not that I've done any such thing recently, as my flab will attest. Perhaps I should re-join, get fit. Sod it. I'm off to bed.

But sleep refuses to come. I lie awake, the image of the guy at the car park looming at me through the dark. The photo: I didn't look at the photo. I fumble on the bedside cabinet till I find my mobile and, pulling the duvet over my head, put in my password and press the photos icon. My photo stream pops up, and there he is. One light touch of my fingertip, and the photo fills the screen. Who is he? The shocked face is a stranger. But what sets my pulse racing again is the reflective flash on what he holds in his hand. It's a knife.

In my haste, I become entangled with the duvet, knock the bedside lamp and tumble in an ungainly crash to the floor. I scramble to my feet, switch on the light and dash to the front door. It's locked. I career through the flat to the kitchen. The fire escape door: locked. I tip-toe into each room, turning on the lights, despite knowing I checked when I came home, but maybe someone is hiding. I fling open the wardrobe doors in Jenny's room, sweep my hand through her clothes. Nothing. In the sitting room, I eschew the sofa, instead nesting myself in the armchair from where the entire room, the doors, everything, is visible. Should I call someone? I was going to call Jenny, wasn't I? It's not even eight o'clock, I still could. Or Theo. No, not him. Not two nights in a row. Sandro. I'll call Sandro. He might come and stay with me.

But Sandro's phone goes to answerphone. No doubt he's still tussling with that recalcitrant piece of walnut. Jenny, then.

'Sia. How're you doing? Any news on the Daniel Rose mystery?'

I tell her, and she listens without interruption.

'So, I'm sitting alone and scared, holding a photo of a strange bloke brandishing a knife.'

'Call the police.'

'I've really had enough–'

'Call them. This is serious. Promise me.'

The risk PC Gorgon might be on duty doesn't inspire me to call. Someone else might be on duty. I could risk it. 'I'll think about it.'

'Sia, if you don't call them as soon as I put the phone down, I will.'

'How will you know?'

'Because you'll call me back. If I haven't heard from you within half an hour, I'm making that call.'

There's a click, and she's gone. I fish DI Smith's card from my purse. Perhaps I should just call 111. I'm not in any danger now, am I? Am I? I can't be sure, can I?

Minutes later, I'm dressing and, with my mobile jammed between my shoulder and my chin, reassuring Jenny.

'He said he's coming straight round. He'll call me when he's at the door, so I know it's him. Christ, I hope he hasn't got the gorgon with him.'

'He won't come alone, will he? You're a single woman, on her own. Text me as soon as you can what happens. I shan't sleep until I hear from you.'

'Go to bed, Jenny. I'll text you tomorrow.'

'Text me before you go to bed, so I can read it as soon as I get up.'

'Okay. Thanks.'

'You're welcome. One of us had to see sense. Love you.'

'Love you, too.'

I make a cup of tea while I wait and set out two more mugs for DI Smith and whoever he brings with him. I've only just settled when he rings. He sits at my table with his sidekick, an older woman I haven't seen before, as I brew their teas and offer them biscuits. They both say no thanks to biscuits. I pull out a chair and sit with them.

He nods towards the woman officer. 'This is PC Clark. Could you explain events again, so PC Clark can make notes? And if you've got that photo handy, it would help.'

I fetch my mobile and show them the photo.

'Quick thinking, well done.' PC Clark smiles and I warm to her. Can't imagine PC Gorgon saying that to me.

We go through the events of the evening again, and PC Clark writes everything in her notebook. She asks questions, wanting more detail, and I remember much more than I realise when prodded. DI Smith doesn't say much.

'It's unlikely, but would you recognise him if you saw him again?' DI Smith leans on his hand, his elbow on the table. His grey complexion runs seamlessly into his hair, his heavy eyelids are rimmed with red. Poor man looks exhausted.

'Honestly?' I stare at the photo, trying to concentrate on his appearance rather than the knife he holds. 'I don't know.'

'Can you give us a copy of the photo? Our people may be able to enhance it, get a clearer picture.'

'Do you want me to send it to you? I could air drop it now.'

'That's helpful, yes.' He turns to PC Clark. 'Got your mobile with you? Mine doesn't air drop.'

She produces a top of the range iPhone, and we do the exchange in seconds.

'Got it.' PC Clark slips her phone into her pocket. 'Sia, can you think of why anyone would suspect you of involvement in Daniel Rose's death?'

'No, I can't. Hadn't known him long, and we got on well. I liked him, very much.' I say nothing of my deeper feelings for Daniel; not sure they'd understand.

'The man who approached you in the car park didn't sound familiar?'

'No, sorry. I suppose he could've been a reporter, but that hardly justifies the knife. It is a knife, isn't it? You don't think it could be his mobile, do you?'

'It had occurred to me. But seeing the photo, it's pretty clear it's a knife. You agree, Jan?'

PC Clark nods. 'That's no mobile.' She looks at the photo on her phone and shakes her head.

'Right.' DI Smith stands. 'We'll do a quick check of the surrounding area immediately. Then, one of our patrol cars will sweep by each hour until daybreak. Contact us if anything else happens – odd phone calls – that spy-hole in the door? Yeah? If someone unfamiliar knocks, call us. In the meantime, I suggest you go to bed.'

'Thanks.' I'm wide awake so will ignore his advice. 'I'll do that.'

'Thanks for the tea.' Good old PC Clark. She should teach the gorgon some manners.

They leave, reminding me to keep my door locked and to get my beauty sleep. Cheek. I close the door, lock it and peer through the spy-hole. It's amazing. The distorted landing stretches as far as the stairwell and the lifts. Doors bend in at strange angles. They could've been plucked from a low budget sci-fi film.

I wander back to the sitting room, leaving the hall light on, collect the mugs and deposit them in the sink. I stifle a yawn as I switch off the sideboard light and pick up my mobile. The text I send Jenny is brief, and she responds straight away, telling me she's coming home on Friday. For the first time since I left the gallery this evening, I relax. With Jenny home, nothing will frighten me, or at least she'll keep me company in my fear.

The dishes are washed and dried in moments, so I amble to my bedroom and slide under the duvet, clutching my mobile. I am asleep in seconds.

CHAPTER EIGHTEEN

JANUARY 9TH

Vic reads the paper. He's trying hard to behave normally after my revelations about the bloke with the knife, but he's not fooling me; I've spotted his furtive glances over the top of the paper. It's been a quiet morning, no bother from the press - a tremendous relief. We agree it must have been one of their number who approached me. Who else would be interested? Only a handful of visitors stroll the gallery, so I've uploaded the photos. Without the computer having a tantrum; thank the lord. I am pleased with them, especially the close-ups. Betty's is still my favourite, but even the Drewitts have interesting features. It was only when I saw Mrs on the big screen, I realised she has a slight cast in her eye. It's not visible from the gallery floor, but it's pronounced when seen in a close-up shot and explains why she's so aloof. She doesn't meet your gaze even though she's staring out of the painting.

Scrutinising her, now, sitting in front of the painting, I am ashamed of myself. She isn't stand-offish, but self-conscious, shy, even. It alters my perspective completely. Dad has hidden so much in his paintings I expect it'll take me a lifetime to discover everything.

Vic joins me and I tell him my thoughts à propos Mrs Drewitt. 'No doubt she found the entire portrait sitting tortuous. No wonder she looks so uncomfortable.'

He stares at the painting, like he too is having second thoughts. 'You may well be right. It'd be grand if she came to collect the painting. We could ask her.' He rattles the paper at me. 'You should read this.'

I take it from him. 'I'll go into the office. Don't want to risk blubbing here.'

'You won't blub. It's good. He's done Daniel – and the gallery – proud.'

'Did he mention a follow-up interview? Or question my involvement with Daniel?'

Vic pats my knee. 'We went through this earlier. No. Why don't you call the Herald? Double check?'

'Don't know. Feels presumptuous.'

'Then you must wait until the police finish their investigations. I assume you've told Theo by now? And Heather? Sandro? Detta?'

'Yes. Should I say, I left messages. The only person I spoke to was Detta. She said she'd be happy to keep me company tonight, so we're going to enjoy a girly evening with a chick film and a bottle of Prosecco.'

'Good idea. Go on, go read that article. It'll renew your faith in the media.'

'I doubt that.' But I do as he says, and head for the office, curiosity and apprehension gurgling inside me in equal measure.

The reporter has an effortless style, like he's having a conversation with the reader. He makes me smile with his observations on Vic, who's portrayed as an eccentric old academic. Anyone not knowing him would be forgiven for imagining a crusty old codger with untidy silver hair and an encyclopaedic knowledge of art. But what he tells the reporter is spot-on with Daniel. It's obvious Vic has known him for years. So why hasn't he ever spoken of him? Until he wanted to interview me? Plenty of art critics visit the gallery. I shall ask him.

The photograph of Mother's portrait dominates the pages. The article is a double spread, with photos of the paintings taking centre stage. Whoever puts the pages together has a good eye; they complement each other. And no mention of my being distraught. Yes, it's a cracking article. I wish the reason for it being written was different. Unbidden, tears well. I pull a tissue from my pocket and snivel into it. Who am I crying for... Dad? Daniel? Or myself? I hope this crying stage doesn't last much longer; I am washed out, and it plays havoc with my mascara.

Without genuine interest in the rest of the local news, I thumb backwards through the paper. It's disputes over funding, and neighbours falling out over unruly hedges. On the inside front cover page, a headline and photograph stop me closing the paper and consigning it to the bin. Mark's face smiles out at me. They have clipped the photo from a larger one, an official school photo by the looks of it. It's grainy, but there's no mistaking him. The article tells me the police found more forensic evidence at the crime scene, which should expedite their investigation, even lead to an arrest. Has Vic read this?

I rush from the office. Vic is back at reception, tidying the desk. He looks up, surprised by my sudden and frantic appearance. I shake the paper at him.

'Have you read about Mark?'

'Oh, yes. I forgot to mention it. Sounds hopeful, doesn't it?'

I am deflated at once. 'It is, I suppose. Theo doesn't mention Mark much, apart from in relation to the memorial service. Do you think he knows?'

'Would imagine so. The police will keep the school informed, and now he's such an important person, no doubt he's in on everything.'

'Mm. You're right. He's doubtless up to his neck in crocodiles.'

'Beg pardon?'

'I'm misquoting Joni Mitchell – he's battling with lots of stuff, none of it good.'

Vic shakes his head. 'She has some unusual ideas, doesn't she?'

'Something for any eventuality. She is a genius.' I spin on the spot, my hands clasped under my chin, the newspaper crumpled and bent at curious angles, and almost knock over our brand-new postcard stand. I clutch at it as it sways, bring it back to upright. 'Sorry.'

He laughs. 'You've never seen her perform live, have you?'

'No. And never will.' I flatten the paper on the reception desk. 'She's always hated performing, so I've read. She's concentrating on her painting now. And she's not been well. Don't blame her, heart-broken though I am.'

'How many of her albums have you collected?'

'Most. Those released in this country, plus a few imports. Imagine, Vic, if we hung Joni's paintings here, in Deerdale, in our gallery? I'd be in heaven.'

The phone trills and I snatch up the receiver before Vic can reach it.

'Wells Gallery. How may I help?'

'Miss l'Ussier, I trust you had a good night's sleep? Our patrols spotted nothing of interest.'

'That's good. I slept surprisingly well, thank you.'

'We think we've nailed the man in your photograph.'

My guts churn. 'Have you?'

Vic looks quizzically at me. I pull a face, hoping he gets the message something important has happened.

'Would you come to the station and view our video identification recording?'

'Yes. When?'

'We're just assembling a collection of individuals to video, for you to view. Could you call after work?'

'Yes, that'll be all right. Is it okay if I bring Dad's agent with me? She's meeting me here and spending the night at my flat.'

'Glad you'll have company. That'll be fine; she can wait in reception while you view the video or accompany you. Your call.'

'I'm sure she'll want to be with me. We close between four and five, depending on how busy we are.' I scan the gallery. 'Think it'll be the earlier time.'

'Good. The desk sergeant will expect you.'

I replace the receiver and relay the conversation to Vic.

'I'm impressed they're so quick.'

'So am I. Ollie, Theo's brother, slags them off – and he's one of them. Mind you, he says they're hideously under-funded.'

'He's right. And it's a thankless job, I'd imagine. What time is Detta coming?'

'She said half four. I'll text her; see if she can come at four. If that's okay with you?'

'Do it. We aren't heaving with visitors, and I'll close up shop.'

Detta agrees to come earlier. Vic and I spend the rest of the afternoon planning the next event, which we hope will bring in the visitors. It's always tricky after Christmas. Everyone's skint - not that it's been a major issue for us, but now we've got merchandise to flog, it's becoming one. We decide to try our luck with a range of cards for Valentine's Day. Vic takes persuading, but he comes round when I press home how alluring Dad's close-ups are.

When Detta arrives, I am full of mischievous ideas concerning what else we might arrange for Valentine's Day. I pull on my scarf and coat, talking like I've not seen Detta for ages.

'And, if Vic is agreeable, I thought we could have swags of flowers – roses are my choice – adorning the arches. I've looked online and you can get fabulous artificial ones. I picture hearts on shiny red strings hanging from-'

'Stop!'

Detta holds up her hands and grimaces at me.

'I'll do it in good taste. Nothing tacky.'

'Sounds like it. And Vic has agreed, has he?'

'Hello Detta. No, Vic has not agreed.' He kisses her cheek. 'I've said yes to cards – they'll always sell. But turning the gallery into a bordello is another matter.'

'How about spring flowers instead of roses?'

Detta nods. 'That would tone it down.'

'Vic? Please?' I use my most wheedling voice, slip my arm

through his and flutter my eyelashes at him.

He makes a drama of uncoupling our arms.

'You, madam, are incorrigible. We'll talk tomorrow. Now, be off with you and don't overdo it on the Prosecco tonight.'

Detta and I giggle like teenagers as we leave. I wave to Vic from the door and Detta blows him a kiss. We giggle even more.

* * *

They take us to a different room at the station. This one has a large screen suspended from the ceiling against the far wall, and rows of chairs facing it.

'We hold our seminars, briefings and whatnot in here. Come and sit at the front; you, too, Ms Jackson.'

DI Smith walks ahead of us down the aisle in the middle of the chairs. PC Gorgon sits at a table fiddling with what could be mistaken for a nineties stereo. She acknowledges her fellow officer, but not us. I could smack her face.

'It's all set up, sir.'

DI Smith gestures we should sit, and I plonk myself on one of the hard plastic chairs in the front row. Detta sits beside me. He switches off the light overhead.

'Thank you, Alice.'

Alice? I suppress a laugh. A Gorgon. I cross my legs and lean forward, my chin in my hands, my elbow on my knee. I grip my jaw in a power lock, so no sniggers will escape. Detta nudges me, her way of telling me to behave.

'Usually, we use a laptop for the procedure, but today we've a problem, hence the big screen. Study the images, which we'll show you twice. Afterwards, should you wish to view an individual a third time, you must tell us. You'll view nine different individuals, each of whom will face the camera before turning right and left. Don't worry if you can't identify him. He may, of course, not be present.'

I nod my understanding.

'We know who you are, but for evidence security, we must confirm your identity. In addition, you will have noticed Miss Sanderson, sitting at the back?'

I swivel in my seat. A young woman nods to acknowledge me.

'Miss Sanderson is a defence lawyer; another requirement by law. A witness must observe the viewings. We will record the session, but you need not concern yourself with that. It's to make sure we are doing our job properly. So, before PC Broden runs the video, please state your full name, loud and clear, for the recording.'

'Artemisia l'Ussier.' Embarrassment curls over any temptation to laugh. The gorgon smirks at me, enjoying my awkwardness at my name; her eyes glitter with amusement.

'Run the video.'

Nothing happens for a second. Then, a huge white cross with blurred edges fills the screen. It goes black. After a moment, a man appears. His lips are full, rosy, his eyes pale blue and there's the ghost of a beard. He looks left and right as DI Smith said. He isn't the man, although I can't be sure, can I? It was dark. A pause. How can I help them? I should have seen the enhanced photo first; would've made more sense. The second man is similar. I study his features. His eyes are closer together, and darker. And it continues, each man becoming more indistinguishable from the one before.

Until man number six. I push back on the chair, unable to stop the gasp. He keeps looking at me as he turns, his expression arrogant and intimidating. I am shaking. I grab the edges of the chair, the roughness scratching my fingers as I grip. Detta squeezes my hand.

I'm not sure I see numbers seven, eight and nine. Oh, I see them, but none of their features register. I cannot push number six from my mind. My fingers still hold the chair, my knuckles taut, when DI Smith speaks.

'Now, the second time. Are you happy to go ahead?'

I can only nod. The gorgon presses a button and the whole

thing starts again.

I hardly register numbers one to five in my anxiety about number six. As the face of number five disappears, my heart knocks in my chest, the muscles between my ribs flex. My whole body is pumped, ready to flee. I grip the chair, my fingers taut and pressing into the plastic.

He is before me once more. I bite hard on my bottom lip, my attention fixed on his face. It's him. Every nerve, every instinct shrieks: it's him. Tears blur my vision as I pretend to watch the remaining faces. As number nine looks back at me, I wipe my eyes with my hands. I grab the tissue from my pocket and try to tidy my face before DI Smith puts on the light.

PC Gorgon halts the video and sits back on her chair, watching me. DI Smith presses the switch and the overhead light flickers into life. I am washed out. It has taken, what, ten minutes? And I am exhausted.

He sits beside me. 'You saw him?'

'Yes. Number six.' My words are breathy and soft. 'Definitely number six.'

'You are sure? It was dark when you saw him.'

'I'm sure.'

'Do you require another viewing of any individual?'

'Should I look at number six again?'

'If you think it'd help.'

'I think I should.' I take a deep breath. 'Why should he affect me so, unless it's the man? I shall doubt myself if I don't see him again.'

DI Smith nods to the gorgon. The faces flash by until number six. She pauses the recording, and he quivers before me until she presses play. He glowers out from the screen. Ridiculous as it seems, he is attractive: tousled brown hair, umber eyes and a sensuous, smiling mouth. But his smile doesn't reach those umber eyes, and the mask fails to deceive.

'That's him.'

CHAPTER NINETEEN

THREE DAYS LATER

Jenny arrives, tired and irritated after her tortuous journey. In theory, a direct route from London to Deerdale, she's suffered bus alternatives (snow on the lines), a two hour wait in the middle of nowhere (points problems) and a bloke man-spreading while chomping through a smorgasbord of fruit and talking at full volume to a colleague on his mobile. She is understandably tetchy, so I pour her a glass of red and get on with supper.

While I cook, she reads the article about Daniel. She'd called me as she left the House, on her way to the station, so I've made her favourite meal – what we call pork slop. It's one of many recipes we've concocted over the years, one of our earliest. It always reminds us of sixth form evenings without our parents when we experimented with food and alcohol. I slide the chopped pork loin into the pan with the peppers, onions and mushrooms. Steam and sizzles fill the kitchen.

I grab my glass and take a good mouthful. It's clichéd, but I love Merlot, especially from the New World. I hover the bottle over the pan.

'Shall I add wine? Or shall we drink it?'

Without speaking, she holds her glass high. I fill it to the top and leave the bottle on the table. Decision made.

The pasta bubbles in the saucepan. I whisk the spoon through the mixture, preventing any from sticking. Not long till it's ready. I rummage through the herbs and spices in the cupboard, pick out the smoked paprika and shake a generous quantity into the meat mixture. The colour changes to a heart-warming terracotta and the smoky aroma makes my taste buds tingle. From the fridge, I fetch the soured cream. Turn the gas low, and plop spoonsful in. I am hungry now. The pasta cooked, I strain it and tip it into the meat pan. Have I eaten recently? The rumblings in my stomach and the juices sloshing round my mouth imply I haven't.

Jenny folds the paper, putting it aside when I take her plate laden with food and place it before her. We dig in and even if I say so myself, it's delicious. It can be a hit and miss affair, depending on my mood, the alignment of the stars. Who knows? But this one's a goody.

'I changed the bed linen after Detta. She only stayed the one night, but I thought you'd prefer clean sheets.'

Jenny grunts her agreement, her mouth full. 'Thanks.'

'Was weird, her being here. Nice, but weird.'

'I bet. Like having your mum stay.'

My turn to grunt. 'Wish that were true. God, can you imagine Mother staying the night?' I shake my head, but the vision is too strong to erase. 'Nightmare.'

'Yeah, sorry. But my mum has. Long time ago, granted. I remember we had a good time.'

'Your mum's a treasure. Detta's similar, so I get your point.'

She waves her fork at the paper. 'The photos are great.'

'Pity the paper scooped the magazine. Their resolution surprised me. I guess their equipment is digital these days.'

Jenny sits back and folds her arms. 'Not like when I were a lass.'

I burst into laughter at her ridiculous accent, and she laughs, too.

'Glad you're home. I miss you.'

'I miss you, too. In fact, I've been considering coming back to Yorkshire.'

'Have you? Seriously?'

She scoops another forkful of slop. It hangs in mid-air. 'Yup. The contract in Brussels comes up for renewal in the summer. I may not apply.' She eats.

'That'd be brilliant. But what will you do? Are there jobs for translators and interpreters locally?'

'In the cities, sure. Leeds isn't so far. It's commutable. Bradford. Even here in Deerdale. You'd be surprised.'

'Have you been looking?'

Her eyes sparkle with mischief. 'Applied for a couple. Got an interview next week. That's the real reason I've come home. Nothing to do with you.' She raises her glass. 'Here's to new beginnings.'

'Boo, you whore! Fancy keeping secrets from me.' I can't stop the grin. I'm light-headed and whizzy.

'Don't raise your hopes. I might not get it.'

'Course you will. Who could compete?'

She snorts. 'Depends on the opposition, and it's a two-day affair. May not get to the second day.'

'Bet you do. God, your CV must be awesome.'

She doesn't demur.

Her words thrill me. She says it's nothing to do with me, but I don't believe her. Friends like Jenny, who'd jack in their jobs to support you, are rare. Would I do the same for her? I hope so, but I'm not sure. She's a better person than me.

'Come to the gallery tomorrow. I want to show you our new merchandise and our plans for Valentine's. Vic's relented. I'm getting my flower swags.'

* * *

'Why don't you buy a laptop? You could work at home when the fancy takes you,' Jenny says, the next day when she visits the gallery. 'You know, when the muse strikes.' She sits in the office going through the card ideas I've mocked up on the computer. 'And you'd have up-to-date software. This ancient stuff must hold you back.'

'I suppose. The range of fonts is limited.'

'You can't use comic sans. Everyone hates it.'

'I don't. What's wrong with it?'

'If you had the latest computer, you could install a proper, made-for-purpose program. With your eye for design, you'd make a killing.'

'I have looked, but the all-singing, all-dancing ones aren't cheap. I'll speak to Vic.'

'Don't. Just buy one – from your own money, if needs be. This antiquated heap,' she gestures at the desktop, 'belongs in a museum.'

She's right. But I will speak to Vic first. It should come out of the gallery budget if it's being used for gallery business but, Lord knows, I can afford to buy the darned thing myself. I'd be able to link my iPad to it, too. That'd be useful.

'You rate my designs, though?'

'They're ever so eye-catching. I'd buy one, if I had a significant other.'

'I hope we're not too late. The shops have had Valentine's stuff on sale for ages, since Boxing Day.'

'Get a move on, then. Use these designs this year, a limited run; if they're popular, sell out, aim big next year.'

'I haven't ordered the flowers yet, either. I'll place fresh ones in amongst the artificial ones – make the gallery an intoxicating experience.'

'Nice. I should go. Must prep for this interview.' She rises from the chair and kisses my cheek. 'I'll see you at home. My turn to cook.'

She leaves, and I stroll over to where Vic is arranging a new mini-exhibition of local children's artwork. Their theme is our city, and the paintings, collages and sculptures bring youth and vitality to the gallery in their exuberant use of colour and materials. I am optimistic for our future artists if only they aren't hindered by the pressure of exams in academic subjects which dominate schools these days. Vic's promoting of the young is inspiring.

'S'looking good, Vic.'

He stands back to admire the children's handiwork.

'It never fails to astonish me how talented our youngsters are. Fills me with hope.'

'Any from St Bede's?' Theo's school usually sends offerings from the youngest pupils.

Vic points to a papier mâché rendition of the Minster. Its towers and stained-glass windows make it look as though its creator plucked it from its foundations, miniaturised and placed it here, on our display table.

'Wow. That's stunning. How old is the creator?'

'Sixteen. Mm, I know. Unusual. The headmaster said in his letter the pupil in question looks forward to a career in architecture. I hope it will encourage them to send more from older boys. Gorgeous, eh?'

'Yes. Does he want it back?'

'Sadly, he does. It will take pride of place in the reception of his mother's firm.'

'Don't tell me. Of architects.'

'Got it in one.'

'Good luck to him. Talent must run in the family.'

'As it does in yours.'

I snort. 'Yeah, right.'

'Don't start that malarkey.'

'Malarkey. Love that word. Okay. I'll say no more.'

'Good.'

'I want to discuss another issue with you.'

'Oh?'

'Is time we ditched the old desktop and bought a new computer.

Jenny and I were discussing it just now. She thinks a modern laptop would make our lives much better, give us more scope.'

'Have you done the research? Done the finances of such a purchase?'

'Only tentatively. They're expensive but a laptop, with appropriate software, will revolutionise our organisation - not just in terms of merchandise. Our records, finances, everything'd be easier.'

'Get prices together and we'll discuss it. We can't decide without the info. But in theory, I agree. It's time we hauled ourselves into the twenty-first century.'

'Thanks, Vic. I'll get researching now.'

I have such a lightness of step when I return to the office, I could convince myself I have lost several stones in weight. Jenny's coming home, Vic's agreed to a new computer and the gallery's future looks bright. I park myself on the office chair, wiggle the mouse to wake up the computer and wait. None of this nonsense once I've installed the new one. How daft am I, getting excited by the prospect of a sparkly new piece of kit?

My mobile, on the desk next to the computer jumps into life, vibrating towards me before bursting into 'Waterloo.' Mother. How to spoil a cheerful mood in an instant.

'Hello Mother.'

'Sia, I need to discuss something important with you. Come home for supper tonight?'

Resignation nudges at my brain, but I refuse to allow it access.

'I could come after supper. Jenny's home and she's made plans to cook for us tonight.'

'Can't she wait? Food'll keep till tomorrow. This is urgent.'

'I don't suppose an hour later will make much difference.' I try to be strong, but the voice in my head tells me I'll submit.

'That won't give us enough time. Sandro can make it.'

'All right.' We sigh in unison; mine in acquiescence, hers in satisfaction.

'Supper's at six.'

With that, she hangs up, leaving me staring at Betty Boo, who's her replacement on my mobile.

Bloody woman. I must stop letting her browbeat me into doing things I don't want to do. And she'll take the moral high ground for contacting me first. Damn, damn, damn. I must explain to Jenny; she'll be miffed I'm letting her down last minute. I search for her in my contacts.

'Sorry, Jen.'

'Stop saying that. It's fine. She's right, the food will keep. I'll have a baked potato. Is no big deal, really it's not.'

'I feel dreadful.'

'Don't. She said it's urgent. You need to be there.'

'It won't be urgent. She's just throwing her weight about, as usual.'

'You don't know that.'

'Trust me. Bet I'm right.'

'If you are, you can cook for the rest of the week.'

'You're on.'

'And I'll provide wine.'

'You are lovely. Thanks.'

'It's what friends are for. Now, bugger off and sort out what laptop you want.'

'I'm gone, I'm gone.'

Her laughter reassures me, and we end the call. When I get to Mother's, I shall tell her she can't demand we drop everything for her at a moment's notice. It isn't fair. Listen to me. I sound like a fifteen-year-old. Grow up, Sia. But I shall have words. Part of growing up, isn't it?

* * *

Mother smiles at us across the table. We're dining in the kitchen for once. The chicken in white wine smells delicious, and I am hungry, but my annoyance scratches away at me, taking the edge from my hunger. Urgent, is it? Then why does she smile?

'What's this for, Mother?' I cannot hide my irritation.

She raises an eyebrow as she takes a delicate forkful into her mouth. She chews, deliberately slowly, if you ask me.

'I want to have a memorial service for your father, just for family and close friends.'

I drop my fork with a clatter on to the table.

'What? You made us alter our plans for this? This is what you call urgent?'

'Artemisia, kindly do not raise your voice. It is urgent. If we don't arrange the service quickly, your poor father will be a distant memory. I can't bear the thought.'

'We had a funeral. Sia held an exhibition. Isn't this one step too far?'

I nod at Sandro. He speaks sense. Why prolong the mourning in public? Isn't it enough to endure it in private?

'I don't remember the funeral. And Sia's little exhibition hardly counts as a memorial, does it? Hijacked by that woman and her sewing.'

'Mother! That woman, as you call her, was grieving for her wife. The wife who died saving Detta, at our studio. And the "sewing" was exquisite, embroidered pictures.'

She takes another forkful of food, makes us wait. I want to stab my fork through her hand as it sits, relaxed, by her plate.

'That's as maybe. But I want something to commemorate your father, just him. Don't you understand?' And her eyes fill with tears. 'I miss him so much, am bereft without him.'

'We know that.' Sandro is solicitous, his tone comforting. 'We miss him, too. What had you in mind?'

'An intimate gathering, a hundred perhaps, in a suitable venue – the Minster might prove too big...'

Her voice trails off, the notion of the Minster not banished. The Minster might be too big? Might be?

'You want a religious ceremony?' Keeping myself civil takes all my willpower. She plays with us, expects us to do her bidding, however preposterous. I stuff chicken into my mouth. She hates when we speak with our mouths full, so it's a good excuse to say nothing for a moment. I regroup my feelings and try not to do something I could regret. The meat desiccates on my tongue. I take a sip of water. Doesn't help.

'The school chapel would make an intimate setting.' Sandro looks at me, his eyes full of question. 'What d'you think, Sia? Could Theo swing it for us?'

Discomfort at his suggestion oozes through my every pore. I keep chewing, keeping at bay the answer I want to give.

'Artemisia, answer your brother's question. Good God, where are your manners?'

'I can't win, can I?'

I take another sip of water and force down the meat. A few strands linger, caught between my teeth. I'm a vagabond, thrown morsels from a restaurant kitchen.

'If I speak, with my mouth crammed with chicken, you'll upbraid me for being common. If I stay silent until I've finished, I'm being rude to Sandro. I don't know about the chapel.'

She tuts, shakes her head, and closes her eyes.

'Theo would have influence, I'm sure, but I hesitate because-'

Her eyes snap open. 'Because what?'

'We aren't...' The words elude me. 'It feels opportunistic.'

'Nonsense. He'd do anything for you. You're going through a tricky spell. This may be what's needed to set the pair of you straight.'

'Could you, sis? For Mum's sake?'

He turns his puppy-dog eyes on me, and I want to scream. He knows what she's doing but is determined to make it easier for her. Of all people, he knows best how she operates. After years of standing by me when she's behaving unreasonably, he morphs into a spineless creep. I can hardly bear to look at him. But I do. I look him right in the face.

'For Mother's sake?'

'Would you?'

She watches us from across the table, her mouth half smiling, half smirking. So pleased with herself.

'If he says no?'

'We find somewhere else. Sandro can investigate, can't you?' She fixes her green gaze on me. 'But the school chapel would be perfect. Ask Theo.'

My rage, concertinaing through me, renders me unable to respond. It explodes in riotous colours behind my eyes and nausea follows at a gallop. I slide my plate away from me; I can't eat any more. Even the smell makes me want to heave. I push back my chair to stand, throwing my napkin on to the table.

Though my mouth is dry and my tongue sticks to my teeth, I muster my strength to speak.

'I will ask. But don't expect me to persuade him. That I won't do.'

'As you wish.' She lifts her cutlery and resumes her meal. I am dismissed.

CHAPTER TWENTY

JANUARY 21ST

A week later, enough time has passed. Mother has called twice and the thrill of telling her I've been too busy to ring Theo has been worth it. Her efforts to be polite have almost been my undoing.

Theo is solicitous and understanding when I call to ask. He agrees straight away to discuss the service with the headmaster. I'm not any less awkward or furious, but I am calmer. In under an hour, he rings me to say they have agreed and asks for me to suggest dates.

I sit in the office, my mobile in my hand, Mother's number ready. With a press of the call icon, I can impart the good news. Who will be lumbered with organising it: liaising with school; getting an order of service printed? Sandro will be far too busy with his walnut David. I press the icon.

'Sia? You've news? Has the school said yes?'

She doesn't say thank you or ask how Theo is.

'Yes, Mother. They want dates, so they can fit it into their *very busy* chapel diary.'

If she hears my emphasis, she ignores it.

'Splendid. Got your pen handy? I can give you dates now.'

I shouldn't've expected otherwise, should I? I grab the ball point from the pot on the desk, turn to the back page of the diary and sit poised. 'Go on.'

She gives me half a dozen dates to offer – her word – the

school. I jot them on the page in between my doodlings and assorted notes whose relevance I've forgotten.

'Right.' I sound weary and resentful. Not surprising. 'I'll get back to you as soon as I've got something definite.'

For an hour or so, I distract myself researching laptops and software packages. I narrow my choices to three, print their details and seek out Vic.

The gallery buzzes with visitors today, drawn to the city by blue skies and sunshine. It gladdens my heart to see so many, and a few show interest in my Valentine's Day cards. Despite the niggle of negativity, I am excited and determined to make a success of our newest venture.

Through the crowd, Vic stands surrounded by a group that doesn't give me the impression they arrived together. It's a mishmash of people of various ages and colours. I wish I were as talented as Dad - it'd make a wonderful painting. Deerdale in its multi-ethnic glory. I smile, and it feels good.

Rather than interrupt, I push towards Betty. The crowd is thinner by her, thank goodness, and I sit on my favourite bench facing her. Harold is moody today, and Betty looks at me with resigned amusement. Her light piano playing in the background is doubtless unheard by anyone but me. I scan the sheets while I wait for Vic to end his impromptu lecture. My favourite's the most expensive, so I don't hope too fervently. Vic isn't parsimonious, but he has to balance the books. Sia, use your own money, for goodness' sake. Vic's not too proud to accept a new computer; he's aware of your inheritance. I smile. Dad's money spent on "Dad's" gallery. I keep watch for when the crowd allows him to escape. He looks my way mid-sentence and I wave the sheets at him. He makes his excuses to the group and strolls in my direction.

'Tremendous turn-out, isn't it?' I glance towards the group he's abandoned; they disperse to look at other paintings.

'Yes, love it. It's why we're here, isn't it?' He sits beside me. 'Been thinking, it's time we held another open night. Daytime events are great, but our opening hours are impossible for swathes of people. Shouldn't we cater for them?'

'Okay, I'll give it some thought. That consignment from France, we might develop a mini-exhibition based on it, something tactile, get the visitors involved. Learn a technique or two.'

'Our long-term planning isn't up to scratch. We should know what we're doing this time next year. Do we know what we're doing this time next week?'

I laugh. 'Sort of. Since Dad's exhibition, it's been, shall we say, ad hoc? You're right. We should hold a meeting to thrash something out.'

'A meeting? That sounds more like it. When?'

'Before any meeting, look at these; tell me what you think.'

I hand him the sheets and he scans the first one. 'I appreciate I said I wanted more gen on these things, but I trust your judgement.' He turns the corners to read the prices and whistles through his teeth. 'Progress doesn't come cheap, does it? Get the one you want most.'

I squeeze his arm. 'Thanks, Vic. I'll get it sorted. I'm certain it will have a tremendous impact on us.'

'So am I.'

We spend the rest of the day dealing with visitors. Vic's words about why the gallery is here add an edge to my enjoyment and the hours slide past. Darkness outside and the dwindling numbers hint at closing time. It's always a fluid thing with us; we never hurry visitors to leave. We prefer to stay later; it encourages them to return. When, at last, the final stragglers depart, it's half-past six. One of our latest closings ever. It's been a grand day for the coffers, too. I've sold all the Valentine's cards.

'Next year, we'll do things on a bigger scale.'

'Bigger than swags of flowers from the arches?'

'You wait, Vic. When you see how it looks, you'll yearn to be seventeen again.'

His shoulders droop, and I wish I could cut out my tongue.

'I long for that every day. Should count myself lucky. Many people reach their death bed without sharing a great love, don't they?'

I pull a smile from somewhere. 'Thought Theo was mine. Goes to show how wrong a girl can be.'

'You don't fool me, Sia. You're still seeing him, aren't you?'

'Not since the night Daniel died.'

'I see. Dealing with this memorial business will be tricky.'

'I'll manage. We respect each other enough to avoid making matters more awkward than necessary. It's harder for him.' I glance at the clock. 'I should call him before I go. Mother's given me dates for him to consider.'

'I'll wait until you've done. Tidy the racks or something.'

'There's no need. I'm not expecting that bloke to make a return visit.'

'I'll stay. For my peace of mind.'

'Okay. Won't be long.'

Theo takes an age to answer his phone, his weariness palpable as he speaks.

'It's me.'

'Has she come up with dates already?'

'Think she had them prepared earlier. Old Blue Peter habits die hard.'

'What?'

'Never mind. Shall I run them by you?'

'Okay. Fire away.'

We settle on a Thursday in two months' time. It'll be tight, getting everything sorted, but it should be doable.

'Sia, talking of Thursdays, would you come to the next dining in night? It's next week.'

'Yes. Thank you.'

'We could discuss the service with the head over supper. Save us having to chat, and you having to make numerous trips into school. Could you talk to your mother?'

'Is the school taking part?'

'The head's keen. Says your dad was a tremendous benefactor.'

'Was he? I didn't know.'

'We award a trophy in his name every summer for exceptional artistic achievement.'

What a revelation. Dad supported the local comprehensive; they award a trophy, too. My mind reels. 'How long have you known?'

'Not long. No reason to, although my ignorance earned me a reprimand from the head. I must pay more attention at awards night.' He's smiling; I hear it through the airwaves.

I smile, too. It's comforting to share his whimsical comments.

'I'll be in touch. Bye, Theo.'

'Bye.' He pauses, his breath tickles my ear like he were standing close and whispering. 'See you soon.'

I stuff the mobile into my bag, switch everything off and, pulling my scarf round me umpteen times, head out to reception. Vic has extinguished the gallery lights. Shadows and lamplight streak the paintings.

'Ready.'

'I'll walk you to your car.'

I give up the fight. 'Do you want a lift home?'

He shakes his head. 'Walk'll do me good.'

We part at the entrance to the car park. I sense he watches as I make my way to the car. As I slip my key into the lock, I look back; he loiters at the entrance, his breath blossoming into the night air.

By the time I reach the exit in the car, he's up the path, retracing our steps towards the gallery. He disappears round the corner as I pull the car into the road. He's a big-hearted softie. Not bad for a boss. The sheets with the laptop info nestle in the top of my bag. When I get home, if Jenny's in, I'll order the one I want on my iPad. Course, if she's not back, I'll have to get stuck into making supper. Let's hope she's home.

The flat is unlocked, the smell of something delicious wafts along the hall to greet me as I open the front door.

'Jen, I'm home.'

'In here.'

I follow the aroma and her voice to find her sitting at the kitchen table doing the crossword, a glass of wine in her hand.

'What's cooking? Smells great.'

'Meatloaf. An old recipe of Mum's. My favourite when I was a kid.'

'Bet it was. It's making my mouth water. How did it go, then?'

She grins. 'Second round next, and only one other candidate. Improves the odds no end.'

'Wow, that's brilliant. You liked the place? Were the people friendly?'

'You ask too many questions. Yes, I liked the place. Yes, the people were friendly. Now, how come you haven't taken off your coat? Aren't you stopping?'

'Nag, nag, nag. Anyone'd think we were married.'

I take off my coat and go into my bedroom, dump it on my bed. Scarf joins it.

'Had a chat with Theo.'

A glass of wine awaits on the table. I take a long, grateful drink.

'And how is he? Charming as ever?'

'Asked me to the next dining in.'

'It's not totally in ashes, then?'

'I reckon so, but it's nice to talk to him. And I'm looking forward to dining in, despite having to sit at the top table and talk to the head about Dad's memorial service.'

'That's happening?'

'Yep. Date's in the school diary. Haven't told Mother yet.'

'Oo, inside information. I am honoured.'

I slump on to a chair and lean on the table. 'Wish it wasn't. Mother will either be inconsolable or hideously prima dona-ish.

Either way, too horrible.'

'I'll be there, and Theo, and Vic. Why don't you ask Kim? It might help her understand your issues.'

'Not sure that's allowed. Imagine how I'd introduce her to people: Please welcome Kim, my shrink.'

'Hadn't thought of that. Right. Better get the veg on the go. The steamer's full of stuff that's good for you.'

'Put hairs on your chest.'

We laugh.

'You said it. I'm getting through no end of disposable razors since going on this healthy eating lark.'

I top up her glass, laughing.

'You should get an electric one. I did.'

She snorts into her glass; wine cascades over her fingers and drips on to the table. We mop up with kitchen roll, unable to contain the laughter.

'Mum gave me her old Ladyshave when I was a teenager,' she says. 'Still got it somewhere. An antique, but it works. That should do the trick. Save any embarrassing conversations with the shop assistant at Boots.'

'Oh, God. Imagine it. "I'm looking for one of those body shavers" – Sandro has one, you know? "Which one do you recommend?" "Does your husband have sensitive skin?" "It's not for my husband, it's for me."'

Our guffaws echo round the small kitchen and, I expect, through the entire block. We struggle to set the table and check the meatloaf, almost too helpless to function. But we don't care. Pity anyone who isn't us tonight.

CHAPTER TWENTY-ONE

TWO DAYS LATER

How brilliant is Detta's news? She's attended several interviews at the police station as a condition of her bail. And now she's free. They said there's not enough grounds, and besides, they've got new leads to follow. She didn't say what they were. I don't suppose the police told her. I sit here, staring at a blank computer screen, grinning. We've arranged to go out for a celebratory meal tonight. I can't wait.

It's good news all round. Jenny sailed through the second day's interview. She starts in two months after returning to Brussels to hand in her notice and sort out her stuff. Apparently, she can quit provided she gives a month's notice.

And I've ordered the new laptop! My cup runneth over. It'll arrive before the weekend. Hurrah. I've read the blurb associated with the software and my heart whizzes when I contemplate what I might achieve. We will spoil the visitors for choice. We should open a coffee bar by reception. Could it work?

I abandon the computer, which senses its approaching demise, and saunter into the gallery. It's busy again, even now; people getting their culture fix early. Vic sits at reception, going through the mail. From the entrance to where he sits isn't roomy; a coffee bar situated here might be problematic. But further in, where we put Tina's table during Dad's exhibition, there's space. But is it enough? For a couple of tables for two. We could up-grade the coffee machine behind reception. Offer tea – Fair trade, obviously.

'What're you up to? You've got that look on your face.' Vic's voice cuts through my musings. I turn on my toes, and smile.

'How about a coffee bar? A small affair, nothing fancy, for two, four visitors? Over there.' I point to where I can envisage a cosy seating area. 'What d'you think?'

'Dear God. You are empire building. What next?'

'People come here during their lunch breaks. It's a natural progression.'

'You think?' He's speaking in his "I'll humour her" voice.

'Yes. We could stock those biscuits you get at car sales rooms – you know, the ones wrapped in pairs. Best part of buying a car, the free biscuits. We'd charge for them, though.'

'I see.'

He strolls over and stands next to me, his chin in his hand like he's considering my idea. It's dead in the water.

'It'd be tight here.' He scans the gallery. 'Makes more sense to develop the stock room. You've got plenty of space. We'd need to pull down a wall, push it back a metre or two, but it's a possibility.'

'Are you serious? That's brilliant! We could go to town and cater when we have our special evenings. Offer sherry or wine. That'd be great.'

'Whoa. Hold on a minute. For a start, if we open a café, we'll need a licence. Serve alcohol? Another licence. We'll also need to employ someone to run it – unless you're dreaming of a change of career? Let's take it one step at a time.'

'Yes, of course. It would be quite an investment in the gallery. Will the finances cope?'

'We'd get a bank loan. Should be straightforward enough.'

'Know nothing about that. You'd have to do that bit. I'll stake out the stock room.'

I push through the visitors, chat about the paintings. A couple of steps before the stock room, I halt. We might avoid demolishing the wall. The door is extra wide to allow us to carry paintings from the gallery to the store, and vice versa, safely. If we removed and widened it further, I bet we'd get away with it. We could reposition the door in a stud wall further in. I unlock the door and step inside. Vic's right. Look at all that empty space; it's a waste. My head is chaotic with possibilities vying for attention. I shall have to write things in a notebook, or I shall forget them.

'Sia.'

From beyond the stock room, Sandro calls. My heart stops a beat. He's so like Dad: his posture, his colouring, his smile. I'm looking into the past and seeing Dad in his prime. I blink to erase the vision from my head. What's he doing here so early? I lock up as I leave and hurry to his side. By the time I reach him, he's frowning. The day was going so well. I steel myself for whatever he has to say.

'What's up?'

'There's been a development. Someone claims they saw a woman skulking in the woods; said they were walking their dog and saw the studio ablaze. They've just come forward.'

'Is that why they let Detta go?'

'Have they? It gets weirder.'

'Eh? Wait, you weren't aware of Detta's release from bail? But-'

'Mother. She called in a state. I'm on my way now. Wondered if you'd come with me.'

'Why is she in a state?'

'That's the thing; I'm not sure. She was garbled on the phone, and angry. Mentioned Detta, but I couldn't make sense of her. I think she needs us.'

Dread slithers through me. I've been waiting for this since Dad died. For her control to snap.

'I'll just tell Vic.'

Five minutes later, we are in Sandro's car heading for Mother's.

Neither of us speaks; too wrapped up in our own fears to say them aloud. If we can get her to take her meds, it might help. What if they don't? If she's taken them? We should contact the unit. I am about to suggest this when Sandro turns the car into Mother's drive. I don't know how we got here so quickly.

The front door is locked. Sandro uses his key, and we step inside. The house is quiet and cold and dark. No curtains are open, no light spills into the hall from the adjacent rooms.

'Mother?' My call echoes, like I'm standing in an uninhabited house. 'Mother?'

Silence. We look at each other. Sandro's face looks as mine feels: frowning with concern and trepidation.

'She's most likely in her bedroom. Shall we?'

'Good idea.' He grabs my hand, and we race up the stairs, taking them two at a time.

At her bedroom door, we stand out of breath. It's ajar, no light from within through the small gap. Sandro pushes the door open wide. She is not there. Her bed is unmade, clothes scattered everywhere, but no sign of Mother.

I tiptoe to the en suite. The door is open. The room, empty. I turn to Sandro.

'Where the hell is she?'

He pulls the curtains aside and stares into the garden. 'In her studio. Now what? Should we?'

'Yes. No time to waste. Come on.'

We run through the house as we did when we were kids, but without the joie de vivre or whooping. The back door is unlocked. We hurtle to the studio, and I hammer on the door.

'Mother! Open up.'

For a moment, nothing happens. But then, she opens the door a fraction and peers out at us, one eye visible.

'What's the emergency?' She slurs her words.

I grab the door handle and pull, but she's got the chain on and links judder as the chain pulls taut.

'For God's sake, let us in. We need to see you.'

'Why? I'm painting.'

Sandro gently ushers me aside. 'Come out for a moment, instead.'

'Why?'

'I was worried after our phone call. Come into the house, brew us a coffee and tell Sia what you told me.'

The chain clinks as it's withdrawn. She slides out and shuts the door behind her, locks it and slips the key in her pocket. She fixes me with a glacial stare.

'Is my daughter concerned for my well-being? We should break open a bottle of champagne.'

I am a child again, shrinking under her disdain. My cheeks blaze.

'Don't be mean.' Sandro takes her arm, and together, they stroll back to the house.

I follow, seething with shame and anger.

In the kitchen, Mother totters as she opens the blinds, sorts out the complicated and expensive coffee machine, fetches bone china mugs from a cupboard and milk from the American fridge. I sit on one of the leather topped stools and wallow while Sandro takes teaspoons from a drawer and asks Mother where she keeps the sugar. It seems so ordinary, like we've called in for a cuppa and a chat. But something is amiss. She is too controlled; her eyes glitter and her smile is iron.

'Mother, why are you dressed in a kaftan?'

I shouldn't ask, but I can't help myself.

The orange, red and yellow kaftan is pressed sharp at the side seams. No creases show signs of her having moved in it at all. She resembles a cut-out-and-dress figure, one from the back of those ancient girls' magazines that Granny had in her attic. And she's clean. Her nails are blood red, manicured to perfection. Not a daub of paint anywhere on her.

'I needed something exotic today. Your father loved me in this.'

Did he? In the seventies, maybe. First time I've seen it, and I don't recollect it in any photos, either. I let it pass.

'Why did you need something exotic?'

She glares at me over the coffee machine, which gurgles and gives off the most aromatic scent. My mouth waters, despite my fury.

'I had some unsettling news.'

She rearranges the mugs, builds miniature columns with the cubes in the sugar bowl. I wait. Sandro, too.

'Detta called.'

'Sandro said.'

Her head whips back, her hair flicks over her shoulders. 'Did he tell you what she said? She is no longer a suspect. The police are following a new lead.'

With each utterance, her voice becomes shriller, until she shrieks at me across the kitchen unit.

'Aren't you relieved Detta's no longer under suspicion?' I try to keep my voice soft but hear its edge.

'But she did it!'

'Mother, you have no proof, and the police-'

'She had the motive. The opportunity. It has to be her.'

'How many of your pills have you taken?'

Sandro's sudden question cuts through the air, bringing us both to silence. We gawp at him. I turn to Mother. She looks away.

'I can't remember. Happy now? Proof your mother is a raving druggie. Why don't you call the unit and have them take me away? That'd solve all your problems.'

He's by her side in a flash and has her enfolded in a tender embrace.

'Don't, Mum. We know it's been hard keeping track since Dad left us. Where's your pill box?'

'In my bedroom.'

'I'll get it.' I scramble from the stool and hurry upstairs.

When I pull back the curtains, pale sunlight filters through the nets, lighting the room with a pastel glow. I search – on the bedside cabinet, in the en suite, in the dressing table drawers, even in her wardrobes. From the back of one wardrobe, I pull out a heavy wooden box. Locked. Jewellery, I imagine. She should invest in a safe. But no pill box. I return to the kitchen.

She's poured the coffees, and they sit chatting. She slides my mug to me, and the sugar bowl; the tiny columns collapse. I don't take sugar. Never have. I take my place on the stool and sip my coffee. Dark and rich, the fragrance overwhelms my senses. For a moment, I am in heaven.

'You didn't bring the pill box.' Sandro looks at me over his mug.

'Wasn't there. Tell you what, though, Mother, you ought to invest in a safe. Keeping your jewellery in an old wooden box won't stop burglars. One swipe with a hatchet, and they'd be in.'

She tuts. 'There's nothing of value in it. Don't nag.'

'So, where are your pills?' I ignore the insult. One comment, made for her benefit, doesn't count as nagging in my book. 'Are they in the studio?'

'Possibly.' She places her mug with great care on the counter. 'I'll go and look.'

'Shall I come with you?'

She looks at me as if I have suggested cavorting round the garden naked.

'Whatever for? I know the way.'

I shrug, and she pads off through the garden.

'What's she hiding, Sandro?'

'That she's taken too many pills. Although she's not as slurry as she was when we arrived. The crisis may be past; won't harm to check the box though.'

'What if she replenishes it before she brings it? I wish Dad was here. He always kept her straight.'

Sandro gives me a hug. I sink my face into his shoulder and let myself cry.

'How touching.'

We pull apart and I wipe my eyes with a manky tissue I find in my trouser pocket. She clutches the pill box in her hand. Don't think she's been long enough to tamper with it.

Sandro takes out his wallet and extracts a small piece of paper which he hands to Mother. 'Are these still the doses you're taking?'

She gives it a cursory glance and hands it back with a nod. 'I could do with more.'

'Then call the unit for an appointment. That's what they told you, if you're not coping.'

'I am coping. It would just help.'

He opens each section and, satisfied she hasn't overdosed, passes it to her. She clasps the box under her arm, close to her chest.

'Do I pass the test?'

He smiles. 'Yes. Put them away.'

While she's gone, I pour us another coffee. I'll reap a small reward from this time-wasting jaunt. I rummage in the cupboards for biscuits. At least they are in their usual place.

'How long has she been keeping her pills in the studio?'

'Since she started painting again, I guess.' Sandro shrugs. 'Why?'

'Seems odd, that's all.'

'Does it? Why?'

'Have you seen any of her paintings? Since Dad died?'

'Sia, what are you getting at? No. She never shows her work in progress.'

But before I can answer, Mother returns. She's brushed her hair and slapped on lipstick. What else does she keep in the studio? A change of clothes? A stash of gin? Who knows?

She smiles at me as she takes up her coffee. 'Lovely. I need this.'

'Are you feeling better now?'

'Yes. I think I may have over-reacted to the news of Detta. Kind of you to visit. Thank you.'

The day just became stranger. Has she ever thanked me, for anything? It's a start, despite the awkwardness inside me.

'You're welcome.'

I catch Sandro's eye. He's laughing into his mug. I want to leave.

'Time we were going. Vic's alone at the gallery.'

'Of course.' She smiles again and my skin crawls. 'Off you go.'

She must have the last word.

In the car, Sandro takes a tremendous interest in the road, the traffic and the conditions. He might want to avoid a conversation, but I must speak.

'Care to explain why we've wasted our time here? You gave me the impression she was in danger. For God's sake, Sandro.'

He doesn't take his eyes off the road. Suddenly a model driver.

'When we spoke this morning, she sounded at her wits' end. I was genuinely worried.'

'So worried you needed back up from me? Didn't take you for a wuss.'

'So worried, I thought you should be present, just in case.'

'In case what?'

'She didn't make it?'

'What? Is she suicidal again?'

'I thought she might be. Sorry. I was wrong.'

I stare out of the window at the passing scenery. Trees morph into buildings, empty roads into pedestrian-filled streets. I thought she'd succumb straight after Dad died but she didn't. Kim says we go through a numbness when someone dies. Maybe Mother's been numb and is now grieving. But she talks about him incessantly. Tells us how miserable she is without him. Christ, it's been hard enough to cope with my grief, let alone hers. Dad, you shouldn't have left her to our care. You're the only one who knows how to manage her.

We pull up outside the gallery. Sandro squeezes my knee and smiles sadly.

'Sorry, sis. False alarm. But one day, it might not be. I'm not sure she'll ever get over it.'

My heart is leaden, hearing the truth in his words.

'I'm sorry, too. Shouldn't have had a go. You did what you thought right.' I lean over and kiss him on the cheek. 'Like always.'

I climb out of the car and stand on the path to watch him drive away. He says she'll never recover from her grief and anger; that she'll take matters into her own hands. He's right. She always does.

CHAPTER TWENTY-TWO

FEBRUARY 9TH

The inquest into Daniel's death opens and is adjourned. It could take months, so Theo tells me, for it to re-open. The police must finish their investigations before it can be completed. Is this gruesome preparation for when Mother takes action? I hope not. Since my conversation with Sandro in the car, I can't erase the notion from my mind.

She's not insufferable at the moment; too occupied with memorial service arrangements and painting to wallow. Her courtesy towards me still makes me squirm. No doubt I should forgive and forget, but I am on edge, wondering when she will blow.

And if that wasn't enough to addle my brain, Daniel's magazine came out today. I had forgotten the precise date, too busy with Mother, but Vic remembered. He bought a copy and dropped it on the desk over an hour ago. I've been sitting here ever since, too afraid to open the bloody thing.

Betty's features blur. I dab under my eye with my finger while I scrabble for a tissue from my pocket. Daniel abhorred such things, but right now, I'm finding them indispensable. The cover is stunning: Betty's wholesome charm radiates from the glossy paper. She shines: the star she should have been. I flick the pages, the tissue pressed to the end of my nose, until I find the article. Mother peers out from the page, her expression shrewd and temptress-like; her cool glamour and mystery even more potent. It's impossible to see her when I regard myself in the mirror; how can others insist on a resemblance? I cannot read what Daniel has written for the words run together. I know what they say, how my reputation will rocket after today, but it's without meaning. How I'd love Daniel to saunter in, proud and confident, crowing over his triumph; teasing me for doubting. I flip the magazine shut and sit, my head in my hands.

I can't shift from my thoughts, clouded though they are, the suspicion of something awry in this. A fear I can't define strokes the edges of my nerves, makes my skin sit as tightly over my limbs as Lycra. I am captive within myself.

'Sia?'

Vic startles me. He's at the door and a young woman, clutching a large brown envelope, stands by his side.

Mascara blotches on the tissue give the game away. I rub under my eyes with my fingers, stuff the tissue into my sleeve and sniff.

'Vic. You need me?'

'This young lady needs you.' He comes in and gestures for her to follow. She reminds me of ancient photos of Mia Farrow. A chin length blonde bob frames her elfin face, and her blue eyes hold me in an unsettlingly steady gaze.

'Oh?'

She extends a hand. 'My name's Jade Hewson. I'm Daniel Rose's widow.'

The office is suddenly airless, like Vic's opened the hatch to my space capsule, allowing the void outside to rush inwards. Vic tilts his head at me and backs out of the room. He closes the door, and it's me and her in the vacuum. I reach out to shake her hand. Its warmth and firmness cut through the unreality.

'Please, sit.'

'You weren't aware he'd remarried?'

'No. No reason to; we had a professional relationship.' But they mentioned her in the articles after Daniel died; my brain wiped that bit of info, obviously.

Jade smiles a half-hearted smile. 'It was rarely that, with Daniel. But don't worry. I'm not here to accuse you of sordid deeds.'

'Why are you here?'

'Did he tell you his history?'

'A bit.'

She holds on to the envelope, frightened I will wrench it from her? Slender fingers make indentations in the paper.

'Did you know he had a fling with your mother?'

'What?' I laugh. What has he told her? 'Their relationship was *unusual*, not a fling.'

'Your mother's told you?'

She lacks any understanding of Mother or her relationship with Daniel. As though Mother might share an intimacy with me.

'Why does this matter to you? It happened years before he married you.'

We're of similar age, so I'm confident I'm right. My conversation with Jenny whispers through my head. She wasn't far off the mark regarding Daniel. I must tell her.

Jade relinquishes the envelope, placing it on top of the magazine. 'You need to see these.'

'See what?'

'Just open the envelope.'

It's heavy as I slide it towards me, my heart thudding to the rhythm of alarm. The envelope isn't sealed, so I fold back the flap and peer into the interior which is stuffed with photographs. I glance at Jade. She raises her eyebrows in silent instruction to go ahead. I tip them on to the desk.

I select a picture. A child of, I'm guessing, seven grins over her shoulder at the photographer, as she digs with her hands into a strip of sand on a shingly beach. I drop it and pick up another: the same little girl. She's dressed to go riding, her helmet pulled almost too low to see her eyes, and a crop held loosely in her hands. In yet another, she's older. Twelve? She stands outside a psychedelic shop front, holding up a pair of dangly earrings. Her delight with her purchase emanates from the photo.

'On the back.' Did Jade speak aloud, or did the order come telepathically?

Every atom of me contracts as though someone has squeezed me into a container half a size too small to enclose me. I turn the photograph, knowing what I will discover.

Artemisia. 1997.

Mother's graceful, whorled handwriting hasn't faded.

I delve into the pile. Birthdays, holidays, dancing competitions, a day in the garden, school plays: none of my milestones is missing. Tears course over my cheeks and I am helpless to stop them. I drop the photo of me holding a trowel, and it flutters on to the pile like a butterfly that's breathed its last.

'Why have you brought these to me?'

'You should see this, too.'

She opens her handbag and pulls out another photograph. She passes it. Older than the rest, it's obviously me. I can't understand why she's kept this one separate. I flip it to read the annotation on the back, but it's blank.

'Mother forgot to write the date. Your point is?'

Jade's cheeks flush and although it defies logic, makes her even more stunning.

'That isn't you. It's Daniel.'

* * *

Detta hands me a mug of tea and edges me towards a chair. I slump into its cushiony softness, thankful to be off my feet.

'How did she find them?'

'She found the envelope tucked into a filing cabinet, when

clearing his things.'

'Daniel denied having an affair with Heather, didn't he? Isn't that what you told me – after the debacle over the magazine?'

'Yes. But the photos don't lie, do they?'

Detta shakes her head and sips her tea. 'No.'

'Bringing me the one of Daniel was a master stroke.'

'Tell you what, though. I don't understand why; her motives. Won't she be scared you might make a claim on his estate?'

'Don't know. She's given me her details so I can get in touch. I liked her. Maybe she liked me.'

'Did you find your birth certificate?'

'Went straight home when she left. It says Dad's my dad.'

'Heather and Frank were married. That's the law. It gives assumption of paternity to the husband.'

'Is that right? That's something. I imagined being disinherited; Mother refusing to let me have what I'm due.'

Detta shifts awkwardly in her chair. She takes a sip of tea. 'I'm so sorry the studio's a problem. You'll get the value of the land, I imagine, once they complete the investigations. A developer'd love to build hundreds of homes on it. You'd make a killing.'

I snort into my tea.

'Sorry. Awful choice of words. But you get my drift.'

'Dad didn't legally leave it to me – just added it to a list of requests he made. Guess he trusted Mother to do the right thing.'

She ponders her tea as thoughtfully as anyone I've ever seen. Tina's death weighs heavily on her, I'm sure, but she never speaks of it.

'Detta, what happened at the studio?'

She sips, holds her mug to her lips longer than necessary, and eyes me over the rim. She coughs and lowers the mug. Her mouth tightens into a thin line. Have I spoken out of turn?

'I've played events over thousands of times, trying to put them in order, clear my head. I made a mind map to clarify just how they occurred.' She laughs without humour. 'Didn't help much, so I binned it.'

'I shouldn't have asked.'

'No, I'm glad you have. At last. I've been waiting for you to and tying myself in knots over it.'

'Why?'

'Because each time I relive it, I wonder if I'm misremembering, if I *did* start the fire. It's nonsense. I know I didn't, but the suspicion won't go away.'

'So, tell me what you remember. Might help to say stuff out loud.' Hark at me, going all counsellor on her. Kim would be impressed. And that woman at Ashgrove Bog.

'I suppose.'

She takes another sip of tea. Her hands cradle the mug. Will she tell me?

'I'd smelt smoke but ignored it. Assumed someone had lit a bonfire.'

She takes another sip of tea; licks her lips.

'I'd located the nudes. Sia, Frank's genius, the portraits…'

Her expression becomes wistful.

'As fresh as the day he painted them. The one occasion in my life I considered myself beautiful.'

Her smile is heart-breakingly poignant.

'I separated them from the rest and tried to concentrate on the others, but the portraits kept distracting me. My younger self, so assured, so loved. The paintings awoke memories long buried.'

If I lean further forward, I'll topple into her. Every muscle pays attention.

She shakes her head as though putting her thoughts in order.

'You can imagine my turmoil. I upbraided myself with comments I expected to come from Heather. I envisaged her crowing, which gave me the impetus to continue.'

As Detta speaks, Mother's voice sneers through my head, her

words edged with cruelty.

'I pushed my emotions from bygone years aside and focused on the task. I focused so effectively it took a moment to realise Tina had burst into the studio. It's possible I was smoke affected, even at that stage. She yelled something - fire? - but it made little sense. I watched her, in a daze, as she dashed towards me, waving her arms and shouting.'

'When did you realise you were in danger?'

'Not till Tina grabbed me and pushed me towards the door. She yelled, "The mezzanine." It was ablaze.'

She closes her eyes. She's reliving the whole thing. Why did I ask?

'I keeled forwards and staggered to the door, assuming she was behind me. Tina yelled again. As I turned, the mezzanine buckled, flames engulfed the spot where I'd been standing, and the floorboards from upstairs cascaded upon her.'

Oh, dear God. She witnessed it. I assumed Tina had gone back in to retrieve the artwork. Never dreamt she'd died this way. Wondered if Detta had created the whole life-saving story to… what was I thinking?

'I watched her die.'

Detta stares into space, the horror of her experience vivid in her eyes. Should I hug her? That's what I'd want, but something in her posture, so upright and contained, tells me no.

'Is that when you rang 999?'

'Not at once.'

What? I have such a strong presentiment what's coming next. She didn't, did she?

'In the doorway, the noise of the fire, its heat, and Tina disappearing into the flames held me transfixed. Then, I saw a rack of paintings where the fire hadn't reached, and I reckoned I could rescue them before the fire spread. I ran to the rack and hauled them out, one by one. When the flames were arcing over me, I decided it was too risky to continue. That's when I rang the emergency services.'

'Why didn't you call them straight away? You must have known we'd manage without the paintings?'

'My mind had entered a domain so foreign; I was under siege. Seeing Tina, an effigy cast into the fire.'

Would I have acted differently? Had I seen salvageable paintings, rescued them before calling for help? Or tried to help Tina? Despite the impossibility?

Detta drains her mug and places it on the table by her chair. She clasps her hands, her haunted eyes fixed on mine.

'Thank you for telling me. I don't understand how you've continued, with such a burden. Despite your fears to the contrary, Tina's death wasn't your fault.'

'I couldn't save her. It happened so fast. But responsibility weighs heavy on me.'

'Kim might help you.'

'Your shrink?'

'Yes. Why not?'

'You'll be suggesting group therapy next.'

'Seriously, she's helped me and Vic.'

She picks up her mug and nods at mine. 'Another cuppa?'

I hold out my mug, and she takes it from me. Her walk to the kitchen, shoulders back, and each step so decisive, tells me this subject is closed. Deliberate sounds of tea making follow, each gurgle, slosh and clunk another full stop.

What were we discussing before I asked her? The studio. That's why my thoughts strayed to the fire. Not surprising. Dad wanted me to have it. He told me on my sixteenth birthday.

'Why was Dad so keen for me to inherit the studio?'

Detta puts our mugs on the table and comes to sit on the floor by my feet. She rests her forearms on my knees, takes my hand in hers.

'The studio? Heather could answer, but I can't. But what I can say, with absolute certainty, is he loved you. From the day you were born.'

'How should I react? Should I be angry? They lied to me all my life. Grateful? For loving me? Nothing is as it was.'

'Everything is as it was. Frank was and is, in every respect, your dad. Heather is still your awkward, infuriating mother, Sandro your brother. That Daniel is your biological father doesn't change you from the person you were.'

No? And why is Mother so hideous yet Dad the one who loved me? Shouldn't he have been resentful, with a simmering rage at being cuckolded, lurking beneath the surface of his toleration? I must have been a constant reminder of her adultery.

'Show me the photo of Daniel.'

I pull the picture from my bag and hand it to her. She returns to her chair and studies it while she drinks.

'Good of Jade to let you keep it. Did you feel she was out to cause trouble?'

'No. She gave me the impression of genuine concern the effect her bombshell might have. Claimed she was unsure of her motives herself but felt compelled to show me. I liked that. Her doubting herself.'

'And she's grieving, too. We both understand how that messes with your head.'

She's right. Dozens in our circumstances struggling to make sense of a senseless world. Of feelings impossible to explain or describe. Which makes us, each of us, alone.

'Why did Mother send him the photos? He wasn't a presence until the exhibition. Of course; that's why he appeared then. Dad was out of the way. Was that kindness or fear? And was it me he wanted to meet or Mother?'

'I can't answer your questions. Heather has the answers you need, but I'm not sure she'll co-operate, are you?'

I finish my tea and clonk the mug on to the floor. 'Huh. She'd be awkward to frustrate me. He said he'd tried to avoid her, at the exhibition. And when I told her about the interview, she never said she'd seen him, so I can only assume he was telling the truth.'

'Don't confront her. Why don't you wait? Until you're used to the idea?'

'Used to the idea? You think that's going to happen? I discover at thirty-four the man I assumed was my dad isn't?'

Detta shrugs. 'People accept many sorts of circumstances – worse than this.'

I could wrench out my tongue. Living with the guilt, the knowledge someone died to save your life, must be worse. I make a swift change of subject; hopefully it'll appear seamless.

'What if he has a clutch of horrible problems hidden in his DNA I should be aware of?'

'Such as?'

'Cancer or something, something nasty lying dormant, only to surface at a particular age. I need to know.'

'Then ask for a DNA test.'

'Can I do that? On a dead person?'

'I'm sure, but check.'

The consideration of practical issues pushes my angst about my parentage and Detta's burden into the corner of my mind for a while. She invites me to supper, I accept, and we spend a pleasant evening during which we sometimes touch upon Daniel but mostly, we talk inconsequential stuff. And we don't mention the studio fire again.

At ten o'clock, as she's clearing away our coffee cups, she glances at the grandmother clock by the lounge door. 'Do you want to stay the night? Spare bed's always made. We'll have a brandy nightcap and go to bed.'

At her mention of bed, my limbs turn to lead. I'm more tired than I've admitted to myself. 'Yes, please. That'd be great. I can nip home in the morning to shower before work.'

'Don't be so soft. I've got everything you need, including a spare toothbrush. Do you want to borrow a pair of jimjams?'

So, after a quick change into Detta's fleecy PJs, I sit cradling a generous brandy in a goblet, needing two hands to hold it. The fire flames into my throat when I take the first taste. And my eyes water.

Detta laughs. 'You aren't supposed to neck it – it's quality stuff. Savour it. Let it roll around in your mouth before you swallow. Take your time with it. And stick your nose in the glass first.' She shakes her head, bet she despairs of me, and I do as she says.

'I'm not cut out to appreciate fine brandy.' The fire water sensation doesn't dissipate when I follow her instructions, but the smell is luscious and the feeling not unpleasant. I could get accustomed to it.

Later, in bed in Detta's spare room, I lie on my back, with my hands behind my head under the pillow. I've left the curtains and window open, so I can stargaze. An icy breeze plays over my face. The last time I spoke to Daniel, he told me his feelings for Mother, and how Dad warned him to stay away. They didn't have a proper affair. I wager, one night, they couldn't restrain themselves and that's what lead to Dad's ultimatum. He might not have known I wasn't his. But Mother knew. Did she tell him?

I turn on to my side, tuck my knees up to my stomach and fold my arms around me. I shall never know the truth. The photos don't prove I'm Daniel's. I shall organise a DNA test as soon as I can.

Sleep sidles towards me, my eyelids heavy and the warmth of the brandy lingering under the mint of toothpaste. It wraps its tendrils around me, and I fall into its darkness.

But a lightning revelation sweeps away my drowsiness. The paintings. Why didn't I notice it? The connection between them is so obvious. Tina Shaw shouldn't have died. Detta was the intended victim; as Vic said, she got there first. Mark enraged with his fawning and sycophancy. And Daniel. Daniel made the mistake of saying no.

.

CHAPTER TWENTY-THREE

The next day, Vic and I stand admiring the St Valentine's swags I've swung across the gallery. When I say Vic and I, what I mean is me. His hands rest on his hips and an expression that says he can't credit what I've done to the place haunts his face. If he's thinking bordello, I hope he keeps quiet.

'Has Jade replied?'

'No. Is that a positive sign, do you reckon?'

He shrugs. 'Don't ask me. Alien species, women.'

He trundles off towards reception. My mobile sits resolutely silent in my pocket, but I glance at it, anyway. Nothing. After how many hours? Oh. Two. I expect she's busy.

Enough of this. I head into the office and sit facing the sparkly new laptop. Anticipation glows within me. Sandro and I struggled to install the design program, but we triumphed, eventually. Now what's required is me to design stuff. How difficult can *that* be? We transferred my photos on to a memory stick before we wiped the old computer. My photos, on the desktop computer, resembled those hand-painted ones of ye olden days. On the laptop, they are vibrant and sharp, and my smugness goes into the stratosphere. Mother has even allowed me to design the order of service. I shove her to the back of my mind, where she sits, a tiger waiting to pounce.

Beside me, my mobile vibrates on the desk, which is on silent because Vic says he's sick to death of 'Waterloo'. When I've got a minute, I shall change it to one of Joni's. See what he makes of her. On the screen, Detta's face smiles at me. Not Jade.

'Have you contacted Jade?'

'Sent her a text first thing. Nothing yet.'

'Oh. When are you going to tell Sandro?'

'Not sure. Putting it off.'

Detta smiles, I can hear it along the line. 'Best not keep secrets. He'd be hurt if he discovered the truth another way.'

'I only found out myself yesterday. Give me a break.'

'Sorry. I meant to ask last night: how's the preps for the big day? Has Heather driven you mad yet?'

Mother smirks at me from her corner, runs her tongue across her half-bared teeth. I slide a heavy grey door and she disappears.

'No, surprisingly. Has been close once or twice, but she's behaving herself. I wish she'd let us see what she's painting.'

'Hasn't she given any clues?'

'Nope. Says it's therapy and she'll never expose them to public scrutiny. Pity. There's been interest in her lately.'

'So? How's it going?'

'Good. Yes. Sandro's been chasing up the people she wants to speak; most have agreed. The school is putting on a buffet for us in their grand hall, and the school choir will sing one of Dad's favourite songs. Mm. It'll be an okay event.'

'An okay event? You've worked wonders, by the sound of things.'

'Not just me. Theo's been a great help. Sandro, too.'

'How many are you expecting?'

'About a hundred.'

'Very intimate. Heather has odd ideas, doesn't she?'

I chuckle in agreement. 'But the guests are family or personal friends. No hangers-on this time. It will be different.'

'She knows I'll be..?"

'Don't worry. She's not got a problem with your attending.'

Mother has not vented her spleen towards Detta in recent days. Am I mistaken to hope she's come to terms with Detta not being the arsonist? I can't be sure. Can Detta hear my doubt?

Please, no.

'If she creates a scene, I'll make a hasty retreat.'

'She's been taking her meds in the right doses – Sandro goes round most days to check. And her behaviour is steadier.'

'I'm glad. Take care. See you soon.'

'Thanks for taking me in. Means so much. Bye, Detta.'

At once, the gallery phone rings, its ringtone bellowing to be noticed. I pick up the receiver. DI Smith. Haven't heard from him in a while and my heart skips when he says hello.

'We haven't forgotten you.'

'No, I understand. You're busy.'

'We are. More suspicious deaths than you could swing a cat at.'

'Pardon?'

'We've a particularly heavy case load of suspicious deaths.'

'Oh. I see.' Swing a cat at. That's a new one. 'You got a reason for your call, or have you missed me?'

He laughs, and I gasp at my impudence. I start spluttering an apology when he speaks.

'Can you come to the station? Answer a few more questions?'

'About the man in the line up? Didn't you arrest him?'

'We did. He's on bail.' He sighs. 'Judge didn't consider he posed a threat.'

'Oh.' This information is disconcerting. I've been carrying on, assuming they remanded him or something. Out of my hair, for sure. 'They've released him?'

'He won't bother you. Too risky when he's on bail. One false move and he's nicked.'

My laughter erupts. 'Real police officers don't say that.'

'You'd be surprised by what we say.' No, I want to talk to you regarding the studio fire, and Mark Hubbard.'

I'm plunged into ice. 'There's a connection?' My voice sounds far away, like someone else has spoken.

'I need to sort out things from both cases, and it's daft to haul you in twice.'

That wasn't a no, was it?

'Okay.' I turn the pages of my diary. Tomorrow, the printers. Next day, lunch at school with Theo and the head, followed by listening to the choir rehearse, my appointment with Kim. 'I could come on Friday. Booked up till then.'

'Right.' He sounds disappointed. I know that tone of voice anywhere.

'After work today?'

'If you don't mind.'

'All right.'

'Thank you. I appreciate you're a busy woman.'

Neither of us speaks for a moment. Has he something more to say? An air of expectancy hangs over me, mine I assume. I am a foolish woman, imagining emotions where none exists.

'Is there more, DI Smith?'

'I could wait till you're at the station…'

My mind riots; what can he have to tell me?

'But you could tell me now?'

He sighs.

'Your mystery man; he's Adrian Rose, brother of Daniel Rose.'

'What?' For all the sense he makes, the inspector could've spoken Japanese. Relief and confusion make a heady mix. 'Why would he threaten me with a knife?'

'A case of mistaken identity.'

'I don't understand.'

'He thought you were someone else.'

'But he called me by name.'

'He mistook you for Daniel Rose's widow.'

My head fills with white light, dimpled with shadows. I squeeze close my eyes, to rid myself of the electric candy floss clogging my brain.

'How did he not realise I'm not Jade? We're nothing alike.'

'He'd only seen her in wedding photos. Said he forgot her name, and it seemed appropriate that Daniel's wife would be someone arty. And the incident took place at night.'

Questions bombard my mind, so many I can't decide which to ask first. He interrupts my internal chaos.

'We've alerted Miss Hewson, but you've no reason for alarm. I don't expect Adrian Rose to cause any more problems.'

'How could the judge consider a knife-wielding man not dangerous? Why was he after Jade? Is she safe?'

'Miss l'Ussier, please. Don't panic about Adrian Rose. He'll more than likely leave the country soon; his work takes him to west Africa. It was a coincidence he was in the country when his brother died. He wants answers, naturally, but he's not required to remain in the UK. We can correspond by email.'

'Isn't he going to be charged? He had a knife, for God's sake.'

His sigh is filled with regret for telling me, thick and viscous as the malt Mother made us eat when we were kids.

'We *did* charge him; that's why he faced the judge. He explained his circumstances in Africa, where everyone in management carries a weapon - usually a pistol. Mr Rose claimed guns make him uneasy-'

He's interrupted, covers the mouthpiece with his hand and I strain to make out the words of urgent talking, but it's like they're under water. Their conversation is unfathomable. Bet it's PC bloody Gorgon.

'Sorry, Miss l'Ussier, I must go. I'll update you when you're at the station.'

He doesn't say goodbye, but the line goes dead.

I replace the receiver, my thoughts in chaos. Daniel has a brother who didn't recognise his wife; how bizarre. Where did the inspector say Adrian worked? Africa. He must have been abroad when Daniel and Jade married. So, why did he want to speak to Jade about Daniel's death? He could be afraid she's after Daniel's money and murdered him.

And why does DI Smith want to discuss Mark? I took for granted, after the post-mortem, I'd heard the last of Mark Hubbard. I told the police everything I could then. Did I leave something out? So much has happened since I can't remember. Has he interviewed Theo again? I grab my mobile. It's the middle of the morning. He'll be teaching or dealing with boys' problems. I shall have to wait. With a sigh, I drop the phone on the desk.

Every time I begin a new task, my head fills with questions about the fire, Daniel's brother and Mark, so I abandon the effort and pour myself and Vic a coffee. Thus armed, I head towards Betty for a chin-wag. There's only a handful of visitors, so I'm safe enough to speak to her – quietly, just in case.

She's thoughtful today, the spark in her eye muted by the cloudy weather, or maybe she knows my frame of mind. I am a basket case, no matter what Kim says. Who talks to paintings? Daniel. Claimed it was one habit he shared with Dad. And with me.

'Do you remember, Bets, when Dad and I included you in that disagreement we had over the redecorating? Said you and I were ganging up on him to persuade Vic carnation pink would contrast well with moss green.'

We were right. The place looks fabulous, and those shades are a perfect backdrop for the paintings. Two years later, the walls are as fresh as the day we painted them. Betty smiles more warmly.

'We're a good double act, you and me.'

My nerves calm as I sit here chatting to Betty. Harold is disinterested, so we've got time. The overcast day gives them a subdued air, as if they're taking a break from the responsibilities of life. Her gaze on the child distant now rather than adoring.

'Just been chatting with DI Smith. Turns out my knife-man is Daniel's brother. Betty! That means he's my uncle.' I hold my face in my hands as the shock of my revelation percolates through my brain. I need to direct my thoughts elsewhere, otherwise I might go mad. My muscles tighten with effort as I try to regroup my scattered feelings. My voice, when I continue the conversation, slithers through my clenched jaw.

'Mother is behaving herself. Which is unnerving. Is she up to something? She may still throw us a curve ball. We'll leave discussing your magazine cover until next time, you saucy minx.'

She twinkles and I drain my coffee. My jaw relaxes a smidgen.

'Got to go. Things to do, blah blah. Catch you later.' As I stroll away, a bloke sitting behind me on the bench facing the other wall calls, 'Cheerio.' I wave. He didn't realise I wasn't talking to him, and I hope he didn't catch my talk about Adrian.

An icy breeze brushes my arms. I scan the windows. None is open. The skin behind my ears prickles and in my throat, nausea. I sit on the nearest bench, icy apprehension breaking out, familiar and dreadful. Rubbing my arms makes no difference, the hairs refuse to be tamed, and they stand to attention under my sleeve. I grasp the mug, my knuckles white, and wait for the sensation to wane. I close my eyes; be gone. The discomfort persists.

I sense which painting I have landed before: the Butterworths in their garden. I picture it without opening my eyes. Edward Butterworth sits apart from his wife and her two sisters. His wife dandles their daughter, Ingrid, on her knee. Behind the women, their brother, Sebastian stands. An awkward group, Dad always says their unhappiness is clear.

I must look.

That Sebastian has gone comes as a strange relief. The prickles behind my ears subside. I tip my mug to my lips, but it's empty, so I sit dry mouthed, cradling the mug in my hands.

Without Sebastian, the painting is not so unbalanced as The Winning Hand. I stretch over to read the blurb. And nearly give myself whiplash when I pull back. I've written about Sebastian. Mentioned the brother, the awkwardness of the pose.

I must tell Vic. Get the photos up on the laptop. Prove I'm

right. I scamper to the office, swipe my finger across the screen and it bursts into colour. Fingers shaking, I open the pictures file and scroll down the icons till I locate the painting. And he's there. I click the icon. The family fills the screen, Sebastian looking at his sister, his hand on her arm.

'Vic. Vic, come here.'

I don't wait for him to reply. I run to reception. He's by the front door, messing about with the noticeboard.

'Vic.'

When I grab his arm, he begins to complain, but something about my expression, I guess, stops him mid-sentence. I drag him into the office, push him on to the chair and point to the laptop.

'Take a good look at that.'

He knows. Before I explain. He knows. He's on his feet and into the gallery in the instant. I sprint behind him, and we stand facing the Butterworths. My ears hum. I wait for him to speak.

'You've been right all along.'

He doesn't look at me but remains fixed on the painting. He reaches up and strokes the space where Sebastian should be.

'Remarkable. No evidence of his existing at all.'

'Apart from my photo.'

'Indeed. What can it mean?'

'Let's go back to the office.'

We stand gawping at the screen. Vic touches Sebastian and the screen zooms in on him, as if to shout out his existence. Vic recoils, taken by surprise, and I laugh.

'I'm going to print it; not taking any chances.'

'Eh?'

'Something spooky's going on. Whatever is tampering with the paintings might decide to tamper with the laptop.'

'Oh. Good idea.'

The printer takes an age to churn out a stripy, pale facsimile of Dad's original, but Sebastian appears.

'He's not as clear as the rest, is he?' I hand the picture to Vic.

'No. Have you got any ink cartridges? Put new ones in. See if that's any better.'

Changing the cartridges is a faff, so I've avoided it, but Vic's suggestion makes sense. I try not to swear as the cartridges fight back. I win the battle and press the print icon.

'Are you thinking what I'm thinking?' I hold my breath.

The printer slowly disgorges the picture.

Vic's hand rushes to his face. 'Oh my goodness.'

As the colourful and damp paper emerges, Sebastian is paler, a ghostly figure in the background. I snatch the sheet and we stare, lost for words.

Vic motions to the gallery. The picture still clammy, we return to the gallery, trying to affect nonchalance as we approach the painting.

A woman in running gear sits on the bench in front of the painting. Her head bobs to whatever she's listening to through her headphones. She smiles, pulls the phones from her head. She nods towards the painting.

'Your description's wrong. Where's the brother?'

'Yes, we've realised our mistake. We're taking it down - wrong painting.'

While Vic engages the woman in conversation, I prise the blurb from the wall and lift the paint, leaving a patch of white. Huh, so much for our pristine, fresh-as-the-day-we-decorated walls.

'I'll dispose of this and fetch the correct blurb.'

Vic makes his excuses to the woman and follows me. We slump on to the chairs, our eyes locked, not in disbelief but in disbelief's cousin - an unknown, unnamed emotion.

'What would happen if you printed more copies? Would he get paler and paler until he'd disappeared?'

I shrug. 'Don't know.'

The screen is black, so I swipe it again. There he is. Whatever is fading Sebastian from the painting and the prints doesn't seem able to erase him from the computer. An old-fashioned ghost. What? Did I really just think that? The cold sensation from before returns, creeping through me.

'Vic?'

'Hm?'

'I'm sure of one thing.'

'What?'

'Someone else is going to die.'

'Don't start that nonsense. We've enough on our hands with a haunted gallery, without you bringing murder into things.'

'I didn't say murder. But it's interesting that you did.'

'Well, we cannot doubt Mark Hubbard was murdered.' Vic blusters. 'And we don't know for sure Tina and Daniel weren't, do we?'

'No. You're right. I don't *enjoy* this hideous certainty, have no desire to knowing murders are imminent. I want nothing to do with it.'

I feel the hysteria in my voice; I don't want to be the manic woman trusted by no-one because she senses horrible events before they happen.

'All I want is a normal life.'

Vic takes my hand. 'I know that. But seems to me, you've no choice.'

'Should we bring in an exorcist?'

He laughs. He bloody laughs. 'Sia, let's try to work things out ourselves first. If we can't, we'll think about it.'

'What about the police? I can't tell them.'

'You're at the station after work?'

'Yes.'

'Say nothing. Kim and I may believe you, but police officers are sceptics. They won't take you seriously. Unless you accurately predict a murder.'

'Jeez, Vic. How am I supposed to do that?'

'Make connections between the disappearances and the deaths?' My mind goes blank, even though I'd convinced myself I could. I shrug my shoulder. 'I dunno.'

'Let's get back to work; lunch time eat something tasty from the market, and perhaps have another codge later.'

'All right. I'll try. I have loads to do.'

'What're you waiting for?' He claps his hands. 'Chop. Chop.'

'I'm on it.'

'I'll finish the noticeboard.'

How, I can't comprehend, but I work. A busy afternoon with lots of visitors no doubt helps. How weird, everything carrying on as usual when my life is topsy-turvy. When Dad abandoned us, I assumed my life couldn't become more confused; I was mistaken. Jade Hewson is the proof. Jade. I've been so occupied with visitors and the latest disappearance, I haven't checked my mobile. I dig it from my pocket, and I have a message from her, so I skedaddle to the office to read what she says.

She says no. Why? Didn't it occur to her I might ask for a test once I'd seen the photos? I wish I understood people better. Sometimes, it's a mystery what makes them tick. Any of them. I chuck my phone into my bag and slouch into the gallery to find Vic.

'Let's shut up shop. Last visitor left, what, an hour ago? No reason for us to linger – and you've got your appointment with the boys in blue.'

'Jade says no.'

'That is a shame. What will you do now?'

'Ask DI Smith if I can bypass Jade and ask the coroner.'

'Good idea, although you might make an enemy in the process.'

'If I can do it, I'll tell Jade. Want to avoid antagonising her. They may have separated, but I got the impression she still loved him.'

'You are so like your father sometimes. I can't…'

My eyes threaten tears. 'Thanks, Vic.'

While Vic does a last check of the windows and lights, I

pull on my coat, apprehension gathering in my gut. Will DI Smith give me more new information? Or make a link I haven't between the fire and Mark? He's not likely to have made the connection I have. Only a crazy person makes those links.

Despite DI Smith's reassurances, I check the entrance to the car park. Deserted. My drive to the station is frustratingly slow. All Yorkshire's ancient drivers, who pootle along at ten miles an hour below the speed limit, have congregated in Deerdale today. I shake my fist at them, impotence fraying my nerves. And, of course, there's nowhere to park. I crawl up and down the nearby streets until I find a space. It's a long, bitter walk back to the station. I've only got an hour.

I complain to DI Smith once we're sitting opposite each other in the interview room. No sign of PC Gorgon. Has she gone on holiday? Hope blossoms. The door opens and in she comes. Hope dashed.

'This won't take an hour. But if you get a ticket, I'll sort it.'

The gorgon grimaces, her lovely face contorted into her usual sneer. She has a note book and pen in her hands. I wait for her to say hello, but I could die before that happens. How DI Smith puts up with her, I'll never know.

He goes through the usual rigmarole, and the interview begins.

'Since we last spoke, our investigations have unearthed an interesting potential lead.'

'I read it in the paper.'

'Hm. Forensics show the murder weapon as being a specific firearm – one smuggled into this country from America. How familiar with guns are you, Sia?'

'Me? Totally unfamiliar.'

His question bewilders me. I've never even seen a gun, apart from on the telly.

'So, if I showed you a similar pistol to the one used, you'd not recognise it?'

'No. Why should I? Am I a suspect?'

'Not at this stage.'

'What?'

This isn't real. Any moment now, he'll tell me I'm the victim of a practical joke, dreamt up by the gorgon. I glare at her, but she's focused on her stupid note book. She doesn't pick up the vibes I try to send to her. Argh.

'Does any member of your family own such a weapon, to your knowledge?'

'No.' I fight the urge to career around yelling, 'No. Make the madness go away.' Instead, I hold my hands up to my head and try not to pull out my hair.

He opens a drawer in the table and places a wooden box between us. He opens it to reveal a pistol. I recoil, afraid it might go off and hurt someone. Me.

'Take it. It's not loaded, and it's not the murder weapon.'

'You want me to handle a gun?'

My life doesn't involve experiences this peculiar but my inner voice scoffs and nudges my memory. Paintings with people missing. My heartbeat drums in my ears, behind my eyes, the crashing rhythm almost visible as I stare at the gun.

'If you would.'

'Why?'

'It'd be helpful for our enquiries.'

The gorgon studies her note book throughout the conversation. She turns the pen round and round in her fingers, doesn't write.

He pushes the box closer.

I reach for the gun with my right hand. My fingers edge round the square barrel, its cold a surprise. I shake as I curl my fingers round it, bring the gun under my palm and lift. It slips from my grasp, dropping with a heavy thump on to the table. I haven't breathed out since I first touched it, but I exhale now, and, breathing in, try again. In seconds, the pistol nestles in my hand, its weightiness comfortable, edging on familiar. I slide my fingers through the bit where the trigger sits. My index finger fits snugly into its curve. How easy it is to hold. My astonishment overrides my repulsion.

'Thank you. You can put the gun down.'

I place it back in the box. 'Why did you want me to hold it?'

'We've little knowledge about American firearms in Deerdale. Our London colleagues tell us this is a weapon ladies choose, being compact, and, so the experts say, having less recoil than most. My interest? Watching an amateur, under duress, handle the weapon.'

'Have I ruled myself out as a suspect?'

'Unless you're a bloody good actress.'

The gorgon looks up.

'Sorry. Pardon my language.'

'But you know where I was the night Mark died.'

'Few alibis are as watertight as you might assume.'

'Is that the only reason you wanted me to touch it?'

'The only reason I'm able to give you, yes.'

'This scenario wouldn't be incongruous in a thriller on telly. You haven't got secret cameras set up, have you?'

He laughs. 'Nothing so sophisticated. And you're sure you've never seen such a weapon?'

'Absolutely.'

'Have you noted that, PC Broden?'

'Yes, sir.' She doesn't look up from her notebook. I'm convinced there's nothing written on the pages in front of her.

'Now, another thing.' He pulls a clear, plastic bag from the drawer. It's sealed, labelled and inside, looks empty. 'Examine this, please. Recognise it?'

I hold the bag up to the light. Inside, is a single, long hair which could belong to anyone, even me. I say as much.

'Forensics found it in Mark Hubbard's cottage.' He drawls,

with a smile, 'Not his.'

'Can they determine when it was left at the scene?'

He grins. 'Good question. On its own, no. They cleaned the cottages that morning. If he'd been entertaining lady friends before that, the evidence will now reside in a Henry or whatever cleaners use these days.'

I hand the bag back. 'Must be thousands of women with that colour hair. Have you checked if it's dyed?'

'Miss l'Ussier, we'll make a detective of you. It is dyed.'

'And can they age hair, like a tree with its rings or a horse's tooth?'

'Afraid not.' He puts the bag into a drawer and pulls out another. 'Now then, perhaps this will jog your memory?'

He pushes the bag across the table. This bag contains a spoon. Or a small shovel? A pretty thing, the shallow bowl is carved into a filigree eye. And the stem buckled in the middle. To lodge it on the rim of a cup, or a tiny bucket?

'It's a spoon or an ornate shovel for a fairy.'

'Very droll. It's an absinthe spoon. Found in the bathroom of Daniel Rose's flat.'

'Is that significant?'

'Could be. Haven't you seen anything like it before?'

'Never.'

I'd remember, I'm certain I would; the daintily crafted spoon would look at home in a museum display cabinet.

'Is it an antique?'

DI Smith frowns. 'Doubt it. They're made to look ancient, apparently, to enhance the absinthe experience.'

What's he talking about? Booze is booze, surely?

'Why might it be important, for your investigation?'

'Absinthe isn't usually a drink partaken alone, but by the nature of how it's enjoyed, a social experience.'

'So, you're saying Daniel wasn't alone when he died?'

'We think it's a possibility.'

'Then someone knows how—'

The gorgon coughs. She taps her watch. My hour's parking runs out in a few minutes, and despite DI Smith's assurances, I'd rather avoid a ticket.

DI Smith takes the bagged spoon from me and puts it away.

'Just quickly, then, the fire. A witness has come forward - claims they noticed someone acting suspiciously in the woods behind the studio; the time tallies with the fire.'

'Right.'

'They said the person had parked a car on the road adjacent to the woods, opposite their house.'

'So, you can trace the car? That's brilliant.'

'We can narrow it down to one in 400,000.'

'Oh.'

'Who'd have thought so many people drive blue cars?'

He holds me in his gaze. I shift my position on the seat.

'My car is blue.'

'And so is your mother's. And half the women in Deerdale. You ladies. Don't any of you prefer pink? Or red?'

'Would that make it easier?'

'Pink would. Far fewer of those.'

I harrumph. 'Not surprised. Who wants to go round in a car that resembles candy floss? Yuk.'

The gorgon actually laughs.

'Besides, when I bought my car, it was blue or blue. No other colour was on offer.'

'Yeah, I wondered 'bout that. PC Broden and I were saying before you arrived. We've both got cars in silver. Bought the same year.'

Where is this conversation leading? The time is ticking past, and I need to return to my car.

'Do you know anyone else who has a blue car?'

He says "anyone" but he means "woman"; of that I am certain.

Detta's is white, Jenny's is horrible gunky grey – and has been locked up in a garage somewhere since she took the Brussels job.

'Sorry. No.'

'Who, apart from Ms Jackson, might have cause to visit the studio?'

'Tina Shaw, obviously. Claire? But she'd come to the front, not sneak through the woods.'

'You reckon the person in the woods was heading for the studio?'

'Don't you? That's a leading question, DI Smith.'

'It's likely. Anyone else?'

'Only me, after the fire.'

He sighs. 'Someone knew of the path to the studio garden. When we searched the grounds, the gate was open. My officers gave it no importance. An oversight, I reckon.'

'Yes, an oversight.' The open gate. Which I closed. Will someone notice and alert the inspector?

'That's the reason you've ruled Detta's out as a suspect?'

DI Smith regards me with a suspicious smile. Jitters play Stravinsky in my gut.

'Something like that. We're done. Thank you for attending at such short notice.'

He and the gorgon stand. Neither asks me to sign the notes as an accurate record. He switches off the tape recorder, removes the cassette and moves towards the door. The gorgon opens it and allows him to go first. She glances at me.

'After you.'

We head to reception along the corridor in single file. Between them, I'm a prisoner destined for the gallows. Bit dramatic, Sia. But what about the notes she didn't write? Was this an official interview? Or has the DI gone rogue? I've been watching too much television.

At the main door, he pulls the great handle, and it creaks open.

Sound effects by Hammer House of Horror. I step into the night, glad to be making my escape. My shiver is a reaction to the temperature. Course.

As I pull out from the parking space into the evening traffic I remember. I've forgotten to ask if I can contact the coroner, bypass Jade. I'll just do it; see what happens.

CHAPTER TWENTY-FOUR

TWO DAYS LATER

I'm no further ahead. The coroner's sidekick to whom I spoke told me I could only request a DNA test if I was a blood relative or spouse. I need Jade's permission to have one done. Since she rebuffed me, we've not had any contact. She can't stop me having one, though, so I spent last evening browsing DNA companies on the internet. Who knew there were so many? The most local firm is in Leeds. That'll have to do, I suppose. And expensive. A hundred pounds a pop. I wonder why it's so costly? My bank balance may be healthy, but resentment at spending a hundred quid of my inheritance eats at me. Had Mother been honest, I'd be splashing out on wine.

The envelope of photos languishes in the drawer. The gallery is quiet, so Vic's happy for me to spend time double checking, and then choosing which DNA place to use. I pull the envelope from the drawer and tip the photos into a messy pile on the desk. Daniel's, I slip from my handbag and prop against the laptop screen. It hardly takes a moment to spread the photos, so each one is visible. Why did she send him so many? Could neither let go? I suppose they had me to bind them. My tenth birthday. I hold the photo between my thumb and finger, squint at it. No. This isn't the one. Back in the envelope with you. This one? We were on holiday in Surrey? Hampshire? Somewhere down south. A vague memory teases me, but I cannot make it come into focus. Anyway, it's not the one either.

One by one, I examine the photos, and each gets consigned to the envelope. When Vic pops his head round the door, the pile is much diminished, and my hope along with it.

'Any luck?'

I hunch my shoulders and try to smile. Caught in the act.

'I have found a DNA place. But haven't ordered the kit yet.'

He strolls in and eases himself on to the chair opposite me.

'Why not? That was the whole point?' He eyes the photos. 'What are you up to?'

My sigh comes from somewhere deep. 'This picture of Daniel. I'm sure there's one of me where I have exactly that expression. It may be in one of Mother's albums, I guess.'

I sweep the remaining photos into the envelope, put Daniel's in my bag and slip the envelope in the drawer.

'Sorry, Vic. Slacking on the job.'

'I'll forgive you if you order that DNA kit right now. No more dilly dallying.'

'I'm on it.'

He goes to leave but stops at the door.

'Have you talked to Kim yet?'

'No. Next time.'

'Good, good.'

I order the kit, spend the hundred quid, and close the laptop. With unidentifiable emotions running riot, I head out to the gallery to tell him I've done the deed. I don't have to complete the test. Although that'd be a monumental waste of money. Should I buy one for Sandro? If Dad is his biological father but not mine, our DNA will be different.

I'm back on the laptop in an instant, on the website, and changing my order. My bank account will complain, but it'll be worth it. No, it won't. Dad's money. There's no squirming my way out: now, I must tell Sandro about Daniel.

* * *

Sandro wears an expression I can't gauge as he goes through the photos, the one of Daniel in his hand. I wish he'd say something, anything. We've been sitting here in his studio for hours. I check my mobile. Twenty minutes since I tipped the photos on to the bench. I haven't mentioned the DNA tests yet. Something in his face stops me.

He drops the photo of Daniel, and it flutters to join the others. I wait. He shakes his head like he's trying to unravel his thoughts. Just like dad. The idea spears me, and I swallow the cry that threatens.

'Is she genuine, this Jade Hewson?'

'I Googled her, and she checked out. Besides, the bloke with the knife in the car park, the man I identified? He's Daniel's brother, Adrian. Police reckon he mistook me for Jade.'

'What? He's after Jade? Did they say why?'

'Nope. They've warned her he's in the country, but say he's likely to go abroad again soon, so he's not a risk. Despite the knife. Makes little sense to me.'

'What will you do now?'

I curl my top lip over my teeth, hesitating, but I must ask. 'I've sent for a DNA kit and requested Jade to arrange a DNA test to be carried out on Daniel.'

'Wouldn't it make more sense if I took a test?'

I can't stop myself grinning.

'You've ordered two tests.' He laughs. 'When will they arrive?'

'Should be soon. Do you mind?'

'Course not. You need answers; I would in your position.'

'Jade has said no to testing Daniel.'

'That makes no sense.'

'I'll ask again, but not by text. I'll call her.'

'Should have done that the first time. People hate being asked favours by text.'

'Do they?'

'Well known fact.'

'Let's hope I'm more successful in person.'

'Go and see her. Even better.'

'I don't know where she lives, unless she's at Daniel's. I can find out his address.'

'Do it, sis. It'd be much better. She'd be able to explain her hesitation and you could put your case more effectively.' He rubs his chin thoughtfully. 'Why not ask this Adrian for a DNA test? A brother's results would no doubt be as convincing.'

I scoop the photos back into the envelope, put the one of Daniel in my bag.

'You're right. I might put that to Jade. Should I call to say I'm coming?'

'Probably, but don't. She might refuse to see you.'

'True. I'm off. Still lots to do. Have you contacted everyone on Mother's list?'

He walks to the door with me. 'Yep. Maurice whatisname has agreed to give an address, so it's coming together.'

'Are you still okay with speaking? I couldn't.'

'I've finished writing it. Now got to practise.'

We kiss on the step, and I hurry through the February chill to my car, more settled than I've been since Jade arrived at the gallery. The city is majestic in the low winter sunshine, the tower of the Minster creamy rich in its glow. Mother would've loved to have held Dad's service there, the grandeur of it pandering to her vanity. The chapel at school will be more fitting and Dad would have preferred it. He'd rather have no fuss, but no doubt he's sitting on a cloud somewhere laughing at Mother's antics. Whoa. Hold on, Sia. You don't believe that guff. Remember?

* * *

Ten days later, Sandro and I sit, the laptop on the table in front of us in my sitting room. I open my email account and there they are, waiting for us to read them.

'Open yours first. You paid for them.'

I click on the email and open the attachment. Various charts fill the page.

'That one.' Sandro points at a table with coloured columns. 'That's the important one.'

I minimise the page and open the second email, and its attachment. It looks the same, but I peer at the table with the coloured columns, searching for discrepancies.

'Can you jiggle the attachments so they're side by side?'

'I don't know how.'

Sandro leans over the computer, presses the keys, and the screen divides in half. Our results sit next to each other, and the differences between them jump from the screen. Sandro's columns are more uniform in their shading than mine, which resemble sticks of rock left to fade in a shop window.

'There's your proof. We can see we're not full siblings. Let's compare our origins.'

He moves the pages to where pie charts show our heritage. At first glance they, too, are identical, but when I zoom in, everything changes. There on my pie chart is a slice of orange missing from Sandro's.

'What does that prove? Possibly, we inherited from different bits.' I sound desperate. 'That's possible, isn't it?' I look again at the screen.

Sandro doesn't reply. He scans the pages, frowning in concentration.

'I don't know. The DNA breakdown graph is convincing, whatever's in the heritage one. That's what you must show to Jade.'

'I'll print them both at work, so she can see the differences.'

He stands and stretches. 'Shall I make tea?'

'Good idea. Gathering evidence makes me thirsty.'

He ambles to the kitchen, and I stare at the charts, none of the information sinking in.

'Do you reckon the coroner will accept a commercial test?'

Sandro comes to the kitchen door, the tea caddy in his hands. 'Yes, why not?'

'I should have asked which ones they accept, before I bought these.'

The idea the tests won't be taken as genuine bothers me. I should have considered that.

'Don't worry. I'm sure it'll be fine. Didn't the website say it was an accredited company?'

'Whatever that means.'

We sit in silence while we drink. Sandro drains his mug. 'I'd best be on my way. Will you be okay?'

'Yes, you go. I'll be fine.'

On my own, I can read the results again. Hope I can make sense of them. Without a test on Daniel, it's still not worth much. But once Sandro has gone, I can't concentrate on the results. I can see the differences, but I don't understand if they're significant. I don't share Sandro's confidence in them. It's not him who's the outsider, though, is it?

A couple of fractious days later, I go and see Jade after work. Daniel's flat is on the first floor, up a narrow flight of stairs. I hammer on the door, the blows echo in the barren landing. She isn't here. This is a waste of time. I hitch the laptop under my arm and head back to the stairs.

'Sia? What are you doing here?'

Jade stands at the threshold of the flat, her hair wrapped in a towel, and her cheeks flushed.

'Oh, did I get you out of the bath?'

She laughs. 'Yes, but it doesn't matter. I was beginning to resemble a prune. You want to come in?'

She turns and walks along the hallway, so I scurry behind her and close the door. Under the scent of something floral, masculinity smokes out of the walls, the floor. She hesitates by a sitting room, gestures for me to enter.

'I'll get dressed and be right with you.'

Floor to ceiling windows make the room appear huge, though it's no bigger than my sitting room at home. Books cover one wall. Two enormous chairs take up most of the floor space. Too small to be settees, their curved backs and lush cushions are like settees for one. What a brilliant idea. I sit and have to curb the instinct to pull off my shoes and put my feet up. Opposite the book wall, framed articles and photos brag Daniel's success. What did his card say? Can't remember the words, but the wall shows their truth.

Jade returns. Her damp hair hangs round her face. She still looks fabulous. Wish I looked half as good with wet hair. She eases herself into the other chair, puts her feet up and wriggles herself comfortable.

'Now then.'

'I came to ask you to reconsider.' There's no point me not saying it straight out. 'I've had a DNA test, and so has my brother. The results are here.' I open the laptop and it fires up. 'Please, look at them?'

She doesn't move. I swipe my finger over the pad and the pages reload.

'I'm sure you'll agree they're conclusive, but they still only tell half the story.'

At last, she slopes, like a cat, from her chair. She squeezes in next to me, so I shuffle along to make room. Her slender body inclines into mine as she peers at the screen. She smells of spring. I slide the laptop over, so it rests half on my knee, half on hers.

'Mm. I see what you mean. I'm no expert, but it implies you're not total siblings, doesn't it?'

'It does. And the pie charts.' I zoom in, optimism daring to bud. 'Do you know if Daniel had any Russian ancestors?'

'Sia, I can't agree to a test on Daniel.' She pushes the laptop from her knee and returns to the other chair. 'Nothing makes sense at the moment. Adrian's turning up in the manner he did unsettled me and there's still loads to sort out here. And the media won't leave me alone; imagine the fall-out if they got hold of this. A daughter the same age as his widow? My life'd be in ruins, more than it is already.'

The tremors in her voice take the edge from my disappointment. Was I wrong to press her, to bludgeon her with my DNA results? It never occurred to me Jade might suffer at the hands of the media. Too wrapped up in my own concerns. I shut the laptop and stand.

'Sorry. I shouldn't have come. It was wrong of me to pester you. I'll go.'

She springs from her chair and grasps my arm.

'Don't be sorry. Believe it or not, I'm glad you're here. It's lonely with only Daniel's ghost for company.'

Her eyes fill with tears, and I'm torn; should I leave, or should I stay a while longer? It's possible we'd be friends, if we'd met in different circumstances, if Daniel were alive. My heart understands her isolation, the way grief cuts you off from others. But am I the person to help her, when she cannot help me?

'Do you want me to stay for a bit?'

She smiles, uncertain. 'Would you like a coffee?'

'Yes, that would be great. Thanks.' I drop my laptop on the chair I've vacated and follow her into the kitchen.

She assembles cups and saucers, fills the kettle and brings a cafetiere from a cupboard; fetches coffee from the fridge, and rummages through a cutlery drawer till she finds a small scoop.

'I don't know why I brought the photos to you. Would've been easier to burn them. Daniel had told me something of Heather and his tangled relationship with her, but never confessed to fathering a child with her. And then Adrian turns up. He can be troublesome. Refused to attend our wedding, claimed Daniel was disrespectful to Julia. God, she'd been dead years.'

'What did he want?'

Jade's sardonic laugh dies as she speaks. 'He's frightened I'll not allow him his due from Daniel's estate. It's a farce; they didn't hate each other, but they weren't close. Daniel has bequeathed him quite a large sum, so he should be happy. The police are encouraging him to return to Africa. Easier than dealing with another knife crime, so they tell me.'

'They told you that? Didn't have the courtesy to inform me; they fobbed me off with him posing no risk. Thought it dodgy.' Indignation swells within me, effervescent and bitter. I swallow hard, trying to rid myself of its rancour. 'You're very at home here.' Will a change of subject quell the anger?

'We lived here together for a while and then used it for holidays. I haven't taken liberties and made myself at home in my dead husband's flat.'

'Ouch. Sorry. Didn't mean it to sound so awful.'

'S'okay. I gave myself a stern talking to - it spooked me knowing he died here, but I was foolish to fear; he can't return from the dead.'

A half-heard snort whispers in my ear.

'My ritual baths are part of it,' she continues. 'That's where they found him.'

Her face darkens as she remembers. My throat constricts. 'Not sure I could do that. You're brave.'

She pours steaming water over the coffee in the cafetiere and fits the plunger on the top. 'Not brave. I pretend he's in the bath with me, holding me in his arms.'

'Can I ask – why were you separated? Sounds like you adored him.'

She presses a timer, the numbers bold on its over-sized screen. 'I still do. We wanted different things. We loved each other, but sharing our lives wasn't possible.'

'I liked him. Had a connection with him immediately.' I laugh. 'Never dreamt it might turn out so close.'

She smiles. 'His greatest wish was to be a father – properly, involved, present. I've never been maternal, never interested in domesticity. But he wouldn't accept it. Kept saying I'd change, it's what's natural. Not for me.'

'Me neither. I know exactly what you mean.'

'Really? But you don't have a nagging husband.'

'No, not quite.'

'What?'

'Theo, my boyfriend. He's keen on the marriage and family stuff, too. Makes life difficult.' A tiny frisson of guilt zings through me. Should I be telling her this? 'I probably should shut up now.'

But standing here talking to Jade feels so natural, like we've been friends for years, despite her refusal to grant my wish for the test.

'Maybe you should. How do you like yours?'

'Men? Or coffee?'

'Coffee. You can share your tastes in men another time.'

We laugh as she hands me my drink, white, no sugar, and we return to the sitting room.

'I suppose if the press finds out Daniel was my father, it'd be awkward for my family, too. I'll be honest, I hadn't given that aspect of my search any thought. My selfishness shames me.'

'Don't let it; in your position, I bet I'd have reacted the same way.'

'There are so many unanswered questions.' I shake my head. 'Does it sound wacky to confess I'm not sure who I am? Detta, Dad's agent, reckons nothing's changed, but she's not living in my skin.'

'Not wacky, no, but your Detta's right. You don't stop being who you are based on new information. Your character, your life experience, your expertise, loves and hates - they haven't altered a jot.'

Her words make sense academically, but my heart remains unconvinced. She would counsel such; it'd stop me pursuing the truth via a DNA test on Daniel. She sits opposite, seeming so composed and sure of herself. For a second, irritation flares, but it dies as soon as it sparks. I mustn't forget she's in the same position as me, trying to come to terms with loss. She isn't confident; it's a guise, a ploy to cover her hurt. I'm not fooled.

'Thanks for the coffee. I must go.'

I can't believe I've told her so much, when we hardly know each other. Isn't Jenny my turn-to in times of need? How would she feel, knowing I've spilled my worries to Jade? I take the cup and saucer to the kitchen, pick up my laptop and stand facing her. She uncurls from the chair, comes to my side, and squeezes my arm.

'You're welcome, anytime. Thank you for understanding.'

'Jade, I must be straight with you: I intend to confirm whether Daniel is my father, somehow.' A voice in my head presses me to tell her I'll ask Adrian if he'll take the test, but the expression in her sad blue eyes holds me back. 'One day, I will discover the truth. And you are responsible for my needing to do so.'

She lowers her gaze. I may have been forceful, but I must make her aware that I'm not abandoning my search.

'I understand.'

She looks up, our eyes meet, and I am certain she speaks with honesty. Jade is a woman of integrity; I want us to be friends. I kiss her on the cheek and hasten to the door, giving myself no chance to see if she's horrified or pleased.

CHAPTER TWENTY-FIVE

MARCH 14TH

'Part of me wants to confront her, tell her I know.'

'And the other part?'

Kim shifts on her chair, tucks a stray hair behind her ear.

'Reckons it best to keep quiet. Mother's getting wound up because the service is fast approaching, despite her only input being to supply names and addresses. She's trying to behave, and the effort is shredding her nerves.'

'What effect is that having on you?'

'Not sure.'

She tilts her head in question, a small frown on her face.

'Two issues rage within me. The one concerning who my father is and the one…' I bite my bottom lip. 'The other one is…' Can I say this aloud? Without Kim calling for the men in white coats? 'Mother has a connection with the deaths.' I can't bring myself to say what I suspect.

'A… connection?'

I should've kept quiet. Now I'm forced to explain, and it sounds barmy. My legs are full of grasshoppers. I spring to my feet and pace the room while Kim sits in a pool of stillness. I need to gather my thoughts into a semblance of order. Order? That would be a first.

'It's always me who sees there's someone missing, and no-one has disappeared from paintings by other artists. Only from Dad's.'

Outside, visible from my vantage point by the window, back-to-back gardens shiver, abandoned in the winter sunshine. Three gardens down, a lone child bounces without enthusiasm on a small trampoline. Even from this distance, the poor kid looks nithered. Why isn't he at school? Why aren't I at work?

'So, if I'm not hallucinating, someone is making this happen. The only logical culprit is Dad. Huh. Logical. Listen to me, gibbering on about logic when there is none.'

'How does it make you feel, this idea your father is trying to contact you?'

'I've told you before, I don't believe in the afterlife, ghosts and such. So, angry. Foolish. Scared. Take your pick.'

Now I've spoken the words aloud, anger rises within me. It simmers in my chest like hot lemonade, acidic and discomforting. How does she expect me to feel? Sometimes she makes me want to scream. How do I feel? For God's sake. I turn from garden gazing.

'I was eight when I decided. Dad knew this, so what's he trying to prove? It'd make more sense for him to contact Sandro. Or Mother.' But if he'd done that, I would have scoffed, told them they were crazy. Christ, his choice makes sense. I flump on to the chair, the anger suddenly gone.

'If I concede there's an afterlife, and Dad is trying to contact me...' My heart clenches. 'He's chosen me because I'm a sceptic. If I believe, so will others. And he wouldn't contact Mother because she's the-'

She's staring at me, the warmth in her eyes replaced with a steeliness I've not seen before. Like she is struggling to maintain her professional persona, like she's battling not to say something she shouldn't. She glances at the clock; her subtle signal I've had my allotted time.

'It's the service the week after next and I'm expecting things to get hectic so, can we skip a week?'

'The following Monday? I can see you at 11 o'clock?' She holds her pen over the page in her diary.

'Yes, that's good for me. I'll see you then.' I put the appointment in my mobile, sling my bag over my shoulder and make to leave.

Kim grasps my arm as I reach the front door. 'Sia?' Her face is grave. 'If you have any suspicions, you must inform the police.'

So, she *did* understand what I was getting at. She's worth every penny of Vic's money.

'Right. I will.'

She still stands at the door when I drive away, and when I look in the rear-view mirror, she's watching. Anxiety creeps through me. She won't divulge our conversation to anyone, will she? Don't be stupid, Sia. You didn't say it, did you? What could she tell them? I've never asked her if the police have questioned her. Would she tell me if they had?

* * *

Vic stands before The Butterworths, his head cocked and intense concentration in his eyes. I sidle up next to him and wait to be noticed. The painting looks perfect. Were it not for my photos, I'd doubt I'd ever seen Sebastian standing there.

'This one's the best yet. No-one could tell.' He shakes his head. 'What's he up to, eh?'

'Have you gone all new world on me, Vic?'

'Can you explain it otherwise?'

I'm not ready to explain my step towards conversion and, standing here, the foolishness I experienced at Kim's pours through me. This intuition stuff is rubbish. Why did Kim allow me to jabber on, not halt my sliding into the ludicrous world into which I sank?

'No.'

'What does your intuition tell you?'

That instinct cannot be trusted; parents pass their foibles on to their children; some things cannot be explained. 'Nothing.'

In my head, the clanging of infinite doors echoes as I slam each one shut. Behind them, intuition, instinct, insight - call it what you will-is muted; its voice murmurs like the ripple of waves on a sandy beach inside a shell.

'Are you sure?'

'Yes, why?'

'You've been so adamant about the others.'

My conversation with Kim plays through my mind. 'Things to do. Better do them.'

I stroll away from him, affecting an air of nonchalance. In the office, alert in case Vic follows me, I open the laptop to stare once more at the photo. Sandro. Is he the next victim? What has he done to annoy Mother? I glance at the calendar; it's weeks since Sebastian disappeared. The other deaths happened within twenty-four hours. So, Sandro could be safe, but I'm not taking any chances. I pick up the phone and dial.

'Sandro, have you and Mother argued?'

'What? No, why?'

'The last disappearance.'

'For heaven's sake, Sia.'

'It's bothering me.'

'Why?'

'No reason. Forget I called. Sorry.'

I drop the receiver on to the cradle before he can respond. The closed doors allow tendrils of ideas to float under them and into the forefront of my thinking. Nothing is defined, yet I cannot dislodge the conviction. Beneath the muddle, the ludicrous twitching of my subconscious, lurks a truth I don't want to acknowledge. I push it back, behind the notions clambering for my attention. But I will be on my guard. If something happens to Sandro, it will be my fault.

CHAPTER TWENTY-SIX

A WEEK LATER

The boys' voices warble the familiar song, coming to a crescendo that echoes in the arched ceiling of the chapel, giving it a lyricism I'd never appreciated. Mother's eyes shine with tears. She lets them tumble down her cheek and splash on to her clasped hands. My own eyes sting, the choir out of focus. The song ends. Hush falls upon the congregation. Feet shuffle and the pews murmur as people reposition themselves.

Sandro walks to the front, the papers in his hand shaking, as he places them on the lectern. He stands straight and tall, faces the gathering. My heart swells with pride and apprehension. We have gone through his speech a hundred times, but here, in front of these people, the importance of his words hits me. I wring my handkerchief in my hands and will him to stay strong. And, from the corner of my eyes, keep watch on the gathering. So many unknown faces. It could be anyone.

'I must begin by thanking you, on behalf of my mother, Sia and me, for attending today's service. It's almost a year since fate took Dad from us, and it gets none the easier.'

He looks at Mother and me, smiles sadly, glances at his notes.

'The public never knew the real Frank l'Ussier. They convinced themselves they did, but their familiarity was with his portraits. The tantalising glimpse shown through his paintings told little of the man he was to us, his family.

'To our mother, he was a constant companion; one who gave her strength in tough times and self-belief in her own artistic talents. A man who adored her yet gave her the freedom to grow into the woman she is today, never stifling her or hindering her career when at the peak of his success. He never stopped encouraging her to greater things. She says she achieved her best work when he nagged, wittered and got on her case. Without him, her muse is gone.'

Mother sobs. I pass her a clean handkerchief and she dabs her face daintily, her slender fingertips muted in their neutral polish.

'But Dad needed her, too, and always acknowledged she was his inspiration, his joy, and his reason for getting up every day.

'For my sister, Dad was a guiding star. When it turned out her talents were not artistic, in the same way as his and Mum's, Dad guided her towards art history. Because he believed in her ability to appreciate art in this different way, Sia is now a successful curator of one of our city's most prestigious galleries.

'He was my everything as I developed my passion for sculpture, breaking from the family tradition of painting. Though *his* chosen medium was paint, he excelled at sculpting. He helped me with my early pieces, so I won competitions and secured a place at the best art school in the world.

'This isn't where Dad's influence ended. The school, whose chapel in which we are gathered, every year awards a trophy in his name for artistic achievement. And so does the biggest state school in our city – the one most often in the headlines for its problems. From that school, eight winners of Dad's trophy now have careers deeply involved in the art world. Children from families where no-one has shown interest in art, never handled a paintbrush, even to decorate their homes, nor moulded a lump of clay into a recognisable shape. Because Dad invested in them, eight such children achieved in ways they dared not dream.'

Sandro's voice rings out, vibrant and strong. Nobody moves, all held in the power of his words.

'At home, he was Dad, but he was extraordinary here, too. A more loving, interested, and interesting man you could never meet. He blessed our home with his laughter, his conversation, and his constancy. For us, he was our anchor, and we are adrift without him. We miss our marvellous, warm and generous father, but we are grateful he was ours to love and look up to, grateful for his guidance and his care. Without him, we'd not be the people we are today, so we ask you to join us in giving thanks for his presence in our lives.'

It begins as a tentative suggestion of applause, but soon the chapel fills with it. Sandro picks up his papers and comes back to sit with Mother and me. The clapping echoes from the walls, rising to fill the arches like the beating of thousands of birds' wings. We sit and let the noise envelop us while everyone behind us rises to their feet. And it doesn't stop. Mother tucks the handkerchief in her jacket pocket, and smiles to herself, radiant as if Dad were here and they were taking the applause together. Sandro looks at me over Mother's bent head. We share a smile.

The headmaster walks to the lectern. He coughs, his hand over his mouth. Those on the front rows take their seats and gradually, everyone sits and the clapping dies.

'Ladies and gentlemen, friends, and family – please join Heather, Sia, and Sandro in the refectory for refreshments. You'll also find the book of memories Sia has designed - please, share yours; we've provided pens. And continue celebrating Frank's life in a more informal setting.'

This is our cue. We stand in unison. Sandro takes Mother's arm, and he leads her through the congregation. I follow them outside into the spring air.

* * *

'Touching words, Sandro. Did your father proud.'
'Thanks, Uncle Isaac. Isn't Auntie Marian with you?'

'No. Someone has to man the fort. Can't trust these stand-ins. Pinch half your takings.'

He leers at me, and I try to smile. Poor Auntie Marian. I'd have liked her to be here, but she's no doubt enjoying the break from Uncle Isaac.

'Where's this memory book? Ought to jot a few ramblings for little brother. Wrong way round, of course. Should have been me first.'

His face crumbles, and his eyes fill with tears. I take his arm.

'Let me show you. I bet you've got lots of cracking stories.'

He laughs feebly. 'I'll say. He was a bugger when we were lads.' He squeezes my hand. 'Not sure they'd be suitable for your book.'

'Why don't we read what others have written? You might have to liven it up!'

'Possibly, possibly.' He scans the gathering. 'Do you know these people?'

'Nope. But Mother does. And that's what matters.'

Mother is surrounded by the great and the good, the beautiful people she's known for a lifetime, who jostle to have her stardust fall upon them. I guide Uncle Isaac to the table with the memory book. Bill sits, writing in his graceful style, a memory in danger of filling a full page.

'Look sharp!' Uncle Isaac erupts into laughter.

Bill stops writing and turns to see who's addressed him. He shrugs, raises an eyebrow at me.

'Oh, it's you. Nearly done.' He signs his name with a flourish at the end of his memory and tucks the Mont Blanc pen into his pocket. 'All yours.'

He kisses me as he makes to leave. 'Very nice service, Sia. You and Sandro have made this a day to remember, especially for your mother. Now, if you'll excuse me, I promised I'd chaperone Detta. Just as a precaution.'

'Wise move, although Mother's on excellent form at the moment.'

'Let's not tempt fate, eh?'

He strolls away towards the refreshments. I can't see Detta anywhere. Until she waves. Bill responds and cuts across the crowd to join her at a far table. A couple, with matching white hair and reminiscent of characters from a Victorian novel, keep her company. Smiles and expansive hand gestures animate their conversation. I shall make sure she's introduced us before the end.

Uncle Isaac scribbles in the book, leaning close so no-one can read over his shoulder. As he's engrossed, I head back to Sandro. He's deep in conversation with someone else I don't recognise: a man who looks like an extra from a sci-fi film. Where does Mother find these people? Rent-a-weirdo?

'Sandro, introduce us?'

The gentleman with the green man-bun dips in a low bow and I try not to giggle. He takes my hand and kisses it. 'Artemisia. We meet at last.'

I pull a face at Sandro.

'Sia, this is Mother's old friend Alan.' He is so not an Alan. Sandro frowns, pretending he's annoyed. 'They were at art school together.'

'Good to meet you, Alan.' I sound about fifteen, my voice squeaky and barely under control. Where's Jenny? I have to introduce her to Alan. 'Have you come far?'

'Civilisation. Surrey. What possessed Frank and Heather to live in the wilds of Yorkshire, I'll never understand.'

'Family history. Generations ago, that's where Dad's family originated. Back to our roots.'

'How ghastly. Some things should remain a family secret. However, I'll admit Deerdale is a sweet little town, and St. Bede's - oh, divine. Love it.' He leans in and whispers in my ear. 'But those accents. Oh, dear.'

I giggle now. Alan is wonderful.

'Alan, how come we've never met? Everyone should have an Alan in their lives.'

'We have met. Don't you remember? When you were little, you came on holiday with Heather. Three, four times you visited us.' He spears me with his playful brown eyes. 'You can't have forgotten those times?'

Something emerges from the murky depths of my mind.

'Did you have a big, hairy, and smelly dog?'

'You wretch. That was Bengo. He was a sweetie, but I recall you never took to him. Bet he reminded you of a woolly mammoth.'

'I remember now, yes. How funny. I'd forgotten. Do you remember those holidays, Sandro?'

'Sandro didn't come. He stayed at home with Frank. Father-son bonding, all that nonsense. If my recollections are correct, he was showing signs of talent, even then, with that malodourous moulding stuff children are so fond of – you know the multi-coloured dough. Always ends up brown.' He wrinkles his nose as though he can smell the offending substance.

'Didn't we ever visit together?'

'No, darling. Heather said travelling with two children was too traumatic. Can see her point, can't you?'

'Suppose. What a shame. We mustn't lose contact after this. Sandro and I'd love to get to know you again, wouldn't we?'

Sandro grins. 'Yes. And Mother, too. Could you bring yourself to come to Yorkshire again? As our guest?'

'You're making free with Mother's hospitality.'

'I know. But don't you think it'd do her good?'

'Darling boy. I shall ask my better half. See what she says. Anything to assist the luminous Heather recover.' He searches the crowd, and his gaze settles on Mother. His adoration is impossible to mistake. 'Oh, there she is, with her now. I shall saunter over and see what she says.'

Sandro and I exchange bemused glances. Mother talks to a

dapper man in tweed, who holds her hands in his, as if they were porcelain, while they talk. It's the man who gave such a witty address in the service.

'She?'

We link arms and thread through the crowd following Alan, to join him, Mother and Alan's better half.

'Sandro, Sia. You've met Alan? This is his partner, Maurice. Come and say hello. They were both hopelessly in love with me at art college.'

Maurice reaches out to shake our hands. He twinkles at us from behind steel-rimmed glasses. 'It's true. And then, we met Frank and fell in love with him, too.'

The three of them laugh, sharing a warmth which makes pangs of envy shoot across my heart. Maurice puts his arm round Mother's shoulders.

'This enchanting creature is responsible for more broken hearts than Helen of Troy and Cleopatra combined.' He stares at me, his expression softening. 'You are the image of your mother. I bet you're a heart-breaker, too.'

Sandro and I speak as one.

'Not me.'

'Yes, she is.'

I dig my knuckles into his side. He topples sideways, pretends he's in agony.

'I am not. Broken no-one's heart. That's your domain.'

He holds up his hands. 'Guilty as charged.'

'If you'll excuse us, we need to do the rounds. Nice to meet you again, Maurice.' I pull Sandro in my wake and head for the food.

We make small talk while trying to balance buffet food on our plates and mingling with the guests. It's fun, strangely. Mother's idea of close friends is interesting. Many of the attendees haven't spoken to her or Dad since God was a boy. I reckon she's gone through an old address book or Christmas card list and filled the place with folk from their history. Not criticising, although it makes spotting would-be assassins harder. I nearly choke on my vol-au-vent. Sandro pats my back while my eyes stream and I try not to spray pastry across those nearest to us. He grins.

'You need a glug of water, or wine. And I must be elsewhere. Don't fret; I'm only nipping out for a minute.'

'But…'

He dashes away. Any reason I can conjure to persuade him to stay with me stuck like a limpet to his side, dying in its infancy.

Jenny approaches, her plate held above her, so she doesn't spill the contents on some unsuspecting person as she squeezes past.

'Sia.'

Her tone is urgent, her expression grave. Now what?

'Sia, you need to come and sort out Uncle Isaac.'

'What? Why?'

I scan the room. 'Where is he?' I can't find him in the obvious place, the bar.

'Outside. With Bill.'

'Oh, God. Are they arguing again?'

'Bill's not. But Uncle Isaac is drunk.'

'I'm on it.'

I shove my plate towards her, and she takes it. 'Go out the side door. That's where they were.'

Their voices come loud through the open door; Bill's more modulated, Uncle Isaac's slurry and hostile, his words running together.

'I'm still waiting. It's been a year, for Christ's sake. How long do these things take? Have you no idea of my financial responsibilities? I need that money.'

'I am aware of that. It's inappropriate to be having this conversation now. Come and see me tomorrow, in my office.'

'You call me to your office, as you might a naughty schoolboy? You should get off your arse and pay me a home visit. Are you aware who pays your wages?'

'Yes. Heather. Not you. Now, please calm yourself. You'll spoil the party.'

'To hell with the party. Didn't a funeral and an exhibition show enough adoration? This is an indulgence.'

I hesitate at the door. Bill sits at a picnic table, smoking a fat cigar. Uncle Isaac, red in the face and his shirt tails hanging out beneath his jacket, stumbles as he blunders around Bill. I cannot just stand here.

'Uncle Isaac, shall we go for a stroll round the school grounds? Take the air?'

He swerves mid-pace, glowers.

'I'm getting air, foolish girl. Go away. Men talking.'

I step out of the refectory. 'Please don't be mean. Come on.' If I speak any more pleadingly, I'll throw up. 'Sort this out another day.'

'Isaac, what are you up to?'

We swing in unison to face Mother, who has crept up behind me and now stands with her hands on her hips, glaring at Uncle Isaac. She marches over to him, grabs him by the shoulders, turns him round and pushes him back into the refectory.

'Leave this to me.'

Bill takes a drag on his cigar.

I sit opposite him. 'He doesn't improve, does he?'

Bill shakes his head. He exhales a great plume of smoke, which diffuses into the air. 'No. And it's a pity. Settlement is close at hand. I understand things at the pub are difficult, but ranting at me won't get matters sorted any more expeditiously.'

'How bad are things at the pub?'

Bill shakes his head.

'Oh, you can't say?'

'No, no. Not that I can't. Not sure if I should.'

'Didn't realise. Thought the pub was a roaring success.'

'The visitors enjoy it. But not enough to cover the overheads. He's made one or two, shall we say, questionable investments? But I've said too much.'

I listen for trouble within, but there's no sign Uncle Isaac is still misbehaving.

'I'll see if Mother needs any back-up.'

Bill laughs. 'She won't. But do check if it makes you feel better.'

I discover Mother and Uncle Isaac outside, on the far side of the building. They sit on a bench. Uncle Isaac cradles a glass in his trembling hands. I hope it's water, not gin, he's drinking.

'Mother.'

She turns at my call and beckons me to her. Uncle Isaac's head droops. His face is flushed, and he sways, so Mother puts a steadying arm round him.

'Sia, I'll take Isaac home. He needs to go to bed.'

'But, it's your do. You can't just leave.'

'Yes, I can. I've had enough. And there's no-one else who can handle him when he's in this condition.'

'We could sling him in a taxi.'

'We could not. He's family.'

I don't know how to respond. She hates Uncle Isaac. What on earth has brought this on?

'Mother, do you really-'

'I'm taking him home. Don't argue. Apart from anything else, I'm the only one here who's sober enough. You can't drive. I've seen you swilling back the wine.'

'That's not true. I've had one glass.'

She hoicks Uncle Isaac to his feet. He drains the glass and drops it on the bench. It wobbles on the edge, held in suspension by an invisible thread which snaps, sending it crashing to the ground. Shards of glass fly in all directions.

'Sort that out. I'm going to take him home.'

They make a sorry pair as they hobble across the green to

the car park. Uncle Isaac's footsteps are heavy and deliberate as he tries to stay upright. His shoulders hunch with the effort. Mother walks with purpose beside him, matching her steps with his to keep their balance.

Something akin to dread washes over me as she opens her car door and bundles him in, like an over-full shopping bag. She slams the door and walks round to her side of the car. Will she look back and wave? She drives away. I dig my mobile out of my pocket and dial Auntie Marian's number.

'Hello dear. How's it gone?'

A backdrop of conversation and laughter, people cheer. A darts match in progress.

'Good, thanks. Look. Mother's on her way with Uncle Isaac. He's worse for wear, I'm afraid.'

'Is he? Wouldn't have thought he'd have time. Oh, well. It's good of her. Had enough, has she?'

Auntie Marian has no illusions about Mother.

'Something like that. Thought you'd appreciate being prepared. He looked pretty sozzled when they left.'

She doesn't respond at first. I wait for her to speak. When she does, she's brisk.

'A good night's sleep'll do the trick. Thanks, Sia.'

'Bye.'

The conversation doesn't comfort me as I expected. I need to find Sandro.

Inside the refectory, I find him and explain what happened. We go together to locate someone who'll have a dustpan and brush. Behind the storerooms towards· the rear of the building, we discover two bar workers enjoying a cigarette. They jump up from their make-do seats on a couple of crates, throw their fag ends on the ground, and stamp on them.

'We need a dustpan and brush. Someone's broken a glass outside the refectory.'

The lad nearest me mutters sorry, and disappears into the bar, to re-emerge with a broom and a large dustpan. 'Where?'

'I'll show you. Sorry to disturb your break.'

He smiles. 'S'all right. S'nearly time to clock off.'

Sandro and I watch him as he sweeps. He makes quick work of clearing up and ambles away to empty the dustpan.

'It's time people were going. Not much point hanging around when the guest of honour's left.'

But inside, no-one's noticed Mother's departure, and the mood is cheerful, so we stay longer than we thought. People have written brilliant comments in the memory book, stories of youthful shenanigans that make us laugh, and wistful remembrances of good times shared with others no longer alive. It is a marvellous treasure. Mother will cherish it, I'm sure.

Theo comes over, dashing in his academic gown. A surge of love for him overtakes me and I wish he'd come back to the flat with me. Love? Or lust? Either way, he undoes me.

He leans on the back of my chair to whisper in my ear. 'We need to get people moving. We'll be using the refectory for supper.'

'Of course. We'll make an announcement.'

'I can do it over the PA.'

'That'd be great. Thank you.'

He swooshes away, like a young vampire, his gown billowing as he saunters across the room. I'd love to sink my fangs into his… oh, stop it, Sia.

'Ladies and gentlemen, honoured guests. It's time to go home now. On behalf of the l'Ussiers and of St. Bede's school, may I thank you for coming and wish you a safe journey home.'

He sounds every inch the headmaster. He may only be deputy now, but he'll reach the top. So much certainty and pride mingle in my heart, I could self-combust.

The party disburses, as a shell picture in the sand dowsed by waves. Alan takes me, and then Sandro, into a bear hug. Maurice kisses us both on the cheek.

'Darlings, we will be in touch.'

Sandro and I stroll to the main door, arm in arm. Tiredness overcomes me. I lean on him as we watch the stragglers chatter and separate, get into their vehicles. He pulls me close.

'Well done, sis.'

'Well done, you.'

'What're you doing now?'

'Collect the memory book and go home. Long soak in the bath followed by wine, food, and bed. You?'

'The same. I'm too weary to work on David tonight. Thought I might, but no.'

'Don't blame you. Jenny went earlier to prepare supper. If I text to say I'm on my way, she'll run the bath for me.'

'It'll be great having her home again, full time, won't it?'

'Reckon. You could do worse, you know.'

'Me and Jenny? Don't think she'd have me. Knows me too well.'

We laugh as we return to the refectory. Staff clear the mess from our do and prepare it, ready for supper. Someone has wrapped the memory book in its velvet bag and left it for us to collect.

'Okay?'

I clutch the book to my chest, its contents warming me by osmosis. I can't wait to get it home and read the rest of the memories.

'Want to take the book? I've got Jenny for company, and you'll be alone.'

'I won't, in fact. You take it, but thanks, anyway.'

'You kept this quiet. Who's the lucky girl keeping you from getting your much needed rest?'

'Claire Shaw.'

I nearly drop the memory book. It slips from my grasp, but I get it under control before it falls to the ground.

'Tina's Claire?'

He nods. 'We hit it off at the exhibition. I've seen her several times since.'

'But, isn't she..?"

'She's bi. That's cool with me.'

'Well, have a lovely evening.'

We kiss and he lopes off to his car. I stand there, the book held against my chest, happy to see him so content and at ease with himself.

* * *

After supper, Jenny and I pore over the memory book. Its stories have us in tucks and in tears. People loved Dad, shared such wonderful times with him. Makes me yearn for the Doctor to transport me back in time to witness them myself. Mother will have an emotional time reading it. And that reminds me.

'Think I'll give Mother a call. Make sure she got to Uncle Isaac's, and home.'

Her phone rings and rings but she doesn't answer.

'It's late for her, and I expect she's worn out after an eventful day, and no doubt dosed up for the night. I'll try again in the morning. I'm weary myself. Time for bed. Thanks for supper, and for the bath. Nice end to the day.'

'You're welcome.'

We hug, and I slope off to bed. The cool sheets are a balm and I drift into slow motion dreams of Theo and Mother and Sandro and Alan. Talk and laughter spill over me. The sun shines and the light is lovely. Joni sings 'Chelsea Morning' and the world bathes in happy colours...

The singing grows louder. Through the blur of sleep, my mobile, vibrating on the bedside cabinet lights up the gloom. I fumble out from under the duvet and slide it towards me. Detta. Four thirty. Detta? I swipe the screen.

'Sia? Sorry to call when you're in bed. There's no easy way of telling you this – Isaac is dead.'

CHAPTER TWENTY-SEVEN

THE NEXT DAY

The dusky morning light pales behind the thatched roof of The Dog and Duck. Mallards complain on the pond when Sandro pulls up in the car park. Cool air clings to my face as I climb from the car. Detta's car is here. We cross the dewy grass to the back door.

White-faced, Auntie Marian meets us in the hall, framed by the narrow walls and low ceiling; her shoulders droop and she wrings her hands. Sandro takes her in a fierce embrace. I hold back, a tickle of envy in my chest at Sandro's ease. Auntie Marian buries her face in his shoulder. She makes no sound.

How long we stand there, I can't tell. Sandro releases his hold on her, and she looks at me with such misery, I can hardly bear to return her gaze. I step forward and she hugs me. I fold her into my arms and hold on tight. It's like caressing a waif.

She pulls away from me.

'Thank you. It's a god-forsaken hour to be awake.'

'We couldn't have not come. Where is he?'

'They took him away.' She shakes her head as if she's struggling to remember. 'To the morgue.'

What a relief. My stomach is in knots from the worry she'd want us to pay our respects. 'They'll take care of him.' A stupid comment, but my mind is mush.

'Come through here. Detta's made tea.'

We follow her along the hall, past the lounge bar and into the part of the pub they call their home. Detta, in the sitting room, comes to us and we share a brief hug, the three of us.

'I'll get more cups.' Auntie Marian heads for the kitchen and I go to follow her. Detta grasps my arm.

'Let her do it. She needs to be occupied.'

The sitting room fire hasn't been lit, so I bank up the coal and logs. It may be spring outside but in here is chilly. Auntie Marian return with a tray laden with another teapot, cups and a sugar bowl.

'You shouldn't do that, Sia. I can do it if you're cold.'

'It's all right, Auntie Marian. I often to it for Mother.'

'Bless you.' She puts the tray on a low table near Detta. 'Would you pour?'

I struggle to frame the question I'm burning to ask. If we knew each other better… ask it, Sia. 'Auntie Marian, what happened?'

She sits on the settee next to Detta, who's playing mum pouring and handing out tea. 'I've heard it. Shall I make us toast?'

'If you like.' Auntie Marian sounds winded; her words come breathy and quiet.

We wait, only the crackling of the fire as it takes hold, and the chink of cups on saucers breaking the quiet. The tea is hot. It sears my throat and burns all the way into my stomach.

'Heather brought him home in a terrible state. I said he'd find the service hard, but he denied it. Said I must stay at home and man the fort.'

Her use of Uncle Isaac's words hits me. My cup rattles on its saucer. I put them on the floor, afraid of spilling tea over myself.

'Was good of her. He's difficult when he's had too much. Pub was busy; I was alone, save for the youngster - who's too daft to leave her in charge, so Heather volunteered to put him to bed. I said I should do it, but Heather said she couldn't possibly serve in the bar.' She weeps, tears plop into her teacup.

'I checked him every so often, but he'd crashed out. I had to keep it secret from the customers. If they found out he's a drunk, we'd lose the business.'

Sandro and I share a look. I imagine everyone had their suspicions.

'After closing time, I headed for bed. My instinct told me something was amiss: the still air, the stillness of Isaac. I tried to rouse him. I shook him, tried to roll him on to his back but he was too heavy.'

A coal slips across a log in the fire, sending flecks of orange into the chimney. I pick up my cup and saucer. Take another sip.

'I knew he was dead. I knelt by the bed and took his pulse, even so. Then, I called 999 and waited for the ambulance. The police got here first. Don't understand why they came. The paramedics confirmed it. Asked me questions. And took him away.'

'How awful for you. I am sorry.' My words ring hollow, but I want her to be sure I've listened, taken in what she's said.

Detta returns with another tray, this time stacked with toast. She puts it on the floor by the fire. 'Come on, help yourself. Quick, before the butter turns to liquid.'

Auntie Marian doesn't move from her place on the settee. I spread a slice with butter and jam and offer her the plate.

'You must eat. Toast is my go-to food when I'm poorly. This is like being ill.'

She smiles, takes the plate but makes no move to eat.

Detta has made a mountain of toast, and I, for one, am grateful. I don't function well on an empty stomach, especially at ridiculously early hours of the day. I munch through several slices.

'What happens now?' Sandro speaks with his mouth full; not a morning person, he's no doubt almost as wretched from being woken as he is from Uncle Isaac's death.

Detta yawns. 'I'm not sure. Marian, shut the pub for a few days. People will understand.'

'Yes. You'll have lots to attend to: legal stuff, practical matters, and you must take care of yourself. It'd be impossible to run the pub.' I hesitate before asking my next question. 'You haven't got a regular stand-in team, have you?' Uncle Isaac said substitute staff put their hands in the till, so he doesn't use them.

'No. We have our own staff, but none of them are full time anymore. Isaac cut their hours.'

'Marian, you look tired.' Detta pats Auntie Marian's knee. 'Why don't you have a sleep? We'll stay, in case anyone official comes or calls. Sia can make notices for the doors, explaining why you're shut.'

'I can't sleep in that bed. Not where he died.'

'Haven't you a spare room upstairs? I remember staying there once when Mother and Dad went abroad.'

'Yes, yes. I suppose…'

Detta takes Auntie Marian by the hand. 'Come on, then. Let's get you to bed. What's your doctor's name? I'll make you an appointment so you can get some sleeping tablets just in case you need them.'

She keeps up a stream of chat about things we can do as she guides Auntie Marian away.

'I knew this was going to happen.'

Sandro finishes his toast. He collects Detta and Auntie Marian's plates. He stacks them on the tray. 'Did you? There's a few slices left. Want them?'

I shake my head. 'Another person disappeared from a painting.'

'Sia-'

'I have proof this time. Photographic evidence. Vic's seen it.'

That makes him take notice. 'You mean, a before and after?'

'Exactly so.'

He squats on the floor and rocks back on his heels. 'Wow.'

'Vic asked me if I could link the victims to the disappeared. And I can.'

'Tell me.'

'It's not concrete, but, well. The first person to disappear, a woman. Not a day later, Tina Shaw died.'

'No. Concrete it isn't. More a coincidence.'

'But the link is their profession. Both women being unusual in theirs. Tina may have been unusual, but the intended victim was Detta. A professional woman.'

'Detta?'

'I can't explain why. Not yet.' What I suspect is too awful to confess now. I put on my best pleading face.

'Hm. Next.'

'Next was Mark. And there, the connection is obvious.'

'Is it?'

'The man who disappeared was a poker player. Mark used to gamble with Dad. Mother gave the impression they were quite a team once.'

'What? Dad gambled?'

'Yes, Mother told me when she was getting cross with Mark at the exhibition. That's why she loathed him.'

'Not because he was an obsequious slimy toe-rag?'

'Sandro! Don't. He wasn't that bad.'

'I'm with Mum on this one, but I get your point. What about Daniel?'

My throat tightens as it always does when he invades my head. The burgeoning friendship between us snuffed out too soon, losing two fathers in quick succession. I swallow hard.

'Sorry, sis. This must be tough.'

I sniff, find a tissue in my bag, and blow my nose. 'The third disappearance was of a man admiring the artwork of his children.'

'That would imply Dad knew Daniel was your biological father.'

He's right; isn't he? Dad must have known, if my wacky theories are correct. What an utter circus. What can I believe? Or perhaps Dad struck lucky on this one.

'Possibly, but as far as it concerns the painting, he was an art critic; someone who regarded art in a, a critical way, as the father regarded his kids' efforts.'

Sandro looks thoughtful. The machinations of his brain almost materialise as he considers my words.

'And there's been a fourth disappearance? Who? A man holding a beer tankard aloft?'

'No. He's a brother. The man who's gone is someone's brother.'

He blenches, falls back on his heels and steadies himself. He frowns.

'Does this explain why I had to shake you off at Dad's do? And the phone call? You thought I was the next victim?'

I nod, and another truth hits me. 'But if Dad had meant you, he'd have erased a son from one of his paintings – from the Drewitts, perhaps. Damn, I should've sussed it.'

'Are you frightened?'

Although the incredulity in his voice shakes my conviction, I have no choice but to continue.

'I am, not just because it's weird but...'

'But?'

'What if the next victim is me?'

CHAPTER TWENTY-EIGHT

MARCH 23RD

'Art Critic Post-Mortem Result: Suicide Not Ruled Out. Inquest Date Confirmed.'

I hate the media. It never brings good, or life-enhancing news. It's an article by the same reporter who interviewed Vic, so I hope it won't be as sordid as the headline implies. Suicide? I can't believe it.

Perhaps I shouldn't read it, but I do. Each sentence wounds. The post-mortem showed deadly levels of alcohol and the drug Xanax. Drugs? Daniel? How can that be true? I didn't imagine him saying he never drank, did I? Another hallucination? Don't, Sia. Kim says no, and Vic's seen the proof. Crazy things are happening. It's not you who's crazy.

I'm ignorant about Xanax, although the name is familiar. From where, I can't think. The article tells me it's a tranquilliser, and a potentially fatal drug to combine with alcohol. I am sure Daniel wouldn't combine drink and drugs on purpose. He wasn't stupid.

I leave the paper on the sofa and fetch my iPad. Do a quick search. And am terrified by what I discover. It *is* a killer when mixed with alcohol. I watch videos, read real-life accounts of Xanax abuse, and am horrified by what I learn. Daniel must've been ignorant, unaware of how lethal the combination of alcohol and Xanax can be or he wouldn't have taken it.

I chuck the iPad on to the sofa and slope into the kitchen to pour myself a glass of wine. But I stop. Do I drink too much? Is it possible to fall victim to drug abuse by accident? If, one day, I'm prescribed Xanax? I put the glass away and switch on the kettle. Caffeine won't kill me - will it?

Jade'll know if Daniel was drinking again. I scrabble for my mobile at the bottom of my bag. She'll be furious with the press for leaking the results. I press the phone icon under her name. After only two rings, she answers.

'Hello Sia. You've seen it?'

'Yes. How are you? It must come as a terrible shock.'

'Seeing it in the paper was, yes. But I've known for a couple of days. I'd be interested in who tipped off the media. Might have been Adrian. I wouldn't put it past him. It was on telly, on the local news. No doubt it'll be national in the morning.'

'So, it's true?'

'There was always a risk he'd fall off the wagon, but the drugs. That was a blow.'

'He told me he never touched alcohol. When he introduced himself at Dad's exhibition. And when we met at the pub – he drank lemonade.'

'It doesn't seem right, Sia. Something's horribly wrong, somewhere.'

Her words echo my own reactions. 'He was on the verge of receiving tremendous accolades for his scoop on Dad's paintings - surely he was too happy to consider killing himself?'

'He was *so* pleased with himself over it. Said it was worth the upset.'

'Upset?' Alarm storms through my head. But it comes to me. 'Oh, you mean the cover? He told you about that?'

'We still spoke most days, despite the estrangement. You'd impressed him with your determination and... dignity. Yes, that was the word.' She chuckles. 'Unlike your mother.'

'Excuse me?'

'She was furious with him. Screamed like a banshee, so he said. Threatened to ruin him, although I don't see how. I suppose that's one blessing; she won't be able to ruin him now, will she?'

'No, I guess not.'

I hold back the invitation to join me for a takeaway. I must process what she's just told me. Another time. Nausea curdles in my stomach; bile leaps up my throat. With my mobile tucked between my ear and shoulder, I make myself a coffee. As soon as the milk's in, I drink it and the bile recedes. Nausea sits in the pit of my belly, a belligerent intruder that won't be dislodged.

'As long as you're okay? I wanted to check.'

'That's kind. I'm fine.'

'If I can help, call me.'

'Thanks. If the media gets too intrusive, I might stay with my parents for a while. Get away from Deerdale, and the possibility of Adrian getting in touch.'

'Wise move. Don't care what the police say, he's a dodgy character. Where do your parents live?'

'Suffolk. They run a B and B.'

'By the coast?'

'Yes, Aldeburgh.'

'Sounds perfect. Wish I could come with you.'

She laughs. 'So do I. Possibly, one day.'

'Text me if you go.'

'Will do. Thanks for calling.'

'Bye, Jade.'

We end the call. I stand in the kitchen, my mind buzzing with ideas I don't want to countenance. Muster some self-control, Sia. Daniel's death was caused by alcohol and drugs, so how can that possibly be construed as murder?

I brew another coffee and sit, cradling my mug, on the sofa. No television, no radio. Nothing. Friday night is a lonely place when you've stuff on your mind. What do I need? I need *Blue*. A quick shufti at the iPad, scroll to Joni, press play. *All I Want*. I crank up the volume to maximum; Joni's ethereal tones fill my senses, submerging me in her words and music. I shut my eyes and listen to her truth. It's my truth, too. And, as she sings, something becomes clear.

Theo.

I must share this revelation with him. His starchy old governors shouldn't dictate how we live our lives. It's the twenty-first century. We can be a family our way. I must tell him about the events in the gallery. I must tell him how much I miss him. I must tell him of my fears. If any of this deters him, I'll accept we're finished. If not, our future is together. *My Old Man* says everything.

I take the iPad and get ready for bed. It's early but I am weary to my bones. Joni serenades me while I clean my teeth, wash my face. I can't believe I pinched this album from Mother, that she worshipped Joni, as I do now. Perhaps we have something in common underneath the skin. What a terrifying notion. Mother, you will not wreck another night's sleep.

In bed, I turn the volume low, so Joni's only a whisper. I lie, eyes open, and let her lyrical music tuck me into sleep. *Blue.*

* * *

Under the pretence of researching a Spanish painter, I spend the morning online seeking information on Daniel. And I call Theo. No point deciding if I don't act on it. We arrange to meet for a drink this evening. My stomach is a whirligig of anticipation and dread. Perhaps I won't say anything tonight. I'll wait to see what kind of humour he's in.

Sandro calls mid-morning to say he's going to visit Mother; did I want to go with him? I take it as a request for my company rather than an invitation I can refuse, so we agree he'll pick me up at two. He says he thinks we should both be there when she discovers Uncle Isaac's dead. No reference does he make to our last conversation; obviously, he ascribes my theories to my being over-imaginative.

I throw together a peanut butter sandwich, grab a packet of crisps, and continue my search. My delving throws up an article with details of Daniel and Jade's marriage. A photo of their wedding tops the page. It crushes me to see them so joyful, looking into the camera with faces filled with optimism as he holds his bride close. She's only three years older than me. Another piece of the jigsaw of my understanding falls into place; in the photo, Jade's hair is dark, not blonde as it is now. Little wonder Adrian made a mistake. Jenny's joke about me having a fling with Daniel whispers in my ear again. I shudder. Still isn't right. The article says they are separated. Nothing new. In the penultimate paragraph, the writer mentions Daniel's first wife, Julia. Who died of suicide the year I was born. The screen blurs. Poor Julia. Was she devastated by Daniel and Mother's betrayal? Jade said he always wanted to be a "proper" father. So, he and Julia had no children. Did Julia crave motherhood, only for Mother to parade her pregnancy before her? The sandwich in my hand loses its appeal. I drop it on to the plate, my appetite gone.

Sandro hammers on the front door and lets himself in, so I slam shut the laptop, wipe my fingers across my face and turn to greet him with the brightest smile I can muster. He plants a kiss on my cheek.

'Is she expecting us?'

'Not sure. I left a message this morning. Not spoken to her since the do.'

'Hasn't anyone tried to contact her before now? Tell her about Uncle Isaac?'

'Yes. She's gone into purdah. Probably needs to recover after the memorial.'

'She will be there?'

'Don't know that, either. Sorry, sis. But telling her is our responsibility. She'll take it better from us.'

'From you.'

'She'll go into shock. She was the last person to see Uncle Isaac alive.'

The image of the Butterworths and their missing brother lights up in my mind. It takes all my might to dull the illumination.

'Let's get it over with, shall we?'

I grab my bag and we make our way out into the March sunshine.

* * *

Mother's front door isn't locked this time. We find her sitting in the kitchen reading the paper. Thank goodness no-one's informed the press yet. How she'd cope reading it in the paper before anyone in the family has told her doesn't bear consideration. She smiles at Sandro, sort of smiles at me.

'Good morning, Mum. You're looking good.' He doesn't flatter; she does.

Her hair is swept up in a chignon, so she's nailed sophistication as far as I'm concerned. Whenever I try it, I end up doing a passable impression of a windblown haystack. In a black trouser suit and a string of pearls, she could be on her way to an executive meeting or grand cocktail party. Her easy refinement makes me feel scruffy and common.

We arrange ourselves at the peninsular alongside her. Sandro takes her hand, and her eyes flash with alarm.

'Why are you here? Haven't you seen enough of your darling mother? Or are you come seeking gratitude and praise?'

'Mum, Uncle Isaac has died.'

She pulls her hand from his grasp, like a snake shedding its skin, and folds her arms, leaning on the counter. 'How?'

That's a bizarre first question. Everyone well knows her dislike of Uncle Isaac in the family, but she always had, despite her scathing descriptions of Auntie Marian, a smidgen more respect for her. I'd have asked how she was. But I'm not Mother.

'We think it's alcohol poisoning, but we're not sure. Suppose it could be a heart attack. Auntie Marian found him when she went to bed after closing the pub.'

'Oh. I assume there'll be a post-mortem.'

'Auntie Marian is in quite a state.' We can't ignore Auntie Marian, the poor woman.

'I expect she is. Must have shocked her to find him.'

'How drunk was he?'

She turns her glacial eyes on me at last.

'Verging on comatose. Just as well their bedroom is on the ground floor. He'd be at the bottom of the stairs, otherwise.'

'She feels guilty because you put him to bed while she carried on in the bar.'

'Does she? She shouldn't. I told her I wouldn't take over.' She closes her eyes and shudders gracefully. 'Can you imagine me serving drinks to the hoi polloi?'

We've done what we came for; I don't want to sit here any longer and listen to her coldness. Sandro didn't need me by his side.

'I must get back. Sandro? Can we go now?'

He frowns. I raise my eyebrows, widen my eyes and gaze as meaningfully as I can. The sound of the penny dropping is thunderous.

'Haven't you brought the book of memories?' Mother fixes me with her emerald lasers. 'You took it home, I presume?'

'I did, yes.'

I stand, but as I step away from the stool, she reaches over and clasps my hand.

'Artemisia, be a darling and bring my book; bring it this evening. We'll eat supper, then look at it together.'

I'd planned to have that special conversation with Theo tonight, even dared hope he might come home with me.

'Can it wait? I've a date with Theo tonight.' Not exactly his words when we discussed it, but she won't know I'm taking liberties.

The green eyes darken, and I realise my mistake. She releases my hand.

'Sorry I suggested it. Please, don't alter your plans for me. Especially an evening with your ex-boyfriend.'

Her words cut into me, and she knows it. Sia, the selfish daughter who always puts herself first, and neglects her long-suffering mother, puts a night with her erstwhile lover ahead of her poor mother's feelings. I cave. Again.

'I'll call him. We can meet another time.'

'Lovely.' Her smile, gorgeous, sweet and sterile, seals my fate. 'Come straight after work.'

'I'll have to go home to fetch the book.' As soon as I utter the words, I curse myself for attempting even such a minor rebellion.

'Go via the flat when you leave. Sandro won't mind the detour, will you, Sandro?'

'No. It's fine. David can wait another hour.'

She tilts her head, and her face radiates affection. 'Dearest boy, you are good to your mother. I would ask you to join us for supper, but it maybe you'd better use the time on that marvellous walnut creation?'

'Let's go.' If I stay any longer, I'm in danger of crying, which always happens when anger grows into fury. There's no way I want her to witness that spectacle.

In the car, Sandro is apologetic, but I don't want to assuage his guilt. I sit, arms folded over my chest, and glower out of the window. He keeps trying.

'Leave it, Sandro. What's done, is done. Theo will understand. He's stood me up enough times, for marking and such.'

Theo will, that's part of the problem. He'll shrug his shoulders and not even suggest another time if I don't hint at it enough. He's never been the most ardent of lovers in that respect. After his initial approach, I made the running, until he wanted marriage. And even then, he enlisted Mother's help. Fat lot of good it did him.

'I'm sorry, sis. You're going through it, aren't you? You were Daddy's girl. This business with Uncle Isaac must make it more difficult.'

I bite the inside of my cheeks. Sandro can be perceptive sometimes, and sensitive. He senses stuff others don't notice. My fury at Mother, the shock of Daniel being my father, my fear concerning the paintings and the hollow emptiness since Dad's death meld together. I can't stop the tears. He lets me cry, making no attempt to cheer me with barren platitudes.

I wish Dad were here. None of these events would've happened if he were. Detta's worries over the nudes – she'd have talked to Dad herself and persuaded him not to show them, avoiding the studio fire. Tina would still be alive.

Sandro keeps his attention on the road, his profile so like Dad's if I squint, I could fool myself it was him.

Mark Hubbard. Not sure whether he'd still be with us. Perhaps. And Daniel? Daniel would've stayed away. I choke again, the loss as stifling as Othello's pillow. I don't know. Am I making connections where there aren't any? Even as the words float through my mind, my inner voice berates me for entertaining them. Of course, there are connections.

Sandro drops me off at home with yet more apologies. He doesn't speak of his own grief, and I am riddled with guilt.

* * *

Mother is all smiles and welcoming. She presents me with beef in beer, complete with dumplings. My anger has subsided but lingers, embers in the grate waiting to be stoked into a fire. She chatters while she serves up, telling me of her day, fishing for praise because she's visited Auntie Marian.

'I hope you weren't wearing that black outfit from this morning.'

'Why not? We're in mourning, aren't we? As it happens, I changed. I spilt coffee on it, so was forced. I wore a sensible ensemble of jeans and a crisp white shirt, but I don't see why I should explain to you. Not exactly the doyen of the well-dressed, are you?'

'Thanks, Mother. Your direct approach sure gives a girl confidence.'

'I don't mean it in a nasty way, you know that.'

Do I?

'But look at you.'

I can see nothing wrong with my wide-legged cropped trousers and lemon sweater. It might be spring, but it can be chilly. And my boots - floral Doc Martens - may not be ladylike in Mother's eyes, but they're perfect for comfort and for avoiding damage to the parquet.

'I like my clothes.'

'You remind me of an intern on her first day.'

'Young?'

'Untidy.'

'Mother. I'm thirty-four, not fifteen and I know what suits me, what I find comfortable. I'll never be another you.'

'That much is true.' She sighs, no effort to hide her disappointment.

'Shall we adjourn to the sitting room? Go through the book?'

'Haven't you done so?' She raises an elegant eyebrow. 'Don't tell me no. Not when you've had it at home.'

'So, the book isn't why you got me to rearrange my evening with Theo?'

Here it comes again. It fizzes subtly as champagne under a half-removed cork. How long can I keep it from popping?

'It was, but now I think about it, I'd better read it alone.' She takes a noisy, deep breath. 'You're aware how I miss your father.' Her bottom lip quivers. 'You don't want to witness another emotional breakdown.'

'Thanks for supper.' I push the chair from beneath me, stand with my hands, white-knuckled, gripping the edge of the table. 'I'll see myself out.'

Must make good my escape before I clock her one. Theo could still meet me, for one drink, but I'm too furious. Certainly not in a suitable frame of mind to bare my soul.

I collect my handbag from the bottom stair where I dumped it when I arrived, dig out my car keys and march to the front door. She doesn't follow me. I slam the door behind me as I leave; one minor act to demonstrate my frustration. I drive, hitting the motorway, with Joni on full volume, singing at the top of my voice. Countless songs later, too hoarse to sing another note, I turn the car homewards.

CHAPTER TWENTY-NINE

FIVE DAYS LATER

'You shouldn't have. These are stunning. Thank you. I'll put them in the sink until we've finished. You go in.' Kim gestures to the consulting room.

'May I use your loo? I should've gone before I set off, but time was against me.'

'Sure. Follow me; I'll show you where it is.'

Off the hall, I glimpse rooms revealing the private side of Kim's life: a dining room with an upright piano, music, propped above the keys, ready to play; a terracotta couch loaded with cushions dominates a sitting room with honey-coloured walls. I could live in such a house. An airy kitchen, with folding doors out to a garden with a riot of spring colour.

'Through there, first door on your left.' She goes into the kitchen and shuts the door. Does she fear I'll invade her privacy if I catch a glimpse? The sound of water cascading into a sink. I dash to the loo.

Back in the consulting room, Kim consults her notes briefly, and begins.

'You talked last time about wanting to discuss your feelings towards Theo. Shall we start with him?'

I sigh. 'I haven't told him my feelings about our relationship. After our postponed date, my anger with Mother was slow to subside. We met, but I wasn't in the right mood. When I went through it in my head, I sounded frivolous and shallow.'

'Why did you think that?'

'Because songs I love have influenced me.'

'The songs express your love for Theo, and your relationship with him? You mentioned this last time.'

'Yes. But he'd not understand it.'

'Why do you have to tell him what caused you to reconsider?'

It's a good question. I've argued with myself over it dozens of times.

'If I'm not honest with him, won't our relationship be based on a lie?'

'Not if your feelings are genuine. What's most important, showing him how you feel or avoiding it because of a desperate need to hold on to the absolute truth? What should partners know about one another?'

'Everything? There can be no secrets.'

'Imagine a secret which might hurt your partner, but not knowing makes no difference.'

'What do you mean?'

'Let's say, for the sake of argument, Theo is a terrific kisser.'

My face burns in an instant. He is. She grins and is serious again.

'Now imagine a future in which your relationship with Theo has ended. You've met a wonderful man who ticks all your boxes. You're in love. But his kissing? It's not so good, and every time you kiss, your thoughts stray to Theo.'

'Wow. Awkward.'

'For you. But this future paragon worships you and wants you to live together. He's accepted you don't want kids but has left you in no doubt he'd be happy if you changed your mind. He tells you it's you he wants. And you love him.'

It's hard to imagine such a scenario. I've never pictured a future with another man.

'Do you tell him he's not the best kisser? Or do you accept his limitations and give thanks for everything else he is?'

'And this relates to me and Theo..?"

'You've a compulsion to be truthful concerning the inspiration for your powerful feelings. You fear he'd dismiss your inspiration - which would devalue your declaration, your desire to fight for your relationship.'

'And?'

'Why tell him and scupper your chances, if having Theo in your life means so much to you? What are you most afraid of? Failure or success?'

That's a question I haven't asked myself. So, I ask it now.

Kim seems to sense I need a moment. She does that stillness thing, when it's easy to forget she's in the room.

If I fail to say my piece to Theo, we will drift apart. We'll continue to see each other until one of us dates someone else. Or until I become too miserable to face him, because we're not a couple, but we're not apart, either. If I say what's in my heart, I might still fail. He might think I'm being pushy and end it. At least I'd have closure. But he might appreciate my strength of feeling, remonstrate more forcefully with the headteacher and whoever. Tell them he wants to live with me, that they should drag themselves into the modern world.

'What have I got to lose?'

'Can you face doing empty chair work? Say it aloud? As we did on previous occasions?' She glances at the wall clock. 'We've got time.'

'That might be a good idea, yes.'

Although my reply was swift and positive, I am nervous as I recall my self-consciousness the first time, trying to picture someone sitting there. It isn't easy. Have I made a mistake? I'm not as angry with Theo as I am with Mother.

'Take your time: consider what you want Theo to hear from you.'

I stare at the empty chair, conjure Theo's features in my mind.

Words present themselves in my brain, behind my forehead, but my skull is like a barrier. My eyes closed, I try to form my words into something that makes sense out loud.

'I've been thinking about us, our relationship.' I'm too woolly and wishy-washy, not strong, like the woman I want to be. I open my eyes.

'Theo, it's time we decided. Either we are a couple or we're not. I don't want to continue the way we are. It is too distressing, and I am exhausted by it.'

Kim listens, says nothing.

'I want us to be together, to live together, grow old together. I assumed you wanted that, too.'

Kim leans forward. 'You want to include Theo's reactions to your words? Use the empty chair for his responses, separate them from yours.'

I nod, and awkwardly slip on to the vacant chair. I'm reminded again of school drama, the silliness of it. Pretend to be your boyfriend. My face reddens, but I know this technique works; Kim explained it to me when we first tried empty chair work. This has another name, I can't remember, but I bet it's just as effective. I gather my thoughts.

'He'd say he wanted it, too.' My certainty comes from somewhere deep. 'He'd tell me he loves me.' A lump the size of the asteroid in Deep Impact forms in my throat. I swallow hard.

'Are you able to continue, if you've more to say? Move back to your chair when you're speaking for yourself.'

I shift back to my chair, clear my throat of nothing.

'You should speak to the governors. Tell them they have no right to determine your private life. Your unwillingness to do it makes me question whether you love me.'

That's a suspicion I've harboured for ages but never vocalised. When I hear it spoken aloud, it brings home the truth. Theo's inaction has me doubting. The confusion is hard to unravel. I'm sure he loves me. I doubt his love. How can both be true?

'I want you to speak up for us, to show the school how important "us" is. I miss you.'

The full-stop is a finger point to my heart. Quiet fills the room. Theo's face comes vividly into my head, a perplexed half-smile on his lips. Kim, like a mind-reader, breaks the silence.

'Does he respond?' She tilts her head to the other chair, and I move.

'He says he didn't realise how much I love him, how important to me he is. He says sorry.'

Tears cascade down my face. Kim hands me the tissue box. I resume my place in my chair, sniffing.

'What's made you tearful?'

'Realising he doesn't understand the depth of my feelings for him. That I could have made it clearer; rather than just insisting I don't want to get married, explained why not.'

'Anything else?'

'It's easy to say I love you. People throw it into their conversations out of habit, but the words are meaningless without loving actions.'

'Yours, or Theo's?'

'I could have offered to speak to the headteacher or governors myself, argued our case. I could've viewed the cottage, instead of dismissing it.'

'Can you tell him why you don't want to get married?'

'If we get married, people will assume we'll have a family. I don't want that because…'

'Go on, he's listening.'

'I, I don't want that… because I'm afraid… I'm afraid any child we have will turn out like Mother.'

I hold my head in my hands to stop the room spinning. My ears hum. Tears drip from the end of my nose, along the sides of my wrists, and fall with a silent plop on to the carpet.

Kim pushes another tissue between my hands. I mop up as

best as I can.

'How are you?'

'Washed out. Relieved.'

'And..?'

'Brave enough to tell Theo.'

She nods again. 'We said this might be our last session – you're coping with your father's death well now. You've shared with me how challenging the relationship is with your Mother, especially since the revelation about your biological father. And you've talked about how things are with Theo. Are you satisfied with your progress, content with your position now?'

It scares me, the idea of not seeing Kim anymore. And if I told Theo I was seeing Kim about Mother, it would add weight to my argument.

'Satisfied with my progress? Definitely. But my issues with Mother remain. I'd appreciate a couple of sessions discussing them. It'll be traumatic.' I laugh a wobbly laugh. 'Much worse than discussing Dad.' I wonder if she remembers when I nearly told her my suspicions? And can I have appointments when Mother is my focus, and keep them to myself? Suppose I can stop the session, if I fear I might divulge something I shouldn't.

'That's why I'm here. Let's make another appointment. You can cancel if you change your mind.'

So, that's what we do. I climb into the car, exhausted. If I give in to it, I'll sleep for a week, and I must return to the gallery. Vic's had an idea regarding our next "big thing", and he wants us to start planning.

* * *

Auntie Marian sits in reception. She stands as I approach, and we embrace. Vic excuses himself and wanders away, towards two trendy looking people, probably students, who are admiring Dad's early stuff that wasn't sold – including the haystack soldiers.

'Lovely to see you here, Auntie Marian. Didn't think art was your thing.'

'You'd be surprised. I've always been an art lover. I've admired your dad longer than I've been married to Isaac.'

'Really? You are a surprise.'

'That isn't why I'm here. Can I speak to you in private?'

'Sure. Come into the office.'

She won't take a seat, so I stand, too.

'It's the post-mortem. I've to go to the hospital for the results. I need someone to support me, and I wondered if you'd come with me?'

Another post-mortem. My life is filled with nothing else.

'Yes, of course I will. I'm glad you're comfortable enough to ask. When?'

'I must telephone to make an appointment.'

'Tell me when, and I'll tell Vic.'

'I hope you don't mind, I told him.' Auntie Marian chews her lip, like she's expecting me to be annoyed.

'He's been understanding. I've taken a lot of time off.'

'If you'd rather not, I can ask Sandro?'

'Don't be silly. It's not a problem. Vic's lovely, and he knows I'll make it up to him.'

'If you're sure?'

'I'm sure.'

'I'll call as soon as.'

She bustles out of the office, reminiscent of one of those Queen Mother impersonators. I am glad to help but Vic worries me. He's been an absolute stalwart, but can I continue taking advantage of his kind nature?

Auntie Marian says goodbye to Vic and takes her leave. He ambles towards me, a sympathetic smile on his lips.

'That poor woman. Tells me she has no family of her own.

She's lucky to have you.'

'Thank you. We never see enough of her. Uncle Isaac always insisted she stay at the pub whenever there was a family do.'

'Must have felt very isolated.'

A pang of guilt. 'Yes. I won't allow anyone to push her aside any longer. She says she told you why she was here.'

'Hm. Post-mortem results. Suppose they make everything easy to understand? For the lay person.'

'I suppose.'

'Why does she want to go? Seems macabre. Couldn't they send her the results in a letter?'

'That's harsh. You surprise me. I'd want to, if it were my spouse.'

'Really?'

'Mm. Make sure everything's legit.'

'Could you tell if it weren't?'

'Probably not.'

He wanders back to the remnants of Dad's exhibition, and I fire up the laptop. I should act on my words, visit Auntie Marian. She's obviously bewildered by events. I expect there're dozens of jobs I could do for her. The screen lights up and I type in my password. Betty's twinkly eyes gaze out at me. They tell me I'm right. Auntie Marian needs my help.

I try to concentrate on the task Vic has given me: to locate the whereabouts of a painting he swears used to hang here but has vanished. Not one of Dad's, thank goodness. That'd be taking disappearances to a whole new level. He thinks he's given it on loan to a school or university, but he can't remember. Blithering thing's only been missing for a decade. And now he wants me to find it and get it back. I best ring round the schools. Or the council? Maybe they have a scheme for procuring works of art for their schools.

The afternoon drags. No-one has a clue to the location of the painting. At four o'clock, after thousands of futile conversations with bored officials, I turn off the computer and walk into the gallery. It's good to stretch my legs, even if my knees complain. Makes me feel I'm three hundred not thirty-four.

The gallery looks gorgeous in the late afternoon light, low sunshine shimmering through the ancient glass. Vic talks to a group of school children. Most look rapt but one lad, about ten years old, gazes round the gallery with ill-disguised ennui. He sees me watching him and grins, turns to Vic and nods as if he's been paying attention all along. Oh, to be ten again, with no worries but boredom. Come on, Sia. You aren't three hundred yet. Two hundred and ninety-nine, maybe.

The group disperses, and Vic joins me.

'More youngsters' enthusiasm sparked by a visit to our gallery.'

'Hm. I saw that. Have they gone away filled with inspiration and the urge to daub?'

'Are you making fun, Sia?'

'As if.'

'Well, if only one of them has, I consider it a success.'

'Me, too.'

'Any luck tracking down my lost painting?'

'Not yet. And lots of offices are closed now, so I wondered if you'd mind if I skedaddled? Thought I'd drop in on Auntie Marian. See how I can help, keep her company for an hour.'

'That's thoughtful of you. I'll see you tomorrow.'

'Okay. Thanks, Vic.'

The pub looks deserted; no lights on and the main doors closed. I park at the front and walk round to the back door. It's unlocked, so I push it open and step inside. The silence is out of place. As I stand on the threshold of the lounge bar, signs of Uncle Isaac I hadn't noticed before stand in stark relief to everything else. Postcards from around the world from famous athletes, his battered tankard sitting on the bar, scores in his untidy hand beside the dart board, the regimented gin bottles, placed in alphabetical order against the mirrored wall. Reminders fill the room, and I bet it's the same in the snug. I swallow hard, my mouth suddenly dry. I turn my back on the lounge bar and head towards the kitchen.

Auntie Marian sits at the table, her chin cupped in her hands, her elbows on the table. If I were to paint the portrait of grief, this would be my inspiration.

I sit by her, my arm around her shoulder, and hold her close. Minutes pass, her hushed weeping punctuated by ticking as the second hand sweeps mechanically round a faux antique clock face. Somewhere outside, birds sing, and a breeze picks up, scratching branches together in a quiet cacophony.

She dabs her face with the handkerchief. 'I don't know what I'm supposed to do.'

'You mean with the pub?'

'Yes. I can't face opening.'

'Then don't. But you need to inform your staff. Shall I call them?'

'But I'm not sure when I'll open again. *If* I open again.'

'I can tell them. Best to be honest, from the start.'

She rummages through a drawer in the dresser and deposits a red leather-bound book next to me.

'I've marked the staff with an 's' in a circle next to the name. Ignore the rest for now.'

'Is everything you do so organised?'

'Someone has to be. Isaac wouldn't know… where to start.'

'Right. Leave it with me.'

She pats my arm. 'Thank you, Sia. I'll just close the blinds in the bar.'

'Before you go. Is there someone I should tell first? A more senior person?'

She hovers by the door. 'Erm…'

'Okay. I'll do it alphabetically.'

I open the book at "A" but none of the names is marked, so I turn to "B". She hovers, like she's waiting for my permission to leave.

'I'm on it. Didn't you say something about blinds?'

'Yes. I did.' She ambles from the kitchen like she's lost her way.

At "D" I find the first member of staff. Joanne Davis. The phone rings a few times before she answers.

'Hello.'

'Is that Joanne Davis? It's Sia l'Ussier and I'm calling on behalf of my Auntie Marian at the pub.'

'I sensed bad news was coming, what with the pub being shut and everything. I saw the police and the ambulance. I don't sleep well, and the lights woke most of the neighbourhood. It's Isaac, is it?'

'Yes, I'm afraid so. He passed away on Friday.' I don't know why I don't say Thursday. Probably because Auntie Marian found him in the early hours.

'Can I do anything to help?'

'That's good of you. Can I get back to you? It's still early days. Auntie Marian asked me to tell you she's shutting the pub. Might be for a long time.'

'So, my job's on hold?'

'It is, but I'd seek alternative employment, if the money's a concern.'

Joanne laughs. 'Bless your heart. I do it to escape the house. Have some adult conversation.'

'You have kids?'

'Four, if you count the hubby.'

'See what you mean. Thanks Joanne. I'll be in touch when the situation changes.'

'Give Marian my love and don't forget to call the moment you need an extra pair of hands.'

'Got it. Thanks. Bye.'

'Before you go, have you spoken to Phil yet?'

'Phil?'

'Mercer. He doesn't work weekends, but he's practically full time during the week. He'll take it badly. People find him tricky, prickly.

Single dad with teenagers. Be gentle with him, but firm.'

My stomach squirms. 'Thanks for the tip. I'll call him now.'
Best ring him next.

I riffle through the pages to "M" and there he is. I press the
first three numbers. Wait.

'Auntie Marian?' I hope she can hear me. 'Auntie Marian?'

She appears at the door. 'Yes, dear?'

'Phil Mercer.'

Her hands fly to her face, her eyes widen. 'Should I call him, not you?'

'I was wondering if we should go to his house. Tell him in
person rather than by phone.'

She pulls up a chair and sits by me. 'He lives across the green.
Isaac never liked him very much – always said he suspected he
had his hand in the till, but I didn't believe it. Phil just doesn't
take any nonsense – even from his employer.' She sighs, but the
expression in her eyes changes. 'Yes. I should speak to him. He's
our longest serving member of staff. It'll hit him hard.'

'That's what Joanne Davis said. Want me to come with you?'

'No. He might get defensive with you there, but with me, he'll
be able to react honestly. I'll go now, while... have you called
everyone between Joanne and Phil?'

I shake my head. 'No. Just her. She sends you her love and says
we must ask if we need anything.'

Auntie Marian pushes herself away from the table.

'She's a good sort, is Joanne. I'll see you later.'

She bustles through to the hall, much lighter of foot than a
moment ago. In an instant, she's back and pulling on her coat.
Her movements more defined, somehow.

'Tell them I'll pay a month's wages, to begin with; that'll soften
the blow.'

'Okay. Good luck with Phil.'

'I can handle Phil.'

She closes the back door with a determined thud and is gone.

I redial Joanne's number. I tell her about the wages. She repeats her offer of help, and we say goodbye.

No-one else in the "D" section.

I'm in the middle of a conversation with Bryony Tozer when Auntie Marian returns. She crosses the kitchen without acknowledging me, her head bent. Anxiety threads through me.

'Anyway, Bryony, thanks for your understanding at this difficult time. We appreciate it. Bye.'

I fill the kettle with water and fetch two mugs from the cupboard. Auntie Marian appears just as the kettle boils.

'Fancy a sandwich?'

'Don't you want a proper supper? There's food in the pantry.'

'This'll do me. How about it? I make a mean cheese and pickle sarnie.'

She nods, so I gather the stuff I need. While I butter the bread, she milks the drinks and removes the tea bags.

'He was difficult, huh?'

'No. Poor man was bereft. Not just because of the job. He seemed genuinely heart-broken about Isaac. You can never tell, can you?'

Her eyes fill with tears. She dabs them with an embroidered handkerchief, and for a moment, Daniel enters my head.

'Here. Take these.' I hand her a plate with her sandwiches. 'Let's eat. Cold calling strangers is hungry work. Funny, texting never gives me an appetite.'

'You are a dear.'

We return to the table, where we eat in silence. Auntie Marian nibbles the edges of hers, but I wolf mine and am finished too quickly.

'Would you be able to face a slice of cake? I noticed an appetising chocolate affair in the larder.'

She smiles. 'I'll give it a go.'

'You pour us another cuppa, and I'll do the honours.'

It's just as delicious as it looks, and it takes no time to demolish the slab I cut for myself. Auntie Marian manages to eat the sliver

I serve her and seems to enjoy it.

'You can live on chocolate cake, you know. Chocolate comes from a bean, a vegetable. One of your five a day.'

We laugh together, and she licks her finger, dabs the crumbs from her plate.

'Shall I come another time? I'd love to help, however I can.'

'You're a treasure. Stop calling me auntie though. Makes me sound a hundred.'

'Got it.'

'I'd better go through the books, see what bills I can pay.'

'Just pay small ones, for now.' Their financial position is a tricky subject but one I must broach. 'We're aware Uncle Isaac had money problems.' She flinches. 'But we'll help you sort them. Don't try to get everything done straight away. Promise me. Don't get yourself into a situation more difficult, okay?'

'Promise. Thank you.'

'Right, I'd better go. Will you be all right? Want me to call later, for a chat?'

'No. I'll be fine, thank you. I'll call you in a day or so.'

'If you're sure? You're okay being on your own?'

'I'll get in touch with one of my choir friends. I'm sure she'll come over.'

'Good idea. But call me – anytime – if you need a chat or company overnight.'

'I will.'

We hug on the doorstep, and I head for home. What a lovely woman. Pity Uncle Isaac kept her apart from the family for so many wasted years, not allowing us to know her better. From now on, I shall be her friend. My heart is lighter as I drive. The low sun shines on the passing scenery, glimmering in its spring clothes. Shall I pop in on Mother, find out how she reacted to the memory book? I catch myself frowning in the rear-view mirror. Perhaps that's a task for Sandro.

CHAPTER THIRTY

APRIL 3RD

T. S. Eliot said April is the cruellest month, but I reckon he must have been going through a rough patch. Three days in, and my April is glorious. My head is unclouded, like the spring air, and life brims with possibilities. Listen to yourself, woman. Eliot will spin in his grave at your poetic stumblings. It's true, though. Helping Marian – don't call me auntie – gives me a boost, and Kim's session on Monday has given me the determination to talk to Theo. Not long till Jenny is home to stay, and gallery developments start. Yep. It's all good, as the sign outside the chip factory used to say. Course, the disappearances put the mockers on my optimism. What a phrase. One of Dad's, not T. S. Eliot's. Under the spring sunshine and the scent of narcissus, dark things lurk, trying to wreck my burgeoning confidence. Admit it, T. S., that's an effective image.

A few people wander the gallery today, showing lots of interest in our new project. Vic's amateur sketches, his scrappy depictions of the gallery once the café's completed, have drawn comments. One of our regulars wryly said he should retrain as an architect. The glint in her eye told the lie of her words. He stood to attention, I swear, so chuffed with her praise; I had to develop a sudden interest in my shoes. Dear old Vic.

I stroll to the bench by Betty and Harold. As is often the case, like people know it's my favourite spot, no-one sits there so I make myself comfortable. She is radiant in the sunshine, and Mrs Drewitt isn't too shabby either. Yes, she's haughty and sneery but there's a softness to her that stops her from being totally unpleasant. My mobile vibrates in my pocket. I take it out and Jade's name flashes on the screen. I tap my security number and open her text. She's in Suffolk. Don't blame her. She's sending me an image? Of the beach, perhaps? Or a stick of Aldeburgh rock? The dots bloom and fade as she sends the picture. Then, it pops on to my screen. It's a selfie, taken at the tide's edge, looking back towards Aldeburgh. A small, hairy dog in her arms licks her face. The way she captures herself, grimacing into the camera, makes me smile. She looks unsteady, about to topple into the waves rippling along the shingle.

Looks fab. Cute dog.

Buster. My parents' spoilt 2nd child.

Haha. RUOK?

Yes. They spoil me 2.

Good.

The dots come again; she's sending me another photo.

To begin with, I struggle to comprehend the image. A blur of white sharpens into focus. A screen shot of an email. To the coroner. She's requested Daniel's DNA.

OMG! Thank U.

Thank parents. They persuaded me.
Sorry I didn't do it sooner.

My hands tremble so much I'm in danger of dropping the phone. I'll get the truth at last. I must tell Sandro; he'll be so surprised as he's not had the faith in Jade I have.

No apology needed. Understood your reluctance. What a bizarre text conversation. Any idea when results available?

Will text ASAP.

THX.

I follow my thanks with a row of stars.

A smiley face, winking, pops up next, alongside two kisses; the conversation ends. I must tell Vic my news; he'll be delighted. I slip the phone into my pocket, and just as I stand, a voice says:

'Is this the lady who plays piano?'

An elderly couple stand next to the bench, their interest in Betty obvious. They wear matching jackets and walking shoes, identical scarves tucked into their collars. I struggle to subdue a grin, forcing myself to hold it at a smile.

'It is. This is Betty Parmenter. My favourite woman from Dad's paintings. We play her music sometimes. Pity not today.'

They nod in unison, reminding me of that couple in the television programme Dad used to enjoy so much when I was little. He used to call Sandro and me Howard and Hilda sometimes.

'I can see why she's your favourite.' The woman tilts her head. 'Looks like she'd make a wonderful friend.'

'That's how I see her – as my friend. Crazy, but true.'

The old woman pats my arm. 'Not crazy, love. She'll never let you down.'

'Shame we missed the piano, though,' Howard says.

'You must visit us again. We're opening a café soon, so you'll be able to stop for a coffee and cake.'

'We'd love to, but we're on holiday. It's a long trek from Colchester for a coffee with music.'

'What a pity. Tell you what, I'll put the music on, just for you. Will you excuse me?'

Their faces shine and I waltz to the office to get the CD player, grinning at last.

The old couple sits on the bench I vacated. I plonk the machine on the floor next to the painting and press play.

'There you go. Watch Betty's smile change as you listen.'

I leave them, their eyes fixed on Betty, who I swear watches me as I walk away. I can feel her gaze penetrate the air.

In the office, Vic sits at the desk, the laptop open. 'I see you've tried the obvious places. What's your next step?'

I sit opposite him. It's weird being this side of the desk.

'Look at this.' I thrust my mobile, the photo of the email open, across the desk.

Like me, Vic doesn't register the picture's importance straight away, but when he does, he breaks into the widest smile.

'Sia, that's marvellous news. You said she was a good'un.'

'I did, didn't I?' I take back the phone. 'Now, what were you asking me?'

'Your next step, locating the missing painting?'

'Putting out an alert on the internet. If I created gallery Bluesky, Threads and Instagram accounts, I could put it there.'

'Do you know how?'

'Vic, come out of the dark ages. Everyone has at least one account. It's easy. I could open one for you, too.'

'Why would I want one?'

'Forget it. But I will for the gallery.'

'What're the advantages? Doesn't it leave you vulnerable to

cranks and ne'er-do-wells?'

'It can do. But we should be safe with official gallery accounts. Leave it to me. I'll put a photo of the painting online. That's one advantage.'

He rubs his chin and nods. 'Yes. Yes, I take your point.' He stands. 'Better let you get on. Is that Betty's music?'

'Yes. My good turn for the day.'

'Jolly good.'

He wanders out of the office without another comment.

It takes moments to open various accounts and to compose my introductory posts. That done, I write absinthe into Chrome and dozens of results spring up. Scrolling the page, I happen upon a link to YouTube with instructions on how to drink it. Bizarre. Stick it in a glass and, what was the phrase Detta used, neck it? Not so. I watch several videos. Sugar cube. Hence the spoon. Drip icy water into the glass to dissolve the sugar and watch the absinthe go cloudy. The men in the videos comment on how refreshing it tastes. Sounds tempting; I'd try it. An odd choice for suicide, though. Wouldn't gin or vodka be quicker? Less hassle?

A Bluesky banner across the screen. Our first alert. I click; someone thinks they've seen the painting. Wow, incredible; a result in under an hour. I love the internet. Oh. I'm too optimistic. I've contacted the college they suggest. I lean back in my chair. What if the college had it and lost it? They might deny having possession, mightn't they? I ask how recently the poster, named Hesperus, saw the painting in situ. Two years ago, says Hesperus. I thank him and promise to let him know if I have any luck.

No alerts ping while I scroll through my personal Bluesky feed without interest. This won't do. People get sacked for doing personal stuff in work hours. Vic won't fire me, but I close the page. The rumbling in my stomach tells me it's lunch time. I grab my purse and head out, ready to do my next good turn, but before I do, I must ask Vic what he knows about absinthe.

'Absinthe?'

'You know the rigmarole for drinking it, all that sugar cube in a spoon nonsense?'

'In my youth, we used to partake. Considered ourselves very daring. In France, you could only buy it under a different name, until recently. We regarded it in the same way as we did recreational drugs. You should try it.'

'I might, one day. But now, I'm just popping out. D'you want your usual?'

He gives me two thumbs up, so I saunter into the warm spring sunshine, the mystery of Daniel's final hours niggling me still.

* * *

Friday morning, Marian calls me at the gallery. She prattles at me.

'It's come. The result of the post-mortem. They've just called. Got to go to the hospital.'

'Slow down, Marian. Now then, when's your appointment?'

'On Wednesday.'

'Time?'

'Half-past two.'

'I'll pick you up at two.'

'Good. Thank you.'

Wednesday. It hasn't taken long for them to complete the report. Does that signify anything? I don't know. We'll find out on Wednesday. I search for Vic; he's telling a visitor what the upheaval is for, as if she hasn't spotted his diagrams.

'So, we've put an ad in the paper.'

'Could I apply? I'd love to work in an art gallery.'

I stand by Vic. 'You interested in our café?'

She's in her twenties, fresh featured with sparkly eyes. 'I'll say. I work in Big Ben's on Government Square. Nice enough and well positioned. But I'd rather work here.'

'What do you do?'

'Everything, if I have to. Cook, wait tables, wash up. You name it.'

'Can you bake?' I cross my fingers behind my back.

'Cakes? My speciality.'

I nudge Vic in the ribs. 'I reckon we should abandon the search and take her on now.'

'The advertisement's gone in. We can't.'

'Tell you what, I'll bake you a cake and bring it in so you can see for yourselves.'

'C'mon, Vic. Give the girl a chance.'

'That might be construed as bribery.'

'I'm sure – what's your name?'

'Nina.'

'I'm sure Nina can fill out one of our application forms *and* bake us a cake.'

He shakes his head, but I can see he's tempted. 'We should wait until the closing date.'

'Which is when?' Nina doesn't miss a trick.

'There isn't one. He's prevaricating. You'll get used to that if you join us.'

Vic harrumphs. 'I think we should stop discussing it now. If you come with me, Nina, I'll furnish you with an application form.'

Furnish? I burst into laughter. He's wonderful when he speaks this way.

I scramble behind them. 'Vic, I came to tell you. Marian's appointment is on Wednesday. Half two.'

He spins on his foot. 'Marian's appoint – oh. So, you'll be off Wednesday afternoon.'

'If that's okay?'

'Course, silly girl.'

He bustles into the office, Nina in his wake. When they emerge, she's folding an application form and stuffing it into her bag. It will be somewhat crumpled by the time we get it back.

'I'll bring this back tomorrow. Bye.' And she's out of the front door in a whirl.

'I like her.'

'You like everyone.'

'I do not.' I struggle but am victorious in my battle against admitting I dislike Mother. 'Most people; not everyone.'

He gives me one of his looks. And I put on my most innocent of faces.

'If that poor girl ends up working with us, I shall have to take her to one side. Warn her, this gallery is simply a picturesque asylum - and the lunatics have indeed taken over. I can see you're going to be a bad influence.' But his voice is laden with smiles.

'We are perfectly balanced then, mister goodie-two-shoes.'

He's chuckling as I leave him to it. I shall be glad when this part of the development is over; there's dust everywhere. No matter how fast we clean up, it forms another layer before we've put away our dusters. Vic doesn't mind getting his hands dirty, either, but he takes ages to clean just one painting or a single shelf.

In the office, the laptop has gone to sleep. It bursts into life with a stroke of my finger, which even after several weeks still gives me a thrill akin to a small child performing a simple magic trick. My latest project is Christmas cards for specific people. I know it's spring, but you must plan. I must contact the estates of the other artists whose work I want to use, and it gets complicated. But what a lot I'm learning about permissions and such like. I could become the gallery's legal expert. And it stops me getting distracted. No, it doesn't. My date with Theo tonight won't settle into the recesses of my mind while I work.

I sit and stare at the screen, at the gorgeous reds and greens of the detail I'd taken from Betty and Harold's background. The colours are rich, reflecting their wealth, but taken out of context, they brim with life and festivity. I'm constantly amazed how paintings offer so much to those willing to look beyond the obvious. Dad's mastery impresses me more every day.

I still haven't said my piece to Theo, despite my determination, and Kim didn't ask at my last session, as we concentrated on Mother. It was as challenging as I predicted, so I'm not yet convinced they'll make a difference, but Kim wants me to stick with it. She says resolving mother/daughter issues takes time. Our initial session was an eternity of pain, but she's an expert, so I'll persevere. For now.

The outfit I bought for tonight hangs – ironed, Jenny was hysterical – on my wardrobe door. If I wear something I feel good in, I'll be more confident when I speak. Right? It's daft, allowing myself to get churned up, given what I'll say is so positive, but it's true. Jenny has lost patience with me, too. Has threatened to "let something slip" when she sees Theo. So, tonight's the night.

Vic pops his head round the door.

'Sia, the fitters are here. Can you spare a minute?'

We spend a while poring over the designs, double checking everything before they start. Fireworks whiz in my stomach. I can picture the outcome and can't wait to see it. Nina will think she's died and gone to baking heaven. If she joins us.

I'll put myself on the roster in the café; it'll give me the chance to chat to visitors about the paintings, as I said to Vic. He likes the idea of intimate dialogue with visitors, reckoning other galleries have missed a trick. We've been doing recces of nearby galleries and museums and, so far, he's right.

By half-past three, I've had enough of not getting anywhere. The inspiration refuses to come while my head is filled with Theo. Besides, the fitters are making such a row I can't concentrate. I switch everything off in the office and seek Vic. He's still with the fitters, the diagrams in his hands.

'Is there a problem?'

'No, no. Thought I'd help.'

The fitters continue working, moving around Vic and talking

in whispers.

'Do they need your help?'

Vic pulls a face. 'Probably not, but they haven't told me to get lost. Have you, gentlemen?'

The fitters laugh awkwardly without pausing in their work.

'I'm going. Important night.'

He springs over and takes me in a bear hug. 'Yes, of course. New dress and everything. Don't lose your nerve, my dear. I need you fully involved here, and ready for anything, not half somewhere else daydreaming of Theo.'

I pull away sharply. 'Haven't I been pulling my weight?' His words cut into me; he's never criticised me.

'Dear girl, of course you have. But the Theo situation has occupied you enormously, distracting you more each passing day when you've failed to say your bit. For everyone's sake, you must do it tonight.'

'You're right. Sorry. I don't know why I've put it off.' But I do. I'm afraid Theo will say it's the end. Despite not wanting to become a school wife, the idea of us parting rips me to shreds.

'Off you go. Make yourself so beguiling he'll agree to anything. You can do it.'

He kisses my cheek.

'Thanks, Vic. See you on Monday.'

*　*　*

Theo waits for me by the bandstand. Was it too corny to ask to meet here, too reminiscent of a syrupy chick flick? Too late. He's here, I'm here. There's no going back. My guts do a jig. Calm, Sia. Calm. See people enjoying the evening sunshine, lounging on the grass, laughing, kissing and, well, doing what we should be doing.

He is so handsome, he could be the hero in a soppy movie. The voice over in my head tells me how rapidly my heart beats, how weak my knees have become. For heaven's sake. I can't stop smiling at the sight of him.

'You look fabulous. New dress?'

'Thank you. Yes. The gallery is knee-deep in dust, so I treated myself in an attempt to expunge the constant sensation of grubbiness.'

'What had you in mind? I hope you didn't want to eat. Had supper at school.'

I couldn't eat a thing. My stomach has knotted as tight as a clenched fist.

'A stroll and then a drink?'

'Perfect. And I won't be too late back.'

We link arms and head towards the path round the lake. He tells me how his week is going, and I pretend to listen. I take in most of what he says but wouldn't pass the exam. I tell him about the gallery.

Dappled through the willows on the bank, the lake glimmers in soft sunshine. The park is Deerdale's jewel, a popular place for all kinds of people, from young mums with their children, to pensioners. I've always loved it.

We stroll past an empty bench. I stop. Theo looks quizzical.

'Why don't we sit here? Watch the world go by?'

He squints at me. 'Okay.'

The bench is cool through the cloth of my dress. I shiver.

'Theo, I need to talk to you.'

'Right. Should I worry?'

'No, but please allow me to explain what's on my mind before you respond. If you interrupt and I reply to a question, I may forget something important.'

'Golly. Should we have brought a blanket and a bar of Kendal Mint Cake?'

We laugh, and my nerves unstretch, just a little.

'No. It won't take long.'

'You have my full attention.' He holds my gaze, his lovely eyes soft and reassuring.

'I thi…' No. Be strong. Be assertive. 'It's time we decided if we are a couple or not. I don't want to continue avoiding the problem between us.'

His eyes widen, his mouth forms an O, but he says nothing.

'I want us to be together, to grow old together. Please, speak again to the headmaster, governors, or whoever - tell them they must accept our relationship, value it, recognise its importance, as it is. I've been pig-headed about the tied cottages, not coming to see them. I'm sorry. I'll do that, consider coming to live at school. Can't promise I'll live there, but I want to consider it. Because I love you and I want you in my life.'

I take a deep breath and Theo raises an eyebrow. But I haven't finished, so I shake my head.

'I feel no different regarding marriage and children, but I haven't been honest with you, given you the reasons for my antipathy.'

He takes my hands in his, pulls me closer. Still doesn't speak.

It was so much easier talking to the empty chair. It didn't have warm hands, nor a frown of concern, nor the power to break my heart.

'I'm afraid. If we were to have a child, I'm afraid it would-'

'Be like your mother.'

I cover my face with my hands. He gathers me into his arms and holds me. I've never felt closer to him, never credited him with the understanding he's so simply demonstrated. If he decides this is the end, I shall be bereft.

He tucks his hand under my chin and pulls my face towards his. He kisses me with tenderness.

CHAPTER THIRTY-ONE

THREE DAYS LATER

Isn't it amazing how happiness can transform someone? I hadn't considered how happy or otherwise I was until Theo and I lay, post-sex, in my bed and caught myself grinning at the ceiling. I've been grinning ever since.

Today, I smile at everything, getting on Vic's nerves. Especially now we're into the third day. But it's wonderful. Even the prospect of this afternoon's hospital visit with Marian fails to dim my delight.

In the meantime, we've a clutch of applications to read, including Nina's. As I predicted, her form is tatty, verging on disgraceful. Despite the creases, she's written a cracking application and I want to offer her the job without an interview.

'We will conduct interviews. If we end up appointing Nina – and I liked her, too – she won't take the position seriously if she gets it on the nod. She must see she's got opposition.'

'Fair enough. How about, when we invite candidates for an interview, we ask them to bring a sample of their baking? We could reimburse them, and negate any charge of bribery, if we choose Nina?'

Vic cackles, leans back on his chair with his hands behind his head.

'You are incorrigible! Superb idea. Let's do it. Sustenance during the interviews, and a café manager at the end. Brilliant.'

We short list four people and I ring them during the afternoon.

They sound delighted to be asked to bring a sample cake. I'm looking forward to meeting them so much and keeping my fingers crossed Nina interviews well.

At one forty-five, I set off for The Dog and Duck to collect Marian. It's been a strange time for her, waiting for the results. She stands in the beer garden, her shoulders round as if anxiety presses heavily upon them. Understandable, I guess. We hug and then set off for the appointment.

'You're still love's young dream? On cloud five hundred and something, number nine way behind you?'

'Theo's arranged an interview with the head and the chair of governors for next week - the soonest they could fit him into their hectic schedules. Bloody people. I think they enjoy keeping others waiting to show how powerful they are.'

'Don't be too hasty, dear. They have lots of responsibilities.'

'I know, I know. I must rein in my impulsive behaviour if they ask to meet me – which Theo says is likely; they'll treat me as though I were his wife.'

'That doesn't bother you, does it?'

'No. Only I think it's a cheek they vet the spouses of their staff.'

'If you're to live in a school cottage, young boys in the vicinity, I imagine they must be careful. Won't you need one of those CBR thingies?'

'The criminal record check? Hm. Possibly. I'll ask Theo.'

We chat about all sorts of stuff until we reach the hospital when Marian goes quiet. She is pensive as I drive up the multi-storey car park, searching for a space. I find one on the third floor. The walk from the car park to the hospital is pretty since they landscaped the grounds using a grant from the EU. In the sunshine, they're dazzling with flowers of various colours. Patients and their visitors sit on the benches provided. Reminds me of the park.

The Coroner Liaison Officer asked Marian to meet him here rather than at the Coroner's Office. We don't know why. In reception,

I ask for directions to the room number on Marian's letter. The receptionist scans the letter and gives us a sympathetic smile.

'I'll get a porter to show you. Easier than trying to follow my directions.' She makes a quick phone call, and a porter arrives within minutes. I thank the receptionist, and we follow the porter through a labyrinth of corridors. He takes us away from the main part of the building to the back offices, where I suppose they do the admin.

'This one.' The porter jerks his thumb towards a door with our number, and he abandons us.

We loiter by the door as there's nowhere to sit. I look at my mobile. Two twenty-eight. Opposite the doors, windows run the length of the corridor, revealing a scrubby square. In the centre, ringed by unkempt lawns and barren flowerbeds, a bench sits next to an empty bird feeder.

'Mrs Isaac l'Ussier?'

'Yes, that's me.'

A kind faced man stands back and gestures an invitation to enter.

'This is my niece, Sia l'Ussier.'

He leans across the desk to shake my hand. 'Loved the exhibition of your father's work. His subjects brim with life.'

If he's being ironic, given why we're here, I can't tell. 'I love them, too. I'm very proud of my dad.'

Marian and I sit, both of us on the edges of our chairs. She rests her handbag on her knee and clutches it with both hands. The liaison officer opens a manila folder on the desk.

'I expect you want me to explain why I am conducting your appointment, rather than the doctor. The coroner instructed me, because we must hold an inquest into Mr. l'Ussier's death.'

Marian gasps, clutches her handbag tighter. Her face is ghostly.

'Why?' I ask because she looks unable to speak.

'Let me interpret the results; clarify matters for you.'

The next half hour passes in a fug of data, his idea of "clarify" different from mine. I must say something; Marian is immobile, her eyes glazed, but the liaison officer speaks before I question him.

'Initially, Mr l'Ussier appeared to have died from alcohol poisoning but, when toxicology reports came back, it became apparent things weren't so straightforward. We found deadly levels of the drug Xanax. Levels which indicate Mr l'Ussier either died by suicide, or we must suspect foul play.'

The words linger in the air like invisible, deathly butterflies. In the silence, an itch in my brain eludes my efforts to define it; too far away to scratch, it remains a profound irritation.

'What happens now?'

'Miss l'Ussier, the matter becomes a police investigation. I can issue a Coroner's Certificate of Death. This will assist the administration of Mr. l'Ussier's estate. Odd organisations won't accept it, so they may delay completion until after the inquest, when you can finally register the death.'

'Does that mean we can't hold a funeral?'

'No.' He leafs through the folder. 'The coroner is satisfied there is no requirement for further investigations. We can release the body to a funeral director of your choice.'

'When will the inquest be?'

'It will be opened and then adjourned until the police complete their investigations. Should the police investigation result in a prosecution, the inquest will be closed.'

I take Marian's hand, which trembles in my grasp. Her haunted expression tells me the depth of her shock. I am numb.

'Do we need to contact you about the funeral directors we choose?'

'No. Any decent funeral director will be au fait with the drill in these circumstances. It's customary for them to make the arrangements on the family's behalf. They collect the deceased from hospital and keep them at their premises until the funeral takes place. Do you have a company in mind?'

'Marian?'

'No.'

'I have an information leaflet here which lists Deerdale and the surrounding area's reputable funeral directors. Also, you might find this useful.' He slides across the desk a thick booklet: Guide to Coroner Services.

'Thank you.'

'I am sorry there is no way of avoiding your distress, in the circumstances, I'm afraid. No way of preparing loved ones for the shock. But we endeavour to be approachable, open; if you've any questions, get in touch. Our numbers are on the reverse of the guide.'

'Will the police want to interview us?'

'Most definitely. Everyone involved. They must be thorough.'

'If it goes to court, will I have to take the stand?' Marian's voice, breaking through our discussion, startles me. I'd almost forgotten she was there.

'I can't answer your question. That's for the police to decide.' He stands, hands me a bundle of other leaflets. 'Take these. They've all the information available. I'm sorry for your loss. Please accept my condolences.'

We both shake hands with Mr Jefferson, whose name I've only just spotted on a discreet lapel badge, and say goodbye. Arm in arm, we retrace our steps through the maze of corridors and arrive at the main entrance foyer where life continues as normal. In the coffee shop, there's a strange mix: out-patients slouching on uncomfortable looking chairs next to tired medics. The charity shop does a roaring trade in assorted knitted objects.

I guide Marian to a bench in the hospital garden. To my surprise, she takes out a packet of cigarettes from her handbag, offers me one and when I pass, lights up. She smokes in silence for a while.

'I thought it was odd.'

'What?'

'Isaac dying the way he did, like he wasn't able to take his drink.'

Poor Marian: the family was aware he couldn't hold his drink, having witnessed his descent into belligerence so often. How he fooled her is a mystery.

'Thought it might be grief, making my mind come up with peculiar ideas. But I've been convinced from the moment I discovered Isaac - something's amiss.'

'Are you saying you think someone killed him? Or do you think he took his own life?'

'We might have money worries, but he loved life, did Isaac. Where there's life, there's hope – a favourite phrase of Isaac's. We've hung a plaque in the lounge bar. His idea.'

The Butterworths' portrait, like an old-fashioned photograph bathed in the red light of a dark room, develops in my mind. I'm convinced there's a connection between the paintings and the deaths, a connection between the deaths themselves. The itch grows, more than the hint of a hunch. Suspicion mutates into certainty. I can't confide in Marian; I need to take her home so I can return to the gallery.

'Shall we make tracks?'

'Yes. Vic will want you back, won't he? He's kind, allowing you time off to support me. I do appreciate it.'

'He knows the importance of having someone by your side.' His comments about Susan whisper through my head. Poor Vic, so concerned other people don't experience the solitude he faces each day since she died. 'Let's go.'

Marian waves as I drive away from the pub. Should I have told her about Jade's change of heart about the DNA test? Might've cheered her up a bit. One person I can tell, who'll be as thrilled as me; at the junction, instead of taking the right turn towards the city centre, I go left and head for Sandro's studio.

CHAPTER THIRTY-TWO

FOUR DAYS LATER

Why can't the media leave families to grieve in peace? 'Tragic brothers' indeed. I'll give them tragic. How do these people discover the details of our lives? I shake the paper, so the double page lies flat on the desk. Vic's voice, gentle but firm as he speaks on the phone, soothes me as I read the article again. We're plagued with heartbreak, according to this journo, whose florid language makes me want to vomit, and we flounder in our grief. Oh. Interesting. This reporter isn't stupid. Who else will read this and link her ideas? She may assume it's background to the story, but she could've been a third person sitting at the table with Daniel and me at the pub.

Vic drops the handset on to the base. 'Sia, you must have read that a hundred times.' He leans over and scoops the paper before I can stop him. 'Don't torture yourself. When are you going to Marian's?'

'Soon. Might as well go now; no point in hanging round here.'

'No. You go. You'll be more use there and doubtless feel better.'

'And you?'

'It doesn't take two of us when we're closed. I'll potter around for an hour or two. Toddle home early, once the fitters down tools.'

'All right. Marian will appreciate the company before the police arrive. And I know for a fact she has cake.'

'Oh?'

'Nina made her one, after she saw Uncle Isaac's death reported on the telly.'

'Lovely girl.'

'Isn't she? Perfect for us.'

'Sia.' Vic frowns at me over his spectacles. 'I hope she isn't trying to wriggle into our good books by corrupting us with cake?'

'Course not. It was a kind gesture, no underhand motive. She's not to know I'm off to Marian's to get my teeth into it, is she?'

'She'd be on a safe bet if she suspected. You're incorrigible. Said it before and-'

'You'll say it again. No doubt.'

'Indeed.'

'I'm taking the laptop; Marian needs to choose a coffin.'

My distaste must show; Vic snortles with amusement. 'As must we all, eventually. Don't let her spend a fortune. Just a waste of money better put towards a holiday.'

'Good tip. Thanks. I'll make sure she chooses the cheapest. So, is it okay, my not hanging around?'

'Of course.'

I switch it off, slip it into its bag, and zip up. 'I'll be off then.'

The drive to Marian's I endure in silence, as silent as it's possible in a jalopy like mine. I toy with trying to drown the noises in my head with Joni or the radio, but I'm not convinced they'd be overwhelmed. More likely, I'd go mad with distraction.

Mother. I'm glad she's painting but, my God, she's hard going. Kim says I have a long way to go before I'm comfortable with my difficult relationship with her. I appreciate how Kim's helped me with my grief for Dad, but Mother? Maybe it'd be better for everyone if I cut her from my life. Then I'd not have this certainty. And what use is it if I can't prove anything? People disappearing from paintings is hardly solid evidence. Can just imagine the gorgon's face when I tell that to DI Smith. 'I see, Ms l'Ussier. You're telling us you believe your mother is a murderer because something supernatural has occurred with these paintings?' Sneer, sneer. Sandro doubts me, too. Only Vic and Kim. And she told me to take my suspicions to the police. Think it through, Sia. If they used gut feelings as evidence, Lord alone knows how many innocent people would be behind bars. It's not enough.

The man in the car next to me grins and nods at the light. Cripes. They're green. He pulls away, and I swear I can see his eyes laughing at me in his rear-view mirror as I put the car in gear and edge forwards. Horns honk and I stifle the urge to stick up two fingers. I must concentrate on the road. Don't want to get myself killed. I have death on the brain. And no wonder.

At Marian's, I park, grab the laptop and my bag, and head round the back as usual. Later, DI Smith will be in attendance, with the gorgon. I've warned Marian. We mustn't get the giggles.

She's sitting at the kitchen table, which seems to be her habit when she's expecting me. It's possible she spends her waking hours sitting there, but I hope not. Her demeanour, her posture, and the liveliness in her eyes reassure me. And my news is bound to interest her, too. I plonk the laptop on the table and unbag it, press the start button.

'Guess what? I meant to tell you the other day and forgot - Jade's requested Daniel's DNA. Soon, I'll have proof, one way or the other.'

She springs from her chair and enfolds me in her arms. I sink into her embrace, still overcome by the notion of discovering the truth, even though I've discussed it and thought about it so much since Jade sent me the text. But today isn't about me. I'm here to support Marian. I pull away from her.

'Right. You're up for our task today?'

She nods. We sit side by side at the table and I click the Chrome button.

'There're websites for caskets?' Her face contorts in a grimace.

'Websites for everything. You name it.'

'Dildos.'

'Marian! That's how most people get them, I suppose. Better than popping into your local sex supermarket, eh? Or that one on the A1.'

She snickers. 'I've seen that one. Do people really stop there, break their journeys to buy exotic items?'

'It's still open, so I guess.'

'We must go one day. For a giggle.'

'You're on. Now, here we are.' I slide the laptop over so she can see the screen. 'Might as well start at the top.'

I click open the first website: Amazon. I can't help myself; laughter wells up. Marian shakes beside me, her hand over her mouth.

'I think I'll buy another Carpenters CD, a book, and a casket. Like you do.'

'I know.' My voice wobbles. 'Would you credit it? Amazon?'

Our laughter fills the kitchen. The screen blurs through my tears. How many times have I cried at this laptop? I wipe my eyes with a tissue.

'Come on, let's be sensible.'

'Yes. Quite right.' She blinks several times, pulls her lips in between her teeth, the effort of controlling herself obvious in the whiteness of her skin. We stare at the screen.

She says in a hushed whisper, 'It reminds me of the Argos catalogue.'

'Marian, don't.' Snort.

'Which would he find most comfortable? Wicker? He'd look like Moses.'

'I went to a funeral with a wicker coffin once.' Watering eyes. Not tears.

'And?'

'The pallbearers couldn't stop it sagging in the middle.'

Splutter. 'Oh, no. Did you get the giggles?'

I bite my lip. 'Disgraced myself.'

I cannot hold it in, and she joins me. We struggle to regain control.

'This must be our reaction to grief.' I wipe my eyes with the back of my hand. 'Apparently, there're various kinds. In the old days, they thought it another form of hysteria.'

And even that's hilarious. We laugh so much a passer-by peeping through the window would assume hysteria was exactly our problem.

It takes a firm push of our will power, but we settle and evaluate the selection before us. Marian doesn't care for any of them, so we look at two other sites before she sees one she likes.

'Don't funeral directors organise the casket?'

'They do, but we agreed we'd research styles and prices before we go, remember?'

'We'd not have enjoyed it so much at the undertakers, eh?'

'Nowhere near. Who'd have thought it?'

I write a memo on my mobile, close the webpage from which we chose a suitable casket and shut the laptop. On the counter by the kettle, I flick the switch, sits the magnificent Victoria sponge Nina made for us. It's not her interview offering, but I don't see how we can employ anyone but her. Yet, Vic's holding out for the interviews. One candidate pulled out. I'm sure it was after the press got hold of Isaac's news.

Marian wanders off to check the lounge. She cleaned yesterday but gave it a quick going over this morning, she tells me. If she polishes it anymore, the space station will pick up the glare. It's where she'll be interviewed by the police, so she wants it spotless. Will they take any notice? Doubt it.

I haven't told her about the paintings yet, but I will; I'm waiting until she's more settled. She has a penchant for the supernatural, reads her horoscopes and such so she won't dismiss it out of hand. No. More likely she'll take it as gospel, start looking for hidden meanings. I suppose she could be a help, be another perspective on things? It's possible.

'Marian, tea's up.'

I pour two mugs and rummage in the drawer for the cake knife. It's a lethal thing with, I shudder, an ivory handle. They've used it for weddings, beribboned and prettified. I've seen the photos.

'Cake?'

'Yes, please. Make it a doorstep.'

The knife slides through the cake with the ease of a surgeon's lancet through supple skin, as smooth as a zip. Marian's slice topples on to her plate with a sigh. I pass it to her and cut myself a smaller wedge. At the table, we savour the wonders of Nina's cake in silence. She's a fast learner, Marian, and never speaks before I do when we eat. It's another reason I've come to love her.

'When will the force be with us?'

She looks at the clock on the cooker as if it will tell her. 'Twoish? If I remember right.'

'Is the lounge ready for them? No specks of dust lurking under the tables?'

'It'll do.'

'Any idea what they'll ask?'

She shrugs. 'Last movements. If he had any quarrels with anyone. Reasons he might have been suicidal.' She breaks off a piece of the cake and stuffs it in her mouth, licks her lips. She speaks with her mouth full. 'There weren't any reasons. I was more likely than him to kill myself.'

'You? Were you unhappy?'

'Sometimes. I got lonely. Room full of visitors, but your uncle out at a family do.'

'I'm sorry, Marian.'

'Not your fault. It's not I wasn't fit to be with you; he preferred to leave me in charge, insisted I organised pub matters better than him.'

'Really?'

'Mm. He liked the idea of a pub more than the reality. I've

always loved it, getting stuck in. I shall be glad to get this business behind me and re-open.'

This is startling news. Only recently, I worried she'd never recover and here she is, claiming she wants to get going again, without Uncle Isaac.

'Will you be able to, after you shut the place? Won't it be hard to get the staff back, and the regulars?'

She tips her plate and the crumbs cascade into her open mouth.

'Love a challenge, and it'll keep me busy. Atmosphere'll be different without Isaac, but I refuse to wallow.'

'You're a tough one. I hope you succeed. Now we've got the coroner's certificate, things will move, won't they?'

'Not tough; practical. That's how I see it.'

I stack the plates in the dishwasher, balance the mugs on its top shelf, and return the cake to the tin Nina brought. I rinse the knife under the tap, making sure I don't wet the handle. Marian's instructions.

* * *

DI Smith and the gorgon arrive on time. Marian and I exchange smirks as she lets them in and takes them to the lounge bar. Both ask for tonic water when she offers them a drink.

'I'll get them, Marian. What do you want?'

'I'll wait. Have a gin after they've gone.' She turns a mischievous eye on DI Smith. 'Don't suppose it's the done thing to imbibe while being interviewed.'

DI Smith smiles but doesn't reply. The gorgon, of course, her face remains stony.

We make ourselves comfortable by the open windows. A warm breeze flutters the curtains. The gorgon takes out her notebook and pen.

'Do you mind if my niece stays with us?'

'No. We'll be asking her questions, too.' He looks at me. 'Just don't answer for your aunt. Don't be offended. You'd be surprised the number of times a "friend" tries to dominate an interview.'

'Okay. Got it.'

'Ready PC Broden?'

She nods. Her hair gleams like spun gold in the sunlight. Why is she such a monstrous woman? A woman of her loveliness should be sweet, sing in tune with the birds, and cause flowers to bloom spontaneously.

'Mrs l'Ussier, may I call you Marian? Thank you. Were the financial problems your husband suffered connected to the pub?'

He's direct; no soft questions to warm her up.

'Many of them. We struggle to make the pub profitable, not unlike most publicans these days. Isaac's ideas for getting visitors in were, shall we say, a little unwise.'

'Did you manage the books together?'

'Officially, Isaac did the books, but I check them, so I can tell you precisely how the finances are.'

'Did you try to rein in his unwise ideas?'

'As much as possible.' She has an enigmatic expression, like she's not saying all she might. What is she hiding?

'But the losses continued?'

'The auditors got aggressive with him.'

'Oh? How did he react to that?'

'He asked Bill Sharp for an advance on his inheritance from Frank.'

So, it was true.

'Did he get it?'

'No.'

'Was your husband angry?'

'Yes, he and Bill had words on a couple of occasions, so he said.'

'What did he say, exactly?'

'To Bill? No idea. Isaac told me he'd asked him to allocate his share of the inheritance when the rest of the family got theirs. He thought the large payment to them organised by Bill undeserved; a smaller one to everyone, including Detta, would've been fairer. I agree.' She looks at me. 'Nothing personal, Sia.'

'I understand.'

DI Smith looks at me, too. 'Were you present when Mr. l'Ussier and Bill Sharp argued?'

'Once, yes. We were at Mother's for dinner. Bill had requested a meeting to outline progress with Dad's estate.'

'Can you remember what was said?'

'Uncle Isaac was angry, and drunk. He claimed to be a closer blood relative than Mother, Sandro, or me.'

'Is that it?'

'No. When Bill said how much we'd get as an interim sum, Marian's right, he said they should split it five ways, not three.'

'How did Mr Sharp respond?'

'He didn't respond. He waited for Uncle Isaac to stop shouting, and just continued. They argued later, but I was with Detta in the sitting room, so I couldn't hear their words.'

'Marian, can I ask you about Mr l'Ussier's drinking habits? Was he a drunk?'

'You may say that. He drank, every day, but it never impeded his judgement.'

'Yet you said he made unwise financial decisions concerning the running of the pub?'

She looks away from the inspector, her gaze focused on something outside, in the distance. 'Yes.'

'And what of his drug habit?'

Her focus snaps back to DI Smith. 'He did not have a drug habit.'

'How do you explain the traces – more than traces – found by the post-mortem?'

'I can't. But Isaac would not have taken enough to kill himself on purpose. He was not that kind of man.'

'Did he ever take illegal substances for pleasure?'

She fidgets in her chair, her fingers entwined, her knuckles taut. 'Cannabis, occasionally. Someone in the village deals, and he sometimes comes into the pub – not to deal; we made it very clear that was unacceptable. But Isaac did indulge, very occasionally.'

We hardly know other people, do we? I've always thought of Uncle Isaac and Marian as staid, dull and not my kind. My time with Marian has shown how wrong I've been, and now I hear Uncle Isaac used to do drugs. She'll be saying next that they're part of a weird sexual cult that meets monthly at the pub for fun and excitement. If I rummage through her wardrobes, will I discover a host of S & M gear hidden behind the twin sets? I zone into the interview once more to find they've moved on.

'Why weren't you at any of the family gatherings?'

She explains, telling him what she'd told me in such a way I'm sure she's practised. Has she got the script perfect in her head because it's what she tells herself? DI Smith nods as he listens, encouraging her to continue.

'Of course, I felt resentful and excluded. Who wouldn't? But I understood he wanted the pub in safe hands.' She chuckles sadly. 'He trusted no one but me.'

'Have you had many dealings with Heather l'Ussier?'

With Mother? Why ask her about Mother? My heart is a clenched fist, flexing its knuckles in my chest. What will Marian say?

She takes a deep breath and exhales loudly. 'Not really. She came to our wedding. The odd Christmas do here. Nothing else.'

The inspector glances at me and continues to question Marian. 'What do you make of her?'

This is an odd question and Marian doesn't answer straight away. How might I answer? How long would it take?

'She's an eccentric.'

That's one way of putting it.

'We've nothing in common, as women. She's far too exotic for the likes of me.'

Yes, she's right there. What does Mother call Marian? Uncle Isaac's munchkin? Marian the munchkin. Bit cruel: Marian's a pretty woman, with far more to her than Mother gives credit for.

'So, how did you react when you learnt her husband's share in the pub goes to Heather l'Ussier?'

For the first time, Marian looks rattled. She turns her gaze to me in question, as if she expects me to have known. And the truth dawns; I knew. Bill told Sandro and me the night of the dinner. I had forgotten. Terrible guilt passes through me; she'll imagine I've betrayed her.

'You knew this?'

'Marian, I forgot. Bill said that night. I had completely forgotten. I'm so sorry.'

She addresses DI Smith. 'It makes life difficult. But not impossible if she doesn't interfere.' She takes a deep breath. '*I* run the pub.'

'She won't – she hates pubs. Remember when she brought Uncle Isaac home from the memorial? You wanted to put him to bed, but she'd hear none of it; said she couldn't possibly work behind the bar.'

'Was that the night he passed away?'

'Yes. It was uncharacteristically good of Heather to bring him home, although she said she was glad to get away. She'd had enough of the reminiscing and fawning over Frank's memory.'

'That's what she told me when she left with him. She looked thoroughly fed up.'

'Why was he so drunk, if he can hold his drink? How close was he to his brother?'

'Can I answer this one, Marian?'

She doesn't reply but shrugs her shoulders like a wounded teenager. I'll have to grovel when the police have gone. DI Smith arches an eyebrow, tilts his head towards me in what I assume is an invitation to continue.

'He wasn't that close, but he always supported Dad – came

to his exhibitions and bought one or two of his paintings in the early days. Dad said he looked up to Uncle Isaac, as his big brother, but worried because he never felt running a pub was the ideal occupation for him.' He never told me, not a hint, Uncle Isaac was a drunk; realised myself over the years.

'At the memorial, he had another argument with Bill about the inheritance, how long it's been since Dad died, saying he should've sorted it. I only caught the tail-end, but he was shouting at Bill. Mother's intervention was the only thing that stopped it becoming nasty.'

'How did she resolve matters?'

'She grabbed hold of him and took him back inside the hall. I worried she'd struggle, but when I checked, everything seemed fine. They'd gone out a side door, and were sitting, talking. Well, Mother was talking; Uncle Isaac was listening. He had a glass in his hand, and he dropped it when she hauled him to his feet.'

'And then she took him home?'

'Yes.'

'What time was this?'

'Towards the end of the do, so late afternoon – fourish? Marian, what time did they arrive? It's only half an hour or so from here, isn't it?'

'Can't remember the exact time, but the lounge was full of people having pre-dinner drinks. We'd a full house for food that night, another reason I stayed home. So, I don't know – half five? Six? I might be wrong.'

Prickles of something unpleasant work their way over my skin. An hour and a half? Two hours? But Uncle Isaac was wasted, which could have made him difficult; not that he behaved difficult when they left. Maybe he threw up in her car. That would delay them. Mother wouldn't have been able to continue without clearing it up. Or perhaps he passed out, and she stopped to waken him. Yes, that sounds more likely.

DI Smith checks his watch. 'We need to be elsewhere. We'll finish this off another time, if you don't mind. Thank you for the drink.'

Marian is on her feet like a whippet. 'You're welcome. I hope we've been helpful?'

The gorgon shakes her head, a grim smile on her lips. DI Smith takes his car keys from his pocket.

'Yes, it's a start. Thank you. We can find our own way out. Good afternoon.'

Marian and I watch them leave, cross the beer garden and get into their car. They don't drive off but sit talking. It looks as though the gorgon is reading her notes to him. After a few minutes, he switches on the ignition, and the car pulls away.

'Marian, I am sorry I didn't tell you Mother inherited Dad's stake in the pub. Genuinely, I had forgotten.'

She walks to the bar, slips behind it and pours herself a double gin. 'Do you want one?'

'Yes, please. You believe me, don't you? Why would I keep it from you deliberately?'

I join her at the bar, sit on a bar stool and take the glass. She pours half a bottle of tonic water into her own glass and passes me the bottle.

'I believe you, Sia. It shocked me, that's all, and it put me off my stride when he asked.'

But she's not looking at me, rather staring into space like she's got other, more important worries. We finish our drinks in silence, and she pours us another. It's my favourite gin, made locally with the flavours of heather and honey. Just the aroma can make my mouth water. Perhaps she believes me. We're neither of us in a normal place in our lives. I should expect unusual reactions to events, shouldn't I?

'Do you want me to go?'

'Go? Go where?'

'Back to the flat.'

'Not yet. Unless you want to. I understand I must be sorry company, and Jenny's home, isn't she? I expect she'd be pleased to have you home.'

'You're not sorry company. I'm glad we've got to know each other. Wish it had happened sooner.'

'Bless you, Sia. I'm glad, too. Shall we put the finishing touches on funeral arrangements? Or are we too squiffy?'

We burst into sozzled laughter.

'Far too squiffy. Let's watch something daft on telly instead.'

'In the daylight? In the afternoon?'

'Why not?'

'No idea.'

And we snort into our glasses, unable to stop our riotous cackling. We stumble our way to her private sitting room, delve through her DVD collection and choose 'Pretty Woman'. Several failed attempts to slide the disc into the slot intensify our laughter.

'Wait,' she says. 'We need more gin. Hold on.'

She totters out, returning with an unopened bottle in her hand, and several bottles of tonic clanking in a bag. She looks as though she's just been on a shop-lifting spree at the supermarket which makes me laugh again.

I fetch two tumblers from her glass-fronted cabinet, plonk them on to the low table, and Marian pours us huge measures of gin. She selects a tonic – elderflower – and shares it between us. We clink our glasses together and settle to watch the film.

CHAPTER THIRTY-THREE

THREE DAYS LATER

The following Sunday, the papers strewn over the furniture, Mother paces the room a colour supplement tight in her fist. She waves it at me.

'Marian has no claim on any of Frank's money. She's a grubby, blood-sucking bitch who'll drain us dry if she can. I will not allow it.'

'There's nothing you can do to prevent it. Dad left the money to Isaac, and he left everything to Marian. You must come to terms with it, Mother.'

She throws the magazine on to the floor and stamps on it. 'I will not allow it!'

'Mother, please stop shrieking and calm yourself. Having a tantrum won't alter a thing.'

'I'll shriek as much as I want, Artemisia. This is my home and I'll do as I please in it. How are you going to help stop this miscarriage of justice?'

'I can't go against the law. You know this. And I wouldn't if I could. Marian deserves the money – it will help her back on her feet and make the pub a success.'

'Deserves? She deserves? More than I? It's where your loyalties lie. How could you? How could you betray me so? I am your mother.'

I wince at her sudden maternalism and hold back from saying the scathing remarks burning in my brain. She stomps across the room, her arms flailing, the sleeves of her kaftan like a giant kite.

Terrifying as she is, her rages are impressive, her extravagance mesmerising. At the open French window, she makes a dramatic turn and gives me the full force of her green eyes.

'I own part of that god-forsaken pub so I can make it difficult for that deserving woman.' She drags her sneer from the depths of her, the words as toxic as a viper's bite. 'She'll regret ever taking the family name.'

'Why do such a thing? The pub's success can only benefit you as a shareholder?'

'It's not the money. I can do without it.'

There's no reasoning with her, and if I mention her meds, she'll only get worse. Withdrawal is the wisest action now. Besides, should I stay longer, I may make a slip and mention my suspicions about her. God knows, it's nearly happened a couple of times. I grab my handbag from the settee and stride towards the door.

'I have to go, Mother. When I next come, I hope you're calmer. Talk to Bill. He'll clarify everything. If there's any way to prevent Marian inheriting, he's your man with the knowhow.' I don't have a jot of guilt – I am certain there's no way to stop Marian getting Isaac's money.

'Don't bother. I don't want a quisling passing through my front door.'

'That's rich, coming from you.'

She pulls herself up to her haughtiest. 'And what do you mean by that?'

'You call me a quisling, yet it's you who betrays.'

Blotches of pink blossom on her cheeks.

'Who have I in any way betrayed?'

'When were you going to tell me Daniel Rose was my father?'

I could laugh. Her eyes open so wide I fear they may tumble on to her beautiful cheek bones. She slinks on to the nearest settee, staring at me like I'm the monster here. Her heat and anger are spent. I grip the handle of my bag tight to stop my trembling from showing and stare right back.

'How did you find out?'

I take Daniel's photo from my bag, pass it to her, and step away. She turns it over, puzzlement in her expression. She thinks it's me. Proof enough.

'Where did you get this?'

'Whose photo is it, Mother?'

'Yours. Where did you get it?'

'It isn't me. It's Daniel.'

'But-'

'You annotated each of the photos you sent him.'

She turns the photo to double check, shakes her head like she's trying to understand why she's not written anything. I'm not going to help. I have copies of Daniel's and my DNA reports tucked in my bag as a back-up, should she dare to deny it.

'You'd better sit down. It's a long story.' She offers me the photo. I snatch it from her and stuff it into my pocket.

I teeter on the edge of the opposite settee, my bag clutched on my knees. She studies her hands, stroking her ring finger between the thumb and index finger of her right hand.

'Your father and I – Frank - Daniel and Julia, we went everywhere together, holidays, evenings out, weekends away.'

The room hushes to listen, my heartbeat quietly thudding a descant to Mother's voice.

'One time we spent a week in France. It was hot, the atmosphere was heady but relaxed. We'd painted, well, dabbled, all day in the sunshine, drinking absinthe and smoking.'

She searches my face, her emerald eyes pleading for a response.

I force myself to be still, not even raise an eyebrow, but one word from her description shrieks in my head. I try, with only partial success, to silence it with a smothering blanket of fog. There's a word cloud boiling behind my eyes, one word - like a lightning bolt-flashing from the murk.

She twists her rings round her finger.

'By evening, we were tired and drunk. We'd taken cocaine. Seemed such a harmless thing to do. No-one else was there. We had the villa. It was private. We played cards or tried to. There was laughter, so much laughter. Daniel and I partnered, but we kept helplessly laughing.'

My blood sprints through my veins. We're approaching the moment. My breath comes in shallow puffs and my head is floaty.

'Frank and Julia wandered off into the garden, looking for fireflies. Daniel and I sat, our hilarity subsiding. I leant into him, and he kissed me.'

She twists her wedding and engagement rings, aligns the diamonds of one with the diamonds of the other. She begins again, each spin the winding of her courage to continue.

'They sat astride the wall at the far end of the garden, watching fireflies in the ravine beyond, sitting so close to one another, I couldn't make out where Frank ended, and Julia began. Next thing, I awaken to sun streaming through the window of an unfamiliar bedroom, with Daniel asleep beside me.'

She looks up again, the silent pleading palpable in the air between us. In my chest, cold fury spreads like a bruise.

'Artemisia, darling. Forgive me.'

No apologies. No remorse. Only a demand that I respond, that I take responsibility for her actions and their repercussions. I will not.

'And that's the story of my conception. What an edifying tale.' I stand, hoping my liquefied knees don't let me collapse. 'Talk to Bill about the pub. Goodbye.'

I sound much more controlled than I am. She can't hear the drumming of my heart or feel the tremble of my fingers as I reach for my keys. I jangle them to mask the shakes, just in case.

In the car, I fumble getting the key in the ignition but soon, I'm heading away from the madhouse towards home. Joni on full blast soothes my frayed nerves and by the time I pull up outside the flat, I've little voice left. But my heart isn't racing, and I've stopped shaking.

Jenny greets me with a hug. I hold on, hugging back like my life depends on it.

'You all right?'

I shake my head.

'What do you need?'

'Doughnuts.'

'This is a doughnut-free zone, I'm afraid.'

We face palm in unison, and I smile despite myself.

'We'll have to go out.' Jenny tugs at my arm. 'C'mon. No time to waste.'

Moments later, we stroll arm in arm towards the parade of shops close by. The bakery will be our downfall, for sure, one day. Especially since it opened a café area at the front of the shop.

'Market research, in case we have to cover for Nina one day.'

'You haven't appointed her yet.'

'You and I both know she'll get the job. It's only Vic who's yet to understand that.'

The bell over the door announces our arrival. Unusually, even for a Sunday, the shop is empty, save for one woman buying takeout sandwiches at the counter. Jenny and I stand beside her and drool over the cakes behind the glass. The doughnuts are the best I've tasted, so our research is to make doubly sure. I select a ring doughnut iced in pink and dipped in vermicelli; Jenny chooses a custard filled confection. We sit waiting for our cakes at a window table. Daft, we could have carried them ourselves, but here, they put them on little doilied plates with a cake fork. I'd much rather just use my fingers and take a great big chomp, but Jenny tells me I'm uncouth.

With the doughnuts, we enjoy a cup of coffee; the perfect combo. The tensions of my contretemps with Mother grow less potent with every bite as I tell Jenny what she said about Marian.

'You staying at the pub tonight?'

'No. Vic wants me in extra early for the interviews, so I'm staying home. Marian has stuff to do. She doesn't mind. And she knows I don't live there. It's only while she gets back on her feet.'

Jenny's expression softens. She's not made a complaint nor said a word to make me guilty for leaving her marooned during her first few days back from Brussels. Guilt riddles me, anyway, and I squeeze her hand.

'Sorry you've been on your own so much. It won't be for much longer.'

'I know. Although I suppose you'll get back and before we know it, be looking at tied cottages with Theo.'

'Jenny, don't. If I move into school – and it's not a done deal – it won't be at least until September. Theo only met with the big guns at the beginning of the week. And they weren't that happy, were they?'

'"It's not our practice to condone cohabiting."'

We snigger into our doughnuts.

'That should be the school motto.'

'It won't affect Theo's promotion chances, will it?'

'Shouldn't think so. He'll probably look for a headship of a smaller school, you know, to learn the craft.'

She picks up the last piece of her doughnut and battles with it between her finger and thumb. The battle won, she resembles an over-fed gerbil, her cheeks bulging. I make a big drama of using my cake fork, my little finger stuck out as I spear my last piece.

We sit back and drain our cups. I clonk mine on to its saucer.

'There's more.'

'Thought there might be. Did you tell her?'

'I did, showed her Daniel's photo. She confessed and asked me to forgive her. Bloody woman.' Tension tightens its grip; I roll my shoulders to loosen the knots.

Jenny squeezes my arm and smiles.

'That was brave of you. Think she's genuine? In wanting your forgiveness?'

'Don't doubt it. To assuage her guilt. But I can't. Not yet.'

'We need something to distract you. Let's finish unpacking my stuff. That should do it.'

We hasten home but discover Jenny has unpacked most of her belongings. Despite that, I find, wrapped in an "I ♥ Brussels" tee shirt, a tasteless statuette of the Manneken Pis. I hold it aloft. 'You're not serious?'

'Why not? It's an icon.'

'So, where do you want it? In the bathroom? On the cistern?'

'Brilliant idea.'

She snatches it from me and runs to the bathroom. I am so glad to be home. It'll be a struggle to return to the pub tomorrow. I sigh. Jenny's remark about the school cottage runs through my head. I wonder if the school would contemplate allowing a ménage à trois?

* * *

I h tell me off when she's gone and lecture me on how to behave during an interview. But it wasn't my fault we ate the burnt offerings with the woman in front of us, was it? I suggested she leave it with us so we could enjoy it at our leisure, but oh, no. Vic had other ideas. My mouth still feels like it's charred, bits of singed crumb are, I swear, lodged between my teeth, and trying to remove them with my tongue is hopeless. Perhaps he'll go easy on me, given my traumatic experience with Mother yesterday.

No such luck. Vic appears, frowning. I steel myself for castigation.

'If you could conduct yourself in a more seemly manner for our next candidate, adopt a more professional approach, I would appreciate it.'

'Sorry, Vic. But in my defence, I said we should try the cake after she's gone.'

'That is what we'll do for the remaining candidates. You expect the poor woman to want us to employ her after your performance?'

'Was she in any danger of getting your vote?'

'That is not the point. We should treat candidates with respect, however unsuitable they turn out to be. How'd you like it if the person interviewing you choked on your cake? And then couldn't hide their amusement?'

'I'd hate it. But I wouldn't bring an abomination masquerading as cake and expect my prospective employers to eat it. Especially if cake making was a prerequisite. Would you?'

'No, but my point is still valid. We've got ten minutes before the next candidate; I need a glass of water.'

He wanders off and I follow him into the gallery. At the far end, the café sparkles in its newness. It enlivens the whole character of the gallery; it's brighter and more inviting. It was a stroke of genius to suggest opening a café, if I say so myself. In congratulatory mood, I stroll towards Betty. She'll understand my reactions to the scorched cake.

The hairs on my arms tug upwards on a shiver, and a prickle behind my ears brings me to a halt. It's not the over-cooked cake making me nauseous. I step hesitantly towards Betty, hoping she's still there. I heave a sigh. She smiles at me, her level of twinkle undiminished by my feeling of dread. I spin round, scan the paintings, can see nothing amiss. I check the time. Eight minutes.

I sprint along the gallery, inspecting the paintings. All complete. At the far end, I stop, gather my breath, and edge along the opposite side. Each painting is perfect. Oh, God. How did I not see it? The woman from the bar. She's gone.

Is it my turn? Has Mother turned her wrath on me after our confrontation yesterday? Mother's wrath? Whoa, hold on, Sia. Just be calm and consider what you're thinking. If Mother is planning to kill me, she must have killed the others.

The day the studio caught fire; she was there. Detta was the intended victim of the fire. Because she'd "got there first". She feared Detta might change her mind, ask me to include them in the exhibition and eclipse her portrait.

She took Uncle Isaac home. Uncle Isaac – wittering on about his inheritance. Insensitive, but a motive for murder? Possibly, if she worried he'd gain too much. Is she that selfish?

Mark. Well, that's a nonsense. Someone shot him. He infuriated her, though, at the exhibition. Christ. Is that why DI Smith had me touch the gun? He suspected Mother. My guts turn to lead. The box in her wardrobe. Not jewellery.

She visited Daniel once; could she have gone a second time? Why? Think. Daniel changed his mind over the photos, wounded her pride. And I bet she worried he'd tell me he was my father. But he didn't. He stayed true to whatever bargain they must have made. In my mind's eye, the image of Mother gazing at Daniel in faux adoration is as vivid as if I were standing in his flat with them, an invisible witness. She plies him with drink; absinthe, naturally, spiked with Xanax. Bewitched by Mother's glamour, his hopes are rekindled. He is helpless; poor Daniel.

I haven't told her how I know. Have I? Did I mention Jade? Oh, God. If I have, it might be Jade she's targeting. I lean on the wall, my head in my hands, trying to force my memory through my fingertips into my brain. I'm sure I didn't tell her how I know. Not a hundred per cent; doubt squeezes through the crack. I replay yesterday's conversation, my eyes closed and seeing the words on a ticker tape across the inside of my forehead. No. Jade is safe. It's me.

'Sia, our next candidate is here.'

'Oh!'

I don't see or hear them approach, but Vic stands by me with Nina at his side. I must force myself back to the real world, but the other holds me fast in its grip. Scrambling for words to avoid sounding like a raving madwoman, I stare at them.

'Look at the painting.' I raise my hand towards Relaxing After Work, my words husky.

Vic's eyes widen as he takes in the significance of my invitation.

Nina must think us strange, gawking in wonder at a familiar painting. Vic runs his finger along the empty bar where she was leaning yesterday, a drink in her hand, the cares of the day etched upon her young features.

Nina looks from Vic to me, and at the painting. She tilts her head; is she weighing up if what she sees is worth such a response? She copies Vic's movements, her neat fingertips edging across the painting.

'Who's missing?'

Vic arches an eyebrow. The cauldron bubbles to a dangerous level. She's guessed? Or does she sense something?

'See the barman? In front of him, the woman wearing the red blouse shouldn't be alone; her friend is missing.'

Nina steps back, folds her arms and studies the painting. Her hazel eyes dart across it, like she's a machine taking a scan. 'I remember now. Wasn't she dressed in a shimmering pale blue dress?' She comes forward again. 'I was struck by how she was haloed, angelic, from the light reflected in the bottles behind the bar.' She narrows her eyes, bends to get a closer look. 'And I don't think the barman's hands were visible, either.'

Nausea overtakes me, impressed by Nina's accurate recollection of the details. I hadn't considered the barman when I noticed the missing woman. Sod the interview. Nina's got to have the job. She's one of us.

Vic puts on his sensible, "I'm in charge" voice. 'Why don't we carry on and conduct the interview? As planned?'

'Good idea.' Nina smiles. 'Slice of cake while we chat?'

'No.'

She looks surprised at my swift reply.

'We had a disaster doing that earlier.' I don't confess I'm too queasy to face cake. 'Shall we save it for after the official bit and then enjoy a slice with a cuppa? Vic?'

'Our next candidate is due within half an hour of Nina's

interview. I don't want to keep him waiting.'

'Him? You got a bloke apply? That's brilliant.' Nina grins. 'I'd better be on top form. Where are we having the interview?'

In the café, at one of the mango wood tables, we settle to conduct the interview. Nina is just as I expected and hoped. I can see her winning over Vic with every utterance she makes. The chap who's coming next will have to be extraordinary if he's to pip her to the post. The interview is over in half the time we have set aside. My nausea has abated, so I suggest we break open Nina's cake. Vic agrees with no reluctance. He even collects plates from the cupboard and directs Nina to the cutlery drawer for cake forks. I pour our coffees.

'So, this painting.' Nina cuts through her glorious chocolate cake with the ease of an expert, each slice exactly the same size as the next. 'Your faces told me you've experienced abduction from paintings before.' She passes me a plate. 'Well?'

'Are you interviewing us now?'

'Maybe.'

'You tell her, Vic. I need to try this cake before I say another word.' Before he can argue, I break off a chunk and stuff it into my mouth.

Nina listens with the interest of a character in a Christie novel at the exposition, not touching her cake or coffee. She whistles as Vic finishes with the latest disappearance. He hasn't mentioned my theory, the connection with people dying, for which I am grateful. Especially as I might be the next victim.

A crumb goes the wrong way, and I splutter, my eyes watering. I take a swig of my coffee and the panic subsides. Did my life pass before me then? No. I must calm down. Nothing here can kill me. Apart from choking.

'Why do you think it's happening? Is your dad having a joke at your expense? Was he a funny guy when he was alive?'

'He was funny, yes. But I don't think the disappearances are amusing. They're more disturbing than funny.'

'You'll put Nina off with such talk. I'm sure there's a rational explanation. There usually is; we just haven't found it yet.'

'Put me off? You're kidding. Makes me keener than ever. Nothing like this happens at Big Ben's.' Her animated face, so alive with energy and curiosity, tells me she's being honest.

'Sia, may I speak to you for a moment? Excuse us, Nina.'

Vic and I wander out of earshot. Fear he'll say there's no way we can employ Nina worms through my head. I bash it with the cudgel of conviction he's taken with her. It retreats but doesn't leave.

'We must conduct the final interview. I'm sure we'll appoint Nina, but we must.'

The cudgel takes a fatal swipe.

'Brilliant.' I keep "I told you so" under my tongue. 'So, what do we do?'

'I don't know. Don't want the poor lad here under false pretences, particularly as he's just finished college.'

I remember; when I called to ask him for an interview, he squealed.

'Is there any chance we could hire them both? The boy as an apprentice?'

'I don't think the finances would run to that. If he were part-time, we could consider it.'

'Let's do the interview. He might be awful and save us the worry. If we like him, we'll be up front and tell him our dilemma. He might accept a part-time post.'

The interviews result in us gaining two new employees: Nina as café manager and Eddie as part-time cook, baker and candlestick maker. Turns out he's happier part-time as it gives him time to spend on his other interest – writing music. He's been composing in his spare time and just getting recognition. In a room at home, he has a studio, and his mum willing to support him if he's earning to help the family purse.

Vic and I are ridiculously pleased with ourselves for finding two exceptional talents to join our team. We spend too much time, when Nina and Eddie have gone, congratulating our talent at spotting decent people. A call from Bill douses our revelry.

'Sia, your mother's just left me in the foulest of tempers. Thought I should alert you.'

I slump on to the office chair, lean on the desk and wait for the worst. 'Go on.'

'She'd asked for a meeting to discuss financial matters in the wake of Isaac's death.'

I knew she wouldn't leave it alone. My advice to her plays in my mind.

'And?'

'When I said Marian will inherit everything of Isaac's, including what he'd inherited from Frank, she lost control. Claimed Marian had murdered Isaac for his money, and she threatened to kill her. She's lost control before but this time her manner perturbed me; thought I ought to inform you.'

A banshee of alarm shrieks through my being. If toes could hear, mine would cower in my shoes. 'Bill, when was this? Was this today?'

'Yes, she's not five minutes ago stormed out on me.'

'Thanks. I've got to go.'

I throw my mobile into my bag, snatch it up and fly into the gallery. Vic looks up at my helter-skelter arrival, stands, his face ashen.

'Sia?'

'Call Detta. Tell her to meet me at The Dog and Duck, straight away. Tell her it's urgent.'

'What..?'

'Mother. The latest victim isn't me. It's Marian. Call Detta.'

I'm on the road, driving faster than any limits, the cityscape passing in a blur. The traffic lights turn red on my approach. I drum the steering wheel. 'Come on, come on.'

I should have listened to my instincts. Dad's been trying to tell me through his paintings. Christ, why did it take me so long to believe? Green. 'Let's go. They're green. Come on.'

I screech to a halt outside the pub, jump out and search for Mother's car, for Detta's. Detta pulls up, brakes squealing, as I comb the street. I can't see it.

'There!'

Detta points across the green to a drive outside an innocuous house facing the pub. She's here.

We bolt through the rear garden, and I hurl myself at the back door. It gives unhurriedly, its weight like a burden. I squeeze through before it's halfway and sprint towards the kitchen. Mother shouts. Marian screams. I must reach her. I must save Marian. Detta's rapid footsteps drumbeat behind me.

I thrust open the kitchen door. Mother has pinned Marian against the counter, the ivory-handled knife in her hand, pressed against Marian's neck. The point pricks her skin. A speck of blood buds at its nib.

'Mother. No!'

She swerves from Marian, who squirms in her tight grasp. Marian tries to bend under Mother's arm, but Mother is too strong. Marian grabs the knife-wielding hand, her knuckles blanched with effort, but cannot put herself out of danger.

I rush them. Go to snatch Mother's arm. I clasp my fingers round her deceptively strong wrist. My nails sink into her white flesh. We struggle for the knife; she twists her hand. The knife connects with Marian's arm. Mother shoves with all her strength and the blade sinks into Marian's flesh, like she were just another slice of cake.

Marian howls. Detta heaves Mother from the fray and thrusts her on to a chair. Mother flops, limp, as if it were she who'd suffered a terrible wound. Marian sinks to the floor, holding her bloody arm. The knife is wedged at an angle, Marian's blood dripping over it, a crimson, half-hearted waterfall.

I grab a tea-towel and tie a make-shift tourniquet round Marian's arm trying, as best I can with trembling hands, not to disturb the knife. Marian sits without a murmur, her pale face vacant, as I minister to her in my ham-fisted, best effort, desperately trying to recall the first aid lessons from school. Her blood soaks into the towel, runs under my nails and into the creases of my hand. I pull more tea-towels from the drawer, and clean up her face, where spots of blood have sprayed across her cheek. She smiles but says nothing.

'Marian, can you lift your arm? Even a bit would help.'

Her nod is almost undiscernible, but she pushes her elbow with her right hand, raises her arm and lets her hand rest on her head. She closes her eyes, leans against the cabinet door.

Sirens, growing louder, punctuate the unnatural silence. I sit beside Marian on the floor, my hand over hers supporting her arm. Mother, folded like an empty glove puppet, sits on the chair. Next to her, Detta rests her hand on Mother's arm, ready to move should she make an escape bid. She won't try. I've seen this before, when I was a kid and they first admitted her to the unit. Her fury is spent, this time.

Detta must have called the police on her way here. Never occurred to me. Their booted footsteps march towards us. Relief overtakes me when the first uniform appears at the kitchen door. He speaks into his radio. Another officer arrives. It takes a moment to recognise DI Smith. Marian and I lean against one another. DI Smith talks to Detta. I hear their words but can make no sense of them. The air feels liquid, like glycerine, sticking to my perception. From nowhere, paramedics squat before me. They speak to Marian. At last she talks, whispering answers to their questions. The jitters in my fingers spread up my arms. My foot taps to an unheard melody which rattles into my calves, my thighs. Despite my head knowing I'm safe, my body's urge is to run. The warning rumble in my gut comes too late. I throw up all over Marian's kitchen floor.

CHAPTER THIRTY-FOUR

JUNE - FATHER'S DAY

Theo grins at me across the lounge bar as he collects glasses from the stacked tables. He chats to Vic, who's obviously made a witty remark. They both turn to stare at me. I pull what I hope is a demure face and finish pouring a pint for Eddie. He goes for his wallet.

'Put your money away, Eddie. It's on the house.'

'Oh, cheers.' He ambles back to the table to sit with Sandro and Claire.

Marian, the scar on her arm still florid, shimmies behind me to reach for a glass. I push forward to give her room, but she still winces. Uncle Isaac smiles out from his silver frame. Thank goodness I persuaded Marian to put his ashes in a private room. Few people, I assured her, would feel comfortable with him attending his own celebration in ash form. Enough folk want to criticise her for not having a funeral, but his wishes couldn't have been clearer in the document Marian unearthed in their bureau: absolutely no funeral; have a knees up here instead.

'Weren't you instructed to keep pressure off your arm? You'll never recover at this rate.'

She waves the glass at me with her good hand. 'Phooey. It's feeling better already. Say what you will, your mother, she cuts a clean cut.'

'Hilarious. I mean it. Go and sit down. We've plenty here manning the pumps.'

'Says you. Why aren't you mixing and a-mingling, then?'

'I will. I enjoy being behind the bar.'

'Stops you having to discuss the paintings. Again.'

'Maybe.'

'Get away with you. I can read you as if you were my own daughter. Face it, Sia. Until you've spoken to everyone, it'll remain with you. It will stay vivid and eager in people's minds because they aren't familiar with the details. I'm right, aren't I, Nina?'

Nina grins. 'As always, Mrs L.' She passes whisky to Bill. 'What d'you think, Mr Sharp?'

'That Sia will take whatever action she deems necessary when she is ready.'

He nods at me and winds his way towards Detta. Is it my imagination, or are they becoming close? Wouldn't that be something? Strains of the wedding march whisper through my head and visions of myself draped in organza, the oldest bridesmaid in history, flit across my mind. Stop it, Sia.

People I love, and a handful of strangers, fill the room. Their interest in me, in my story, exudes from their eyes, even as they try to hide it. But I'm not ready, not yet. I long to be ordinary, living a life so dull it interests no-one. I yearn to empty my mind of paintings with missing figures and murders disguised as suicide. Perhaps, one day in the distant future, when we need the publicity, I'll take up Look North's invitation for another interview.

Where's Jade? Sitting with Detta. Bet Detta's telling her a few rum stories of when they were young. She has memories of Daniel, too. Jade getting in touch was such a shock, especially when she showed me the photos, but I'm glad she did.

While everyone's busy, I slip out to the rear garden and sit in the warm June air. Funny, today's Father's Day. The first without him. Has Sandro remembered? Probably not. Typical man. I suppose Mother stopped me needing to buy two lots of cards and presents. Consolation? No. If I'd grown close to Daniel, might I have regarded him as a father? Too odd, but as a friend, amazing.

It doesn't matter Dad isn't my blood father; he'll always be Dad to me. Daniel never fought for me, never tried to tell me he was my father. I'm still who I thought I was; still Sia. I owe him nothing, except for the friendship we had in the weeks before his death, for which I'm grateful, and the publicity his article brought for the gallery. And he brought Jade into our lives; that's a good thing. I can sense it.

I even pity Mother. If she discovers Daniel has a young, beautiful widow, I can guess how she'll react. No. Jade is safer this way. While the stories still interest the media, I requested Mother not be given access to newspapers. The unit is supportive, but what happens to her once they complete the assessments? I don't expect she'll be free again.

Was it the last disappearance that exposed her or did it confirm something I recognised as true? How I've raked through the events trying to discover the answer. For months, I tried to ignore the itch in my deep consciousness, to disregard the unease I registered because I didn't understand it, to deny my instincts. Of course, hindsight is a marvellous thing. I could have gone into her studio, seen there were no paintings. I shan't forget the day the police came to search the house, and stepping into that lair of hers, where I'd assumed she'd been so busy. Nothing. No splashes of paint, no sketches, no traces of the giveaway smell of turps. And those tablets. She could have laid low a battalion of men with what she'd amassed. It was all there: the pills, the gun, the absinthe. She was so confident of getting away with everything, she hid nothing. The police only needed to open the cupboards to find the evidence. It could be something out of a third-rate crime film.

I shiver in the early summer breeze, which carries a summons to the gallery. I sneak into the kitchen, grab my bag and scurry to the car like someone with a guilty secret. Jenny stands at the kitchen window. She waves, giving me permission to leave. Ignition on, Joni full blast, I'm away.

* * *

Soft afternoon sunshine spills through the windows. The paintings look their best in early summer, when sunlight dapples at that angle across them. I lock the door behind me, dump my keys and handbag on reception, and stop dead.

Someone is in here. A man, surely not a burglar, studies the paintings. He has his hands in his pockets, is head tilted in thought. My breathing stops. I stand very still. I recognise that posture. As if he has just sensed my presence, he turns. I knew it was him.

'Dad.'

My voice is a little girl's. The corners of my mouth strain as I struggle not to cry. My eyes brim with tears. I take a step forward. He mirrors me.

'Dad.'

'Sia. My lovely Sia.'

'Oh, God. Dad.'

'You got there in the end. I was sure you would.'

'The paintings.'

'My only avenue of connection with you. Until now.'

He is utterly there, no transparent ghost of a man but fully formed, vibrant. I want to reach out and touch him. 'Come nearer, let me see you.'

He steps forward and the reality of him storms my heart. A sob erupts in my throat.

'You are in every way, my daughter. You always will be. The daughter of my heart.'

His eyes shine, profound and wise. 'Try not to hate your

mother. Life was never easy for her.' He smiles. 'Perhaps death will be more forgiving when her time comes.'

'I, I don't hate.'

'That's my Sia. I am so proud of what you've achieved, so proud of you. Proud to call you my daughter.'

Unable to keep from weeping any longer, I bury my face in my hands.

'I love you, my darling Artemisia.'

'I love you, too, Dad.'

The warmth of his arms around me comes as a sweet surprise. My tears abate and the sobbing subsides. I fall into his embrace, let him comfort me as no-one else ever could.

'I'll always be with you.' He pulls away, and gestures to the paintings. 'At the gallery, in the car with Joni, at home. Whenever you're lonesome. Not stalking you, obviously.'

A tearful laugh bubbles up my throat.

'I'll be by your side whenever you need me. Forever.'

'That's good to know.'

He takes another step from me. I squint, focus hard, but the paintings behind him become more and more visible, till I am looking through him.

'Dad?'

Where he stood, the air shimmers, like the day has stretched its back. I stand in the gallery alone.

I wait for the tremulous air to lose its glister. Certain he is gone, I step back until my calf brushes the bench and I sit. In the corner of my eye, something bright catches my attention, like a forget-me-not bobbing on a spring breeze. It's the young woman by the bar. She stands, smiling out of the painting, her glass held aloft in a toast. It's a Friday night, and she's ready for the weekend.

ACKNOWLEDGEMENTS

It's often said that writing a novel is a solitary business, and the notion holds some truth. However, an author achieves nothing alone. Without a support network, we'd all be staring at our computers, wondering what day of the week it was.

My support network grew from my family. I soon added others from the writing community and experts who gave me invaluable advice about stuff I know nothing about but included in my novel, anyway.

So, I must thank the following people for their part in bringing The Art of Murder to life:

Judith Waring, psychotherapist, was generous with her time and expertise so I could make the relevant sections in the novel as genuine as possible. She also read these sections and put me right when I'd made mistakes.

My ignorance of the art world was pretty total when I started writing The Art of Murder, so I thank Deanna Dawkins of York Fine Arts for her advice about art galleries and painting care.

Artist Gwenn Seemel has simply been marvellous. One of their paintings was the inspiration for the family portrait that features in *The Art of Murder*. Gwenn allowed me to use the original in my newsletter, so I could share it with my subscribers.

Another area of ignorance was guns. Sam MacArthur from Viking Guns helped me out here, guiding me in the right direction so that I didn't include a blunderbuss when a pistol was the more obvious weapon of choice.

From the writing world, I must thank my writing groups who have kept me going with their affection, expertise and generous support.

My lovely NaNas – where would I be without you? Particular mention must go to Marilyn Groves and Mim Landor who read very early versions of The Art of Murder. Their faith in me and in the novel enabled me to press on when I had moments of doubt.

Also, I must thank David Gladwin from the Beverley Writers group for his unfailing and cheerful support.

Another fabulous community of writers is the Best Seller Experiment family. Their expertise, humour, and understanding of the highs and lows of being a writer have kept me sane. Mark Stay gets a special mention here. His knowledge of the publishing world is second to none, as is his generosity in giving of his time and his writing expertise.

Almost finally, thank you James, Ted, and Amy at Northodox Press for taking on my novel.

Finally, finally I must thank my husband, Simon, and my sons, Robert and Tony. Their unwavering belief in my writing, given with a plentiful supply of humour, has made this journey to publication one of celebration. And I must mention that The Art of Murder is the title Tony suggested from the get-go. He never liked the working title I clung on to for far too long!

Printed in Dunstable, United Kingdom